MEN·ON·MEN
5
·BEST·NEW·GAY·FICTION·

EDITED AND WITH AN INTRODUCTION BY
DAVID BERGMAN

A PLUME BOOK

PLUME
Published by the Penguin Group
Penguin Books USA Inc., 375 Hudson Street,
New York, New York 10014, U.S.A.
Penguin Books Ltd, 27 Wrights Lane,
London W8 5TZ, England
Penguin Books Australia Ltd, Ringwood,
Victoria, Australia
Penguin Books Canada Ltd, 10 Alcorn Avenue,
Toronto, Ontario, Canada M4V 3B2
Penguin Books (N.Z.) Ltd, 182–190 Wairau Road,
Auckland 10, New Zealand

Penguin Books Ltd, Registered Offices:
Harmondsworth, Middlesex, England

First published by Plume/Meridian,
an imprint of Dutton Signet,
a division of Penguin Books USA Inc.

First Printing, October, 1994
10 9 8 7 6 5 4 3 2 1

Ⓟ REGISTERED TRADEMARK—MARCA REGISTRADA

The Library of Congress has assigned this title the following ISSN: 1074-1372

Printed in the United States of America
Set in Janson
Designed by Leonard Telesca

CONTENTS

MEN ON MEN 5: INTRODUCTION

• DAVID BERGMAN •

Diversity and excellence are often conceived in the public's mind as opposing forces. Some people think that representing a diverse group of writers waters down content and lowers artistic standards. But my experience has been quite different. Perhaps the difference derives from the nature of the gay writing community—or rather gay writing communities—and that their strength is in their diversity, in their ability to speak eloquently, movingly, powerfully about an enormously wide range of experience. Perhaps I am reaping the benefits of the late George Stambolian's tenure as editor since his high standards of literary excellence and inclusiveness have moved the best writers from all parts of the gay literary world to send me stories. Perhaps I am merely lucky that I am editing *Men on Men* at the very moment when gay writing is the most exciting force in American literature. Whatever the reason, I never felt while selecting the stories in this book that I had to trade off diversity for excellence. Indeed, I was often overwhelmed in the nearly two years in which I read manuscripts by the rich diversity of voices that spoke to me about lives and experiences far from my own. Rather, the problem I faced in putting together the final selection was not finding stories varied enough, but choosing ones that would complement each other and provide the book as a whole with coherence and shapeliness. *Men on Men*, I felt, should be more than a grab-bag, even if that grab-bag contained only literary diamonds.

No doubt some will think that *Men on Men 5* is still not diverse enough—such criticism has haunted the series since its inception a decade ago, and no doubt it will arise again. My response to such criticism—as was George Stambolian's response before me—is that twenty stories could never reflect the enormous variety of gay writers in this country, and no collection worth reading could be merely a reflection of gay demographics. No greater disservice to the richness of gay writing could be done than to hold up a clipboard and check off entries against a predetermined plan based on their authors' ethnic, racial, or class origins. The sheer strength of the writing defeats a quota system.

In the decade that George Stambolian edited *Men on Men*, he established the series as the foremost venue for short gay fiction. Virtually every important gay writer in America has appeared in its pages, and George had an uncanny ability to detect emerging talent. George set up standards and procedures that I have endeavored to follow. First, like George, I have not used readers to screen stories. I have personally read every one of the over 450 stories submitted and handled all the correspondence. Only with this involvement could I be sure of the fullest picture of the work submitted. Because I read everything myself, famous writers and unknown writers got the same attention. When the final list was assembled, it contained only three writers who had appeared in *Men on Men* before—Gary Glickman, Richard McCann, and Peter Cashorali—and several writers who have never appeared in a national journal or in book form. *Men on Men 5* seems to me to announce a new generation of gay writers and it contains several men who, I believe, are destined to be major figures. One of the most exciting aspects of editing *Men on Men* is the chance to bring young, remarkable writers to the public's attention. As a realist, I know that every reader won't find all the selections of equal value, but I can't imagine that readers of taste, sensitivity, and intelligence—the kind of readers *Men on Men* has always had—won't find this group of young talent unusually exciting.

When I began editing *Men on Men 5*, agents and authors wrote asking what kind of stories I was looking for. I didn't know what to tell them except that I was looking for stories that knocked my socks off. The good editors I know have what I call a "wow meter," which goes off when they read something of enormous skill, or emotional intensity, or unusual insight or beauty: stories that explore new subjects, or find new ways to envision old ones; stories that stretch our understanding or throw old beliefs into confusion; stories whose power, beauty, and strangeness make us sit up and take note. I was looking for those stories, which by their very nature defy a formula or classification. All of the stories in this collection set off my wow meter, and I feel confident that most of these stories will excite you. As a consequence, I haven't tried to arrange the stories in any particular order. They appear in the alphabetical order of the authors' last names, which seemed the fairest way.

Only toward the end of the editorial process did I begin to see some pattern in the works that most affected me. Or rather, because I'm still surprised by what turns me on, I began to figure out which stories failed to make an impression. In retrospect, I now see that I avoided stories with nice pat endings. These highly predictable conclusions packed no surprises or discoveries. I also avoided stories that were politically correct but not particularly heartfelt. I find politically correct stories generally dull because they allow the expression of only the "nicest" sentiments, attitudes worked out far in advance and to some formula of what one *should* feel. Our lives are far more complicated, our feelings far more intense and uncontrollable, our actions far less predictable than politically correct stories allow them to be portrayed as being. Human existence is a messy affair, and I'm not drawn to those works that try to tidy it up. I also avoided stories that contained the kind of happy ending one sees in sitcoms every night of the year.

Yet I'm not averse to stories with happy endings that come to a close with a tight resolution. In fact, I've always liked stories that feature that mythic figure the trickster, a figure that has appeared in literature from its very beginnings and is very much a part of gay literature. I received a number of wonderful stories in which the central character or characters are playing tricks. Unfortunately, I could not publish all of them, but D. Lee Williams' tale "Toilet Training," Brian Kirkpatrick's "Hot Chocolate Drips," and Robert Rodi's "Tricked," stories very different in other ways, revolve around tricksters, and the endings of these stories work out with a kind of "click" that I find delightful and surprising despite their classical narrative structures.

Reviewers in the past have looked toward *Men on Men* as a kind of snapshot of the state of gay culture or as a volume that tries to take the pulse of contemporary gay life. I've tried to avoid selecting stories in that way. I suspect that no anthology—at least one as small as this one—can accurately reproduce the gay zeitgeist or gauge the temperature of the various gay communities. Good writers are in general far too individualistic to be good sociologists. It may be possible that at some time in the future, a critic will look at this volume and see in it some sign of the times, but I think we are—at least I am—too close to the moment to act as a gauge of the social climate. However, at times I encountered such strange coincidences that I wonder whether I was watching the emergence of a new gay cultural phenomenon. For example, within a three-week span I received three stories about lovers breaking up during trips to Latin America. What's going on? I asked myself. Are these stories on the cutting edge of some new and important phenomenon? Should I contact travel agents and warn them not to send gay couples off to Mexico and Peru? In the end, although all three stories had elements that were very good, none of them set off my wow meter. However, there are two stories about Latin Americans in the United States—Jaime Manrique's "The Day Carmen Maura Kissed Me" and Paul Bonin-Rodriguez's "Talk of the Town." I have also included two stories about Americans abroad—Liam Brosnahan's "Banshee Music" and Richard McCann's "Some Threads Through the Medina." These stories on what Henry James called the transatlantic theme continue one of the persistent subjects of gay American writing. Justin Chin's "A Sea of Decaying Kisses" is an example of a relatively new phenomenon in American writing, the transpacific theme.

One criticism of earlier editions of *Men on Men* is that they overly represented New York or West Coast writers. Since gay men move around a lot, where someone lives and what region he writes about can be very different, but I have noticed—

perhaps because I've lived in Baltimore for the last twenty years—that stories with Southern backgrounds were underrepresented in earlier editions of *Men on Men*. I should say that I was born in Massachusetts, raised in New York City, and went to college in Ohio, so I'm not a Southerner by birth or inclination. I didn't actively go out to redress this imbalance, yet I'm delighted to have found several stories—"Out There" and "All Who Are Out Are In Free"—that are set in the South, and one—"Talk of the Town"—set in the Southwest. In fact, the stories tend to be set in every region of the country. " 'Summertime, and the Living Is Easy . . .'," "Boys on Fire," and "Tricked" take place in the Midwest; "Toilet Training" in the Northwest; "Land of Love" and most of "Sagrada Familia" in New England; "Spirit House" and "Leaving the Beach" are set entirely or in part on Long Island; and finally "Hot Chocolate Drips," "A Sea of Decaying Kisses," and "The Cemetery" take place in California.

Selecting stories for *Men on Men* was complicated by the fact that gay fiction often concerns itself with a few well-explored subjects, and therefore I received several stories that seemed to retrace the same or similar material. For example, I received a large number of coming-out stories, stories that record a young man's first dealings with his homosexuality. Many of these stories were well written and moving, but over the twenty-five years since Stonewall, it has become increasingly difficult to say something new and fresh about coming out. I've included only a few such stories in this collection—Adam Klein's "Club Feet," Joshua David's "Land of Love," and Michael Lowenthal's "Delivery"—all of which are unusual variations on the theme.

Klein's story seems to be linked in my mind with David Rakoff's story "Sagrada Familia," which represents yet another frequent kind of gay tale—the AIDS narrative. Nothing proved harder for me than selecting among the many stories about AIDS, even the weakest of which often contained something that cut through to the heart. Four stories are directly and centrally about AIDS, but in many of the other stories—"Out There," "Boys on Fire," and "Banshee Music"—AIDS forms a central fact that defines the limits of the characters' powers. Moreover, even in stories that never mention AIDS—"Spirit

House" is a telling example—it is a central if silent presence. In fact, most of the stories in *Men on Men 5* are about trying to form relationships and about those relationships falling apart. Although early gay fiction was often about falling in love, it spent little time on the difficulties of an ongoing relationship or how to keep going after a breakup. Yet current gay fiction seems obsessed with these themes. It strikes me that AIDS is one of the reasons romance has taken a backseat to the care and maintenance of relationships, and even when stories are about romance (such as "Hot Chocolate Drips"), they are about how AIDS has made romance difficult.

As you can see, theme played an important role in making the final story selections. To give the volume coherence without uniformity, I wanted stories that would talk to one another, narratives that would enter into a kind of dialogue. For example, "Spirit House," a story about the appearance of an unfriendly spirit, seems to have a lot to say to "The Cemetery," about the appearance of a friendly spirit. "All Who Are Out Are In Free" is yet another kind of "ghost" story. Indeed, ghosts weave themselves in and out of several stories. Another mirroring pair is "Out There" and "Leaving the Beach," which both have main characters who are helped to understanding by their women friends.

The subtitle to *Men on Men* is *Best New Gay Fiction*. Clearly the judgment of what is "best" is highly subjective, and the selection probably speaks more about my tastes and values than it does about the state of gay fiction at the present time. And yet I come to the editorship of *Men on Men*, like George Stambolian before me, not just as a writer, but as a student of literature. George was a professor of French and a distinguished Proust scholar. As an English professor, I have focused on British and American literature. What George and I could see from our double perspectives as both editors and scholars was that we are living in a remarkable period of gay fiction, an unprecedented flowering. The emergence of gay fiction today is comparable to the emergence of Southern literature in the forties, Jewish-American fiction in the fifties, and women's literature in the seventies. *Men on Men* contains not just remarkable gay fiction, but remarkable American fiction. It represents what I think is the most vital movement in American literature right

now. Just as gay plays are widely recognized as the most exciting element in contemporary theatre, these stories rank with
the finest fiction being produced in America.

Baltimore, November 1993

TALK OF THE TOWN

• PAUL BONIN-RODRIGUEZ •

Wednesday is Christian Steak Finger Basket Special at Dairy Queen. For two-fifty-nine and believing in the Lord, you get four steak fingers, a heaping helping of fries, two Texas toasts, a dish of milk gravy, and all the tea you can drink included. I used to dread working it, because in my experience, it's the holy groups that are always the hardest to please.

Ever since the Domingos opened up the Dairy Queen right by the football field last May, all the Baptists, the Methodists, and the Church of Christs have decided they don't need to plead the blood of Jesus any later than eight o'clock on Wednesdays, if they're gonna make it in time for supper. You know, it wouldn't be so bad just having them come in and eat their plates, but they all want extras with their specials.

"Extra milk gravy," they say, "to cover up my fingers." We give it to them, no charge. "Extra catsup," they say, "to cover up my fries." We hand them a few more packets. Five minutes later they're back. "Extra bread," they say, "to sup up that catsup and gravy."

The Catholics don't have church on Wednesday, so they come early, about six. I guess so they can go home and drink. I want to say that I don't see them taking any more gravy or toast than they need, so for right now, they're my favorite religion. But I'm also pretty grateful to the Pentecostals who let the Holy Spirit keep them occupied until after we close, or we'd be really swamped. Just once, though, I'd like to see them all come in and order up some Hungr-Buster Platters, say grace, maybe break into tongues. I bet it'd sound like this: *hamburger, hamburger, hamburger, double-meat hamburger . . . Amen!*

Manny Domingo, the owner, says a month of Christian specials could bankrupt us at this point, but I told him it's all this extra grabbing that's really costing—and the fact that we don't use bulk catsup. He and his wife, Modesta, think they've got to be nice to everyone, sort of court favor to make everyone feel at home. So they don't say anything when they see people loading up with extra napkins or Sweet'n Low packets.

Now I know they saw Cherry Flanary put five napkin-wrapped slices of Texas toast in her purse before she walked out this past Wednesday. And I know she didn't take them from anyone else's plate. She came up and requested every last one. I told her we'd have to start charging her after the first dozen, and she said, "Don't you get uppity with me, Johnny Ray Hobson. You may have been brought up without much love or guidance, but pretty soon you're gonna have to learn something about respect, and I will not hesitate to make a complaint!"

She doesn't know what she is talking about. My middle name is Roy; and if there is one thing I am not worried about, it's my position at Dairy Queen. I was one of the first ones hired, and I know I'm the best cook they've got. If it weren't for the Domingos' five daughters and one son all working there, I bet I'd be assistant manager by now. As it is, they're talking of letting me run it when they go to the Rio Grande Valley to visit their kinfolk this Christmas.

I hope it happens. Maybe nobody'd come in, except my old friend T.J., and I'd get to spend the day making the things we like, eating, getting things straight between us. It's been six months since we were regular friends. And there's a lot I have to tell him now: about stuff I learned because of him, not only because he was so book smart but because he left me a heap of trouble after fighting with the football boys over the talk of the town.

I learned a lot all right, but hey, you know what they say, "If you can't stand the heat, get out of the D-Q kitchen."

The D-Q kitchen has helped to keep me out of trouble and the places I don't belong, like football games and church, where Momma and Brother Bill are still intent on me re-rededicating my life to Christ. They're dating seriously now, and it looks like the wedding is on just as soon as his last wife's been dead long enough for it to look good to the Southern Baptist Convention. I give them two months tops.

That's why I've got to work fast. I'm saving up enough money to buy a car and get my freedom. I'll be sixteen next month, but because of my T.J. trouble and detention last year, I can't take driver's education until this spring semester, so I know that for a little while, I might have to put up with him.

Momma and Brother Bill don't come to eat the Steak Finger Specials. They eat at his house every night. Momma refuses to come to the D-Q period. She doesn't like it that the Domingos changed their name from Dominguez to sound less Mexican, or that they run a restaurant serving Southern food. She says that, soon enough, she bets they'll have me in the back making tamales and pralines.

Brother Bill reminded her that Domingo still means "Sunday" in Spanish, even if does sound Italian. He thinks the Domingos set a fine example now that they've started coming to his church on Sundays. He's hoping to get enough Mexicans to open an Iglesia Baptista so they can all worship with just each other, rather than letting the Catholics "lead them away from salvation."

Brother Bill gets to D-Q about forty-five minutes after everyone else on Wednesdays. Manny offers him anything he wants—on the house—but he just orders a Diet Coke and a Dilly Bar and then walks around saying "Hi!" to everybody. I try to stay in the back, hoping I won't have to talk to him, but he'll usually ask Delaphine, or Dora Dean, or Delinda, whichever Domingo girl happens to be working the front, if I am in the back, and they'll come back saying he wants to see me.

Maybe I should say he wants to be seen seeing me. Then all the congregations present at D-Q will think that he's Christian enough to welcome this shameful sinner into his fold. That's the latest piece I heard from his corner. Deacon Rice was in the other day, having coffee with some Ladies of the Eastern Star, the women's Mason group. They must have just had a meeting, because they were all wearing their blue chiffon dresses and wigs. They must have thought I was cooking back in the kitchen, but I had moved out to bus some tables.

"He thinks that boy's been too long without a man's stern influence," Deacon said. "It's not only the boy's temper that the Brother's worried about but his shameful inclinations. It's enough to make him worry about marrying Tressie."

When I saw the wigs nod in solemn agreement, I knocked an ashtray from the table I had been wiping, so that it shattered on the brick floor next to Deacon's feet. One of the ladies let out an "Oh, my!" And I faced Deacon Rice, who looked down as soon as he saw me back.

"Is there anything else you'll be wanting out of me?" I asked.

I'm waiting for the day when someone else has the nerve to call me a name to my face. Now when I come up to the front to face Brother Bill with his lacquered-back hair, his tinted glasses, his gray gums and capped teeth, all smiling at me, I wonder just when he's gonna be man enough to tell me the things he says behind my back.

"They making you work all week?" he asks.

"No sir, I choose to work all week," I say.

"We'd love to start seeing you at church on Sundays and Wednesdays," he says. Then he just smiles at me, probably hoping I'll break down and ask to be saved right there in the heart of D-Q country, or maybe he's hoping his beeper will go off so he can respond to a crisis and face someone who will look at those tinted lenses with a look of belief. But all I see is a man who would fear anyone who could doubt him.

And you know, right then, I really get to feeling sorry for my mother. Because after all this time of being alone, I believe she is deserving someone truly strong and good, whose livelihood does not depend on lording over the weaknesses of others. Even so, if she marries him, I'm hoping that my Momma goes to live with him in the parsonage and leaves me in the house, which would spare us all the trouble of having to make ourselves pretend to like each other. Then I could have my friends over.

Oh, I've got me a new friend, Donnie Domingo, the owner's son. We both cook at D-Q. He just turned fifteen, a gangly, tall kid with big ears and feet, and thick glasses that he has to tie to his head. He's a freshman this year, and it hasn't been easy. He's been getting teased a lot. At school, they call him "Periscope," which is based on something that happened to him when he was swimming at Cedar Dale Park last summer. It's the same sort of thing that could have happened to any other guy—you know, an erection. A football guy would use it to brag, I swear. But it's really marked Donnie, mostly because so many people have picked up on it.

One day, Donnie was walking out of a pep rally right by this group of cheerleaders and assorted ugly kids. One of those cheerleaders—I think it was Donna Cox—yelled out, "Hey Periscope, been poking out anywhere lately?" And all those kids started to laugh, like it was some big joke and they expected him to get it and laugh right along. Donnie just froze in his tracks and waited for them to walk on by. And when they had passed, he leaned his head against a trophy case and squeezed his face so that he wouldn't cry. And I knew what he was feeling: naked even then, like everything he wanted kept private had been exposed.

Donnie's not used to it like I am. I wanted to go over and help him, but as I explained to him later on, us being friends in front of those guys would probably only make it worse on him. They'd call me "Periscope's girlfriend" or something like that. So we save our friendship for the D-Q kitchen, where, Lord, we have us a time!

We've got these games going. We've got this one called "Name That Meat," where you have to determine, just by instinct, without forking it, whether a patty is rare, medium, or well. I can get about nine out of ten, whereas Donnie can get only one or two. I think I just see shades of gray better than most people.

Or sometimes, we'll cut up bread, or something else, fry it up with the potatoes, and try to sneak it in with an order of fries. The trick of the game is to not get caught. We call it "Hidin' in the Fries." To this day, I've had to answer to only one breadstick, and that was to Cherry Flannery who, of course, liked it that way and wanted some more!

That day Donna Cox said that in front of those people, she came waltzing in for a late lunch, and for the first time Donnie realized that he could spit on her meat and not get caught. I haven't named that game yet, because I don't want to encourage it, but I understand him doing it.

Most of the time, though, we just slip and glide on the greasy floor, like we're a couple of ice skaters, and talk about the Judds—my favorite subject—or the English royal family—his. Donnie's got this thing about the English royal family, especially Princess Diana. He knows everything about them, buys every magazine that has their picture.

I think it's kind of silly, personally. And I told him, "Just what does a princess do but go around waving at people?"

"She gives of her time, her support, her compassion to the causes that make people feel good," he said, sliding in to cheese some patties on the griddle. "She was one of the first famous people to hug a man with AIDS."

Donnie wants to change the name of Dairy Queen to "Diana, Queen!" just as soon as it becomes official in England. He figures it's the only way we will get her to come here. I told him, it's probably not a good idea. After all, Dairy Queen is a franchise. Plus, I'm beginning to think that having someone famous around is not all it's cracked up to be.

Just this Wednesday, Lady Bird Johnson stopped in for a late lunch, and Lord, you should have seen the needless commotion that caused. The one thing I can tell you about famous people is that they do not travel alone. She showed up with four men in blue suits and black sunglasses—Manny told me they were Secret Service agents, required to protect her from assassins. Those men walked in and cased the joint, going under the tables and looking in the bathrooms.

Dessie May Hightower and Louelle Rhodes were in breaking their diets, eating Big Meal Deals and drinking Blizzards. The agents asked them their names and what they did, and Dessie May started telling them, "I'm not doing anything now but I'm planning on taking my daughter, Tandy Rae Renee, out of seventh grade and home schooling her, because I figure I can better guarantee helping Tandy become a woman of godly character and precious maintained virtue by keeping her away from school—where she's not even allowed to pray, thanks to atheists down in Austin—and away from those sex-crazed football players!"

Me and Manny were the only two behind the counter. I have my last period free and permission to work then, so I get to D-Q before the Domingo kids. Modesta had just gone to the I-G-A to buy bananas for banana splits, and Manny was trying to figure how he could call her there without being noticed by one of the Secret Service men.

Those men came right into the kitchen, where I was working, and started looking around for guns and bombs. I had to explain that the lye was for cleaning the stove, and we didn't use it except at the end of the day. Manny told me just to stand back and let them do their job. So I figured I'd move up to the counter and listen to what Lady Bird had to say, and one of those blue suits followed me.

Lady Bird was looking up, pondering the menu. "Are your fries cooked in vegetable oil?" she asked. I looked at her closely. Her signature dome-do had flyaway gray hairs, like she had been posing for pictures, standing in a patch of wildflowers along the highway, in the wind. But her eyes weren't watery. They were black and direct.

"Yes ma'am, White Swan, purest vegetable," Manny said with an air of pride. "Would you like to see?"

"Oh, heavens no," she said, though before she could get it out, I saw one of the security men hold up an oil can.

"I'll have a hamburger, medium-well, and fries," she said. "Hold the onions on that burger and put some mayonnaise on it, too. Oh, and I'd like a chocolate shake and a glass of water."

Manny rang it up. I was moving to go cook her sissy burger when he said, "I'll get this one, Johnny." So I figured I'd make the shake. "I'll get that, too!" he called out.

So I just had to stand aside and let him do it all, knowing full-well that Manny had never cooked a day in his life, and if there was anyone who would probably have an ice-cube's chance in hell of naming that meat, it was him. It was probably just as well though: me and T.J. used to talk about politics a lot. Once we had "a heated discourse" about LBJ's fault behind the Vietnam War. In my anger, I might have given Lady Bird a breadstick or two and got us in trouble. Considering my own Momma, though, I guess I shouldn't hold any woman accountable for the man she marries.

Once Lady Bird got her food, those Secret Service agents searched her burger from bun to bun. Then everyone took a position to watch her eat. I still sort of hoped to see her choke on a piece of gristle and get the Heimlich maneuver from an agent who would then make Manny lie on the floor for an interrogation about it. As it was, Lady Bird finished her meal, said "Thank you," and walked out. Louella moved in to snag the left-behinds for souvenirs, and I had to explain to her that the plastic basket is Dairy Queen property.

Manny spent the rest of the day at the register telling everybody how they had just missed the "First Lady of Texas." News must have traveled fast, because it seemed like everyone was there before church even started, buying Blizzards and the Christian Steak Finger Special, asking him to tell the story again, saying, "Sure enough," and "Is that right?"

Delaphine, Dora Dean, Delinda, Darla, Donnie, and Dulcinea all came in to help their parents handle the crowd. Manny started talking about putting a special message on the sign, "Cedar Springs D-Q Welcomes Lady Bird J. Anytime!" but I reminded him that, strangely enough, and surprise-surprise, we don't have enough *D*s or *R*s.

Me and Donnie were both busy in the back, cooking away, which was just fine with me. I was sick of hearing Manny's version of the story only. To tell the truth, I was a little bit bothered by it, too. I could think of no one in life who cared for my side of the story. Donnie hadn't asked. All the churchgoers and customers were Manny's people. Even my own Momma would rather hear it through one of them than to have me talk about work. And right then I realized something I had tried to forget ever since going to work there: in my world beyond Dairy Queen, I was completely alone.

Then Donnie started talking about Lady Bird having lunch with Princess Diana in Dallas last month.

"I would have just loved to have been there," he said, sticking some buttered buns on the grill. "I bet everything her royal highness knows about Texas, she knows from Lady Bird. . . . Hey, do you think it's a royal title? 'Lady Bird,' like Duchess of the Pedernales, or something?"

And I tell you, I was really ready to hit him or say something nasty, when Delinda asked me to get the drive-up window. The

Domingo girls were busy making shakes for the whole pep squad, and Manny was telling his story to Sheriff Parham. I looked out and saw this red convertible, and I thought, "Who owns that?"

I leaned out the window. "Welcome to Dairy Queen, m'elp you?" I had to yell. The top was down, and he was listening to his music so loud that I almost didn't recognize the tune. In six months, I hadn't been able to listen to the music T.J. and I shared. But here was this stranger bouncing in his seat and singing a song I knew all too well.

Talk is up, he's become my lover. People say he's now more than a friend, and 'fore this goes much further, I need to get his intent . . .

His long blond hair was straight and thick and blown evenly across his shoulders. And even though it's the middle of October, he wasn't wearing a shirt. His muscular chest was hairy and golden, and he had sunglasses like the Secret Service men wore. He looked right at me, but he kept singing.

He's a strangely quiet man. Kept his love for me captive to his plan. Folks got eyes for things I just can't see.

I might have sung along with him, showed him I knew every word, too. But, frankly, I was a little shocked, so I rested my hand on the order pad and listened. What I noticed strange is that he didn't change any of the "he's" to "she's," like a guy's supposed to when he sings a girl's love song.

Delaphine yelled out, "*Cállate!* Tell him to turn that *música* down. We got a jukebox in here, we don't need his *canciones!*" But I didn't have to, either he heard her or figured out what she said, and he turned it lower without my asking.

"Sorry, I just love the Judds, I sort of get carried away." He looked inside. "Let me guess, all the churches let out early for your Christian Steak Finger Special?"

He must have been driving with the top down for a long time. His skin was pink on top of tan, chapped by the wind. And his lips were dry, with white around on the edges. He gave a nice even-toothed smile, even though it must have hurt his lips. I wanted to tell him that I loved the Judds too, knew all the songs, had all the records. But he had already changed the subject.

"Well, partly," I said. "But they came extra early because Lady Bird Johnson was in here today."

"Sure enough? Is that right? Did you see her?"

"Yeah," I said, "and it was nothing, really, just a few Secret Service agents and Lady Bird Johnson stopping at D-Q for a burger and fries." And then, I don't what came over me, I became bold and leaned deep into the window and said, "Of course, if you ask me, LBJ, even though he was a Texan, was one of our more underhanded politicians. Though that's a redundant statement. I mean, underhandedness is the credo of contemporary politics."

It was a statement that T.J. used to make. Now I said it, with the suredness of a true personal opinion, even if the language wasn't my own. And it did what I wanted. It shifted the topic of conversation to more important matters, like why people are famous, instead of what they look like or wear or eat.

He smiled. "Is that right? Boy, I hope they don't plan to keep you here forever. I hate to think of the world being deprived of you. What's your name?"

He lifted his sunglasses, and I stared into those deep blue eyes.

"John Roy Hobson," I said.

"Well John Roy Hobson, I'll have me a pink lemonade. Large."

I gave him an extra-large, stuck some cookies in the bag, and a coupon for a free Blizzard and a free extra burger-patty on his next visit. I was thinking of how to ask him stuff about him and get him to say my name again, when Delinda said, "You better *andele pronto con sus ordenes*, you got two cars pulling up behind that order!"

"Here, just take it," I said, handing the bag to him. "And please, come back."

"If you're here, I sure will," he said, and he smiled. As he drove away, I leaned my head out the window to grab a look at his plates. Texas, thank God!

We said "Bye-bye, come back" to the last Methodists at ten-thirty. I hurried through my cleaning, thinking that maybe that guy had not gone far and come back.

In my mind, I saw that shimmery-red convertible parked by the Dumpster, just waiting for me. The top down, the passenger door open, I would get in and my new friend would take us on a starry night ride with accompaniment by the Judds. There, we would talk about the things we had in common. For the first time in a long time, Cedar Springs would seem different to me, better, part of the world of the good things to come that I had maybe stopped believing in.

But the parking lot was empty, except for Manny's truck, and because of clouds that floated fast above, there weren't any regular stars. I started walking home on Football Field Road, slowly, in case the stranger would still drive up.

The sprinklers were on in preparation for Friday's game. The water danced off the moonlight like the magic fairy dust that Tinkerbelle used to spread on "The Wonderful World of Disney." I stood watching it, wondering which direction I would go searching for that stranger once I got my car.

"Hey, wait up!"

The voice came from behind me, at the Dairy Queen, where the light on the sign had just been turned off. Donnie came running through the field that shortcutted the path from the restaurant, his glasses bouncing off his nose.

"Don't you have a ride home?" I asked.

"I told my Daddy I wanted to walk," he smiled, and for the first time I noticed that he wore a retainer, too, maybe because he put it on only at night.

"Are you OK?" he asked. "You don't seem right."

"I'm fine," I said.

"That was some car, wasn't it? That red convertible. I saw it," he said. "It takes a lot of money to buy something like that. The English royal family, they mostly use big cars like Bentleys and Rolls, but Jaguars used to be made in England, and they make sports cars. That wasn't a Jaguar was it?" he said.

I ignored him and looked at the fields.

"They're not supposed to leave those sprinklers on all night," he went on. "Sometimes Coach Schull forgets to turn them off and calls my Daddy from Iredell, where he lives. My Daddy knows how to turn them off."

"Was your Daddy coming to do that?" I asked.

"No, he's going home to write a letter to all the state legislators and their wives, inviting them to come to D-Q on their next stop through town. He's got an idea that this could become a real political stomping ground. We could turn them off," he said.

I started following him toward the clubhouse. "In England," he began, "they have football, too, but it's really soccer. They just call it that. I don't know if you've ever seen it or not, but it's not a bad or a mean sport. All the princes—Charles, Andrew, and Edward—used to play, though I think Prince Edward dropped out to do drama. Anyway, you have these two teams, and what they have to do is run and kick the ball into the other team's goal, which is at each end like our goal, only it's shaped like a big basket and not a *Y*. Doesn't that sound fun?"

"I don't know," I said. "I've never been much for running and kicking."

"There's none of this hitting that you see in our games," he said. "They don't even have to wear the heavy padding. Heck, they don't wear anything but shorts and shirts and tennis shoes in that game. Once I bought this French magazine, 'The Paris Match,' because it had some pictures of Princess Margaret, out drinking with her racy friends. I couldn't read any of it because it was all in French, but it had this picture of a soccer tournament, and these two men were both trying to kick the ball at the same time. Well, one of the guys had reached out to grab the other to keep him from kicking the ball, only he got a handful of shorts instead, and was pulling them so that the other guy's you-know-what was hanging out. That must have been terrible for him."

"Why?" I asked.

"Johnny, because it was out there, in front of God and everybody!"

"It might have felt good," I said, "the wind all over his down there. You never know until you try."

"I could never," he said, "I mean, not after. . . ." He put his hands in his pockets and looked back toward D-Q.

"Donnie, nothing happens that's not supposed to," I said. "At least, you know it's working . . . and speaking of work, I'm gonna wash mine off."

I pulled my collar away from my neck, then peeled off my shirt. Donnie looked at me in disbelief, so I kicked off my shoes and undid my pants. "This is how they do it in England!" I said. It was like a dance to imaginary music, and I was just shimmying and twisting without the slippery floor. Like the man in the Dairy Queen window I was performing for an audience of one, doing exactly what I liked. I pulled off my pants. "This is how they do it in France," I said.

Donnie liked it, too. He looked around, then looked right at me. I walked over and pulled off his shirt, inhaling the sweet-salt smell of sweat mixed with catsup. "This is how they do it in Texas," I said.

I unbuttoned his pants and pulled them to his knees, then waited for him to kick off his shoes so he could step out.

I could tell he was busting to get out of that underwear, but I left him to make that choice. Because that had been his own battle over the fear of who he was and what his body did. His own game of "Hidin' in the Fries," of trying to hide what made him feel different and badly famous, when he was just like the rest of us all along.

"Look at mine," I said, pulling off my underwear, "in the wind and the night it's hard not to get hard."

Donnie pulled his underwear down. There we stood, naked, facing each other. His body was thin and dark all over, hairless, except where his privates were. I reached out.

"Please don't!"

"Give me your hand," I said. I took it, and together we ran toward the sprinklers for a baptism of flesh in the waters of love.

We darted in and out of the waterline that ran the length of the field. I felt the jets against my thighs and arms, shooting across my neck and into my nostrils. I was laughing and, for the first time in my life, running completely free.

Donnie ran ahead of me, yelling out, "Long live the Queen! Long live the Queen! Long live Diana, Dairy Queen!"

"Long live us!" I said, and as I said it, I knew that it meant me and Donnie, or me and any friend who was willing to make it work with me.

Donnie's glasses must have been covered with water. He weaved unsteadily back and forth on the path, only crossing the waterline at the points where the spigots shot out of the ground. At the thirty-yard mark on the opposite side, he tripped on a sprinkler head. Before I could stop, I ran into him, and we both fell to the ground, laughing, hugging and rolling. His body felt good pressed against mine, a warm surface that made the chilly ground bearable.

"The Queen's down at the thirty," I said. "Now she must roll with the lowly subjects!" Donnie laughed harder.

We rolled again; then I crawled on top to face him. I realized he could barely see me through the mist on his glasses, so I slid them onto his forehead and gazed into his brown eyes. And there we breathed the warmth into each other's faces.

"I think I'm hurt," he said.

Donnie raised his foot to the light. I could see a slice of skin raised up above his big toenail, the blood beginning to ooze from beneath it.

"It looks pretty bad," I said, offering my hand. "Let's get you to a sprinkler to rinse it off."

I helped him up to a spigot where the water dribbled out gently on the side. We rinsed it there. Then I wrapped his arm around my shoulder, and we began making our way back to the clubhouse against a row of bleachers.

I thought of football players who help each other off the field this way, when one of them's hurt. The crowds yell and the girls all shout, "He's rowdy, he's rough, he's big and mean and tough!" And all the while, two guys are walking, touching out of need, just like T.J. and I did that day on the merry-go-round, only no one had been around to tell us it was okay.

Here, I wanted to touch Donnie more. I wanted to hug him again and feel his warm body pressed against mine on a cold ground. But that would have been like grabbing extras: extra toast, extra gravy, even an extra chance at salvation when the one we've been given should be enough.

And so I contented myself with what I had, and I prayed that this one night would not be the end of the new things that were happening to me. That more performers would come to my drive-up window. That I'd see more famous people and think less of them. That Donnie and I would find new places to run. Like the county fairgrounds on a full-moon night. The town cemetery on a windy autumn one. Us running from the white to the Mexican end, past my ancestors to his, all goose-bumpy, just kicking up leaves and laughter. Maybe we'd get caught by Brother Bill giving our own little testament to life under the watchful eye of God and the dead, who both know that life's too short to make pain for others, to miss the pleasure, or to worry what others will have to say.

BANSHEE MUSIC

• LIAM BROSNAHAN •

Griffin Riordan, as a first-time flyer, was surprised to learn how clearly whispers travel in the cabin of a plane. The droning engines, so near the spot where he had fallen (*Connaught*, read a sign overhead), failed to damp a single consonant of the murmuring brogues that were vaulting the narrow aisle above him.

"—gray as the carpet beneath his—"

"—could make a young man so sick—"

"—ber gloves if I had to touch anybo—"

"—really think so? Why, he looks perfec—"

"—cause God knows what's going arou—"

"Mr. Riordan? Mr. Riordan, isn't it?"

"Yes," answered Griffin faintly, his eyes still closed.

"What seems to be the trouble, now? Did you trip and hit your head, Mr. Riordan, is that it? Or are you ill?"

The murmurers rushed to answer for him.

"He was grayer than the Rock of Cashel even before we took off."

"He's alone, American, and look at his left hand: unmarried. Best not to touch him, dear, if ya know what I mean, till ya find out how long he's been—"

"Mr. Riordan? Are you still with me?"

"Yes . . ."

"Can you tell me what hurts? Can you sit up? There's an empty seat righ—"

"He can have my place," cut in an American woman's voice. "I'm not sitting near any—"

"Ladies and gentlemen, please return to your seats. We're taking care of things just fine, thank you. Eileen, find out what the folks'd like to drink. Thank you all, now; thank you. Mr. Riordan?"

"Still breathing . . ."

"It's a great relief to us all, I assure you. Now . . . can you open your eyes? Can you do that for me, Mr.—oh, you look too young to be a Mr. anything. What's your first name, love?"

"Griffin."

"Griffin Riordan . . . and a fine Italian name it is, too. Can you open your eyes for me, Griffin?"

The flight attendant's angular face loomed upside down above him.

"Ah, what nice gray eyes. Griffin, can you tell me now why you're napping in the aisle? Are you sick?"

Two more faces hovered into view like nosy balloons.

"Um . . . I thought I was . . . going to throw up, and—"

"He was passing my seat when he dropped," volunteered one balloon, whose dentures made her whistle like she'd sprung a leak.

"*Thank* you," insisted the attendant. "Griffin, what's hurting? Were you just dizzy, or are you on some kind of . . . medication?"

Griffin blinked several times as his eyes fixed on the woman's nameplate. ANNE was being helpful and sympathetic, but the nervous Babel of accents was swelling around them.

"—to share air for all this time, when he mi—"

"—thing catching, like the flu—"

"—meningitis—"

"—who says tuberculosis is on the rise agai—"

"—at his left hand, I tell you: *no ring.*"

"—or AIDS—"

"—AIDS?"

"—ya hear that, Jack? Jaysus, it's—"

"AIDS!"

"AIDS?!"

"AIDS! . . ."

The fact that it wasn't remained Griffin's secret as he succumbed to a fit of dry heaves. Grim new statistics on the plague were featured in almost every magazine on Flight 104, and a hangnail on one's neighbor was nearly inspiration enough for some to look for parachutes.

Griffin's eyes blurred and closed again. He had become, as he lay there on his back, peculiarly aware of the vibration of the plane and, particularly, of its sense of forward thrust. His feet were compassed at the cockpit and Shannon, and for the first time he felt like something—comet, knife, snowball—that was actually hurtling across the sky. This in turn made him think, for the first time all day, of Ben Óg.

Did the soul, as he'd been taught, really stay within the body until it is laid to rest? Sixteen months ago, then, had Ben Óg felt the wind's drag beneath his coffin on his last trip home? Somewhere, Ben Óg was probably watching this scene and enjoying it, as he would say, "right down to the ground"—an unfortunate phrase to remember at 30,000 feet.

"Griffin? You still with us?" said the stewardess, momentarily forgetting to sound blasé.

"Yes . . ."

Griffin opened his eyes again and tried to sit up.

The forward aisle was clotted with nervous passengers, who had already found and interposed a plainclothes bishop between themselves and Griffin. A narrow purple stole yoked the prelate's neck, signalling his readiness to say last rites, and rosaries were swaying like Spanish moss from several sets of hands. Griffin groaned and sank back to the floor.

"Griffin, tell me: *do you know* what's made you sick?"

Signs of the cross flew around the torsos of the frightened.

"Yes," wheezed Griffin. "I've never flown before . . . I have a phobia."

A deep voice came from behind His Eminence. "You mean it's not . . . you're sure it's not AIDS?"

"If you're phobic," sighed the much-relieved flight attendant, "what made you take this flight?"

Griffin took a large gulp of air. "I'm about to become a . . . I'm trying to get to Marychurch before my child is born."

The cabin resounded with relieved laughter.

"Phobia, my foot," said a nearby woman. "My husband, God

rest him, was just the same. God bless ya, darlin': you're in labor!"

In a trice, Griffin traveled from pariah to mascot and thoroughly hated the trip. The very hands that seconds before would have flung him from the plane were suddenly helping him from the floor, to the john, back to his seat, and proffering Dramamine and Dubonnet in gratitude for being someone they thought they could approve of.

"I'm not thirsty," he said curtly to a woman who held out a glass of something bubbly. He declined with equal terseness a cigar from a newly palsy man behind him. Glances of confusion intersected all around him.

"Nervous, eh?" said the man. "Your first, I suppose. I've got eight. I understand how—"

"You don't understand shit!" snapped Griffin.

"Well!" began a woman. "Pardon some of us who—"

"Hypocrites!" hissed Griffin, his head still spinning.

The cabin around him went library-still as the plane's shadow grazed the shore of Skellig Michael. The silence reigned intact for the brief descent to Shannon.

Ben Óg O'Brien had proclaimed the Deatharama. Inside his oxygen tent, the once-chubby patient raised a contraband Guinness like altar wine, to the shock of his friends from Alcoholics Anonymous. Turning up his broque, he intoned, "Lads, I give you . . . the Deatharama!"

His toast fell flatter than the tepid stout, as one of his and Griffin's visitors was already "showing," and two more—*merely* HIV-positive—were living each minute like the last verse of Musical Chairs.

Griffin, Macky, and Alonzo were left to volley winces of survivor guilt across the bed, while Ben Óg tried to goad Kayo, Chip, and Duncan into communal nose-thumbing at the nasty fate they shared. He failed, and their guests had evaporated before he finished his pint.

Griffin was too tired to give Ben Óg the fight he was angling for and affected interest in some part of the view outside St. Vincent's.

"Fuckin' Yanks've got no fuckin' sense of humor," prodded Ben Óg.

Griffin did not reply.

"Want a sip of kryptonite?" Ben Óg persisted.

"No. But I'll go find you a glass, if you'd like."

Griffin had been so emotionally numb for weeks that nothing his lover said—and Ben Óg tried many ploys before visiting hours were over—could rouse him to rise to the bait. As he expected, the effort soon tired Ben Óg, who drifted off shortly after unveiling another failed outrage: using multicolored markers cadged from the nurse, he had mapped constellations among his galaxy of lesions. Griffin buttoned Ben Óg's pajama top before he left and then went home to call Macky, his AA sponsor, to apologize for Ben Óg and recite his litany of daily affirmations.

Deatharama. Ben Óg, after days of delirium, died in his sleep one week later, followed in shockingly short order by Chip (who'd been showing) and by Duncan, one of the positives, who surrendered to his illness overnight as meekly as a teacher's pet. Kayo, the other positive, didn't die for another fifteen months, though his lover Macky waited only another fifteen seconds to part the curtains and follow Kayo's soul out the window.

Alonzo, whom Macky had also sponsored in AA for nine years, moved back to the Maine woods in shock and drank himself to death. Griffin attended three meetings a day for months and more or less survived.

It was as he sat watching Ben Óg's last home video for the dozenth time that The Idea actually came to roost. The Deatharama had been expanding recently with the deaths of Kayo and Macky; Griffin's old calico cat; most of his houseplants; an elderly neighbor; his secretary; his VCR; everything around him, the breathing and the merely mechanical, seemed to be dying. Late one night, within seconds of each other, the bulb in the floor lamp he was reading by went *spink* and the snap of a trap beneath the sink boasted two more for Deatharama; the lightbulb and the mouse both were cold and gray. Griffin grabbed his coat and fled the apartment, arriving at the stoop just as an ambulance pulled screaming away from two fresh chalkies on the sidewalk.

If not for the coroner clucking his tongue nearby, Griffin might have convinced himself that Keith Haring's ghost had merely returned to New York for some nostalgic doodling on the pavement ... and The Idea to strike back against Deatharama would not have been born, would not have inspired a revenge that, nine months later, could backfire so very publicly on the floor of a 747.

"Have you people comin' for you, Mr. Riordan?"

Anne, the ministering angel from Flight 104, had pulled her car up to the curb outside the terminal, where Griffin was sitting on his luggage, inhaling the damp April dawn and fighting the urge to fly right back home.

"Excuse me? Oh, it's ... no, nobody knows I'm here," said Griffin.

"Well, where's the blessed event taking—ah, Marychurch, didn't you say? On the Ring of Kerry. Your missus is a Kerry girl, then?"

"We're not married."

"Sorry ... sorry. Didn't mean to pry."

Griffin chuckled to ward off the sob that was climbing his windpipe.

"No offense taken." He exhaled noisily. "I've just awakened in a sort of kelly green nightmare of my own construction."

Anne spoke delicately. "But now you've come here ... to do 'the right thing'?"

Whatever that is, Griffin said to himself. The woman's eyebrows were as pitched as the sides of a tent as she awaited his reply.

"Do you pray?" Griffin asked.

"This *is* Ireland, Mr. Riordan ..."

"Right. Well, could I ask you to say a prayer for me tonight?"

"I can do a little better than that. Let me give you a lift into Limerick, and we can say the rosary together on the way, if you'd like."

"Thanks, but I'm going to just sit here awhile longer ... though I will hold you to a Hail Mary as you go on your way."

Anne studied her former passenger before speaking.

"If you don't mind my asking, Mr. Riordan ... what do you do back in America?"

Griffin smiled sheepishly. "I own a travel agency."

The woman's head shook just enough to notice.

"You know," she said, "I think I'll go catch an early mass. God go with you, Griffin Riordan. And your baby, too." She waved and drove away.

Griffin noticed that Anne's blessing omitted the mother to be and he wondered if it was an omen. Seconds later, the dry heaves returned and his stomach emptied until, physically at least and at last, the expectant father concluded that he just might live.

"All better this morning, dear?"

Griffin walked into Mrs. McGillicuddy's wallpapered dining room and, sitting at the small linened table she indicated, assured his hostess he was much improved.

"Twenty-one hours," said the landlady approvingly to her only other guests, an Indian couple, both physicians, whose generous smiles conveyed a complete lack of interest.

"Jet lag!" crooned Mrs. McGillicuddy. "Our young man here slept longer than any other guest I've had all year."

"Do I get some sort of prize?" said Griffin. The others blinked at him for a count of three and then chuckled politely.

"Tea or coffee?" asked Mrs. McGillicuddy.

Tea was ordered along with the traditional Irish breakfast that one guidebook dubbed Death By Cholesterol: oatmeal with cream, bacon *and* sausage, fried eggs, blood pudding, grilled tomato, toast, butter, marmalade, brown bread, tea, and orange juice. As Griffin ate, trading travel pleasantries with the Drs. Chowdhury, the doorbell rang, and moments later there were three new guests, rainsoaked and freshly arrived from Shannon Airport. The twentyish girls and their slightly younger brother (as it turned out) were blue-jeaned, blonde, and blue-eyed Swedes with matching red backpacks. One of the girls was having a coughing fit as they entered the room, and the boy was pounding her back with a rag-bandaged hand. A vivid red stain there caught the attention of the Chowdhurys, who resignedly escorted the three out of the room, over numerous apologies, to examine and treat them upstairs. Griffin was relieved to finish his meal in solitude and to watch the rainstorm raging outside the bay window.

"Will you be staying again tonight," said Mrs. McGillicuddy

as she returned to clear the doctors' table, "or are you going right on to see your family?"

"My family?"

"Cousins and such, you know. You said when you arrived it was your first time across the water, and, with a good Jewish name like Riordan, I figured you'd be looking for your roots. Most Americans do."

Mrs. McGillicuddy told her guest about the national genealogy office in Dublin where he might get help in finding "the source of the river Riordan" (Griffin chuckled obediently), about local points of interest around Limerick, and about the McGillicuddy diaspora, much of which had settled in Griffin's hometown of New York.

The landlady was an astute conversationalist with an almost surgical interrogative technique, the product of decades of practice on polite, weary strangers. Her chatty style conveyed the impression that her favorite topic was Nora T. McGillicuddy, but deftly placed *Don't ya find*s and *You probably think*s invariably nudged her guests into leaking virtual dossiers on themselves. Griffin had admitted to being an only child, owning Timely Travel, and living just off Central Park before the grandmotherly woman had even finished crumbing his tablecloth.

It was the transparent "And is your wife of Irish descent, too?" that made Griffin sit up straighter.

"What makes you think I'm married?" he asked with a forced playfulness that was not lost on his questioner.

"I just figured a fine-looking young American with a full head of hair and his own business would've had his pick o' the pack," cooed the woman, who boldly continued by asking her guest point blank about his age.

"How old do you think?" countered Griffin, who was determined to ask all the questions from then on.

"Thirty-six," she immediately replied. Her quickness—and her accuracy—caught Griffin by surprise.

"You're good," he allowed.

"A young thirty-four," she amended consolingly.

Griffin's breathing was a little forced, as if he had just played a set on the tennis court. His landlady, however, was smiling serenely.

"So . . . will you be heading straight on to Marychurch?"

Griffin swallowed. "I haven't—how do you know about Marychurch?"

"You left your Frommer's on the desk yesterday when you checked in. I didn't notice it till later on," she hastened to assure him. "Marychurch was circled on the map. You'll have to go by bus to Killarney and switch there to one of the buses that goes round the Ring. I've got all the schedules."

Though Griffin would have liked to put off the trip—for anywhere from a day to a decade—he thanked Mrs. McGillicuddy for her help.

"Do you—"

"Now the Lindens just closed its doors last spring, when the Shanahans retired," the woman cut in, anticipating Griffin's question. "Arbutus House isn't ITB-approved, and Amber Lodge has only been taking guests by recommendation since poor Pauline died."

"How do you know so—"

"I'm from Caherciveen, the next town back," said the woman. "There's nothing else for a dozen miles but Amber Lodge, and the rooms are all *en suite*. Shall I ring them up and see if they can take you?"

Griffin nodded perfunctorily, certain Mrs. McGillicuddy could just as easily have read his mind.

"How long's it been since your last drink and what do you know about children's books?"

"Three years, eight months, three weeks, four days, and not a blessed thing."

"Good man. I'm Ben O'Brien; my friends call me Ben Óg."

"Griffin Riordan. How long since your last drink and why would they call you 'Ugh'? You're not *that* bad . . ."

The Irishman laughed delightedly. "One year, one month, a week, one day, and it's 'Óg', not 'ugh.' Means 'little' or 'junior,' sort of. Riordan, eh? Don't you even recognize the mother tongue when you hear it? What are you, half English or something?"

"*Póg mo thóin*, Ben Óg."

"Ah, the three words even the most diluted mick knows. *Kiss* it? I'll bite it if it's pretty enough. Turn around and let's have a look."

Griffin would always claim that by that point in the conversation he was already in love.

As the Bus Eireann coach passed the halfway point to Marychurch, Griffin slipped in and out of dreams of Ben Óg (which all, happily, predated his illness). These gave way abruptly to sinister phantasms of the woman he had followed to Ireland. Thief, harpy, stalker, ghost: she was each of these in turn and then simultaneously until the cruelest dream began.

Ben Óg was seated at their favorite table at Radio Daze as Griffin came in. He was grinning broadly despite being Dalmatian with lesions and attached by tubes to a shiny chrome machine that hissed and beeped, sitting in the spot where Griffin's chair would normally be. Griffin sat beside Ben Óg on the banquette.

"You order yet?"

Ben Óg ignored the question. "There's someone I want you to meet . . ."

"Aren't you hungry?"

"I don't see her . . . wait, here she is!"

Ben Óg began to fade as a jagged shadow fell across the table. "What's happening? Ben Óg! Wait!"

"Griffin, my own, I'd like you to meet . . ."

He vanished completely.

"So you're the one," said a velvety voice.

"Tara!"

The restaurant shattered into atoms as Griffin bolted from the dream, relieved to find that the panicked shout had not made its way out of his head. Or so he thought.

"Excuse me," said an old woman in a floral scarf from across the aisle. She leaned forward, her eyes gleaming. "Would ya be goin' to Marychurch?"

"Yes, I am."

"You were whisperin' in yer sleep, y'see, and we couldn't help overhearin' . . ." The woman's companion, similarly scarved, was also watching intently. "Are ya a friend of our Tara Power?"

"You know her?"

In all his life, Griffin had never told a joke that had the effect of his mere three words. With the bus ringing with laughter louder than air-raid sirens, he looked anxiously out the window across a field at a scaffolded spire, his first glimpse of the village of Marychurch.

"I take it, Mr. Riordan, that you are not from Down Under?"

The cardiganed man on the threshold of Amber Lodge was eyeing Griffin intently and made no move to admit him.

"Australian? No, why do you ask?" said Griffin, pretending not to mind the rain that was starting to soak his shoulders.

"And you aren't some kind of . . . cowboy?"

"I'm a travel agent. Look, didn't Mrs. McGilli—"

"Is that our Aussie?" came a thrilled shriek from deep in the house. Seconds later, the white-haired man was rudely nudged aside by an excited young girl who looked at Griffin as if at the answer to a prayer.

"So you're the rope twirler who's scared off our cow!"

Before he could answer, Griffin was yanked into the front hall of the Georgian house.

"G'day, mate! *Cead mille failte* and *cead mille* thank-yous!"

"He's not Australian," said the old man, shutting the door.

"Aah," said the girl as she circled the newcomer appraisingly. "Then he probably isn't any of the other things we've heard."

"Um, what have you heard?"

"Left-handed ex-convict ranchhand with a tattoo—I shan't say where—that reads 'Say Your Prayers'?"

"Well . . . I am left-handed . . ."

"But you do know Tara?"

"It's starting to look like everyone does."

"And it wasn't . . ." The girl looked at Griffin with what looked like disappointment. ". . . rape?"

"Fidelma!" shouted the man.

"Actually," Griffin shot back, "it was a test tube."

His hosts were too surprised to reply, for which he was grateful.

"If I can just put my bags in my room, I'd like to go find Tara. Can you tell me which is her family's house?"

"You're standing in it," said the girl. "My name is Fidelma, but do you want to call me Sis?"

Fidelma looked little like her half-sister. Her hair, though long like Tara's, was *merely* long and an indifferent dark blonde disposed to knot, unlike the molten lava that tumbled so symbolically from Tara's scalp. Her complexion was buckshot with acne, and, above brown eyes that knew no midpoint between squinting and popping, she had brows like caterpillars. She was almost seventeen, she informed Griffin, though she looked a good two years younger.

The white-haired man stepped forward. "Fitzgerald," sighed Tara's stepfather, almost grudgingly extending his hand. Rory Óg Fitzgerald looked like someone too accustomed to shaking hands with trouble, and Griffin could easily guess why.

"So where is Tara?"

"Gone, gone!" cried Fidelma, breaking into a jig. "She heard there was a Mr. Riordan on his way and she had her bags out the door before you could say 'Australian cowboy.' "

"What did she tell you about me?"

"Fidelma, shut your trap and go put the kettle on."

The girl frowned and rolled her eyes but obeyed at once. Her father showed Griffin up to his room and gave him towels and keys while relating his stepdaughter's tale of living on a cattle station in Queensland, where she was date-raped by a cowhand who was now in prison on a drug charge.

"Christ," said Rory Óg, "it sounds like the plot of a bad operetta, doesn't it? It's more likely that *she'd* rape *you*."

The God's truth of that statement went unaddressed as Griffin followed the older man back down to the parlor, where a comforting fire crackled behind the tea table that Fidelma was setting.

Over a pot of Darjeeling, Griffin gave the Fitzgeralds a heavily edited abstract of his life. He squirmed through it, though, since even back in Prestonia, West Virginia, he had shunned the closet and had even less need for one after moving to New York. Ben Óg had often remarked with uncharacteristic bitterness, however, that "a chiffarobe at the least" was imperative for a stranger in Ireland. Therefore, Griffin merely acknowledged hailing from Prestonia and Manhattan, that his parents were deceased, that he loved Irish music, was left-handed, and was the father of Tara Power's child.

He did not mention the Deatharama. Fidelma and Rory Óg merely heard how Griffin was befriended by the beautiful redhead after the untimely death of his best friend.

"She started waiting tables at my favorite restaurant. Her accent reminded me of my friend's, and we just hit it off. We began going to movies, flea markets, concer—"

"Cut to the chase, please," said Rory Óg. "One romance is much like—"

"It was never a romance. We were simply friends."

"Well, then, where's the test tube enter the picture?" asked Fidelma.

Griffin described the day that Tara announced, with convincing nonchalance, her decision to become a single mother since, at thirty-two, her biological clock was ticking—

"The cow is only twenty-six," said Fidelma.

—since she was more prepared for "middle age" now that she had her green card—

"She didn't," Griffin interrupted himself to confirm.

—and since she valued her independence above all.

Rory Óg sighed. "How much did that particular lie cost you?"

"That's not important," Griffin replied, lying only by half. Avoiding any direct mention of Ben Óg, Griffin said there had just seemed to be too much death around, and so he had volunteered—

"So you thought," murmured Fidelma.

—to be the sperm donor for Tara's child.

"You poor lads always think they're your ideas," said Fitzgerald wearily. "Tara could plant a tree so's the soil wouldn't notice."

Griffin didn't know whether a brotherhood of chumps should make him feel better or worse. "Do you know where she's gone?"

"Not a clue!" cheered Fidelma.

"She can't go too far, though," said Mr. Fitzgerald.

"Why not?" said both Griffin and Fidelma.

In answer, Rory Óg held up a dark green passport.

"Dad!" shrieked the girl. "You're daft! Why didn't you pin it to her jumper and buy her a one-way—"

"Mr. Riordan," said the man, ignoring the outburst, "Tara's not my child. She was my wife's by her first husband, an arrant fool named Tully Power. Pauline struggled through four years of marriage before he deserted her and the child. He'd come back unannounced for visits around once a year like Santa

Claus—anyway, that's how the girl looked on him, even though he abandoned her over and over. Finally, your man had the courtesy to break his neck on a staircase and free my Pauline to remarry. But Tara refused to let me adopt her legally."

"Why?"

Fidelma leapt to her feet like a cheerleader.

"What's the world's most precious gift? Tara Power. What gives any room a lift? Tara Power. What energy source will never drift? Tara Power!"

"As you can see, he wasn't much of a poet, either. All he left the girl was a hunger for control and a short attention span. The only thing she's ever been sure of is what she *doesn't* want."

"She seemed to want this baby, at first," said Griffin. "But just a week after we learned we were pregnant, she went into an emotional tailspin that was the scariest thing I ever . . . she informed me that the pregnancy was a mistake and she was going to have an abortion."

Fidelma started at the word, one vastly more loaded in a country that did not even have legal divorce. Griffin plowed on immediately to avoid a debate rendered insignificant by the circumstances.

"I talked her out of it."

Griffin blushed at the memory. Rory Óg and Fidelma didn't know of Deatharama, but Tara had, and the symbolic value of her pregnancy became her magic wand. She wielded it over Griffin whenever she was feeling bored or ignored, and Griffin went hoarse pleading and cajoling. Faced with abortion of his child—his battle cry against Deatharama—Griffin grew desperate. As he discussed "the abortion option" with Tara (who savored that phrase like a rich dessert), Griffin fought to conceal both his swelling panic and his shame at the politics of his position.

"I'm ending the pregnancy," Tara proclaimed (the first time), " 'cause face it, we made a mistake."

Agreement danced on the tip of his tongue before being banished to a far canyon of his psyche as, on the wall over Tara's shoulder, Griffin thought he saw the silhouettes of all his dead and made a silent, guilty vow to tithe his income to Planned Parenthood for the rest of his life.

"You know, don't you, that it's probably for the best, now?"

Tara had left the door slightly ajar. By the end of the conversation, Griffin concluded that "probably" had to be Gaelic for "make me an offer."

"How long's it been, Mr. Riordan, since you saw Tara last?" said Fitzgerald.

"Please, call me Griffin, both of you. It's been twelve days. She just disappeared in the middle of the night."

"So the two of you were living together," said Mr. Fitzgerald calmly.

"The *three* of us were, yes. She lost her apartment—"

"Why?" asked Fidelma.

"She stopped paying her rent." As Fidelma mouthed a silent *oh*, Griffin continued. "She also wasn't taking care of her health, what with her smoking and her junk food, which meant she wasn't taking care of the baby. So, as you can see, I didn't have much of a choice."

"That's our mantis," said Fidelma.

"I thought she was your 'cow,'" said Griffin, who already felt connected to the girl through the anger they shared.

"She is. She's our cow, our cat, our pig, our goat—"

"Fidelma . . ."

"—and the only snake in Ireland," said Fidelma, ignoring her father. "But right now she strikes me as a mantis, 'cause she's definitely the kind who'd eat her young. Christ, I've got scars where she's taken nips out of me. You'd better be there the second she gives birth, Mr. Griffin Riordan, and grab your baby and run like hell!"

Rory Óg was about to warn her about her mouth, but before he could utter a syllable, the girl had dashed from the room and, the front door slamming after her, from the house.

An awkward silence reigned as the two men finished their tea, staring fixedly at the fire to avoid looking at each other, until Griffin stood up and changed the topic to something neutral.

"May I pay for my room by credit card, Mr. Fitzgerald, or do you prefer cash?"

"With everything our family's already cost you, you think I'd be taking another penny out of your pocket?"

"You're not responsible for anything that Tara—"

"Please, young man, please; the devil's laughing loud enough already. If you fancy another reason, let's just say you're practically the stepson-in-law I never had."

"Well, then . . . thanks for your hospitality."

"*And* maybe you'll feel just grateful enough not to sue us later on."

The older man got up stiffly and walked across the worn Oriental carpets to a mahogany armoire that proved to be a liquor cabinet.

"So, now, Griffin . . . what's your pleasure?" said the host.

"Just some Ballygowan Water, if you've got it," said the guest.

Rory Óg took Griffin to the kitchen, where he found the bottled water and served it on the rocks and then gave him a tour of Amber Lodge, which was larger than Griffin had expected from outside. Besides Griffin's, there were eight more bedrooms on the upper floor, where an immense, round-arched window on the landing overlooked a garden, fields, and, in the distance, the same scaffolded spire Griffin had seen from the Bus Eireann coach.

"St. Munchin's," said Rory Óg, who reciprocated his guest's first-name informality. "There's a novena going on there later tonight—Christ, when isn't there!—to pray for the conversion of the Somalians . . . or the Ethiopians . . . anyhow, somebody dark and far away. The signs are plastered on everything but the cows."

"Are you going?" asked Griffin, who wasn't really interested but didn't want to appear disrespec—

"Wear out the knees of my best trousers with those superstitious mugwumps? 'Opiate of the masses,' indeed; Marx may've been a bloody Communist, but he hit that pin right on the head, smashing a dozen angels that were dancing there. What about you? You're not a Jesus jumper, are you?"

"No, but I'm not quite an atheist; more like an agnostic and a half."

"That's a good one, very good—I'll have to write that down. No, the way I see it, religion is less about the need to believe than the need to belong."

For decades, Rory Óg had uttered that well-tooled aphorism at least once a week, each time as if it had just come to him. To his regret, no one had ever asked to write it down.

"Well put, Mr. Fitz—Rory. You'd better write *that* down before you forget it."

The philosopher nodded weakly; it just wasn't the same.

"Rory *Óg*," he then gently corrected, changing the subject. "Everybody here and about still thinks of me as Little Rory, 'cause my old man—Rory the First—only died last winter. So he was always the real Rory, and I was just his Óg."

At that moment the front door slammed again, and Fidelma called from the downstairs hall.

"What passes for dinner will be served in exactly thirty minutes. Latecomers will not be seated till dessert. You have been warned."

"My daughter's idea of cooking will make Tara's sins look venial by comparison," said Rory Óg. "You have been warned."

Rory Óg excused himself, and Griffin followed the sound of banging pot lids back to the kitchen.

"Can I help?"

Fidelma didn't look around from the porcelain drainboard where she was chopping vegetables. "Trying to ingratiate yourself?"

"Trying to save myself. Your father says that your cooking is a felony."

"Can you cook?"

"A little. Probably enough. What've we got?"

With Fidelma's help, Griffin turned a leftover roast and the vegetables into a near-stroganoff, which he served over vermicelli, the closest thing to noodles they could find in the pantry.

"Where's the spice rack?"

"You're shaking it." Griffin was holding the salt. "Wait a second. I think . . ." Fidelma went back to the pantry and rummaged through drawers and cabinets until she cried, "Aha!" and emerged holding a never-opened tin of ground coriander that looked old enough to vote.

"Interesting flavor," said Rory Óg later with an unreadable expression on his face.

"Maybe Fidelma could show me tomorrow where I can buy some other spices."

"You staying long enough to use 'em?" asked the girl.

"Well . . ." Griffin was blushing again, though even he was

unsure why. "I figure Tara might come back in a day or two, thinking I've given up and—no, huh?"

Rory Óg was shaking his head. "She won't come within two counties until she knows you've gone. And, though we might be able to fool her—"

"Though God knows why we'd want to," murmured Fidelma.

"—she just has to make one other call to find out if we're telling the truth."

"To whom?"

"Her cousin Finn. From the Tierney side, her mother's people. He's always been a sort of big brother to her. He's the one she'll call before she comes back here. You have any hope of getting to Tara, it's through him."

"Where do I find him?"

"Dublin," said Fidelma. "He went there yesterday on business. He should be back tomorrow, though. I'll take you round to see him."

Nothing more concerning Tara was said, and the remainder of the meal passed very enjoyably. Griffin's coriandered concoction was succeeded by lemon sherbet, though he declined the brandy that Rory Óg surprised him with.

"Not a drinking man, then?"

"I had hepatitis ten months ago," Griffin lied. "Bad shellfish. I'm not allowed to touch anything for another—"

"You fathered a child while you had hepatitis?"

"I—no, I mean . . ." Griffin's cheeks were glowing again. "God . . . I've always been such a lousy liar. Ben Óg always used to say I—"

"Who's Ben Óg?"

Griffin's jaw actually fell as the boiling blood in his cheeks took to even higher ground. The hepatitis lie, barely seconds old, already stood brazenly upstaged. Over the course of one pleasant meal he had become so comfortable with the Fitzgeralds that his guard had not only dropped but had briefly blown away. He already felt as if he knew them. Lack of practice with the closet, however, had made him forget that they didn't know *him.*

"Something wrong?" said Fidelma, returning from dishwashing and seeing Griffin's stricken look.

"No, I . . . your father just asked about someone I mentioned."

"Another Óg!" said Fitzgerald.

"My best fr—my roommate."

"The one who died?" said Fidelma.

Recollection took three interminable seconds. He *had* told them—just—that Tara had met him and cheered him up (Tara actually had created some good old days) after a "close friend" had died.

There was no time for relief. "Yes. He died sixteen months ago."

"So, what about the hepatitis?" said Rory Óg, lighting a pipe. "Is that what you were a 'lousy liar' about?"

"Yeah."

"Then you didn't have hepatitis?"

Griffin wanted to ask if the man was related to Mrs. McGillicuddy. Rory Óg, however, wielded no conversational scalpel. Griffin's ad hoc excuses conflicted so obviously no curiosity was required to see through them.

"I have never had hepatitis. I refused your liquor because I used to have a drinking problem."

"And *that* embarrassed you? Lad, check your passport: your chair is in *Ireland*! I toast you for buckin' the stereotype, but any Irishman—even a foreign one—who's put down his pint has no need to be ashamed. More power to you!" said Rory Óg, raising an ironic snifter in salute.

"There's AA in Ballykeena, if you need it," said Fidelma.

"Thank you," said Griffin, still a bit unnerved.

Conversation reverted then to less stressful topics, and over the course of the next hour the man who'd only experienced tourism by proxy impressed his hosts with how much he knew about a country he'd never seen till Tuesday. In phone calls and thank-you postcards to Timely Travel, hundreds of happy clients over a dozen years had described every hill and pub and bog in Ireland, and Griffin, heir to his immigrant grandparents' nostalgia for the isle, inhaled each story like the perfume of burning peat.

Griffin Riordan knew how the term "lynch law" originated in Galway town; how far back one was lowered to kiss the Blarney Stone; that Charlie Chaplin had spent part of many a summer in Waterville; how near to Bunratty Castle stood the door to Durty Nelly's; what it cost to rent a jaunting car in Killarney; how long it took to get from Dublin down to Bray.

Griffin also knew, though he didn't say, how fast a homosexual son could be disowned in Ireland and driven to emigrate to a city he didn't like in a country he couldn't love. Griffin had inherited Ben Óg's stories also, and, thereafter, longing and loathing combined in a diphthong of emotions that he'd been "hearing," more intensely than ever, since the moment he had first arrived at Shannon.

"Why's your business called Timely Travel?" asked Fidelma. "Are all of the flights you book guaranteed to leave on time or something?"

"Actually, it's named after a character—"

"From the Clockinvar Chronicles?"

Griffin swallowed a gasp. "Have you read them?"

"Those were the first children's books my Pauline ever bought her," said Rory Óg, "and the only ones she ever wanted to hear . . . over and *over.*"

"*Hourtown,* is my favorite," said Fidelma, except for *Morning in Minuteapolis,* or maybe *The Saga of Synchroni City,* or—"

"Written by an Irishman, so they say," said Rory Óg, "though that pseudonym, 'Clockinvar,' didn't sound very Ir—"

"*The Saga of Synchroni City,* definitely," said Fidelma. "It's the best, though only by a hair. Wait, I forget. How'd we get onto Clockinvar again?"

"Timely Travel."

"Oh, right. So, what, did you read 'em to your nieces and—no, you're an only child, you said."

"Only child, lonely child," quoted Rory Óg, whose eyelids were starting to sag.

"Don't I know it," said his daughter.

"You have Tara," Griffin reminded her.

"Nobody *has* Tara, I'll thank you to be remembering, though we've all been had by her."

"Very quick with the quips, aren't you?"

"When God flipped the coin, the French got the lips but we got the tongues."

"What a lawyer you'd make," said her guest admiringly.

" 'The first thing we do, let's kill all the lawyers,' " she quoted.

"Is that Shaw?"

"Should've been. He was Irish. But no, it's *Henry VI, Part 2.* We've just read it in school."

"Whatever happened to *A Midsummer Night's Dream?*"

"We finished the comedies a year ago."

"Oh." The excellence of Irish education thus reaffirmed, Griffin, who could barely remember the difference between Brutus and Benedick, was relieved when Fidelma excused herself to do her homework. Rory Óg also bade Griffin goodnight and went to bed.

It was only 8:00. Griffin flipped through some outdated magazines on the coffee table and then turned on the television. For an hour he played with the remote, flipping from RTE to Sky 1 to the BBC, puzzling at the bland Australian soaps and American sitcoms that aired in place of native programming. One home-grown broadcast did turn up, a quiz show for children, though the host and the contestants spoke exclusively in the Irish language. Griffin watched anyhow, fascinated as always by the way that the words, though not understood, still managed not to sound foreign to his hopelessly American ears. Years before the first time Ben Óg had rasped his "nighttime Irish" into his lover's ecstatic ears, Griffin had borrowed a recording of Celtic poetry from the library and listened in fascination to the vocabulary that British kings and famine flight had denied him. The mother tongue was the one thing that even Timely Travel's most grateful clients could not help him understand.

The team of students from County Roscommon were apparently being declared the quiz show champions as Griffin turned off the television. The china mantel clock said nine, but his internal clock was still on eastern standard time. Sleep was hours away.

Minutes later Griffin was passing St. Munchin's, from which the amplified novena was struggling to be heard through blasts of ear-splitting feedback. A guilty trickle of newly deaf parishioners was leaking from the baptistry door and wobbling diagonally across O'Connell Street to a pub nearly as noisy as the church. Griffin considered going inside until a rift in the clouds enabled the full moon to frost the town and the hills beyond with a silver shimmer that traveled like the glow of an usherette's flashlight. As if limning the way to where Griffin's own private needle and haystack were waiting, the light continued down the street and out of town, disappearing over the crest of the nearest hill.

THE CEMETERY

• PETER CASHORALI •

"What about Tyrone Power?" Mark asks, stopping by the grave. Tyrone Power's monument is white marble—a huge book, a scroll and a bench you have to sit on in order to read the scroll.

"Who?" Ricardo asks, walking a few yards away.

"An actor," Mark says. "See how it's a bench? He liked to have guys sit on his face."

"Really?" Ricardo says, momentarily interested, then dismissing it. "No. I don't need actors."

"Pity. There's a lot of them here." He moves on. They're in Hollywood Cemetery, the first visitors on a Fall of the House of Usher morning, the sky full of grey cotton, the sounds muffled. The layout is vaguely familiar to Mark: a friend once brought him here on a tour of famous graves, showing him Tyrone Power's bench, Peter Lorre's niche in the big mausoleum, Douglas Fairbanks's Olympic-size pool. The friend said that Valentino was here someplace, but he didn't know where. Valentino was the only one Mark was really interested in seeing. "Here's an army officer," he says.

Ricardo comes over, teaspoon in hand. "Let's see," he says, reading the information off the headstone for himself. "Give me one of the bags." He squats down and puts three spoonfuls of dirt from the base of the stone into the small paper bag, then drops three pennies into the hole. Mark looks around to make sure no groundskeeper is watching from the other side of the

miniature lake. Ricardo stands up and smooths the hole over
with his foot. "Just his name and what he was. I don't need his
dates," he says, twisting the bag closed. He hands it to Mark for
inscription.

"What about his being a Beloved Husband?" Mark asks,
printing "Captain of Infantry" on the bag.

"No. Now see if you find a priest. I need a priest and a judge.
And a policeman," Ricardo says, resuming his hunt among the
graves.

Mark stows the bag in his jacket pocket with the other two.
"So is this going to kill her?" he asks. Ricardo's landlady at the
shop warned him she's going to raise the rent again this year,
trying to crowd him out so her own costume business can break
through the wall and have his space.

"I wish," Ricardo says, taking out a cigarette. "Maybe." He
lights up, inhales, blows out smoke. "This is going to make her
own evil turn around and come back to her. All I need is the
seven earths from the cemetery." He showed Mark all the other
ingredients for the spell as they drove here—sticks of wood
with names like "Conqueror," "Shirt-ripper," "I-can-more-
than-you," tiny bottles of mercury ("So that things start
moving—") and gunpowder, a little packet of black salt ("They
take sea salt and burn everything away and black salt is what's
left."). He hit every botanica in Silverlake last night, some of
them staying open especially for him, each old woman recom-
mending her own special addition to give the recipe some kick.
"She'll know who she's fucking around with," he says, grim as
granite. A tiny kestrel nicks down to the lake, nabs something
and flies to the top of a cypress tree.

When Mark developed his first opportunistic infection—
candida—Ricardo took a lump of alum out of the cabinet where
he kept his Santeria supplies, dissolved it in a glass of water and
told Mark to brush his tongue with it every morning. When he
had diarrhea, Ricardo put handfuls of rue, mint, pepperozine
and a garlic clove in the blender ("Forget it. Jesus, it smells awful.") and made him drink two full glasses. One night Mark
woke up and heard Ricardo in the next room, talking to one of
the orishas in the African language santeros pray in. He heard
his own name in among the foreign syllables, and then Ricardo,
furious, saying, "Don't let him be afraid. Just fucking don't let

him be afraid," like a dog growling instructions to an approaching thunderstorm. But now Mark's developed herpes on the sides and bottom of his tongue, and though Ricardo cleansed him with duck eggs and then with a rooster, Mark's had to resort to Zovirax capsules. They're not working as quickly as Ricardo's remedies. The herpes are unpleasant to come in contact with, but the worst part is that they're just a calling card from larger visitors on their way.

Last night while Ricardo and his *ahijado* were out on their botanica-crawl—because Ricardo, fledged in Santeria, now has a student of his own—Mark stayed home. Even the idea of getting into the car and turning the key in the ignition was exhausting. And so, though the imperative "Go out! Go out! Go out!" thumped in the back of his head, his body had its own way, and he sprawled across the bed turning the pages of the *LA Weekly*.

He came across an article on the Grammys, which didn't interest him, but there was a list of who had won for Song of the Year since it began, and who the *Weekly* thought should have won. Mark's never paid much attention to what music's been playing around him, so he was surprised that he knew all the songs up to 1987. Not only knew them, but could hear them as he read the titles. He did that for a while, face propped in his hand, running his eyes up and down the double list, just letting the songs play. After a while he noticed it wasn't just the songs that came but complicated bodies of feeling as well: not quite emotions, not quite sensations. Spirits, maybe? Spirits of the times.

In a way it was like having a cleaning service come in and put everything in chronological order—not just papers or photographs but Mark himself, or at least his memories. When his eye hit "Falling," by Fleetwood Mac, Mark heard the music and was back at the YMAC on Melrose where it had always played that first spring he started going to the baths—alien as a Martian folksong at first, but soon as familiar as the anthem of his home town. He saw "YMCA" by The Village People, and then heard it, and though he'd always hated it, the song brought Paul back after years of not thinking of him. How eagerly Paul had embraced clonedom, so thrilled to get his hands on the signs of maleness that were up for grabs in the 70's—moustache, muscles,

501s. Paul had swaggered and strutted and talked tough and Mark had done it with him, just as happily, and staring down at the *Weekly* Mark tried to tell what chance if any Paul had of still being alive.

As the songs played and called memories and stamped them one year or another, Mark was surprised by how much everything hurt, though what he remembered wasn't anything terrible, for the most part. Perhaps it was just that the past was gone and still here at the same time, but here in a way that couldn't be touched, like ghost-pain not in one amputated arm or leg but in innumerable limbs he hadn't known he'd either had or lost, all at the same time. He didn't doze off, he fell asleep the way he had in the days when he'd binged all night on cocaine and sex, like a spark going down into water that couldn't extinguish it, descending into stranger and stranger territory without being able to lose consciousness. He must have finally gone out for good, because then it was morning, he was under the covers still dressed but with his glasses and Reeboks removed, and Ricardo was awake and frisky and climbing on top of him, saying, "Let's go to the cemetery."

Mark was ready. He loves being up in the morning with Ricardo, who rarely rises before noon. The cemetery is soothing, more like an enormous board game than anything else, and the stillness is what you'd expect while someone meditates on his next move. The distance is so filled in every direction with angels and obelisks and palm trees that it's almost impossible to pick out the vine-covered walls, and only the Hollywood hills rising up in the north say that the cemetery doesn't go on forever. A pair of kingfishers swoop across the lake and perch together on the same cypress. Mark wonders what there is for them in the lake, which is only a few feet deep and under the algae and lotuses lined with concrete. He walks into Ricardo, who's watching him. "You're talking to yourself again," Ricardo says.

"Oh. Sorry," Mark says. "Look, kingfishers."

"Uh-huh. Give me a bag." He's found a priest, and spoons some dirt into the bag, drops his pennies. "There's a heron here, too. A little one. They know where there's water." He closes the bag and hands it to Mark.

"Yeah, but what do they find to eat here?" Mark asks, copying the name off the headstone. It's incised in both English and

Armenian? Ukrainian? An alphabet like broken paper clips, and he copies that as well.

Ricardo considers the question for a moment. "Little, like, fish-things that grow there," he says, one of the last supporters of spontaneous generation. "Give me some of the bags if you're not going to keep up with me. And be looking for a judge. Do you have some pennies?"

"Yeah."

"Don't forget pennies. You have to pay Oyá for the dirt or she thinks you're stealing from her." Oyá is the orisha of cemeteries, generous and powerful if she likes you but easy to offend.

"I watched you. I know what to do."

Ricardo walks off slowly, scanning inscriptions, and Mark begins to wander. It's hard for him to keep in mind that these stones and little Roman temples mean dead people. Not going anywhere in particular, he makes his way to the asphalt road and crosses into an older section.

These graves aren't well visited. There are a few foil-wrapped flowerpots but they're usually holding dead stems. The stones are modest, many of them set flat in the ground and disappearing under the grass. The ground itself has been allowed to become uneven here, and some of the stones meant to stand up are pitched to the side and sinking, oddly like torpedoed ships. Mark relaxes and lets the obscurity pull him toward the corner, where the dates leave the twentieth century and even the tough Bermuda grass gives way to cracked dirt and dandelions. The groundskeepers don't get back here much, and the amount of trash is spectacular. Does it blow here from the rest of the cemetery? or just get thrown over the wall from the street?

He spots a Jack-in-the-Box bag and starts picking up Kleenex, gum wrappers, cigarette butts off the grave in the corner, pretty certain that Ellen Murphy, died February 22, 1906, isn't receiving any direct benefit from this trash removal. On the other hand, who knows? "On the other hand," he says reasonably, getting up at least the larger pieces of a broken bottle, "Who cares?" When the bag's full he walks back to the road, where there's a trash can concealed in a cement tree stump. Inside, there's a wadded-up shopping bag, and he takes that and goes back to the corner.

There's something awful about thinking that Ellen Murphy, wherever she is, if anywhere, would give a shit about the condition of her grave. When someone you love more than your own life dies, it's like they're held hostage in their grave, and you go there and cry and mourn, but eventually they dissipate, and it's just a stone you come to look at sometimes or a little plot of garden you work at on the weekends. But the idea that poor Ellen might have been concerned about this tiny bit of land since 1906, might be bothered because no one's brought flowers since 1950 or because the groundskeepers don't throw down a little grass seed for God's sake, makes him feel something like claustrophobia. He picks up pages from a sex newspaper, a surgical glove, an empty Similac can. "Endless job," he says to himself. "Pointless, too." He picks up a silver lamé high-heeled shoe. There's a deflated red schoolyard ball, and that goes into the bag, and a lot of used Kleenex. Whenever the bag gets filled he goes back to the trash can and empties it. Under a lantana bush next to the wall he finds a bag full of toasted corn, corn meal, hard candies: a Santeria offering, though he can't tell which orisha is involved. He leaves it where it is. On his fourth trip to the trash can he pauses and looks for Ricardo.

He spots him walking among the graves on the other side of the lake, where there are so many statues of angels. Ricardo's white denim jacket leaps out from the green lawn, even on such a muted morning. The sparkle he has when he's around people is turned down, and it's like seeing what a star would look like if it stopped emitting light—calm, dark, almost velvety in its richness. He's taking his time, not something Mark sees him do often, his hands clasped loosely in front of him. Now he sees something on the ground and picks it up to examine it, turns it in his hands like a little boy with a seashell, puts it back down. Mark never gets tired of looking at Ricardo, whose beauty through the years hasn't faded so much as been replaced with who he is, what he means. But this morning it seems like Mark's receiving new information about his lover. He watches and waits for enough to accumulate for him to know what it is.

Ricardo looks so much like Ricardo—that slight forward hunch to his shoulders, the delicate way he places his feet, his chestnut hair. Is it that he looks like he doesn't need anyone? But that's not true, of course: he needs people to talk on the phone with late at night, customers in his shop, Mark to hold him in bed. But he doesn't need anything in order to be Ricardo, to be complete. Mark stuffs the bag of trash into the can.

"Hello," someone says, except it's more like "Eh-yo." Mark turns around. A very old woman dressed in tattered black is hobbling toward him, a scarf tied gypsy-style around her head, a man's hat at an angle on top of it. She's handsome, ancient; the leotard she's wearing even on this chilly morning exposes the skin-cords-and-bones of her upper chest, and she's grinning at him as if they already share a joke. As she comes up, Mark sees that her skirt isn't quite as full as he'd thought, she's actually carrying a long black sack in one hand. Mark, not usually comfortable with strangers, finds himself smiling back. "Hello," he says.

"Do you wan do see a pishur of my ehusbey?" she asks expectantly.

"Your husband?" Mark ventures, taken by her eyes, which were blue once but almost clear now, and her eyebrows, which arch up on her forehead and are drawn on with orange pencil lighter than her skin. "Yes, I'd like that."

She's delighted. "Come," she says, catching the word back into her mouth as if it's too good to lose. "Come," she says, looking back at him over her shoulder as she crosses the road, making pulling gestures with her free hand. He follows her to a small mausoleum that faces the lake and sits next to her on the steps. She undoes the knot in her sack, which turns out to be a silk shawl, the fringe fine as a young girl's hair, and spreads it open. It's chaos inside—used Kleenex, bits of junk, a paperback with the cover torn off, and an empty record jacket. She lifts the jacket out carefully, so the baby's breath taped to it doesn't come off, and hands it to him. "My ehusbey," she says. "Carlos Gardél. You know him?" Mark shakes his head. Her voice is deliberate, stately, the words at first almost unrecognizable, but as she talks his ear becomes educated. "He was the most famous singer in Mexico," she says. "He brings the tango here."

The face and upper body of a girl had been cut carefully out of an old photograph and taped beside Carlos Gardél. The bottom half of her body is painted in, with water color, perhaps, because Carlos Gardél's legs show through one of hers. The baby's breath forms an arch over the couple. Mark taps the young woman lightly and says, "You."

"I was very young when I meet him," she says, and incredibly she becomes a young girl, flirtatious and modest. "He was killed," she says.

"I'm sorry," Mark says.

"He kiss me once only, here," she says, touching her fingers to her forehead with reverence, pride. "The Justice of the Peace, he say, 'Kiss your little bride. Kiss her on the mouth.' But my Carlos tell him, 'No. When I come back I will marry her in the cathedral and surprise the world.' And those bastards, those dirty bastards, they leave him to burn in the plane." Suddenly she's crying, tears rolling like beads over the pink rims of her eyelids, and Mark notices she doesn't have eyelashes. She gives herself to it, not sobbing but sighing, as if an underground river had selected her to issue from. Then she takes one of her Kleenexes, blows her nose and wipes her eyes. " 'My little star,' he called me," she says, smiling, and the crying must have refreshed her because her smile is gold. "He wrote me poetry every day, on green paper, in a green envelope, in those days at the post office you could get green stamps."

Mark wonders if this is what he's been missing every time he's walked away from a bag lady on the street or excused himself to a different bench at the Laundromat. Ricardo talks to women pushing their belongings in shopping carts or wearing five sweaters all the time, giving them pennies or scissors to cut their hair—his mother still tells the story of the time three-year-old Ricardo licked the beggar woman's foot in Honduras. But Mark avoids them, thinking, "Crazy," but meaning he's afraid listening to them will make him liable for them somehow. The story she's telling doesn't find any resistance in him, if anything something like memory answers back, though he's never heard it before.

"Three months later," she says, "I was living with my mother in the Waldorf-Astoria. You know it? It's a good hotel. I was drying the dishes with her when suddenly! I feel a hand on my shoulder! Pulling me down! And the dish flies into the air! My mother, she cries to me, 'Oh my little daughter, my little daughter, what's happening to you?' " She stops, her face wide open with amazement, her eyes empty as hallways, and Mark hangs, waiting for what's going to emerge.

Finally he says, "What was?"

But it passes. Instead, she says, "One day I turn on the radio. This is in New York City, where I danced and the men covered the ground in front of me with roses. And I hear a man, singing. His voice is like an angel in heaven, and I say, 'Who is that man?' 'Don't you know?' they say. 'That's Carlos Gardél.' Right away I say, 'That's the man who will be my husband.' The Justice of the Peace, he says, 'Kiss her, kiss your little bride,' but my Carlos tell him, 'No, when I come back I will marry her in the cathedral and surprise the world.' And he kiss me just once, here." She touches her forehead and surrenders herself not to the memory of the kiss but to the kiss itself, and while her fingers are pressed to her forehead she's transformed from a sunstained old woman to some unbelievable substance like essence of roses. She lowers her hand.

"The seat belt wouldn't open," she says, and Mark hears the river rise up quickly in her voice. It makes him suddenly aware of the herpes in his mouth, tiny burning cuts covering his tongue like the time he broke a piece off a cactus and tried to suck water from it. "And they left him there to burn, in the plane, in the jungle, my Carlos," she grieves. Tears spill out of her eyes with such force they don't run down her face, they just drop, and she reaches for her Kleenex. But this time instead of using it she holds it in her fingers, and her face hardens with, not anger, not rage, but wrath, one of the few times Mark's ever seen it, and he holds his breath. "They left him there, all those *ones* he did everything for. They saved *themselves* and left him there to burn, those bastards, those dirty bastards, I *spit* on them." She spits, like a cobra.

While Mark sits and listens, his ass growing numb on the marble step, she repeats each section of her story five, six, seven times, mixing and matching them, introducing new portions, but always crying, raging, shining in the same places. He understands this isn't just a story, that it's an ongoing event for her, looping back continually. And probably unchanging in its details, while she grows older and older. In that sense the story will outlive her, though he's not sure who will tell it when she's dead. Maybe no one, and the story will come back again and again to be told, but, finding no mouth to tell it, will keep happening, but in silence.

Then something odd happens. She reaches the part where the plane is burning in the jungle. "His seat belt! Won't open! And they leave him there to burn!" she says, and then falls silent. Mark waits for her to start crying but she doesn't. When he looks, her face is contorted but empty, as if she's been pulled out of it from behind, and her eyes are moving back and forth. Mark sees the plane, crumpled, red flames in all that green vegetation, and all the wrong people running out of it. For whatever reason the story's stopped and left her not here but there. The minutes continue to pass and still she doesn't find her way back or continue.

Finally, anxious and wanting to do something that will release or rescue or restart her, with no idea what that could be, he says, "I met him on the bus. I'd seen him at school but I didn't pay attention to him. I don't know why, but he started talking to me on the bus that morning." It's the story of how he and Ricardo met, something he hasn't recalled in who knows how long but here it is again, back fresh and ready from almost twenty years ago. "But he had something, this sparkle you see sometimes. You know that sparkle, don't you? Later on I saw him again in our, what was it, *folk* dance class, and I'd taken off my sweater. This blue sweater I had then. He came up to me, and he kind of frowned like he was really trying to figure this out, and he said, 'Do you have a brother? Because I was talking on the bus to someone who looked just like you, only he had a blue sweater on.' And it was so *obvious*, it was like a little kid doing a magic trick thinking he's going to fool you, and he's so transparent that you're charmed by it, and the trick works. I mean, I actually spent about twenty minutes explaining to him that no, that'd been me on the bus, and I took the sweater out of my satchel to prove it."

At some point—Mark missed it, taken by his own narrative—she started listening. She says, a little uncertain, "Did he write you poetry on green paper? Poetry every day?"

"Yes. Yes, he did," Mark admits, surprised by the correspondence but remembering those phone calls late at night, waiting for it to be midnight so he could call Ricardo and have that voice in his ear. "Beautiful poetry. Like no one ever wrote to me before."

" 'My little star,' he called me," she says, then leans over and puts her hand on his wrist. "I want to tell you something," she says. "My mother was the Mysterious Lady in Black. You know her? She and Valentino love each other. When he die, she comes every day to his tomb to put flowers. Because her love is bigger than his death. When she die, *I* come every day to put flowers, because her love is bigger than *her* death. I'm the Daughter of the Mysterious Lady in Black. If anyone asks you, 'Who is that woman?' you tell them, 'She's the Daughter of the Mysterious Lady in Black.' " She ties her black sack and stands up, gesturing to Mark to do so as well. He does, though not as easily as her, his knees cracking. She walks around the side of the mausoleum where there's a view of the big mausoleum up the road, and Mark's car, parked in front of it, and points. "He's in there. Go in, go to the left, walk past the first two halls, go down the third one. He's there at the end. You'll see the flowers. Did you know that?"

"No," Mark says, shaking his head. "I knew he was here someplace, but not where."

"This is my gift to you," she says. The idea seems hilarious to her and she laughs delightedly. "My gift," she says, then turns and starts walking away.

"Uh, lady?" Mark calls after her, and she turns. He doesn't know why he spoke, can't imagine what he could say to her. Nice to meet you? Thank you?

She comes back, and for a moment he thinks she's going to ask him if he wants to see a picture of her husband. Instead, she raises her hand over his head, palm down, and says, "The Daughter of the Mysterious Lady in Black blesses you, and sends you every success, and hopes that you find a beautiful young girl to hold your heart." Then she gathers her skirts in her hand and goes off over the grass, careful of her footing.

Mark stares after her, not sure how he feels about being blessed. He looks away and scans the view for Ricardo, doesn't see him—though a few more people have arrived to tend graves—then turns back to look again at the Daughter. But she's gone, already out of sight behind one or another of the mausoleums. He starts walking, thinking this must have taken longer than he thought and Ricardo's probably at the other end of the cemetery by now. But as he rounds the lake he sees him on the little bridge that leads to the island where a miniature bank building stands. Ricardo's motionless, completely taken by a miniature blue heron grooming its plumage on the edge of the island. Not wanting to startle the bird away Mark pauses, watching Ricardo.

He's seeing it again, some information about Ricardo he doesn't know how to translate into sense. Ricardo, rapt, picks his nose briefly, then dusts his hand on his thigh. Mark grins fondly, thinks, He wouldn't do that if I were there. And then it hits him like a kiss of cool air: he's seeing what Ricardo looks like when Mark's not beside him, what a world without Mark looks like. "I'm not there," he murmurs in amazement, and suddenly he's not anywhere, though everything else—a man in an oversize white jacket, a blue heron, water mirroring the sky, grass beyond the water—still is. And for a long time, that's all there is. Then Mark's back, watching his lover watch a blue heron launch itself onto the air, skim the water and lose itself to sight among the graves. But it's as if Mark's left some heavy burden wherever it was he went, some responsibility to the world for maintaining it by his presence, and he feels as light as when he was a little kid and owned nothing, not even his toys. "Hi," he calls, coming up the arch of the bridge.

"Hello," Ricardo says, smiling at him. "Did you find me a judge?"

"Huh-uh."

"That's alright, I don't need your help," Ricardo says, pleasantly, patting both pockets. "I got everyone I need. What were you doing?"

"I cleaned trash off some graves. And I met someone." He tells Ricardo about the Daughter of the Mysterious Lady in Black.

Or he starts to, because Ricardo doesn't wait to hear the whole story. "My God," he shouts. "My God, that was Oyá. You just met Oyá, the owner of the cemetery."

"No, no," Mark begins to assure him, but then stops. His certain knowledge that whoever she was, she wasn't an orisha, suddenly isn't there. And it's not that the world of Santeria whose edge he's stood on for so long, looking in, has thrown out a loop and claimed him. It's that suddenly whether or not she was Oyá doesn't matter, and because it doesn't the two possibilities cease to crowd each other, and Oyá can look out for a few minutes from the eyes of the Daughter of the Mysterious Lady in Black. So instead Mark says, "She gave me her blessing, and I'm sure there's more than enough for both of us. Do you want it?"

Ricardo gets down on his knees immediately. "What are you doing?" Mark laughs. "Come on, get up."

"Will you just give me the fucking blessing, you asshole?" Ricardo says, glaring up at him. "You don't even know who you were talking to. She's the heaviest orisha going." He bows his head.

Mark holds his hands over Ricardo, palms down. The herpes are beginning to pain his mouth again, but he says, "The Daughter of the Mysterious Lady in Black blesses you, and sends you every success, and hopes you find a beautiful young girl to hold your heart. Sorry, pal, but that's the way she said it."

Ricardo's not listening to this part. He taps his own head and says, "*Salve le ri, salve le ri, hequa he llansa. ¡Hequa! ¡Hequa, mi madre!*" He's silent for a moment, then holds up his hand impatiently for Mark to pull him up. Mark does, not as easy a task as it once was. Ricardo brushes his knees, and as he does, not looking at Mark, he says, "I shouldn't have brought you here."

"Why not?"

"Because Oyá likes company."

"Yeah, I noticed," Mark says.

"No," Ricardo says. "I mean if she likes someone, she wants him to come and be with her." He looks Mark in the eyes, not something he usually does for more than a few seconds, and Mark sees hospital waiting rooms, banks of flowers at a funeral, the cemetery.

"Oh," he says, then nods. "Yes."

"It's just that," Ricardo says, trying to back up, wanting to be disagreed with now, for once, "if she were claiming you for Santeria, she'd do it at a mass, or when you went to get your shells read. But when she just shows herself to you . . ." He stops, frowning, unhappy.

"It means I'm going to die?" Mark finishes for him, turning it into the slightest question, so it's gentler. He raises his eyebrows, which makes him look like the old man there's less and less likelihood he'll be. "Well. You know, that is what it means." Ricardo continues to hold eyes with him, surely one of the longest looks they've ever shared, waiting. "And the grass means I'm going to die. And the heron. And if they find a cure for AIDS tomorrow, pal, that'll mean I'm going to die, too." He shrugs, as if the wasting of his body, his mind, were no longer a burden he's been chosen to carry. And then for no reason he can see, just a gift from somewhere, he's grinning, uncontrollably, like brushfire leaping up on a dry hillside. "Listen," he says confidentially, leaning toward Ricardo. "Are you hungry?"

"Are you?" Ricardo counters, and though he's still watching Mark he begins to grin back.

"I'm starving," Mark says. "I'm ready for a breakfast that will surprise the world."

"I want pancakes," Ricardo says; pancakes are his favorite. Then he stops smiling, and says, quiet, shy almost, "Are you treating me?"

Mark runs the tips of his fingers down the curve of his lover's face. "Oh, yes," he breathes. "This is my treat."

LEAVING THE BEACH

• CLIFFORD CHASE •

1. THE DOG

The train began to move, and Megan took out her Spanish comic books. About the same time that things started going badly with her boyfriend, Ramon, Megan decided to teach herself Spanish. Since I had recently broken up with my own boyfriend, Megan and I began seeing a lot of each other. This was in June, about a year and a half after my brother died.

She opened the comic book and pointed to a crudely drawn blond woman. "See, Cliff? It's interesting, the blonds are usually the heroines."

"Does that make us heroines, too?" I asked.

Megan fluffed out her hair. "I'm a bottle heroine."

Haltingly she began translating aloud, guessing at the words, proceeding with what seemed to me infinite patience. "*I cannot ever marry with you*—She's sending her boyfriend away. Oh, wait, this is the flashback," Megan said, pointing. "I already read this part. This is where she gets raped. *My friend and I went walking in the country. As a trick—a joke—we threw some stones at some men by a*—hmm—*a lake. The men chased us and one caught me. . . .*" The girl was shown struggling in the man's arms.

"Always sex and peril," I said. "I like the black lightning bolts around her head."

Ashamed, the girl hid at the house of her friend for several days. After her family found her, they had to hide their—

"something. Sin. Shame. Evil," Megan said. "Something like that."

I looked out the window. The train was completing its turn, passing slowly over the highway in a wide arc. I saw the track we were leaving stretch straight on to the left, out to the wilder regions of Long Island. The train creaked and tossed now, like it had given up.

It was as if we had turned off onto a toy or dream railroad. The big silver train floated along the narrow track, and it seemed like we were going places a train wasn't supposed to go—first squeezing between backyards like a boy on the run, then past burned-out factories and littered industrial lots, and finally across marshes and lagoons, tall grass blowing alongside, and our way grown so spindly and dreamy that it seemed there was no track at all.

The station was just two blocks from the water. Behind a boulevard was a neighborhood of low, suburban houses, the newer ones covered in raw wood like country homes. It looked like California, the town where I went to school, or San Diego, where my brother had settled, the city I didn't reach in time to see him before he died.

"It's strange how beach towns all look the same," I said to Megan.

My sister called and said she thought I had better come. "He can barely sit up for a half hour, and he sleeps almost all the time. Sometimes he's more lucid than others. I read him the newspaper this morning, and he was laughing at funny things in that. Then Mom said, 'You're tiring him out, let him sleep.'"

"So, is there any news?" I asked, hoping for the refuge of objective, medical facts.

"It's so hard to get any information! We finally talked to the visiting nurse yesterday." Carol began then to speak in the calm but concerned tone of a doctor or a kind policeman. "She said the dementia is intermittent but basically irreversible, and it will only get worse. He'll be completely bedridden soon. . . . They don't know, but he probably has about two months." I was silent. The urgency had crept into her voice again. "I think you should come as soon as you can."

"All right," I said, trying to comprehend. "Yes, that's what it sounds like." So my brother would not recover from this bout. He had

recovered once before, a year ago, and he had even gone back to work. But not this time.

I heard Carol respond to something. "Oh, he's up," she said to me. "Hold on. I'll bring the phone in there." I heard her saying, "Ken, it's Cliff on the phone. It's Cliff." Then to me, "Here he is."

There was a rustling and then nothing. "Hi, Ken," I said nervously.

It took a minute for him to respond. "Hello." His voice was slurred, far away, spoken with great effort. Then a long silence.

"So, Carol was there for your birthday?" I had the feeling that if only I asked the right questions, he would somehow become coherent again. If I said the right thing, his mind would be sparked and he would have a lucid moment. "So, how was your birthday?"

"Fine." Though he spoke in a monotone, he sounded almost defensive, like a five-year-old with an officious stranger.

I cleared my throat. "Well, I'll be visiting you, too—sometime this month." I wasn't sure when I was coming, and I didn't want to make promises. But I wasn't even sure he could understand "this month." Today, next week, this month—what did that mean? I wasn't sure I was getting through at all.

"I love you," I said.

I heard him breathing with difficulty, as if I could hear him trying to think.

"Come soon."

That was all he said.

"OK, OK, I will. Yes." I tried to fill the silence. "I love you," I repeated, feeling the same embarrassment I always felt when I said that. There was a rustling, and a staticky sound. "Ken? Ken?"

"Uh-huh . . ."

"Ken, can I talk to Mom now? Can you put Mom on?"

"Uh-huh."

The sky was cloudy and the beach wasn't crowded. It was our brilliant idea that summer that you could go to the beach on cloudy days as well as sunny ones. Megan and I settled down and looked out across the sand.

Shortly a young couple prepared to make camp behind us. The man, who was olive-skinned and finely muscular, stripped to a small, green and black striped Speedo. He went down to the water, his taut back small and neat at the waist.

"So, are you going to fix me up with anyone?" I asked Megan.

"I don't think I know anyone."

It was only a perfunctory question, and she knew it. My boyfriend, Glenn, had left me only a few weeks ago, for someone else, and I was still trying to digest this. I had been with him two years, longer than I had been with anyone. It was no effort to conjure him: medium dark complexion, full jaw. Shorter than me, heavy shoulders, narrow waist. Soft-spoken, a tilt to his head, a very kind manner, but elusive. . . .

"Well, at least now if I come out to my parents, I don't have to tell them my boyfriend is black," I said. Megan knew what my parents were like, but she only grunted at this sour joke. I sighed, trying to sleep. In the year and a half since my brother's death, there had often been times when I felt Glenn had let me down, and it seemed I was always begging for his attention. Then, this spring, just as I was beginning to feel better about life, he had started seeing someone else. I knew it wasn't working out between us, but still it seemed like one last thing had been taken away from me.

I opened one eye and looked at Megan. "How's Ramon?"

"Oh, he stood me up again." She waved her hand. "Otherwise he's just fine."

"Shit." I tried to make the word sound especially sympathetic.

Megan fell silent, and I let the subject drop. Somehow it was easy for us to be quiet together, and that was one reason I liked so much going to the beach with her. It gave me a lot of time to think.

I decided to take a swim. It was only June, there was no sun, and the water was very cold. Cables with colored floats strung parallel to the blackened jetties kept people away from the rocks. I swam to the far cable and back again, which because of the waves was hard going. I thought, "Well, at least I can go to the beach and swim in the ocean." This was life. It was cold, my head and the rest of me was all wet, the waves were pushing me, and I was swimming. It seemed like some kind of compensation.

Back at our blanket, I dried off noisily—"God, Megan, that was great!" I felt like a child telling his mother his adventures. "You should go in, Megan!"

But she would have none of it. "How can you do that, just run right into freezing cold water?" Her eyes were still closed. "Oh, it's bracing," I replied.

There was a muffled noise, as if the phone had been dropped in pillows, and more rustling and then my mother came on.

"Hello, yes," she said, with strained efficiency.

She and my father had been caring for Ken at his home for the past month. She said they were looking for two nurse's aides to help them. "There's someone coming Tuesday. The county is sending him over." She and my father had found a residence hotel; once the home aides were hired my parents would stay at Ken's only during the day. The hotel was nearby and was not expensive, she explained. "I have to get some rest," she said. "I can't do him any good if I don't sleep!"

I tried to reassure her. "Yes, that's true." Instinctively I knew it was imperative to keep my mother from panicking. "It sounds like that will be much better."

She cleared her throat. "It's just very hard to find someone you feel you can trust. The last one they sent—ugh, gee."

She meant the nurse's aide. "Oh, God," I said. "Yeah." I was speaking automatically, thinking. "But I'm sure you'll find someone soon. Hopefully this next one."

"Hopefully. . . ." She sighed and jumped to another idea. "Ken didn't even recognize me this morning. 'Where's Mom?' he kept saying. 'Where's Mom?' I was sitting right next to him."

She was trying not to cry, so her tone of voice was strange, as if she were talking about a rude clerk in a store—as if all of this were some kind of terrible and inconsiderate mistake. I paused a minute, wondering how my next statement would hit. "Mom, Carol says I had better come . . ."

She hesitated, sighing. "Yes, I know." I was surprised at how calm she was. "When were you thinking of getting here?"

I flopped onto my stomach and periodically watched the young couple behind us. I could see the foreshortened bulk of the man's torso, the line of the pelvis curving from the side of the hip and into his Speedo. At first his girlfriend, who wasn't particularly beautiful, lay with her arm over his belly. Then she had one white, doughy leg over his. Then she had both legs over him. Then she was lying almost on top of him, both of hem pretending to sleep all the while.

I stood to go swimming again, looked stealthily once more at the pair and saw the book they had flung on the beach blanket: *Honeymoon Getaways.*

A year before I met Glenn, his mother had died of cancer. I thought he of all people would understand what I was going through over the past year, but instead he seemed only to have reached his saturation point. His brother had helped a little, but it was mostly Glenn who took care of his mother in the months before she died—bathing her, taking her to the doctor, helping her in and out of bed.

I fled into the cold water, diving into a greenish swell. Would my troubles have been hard on anyone? For more than a year after Ken died I saw only Glenn and one or two other friends. Everything irritated me, and I was always telling Glenn he had said something that hurt my feelings. I walked the streets murmuring, "My brother died, my brother died." Or I'd just miss a train and, waiting there on the empty platform, find myself thinking, "No one loves me."

Glenn stopped looking at me in the eye about a month after Ken died. His small, black eyes stared off to the side, his dark, heavy jaw impassive. He just nodded "uh-huh, uh-huh" to everything I said, showing no emotion. "What's the matter?" I would ask. He always said he was tired, that was all, and I sat brooding, trying to figure out what he could mean, as if his few words were some cryptic message from a ghost. Or I might bring up an old topic: "When are you going to take the test?" I had taken mine and it was negative, but Glenn kept putting it off. "I'm just not ready to confront that yet," he would say.

I thought now maybe I could see how Glenn might have wanted to take a break from unpleasant topics, and therefore from me. A day at the beach with Megan was like that, a vacation from bereavement. I almost never spoke of my brother with her. That summer even a neutral sort of happiness seemed so tentative. Ken's death and illness dogged me, and almost anything would bring the awful details to mind. Sometimes at the end of a day, lying in bed, I'd say to myself nervously, "I felt OK today." It was like when you're afraid to say, "I don't have a headache anymore," because then you'll notice that in fact you still do.

As it turned out, the fare to San Diego would be nearly a thousand dollars. "But this is an emergency," I told the airline. "Isn't there anything that can be done?"

"I'm sorry, sir."

I had a credit card, but in my panic I was determined to find a cheaper way to go. I called every airline I could think of, and they all said no. It was like I was fighting the implacability and unfairness of my brother's illness, as if by beating the airline industry I could somehow defeat death—or maybe I thought I could somehow lessen the cost of losing him.

Finally I called a tiny ad in the Village Voice. *The fare was three hundred. The woman said I had to pay by cashier's check, and that the ticket would be issued when the check had cleared.*

I hesitated. "So, OK, and what assurance do I have that my ticket is good and that this is all legitimate?"

"Oh, here it comes," said the voice. "I have been operating this business for ten years, and my clients are all over this city. If you're going to start in on that, let's just forget the whole thing now."

"Well, I just wanted—"

She hung up on me.

This beach was not our intended destination. Earlier, Megan and I had discovered our tickets were wrong, but the conductor had already punched them.

"Well, I guess it's Long Beach," Megan had said.

"But Long Beach is practically in the city," I cried. We were supposed to go to the state park two hours away. "Come on, let's at least try to exchange them. They sold us the wrong tickets."

We got off at the next station. I spoke to the conductor of the train to the state park, several other conductors on the platform, a woman in the ticket office downstairs, and finally the stationmaster, who had to be paged. All of them refused to exchange our tickets, and we didn't have enough money on us to buy new ones. Each time Megan wanted to give up, but each time I said let's try someone else. Finally we sat down again a half hour later, resigned, on the next train to Long Beach.

Megan looked at me closely. "You're very persistent."

I stared at the dirty beige seat in front of me. "I really had my heart set on going to a real beach today," I said, trying to take this small defeat in stride.

I booked a regular flight and called my mother that evening.

"The ticket is going to be really expensive," I said. Quickly I wished I hadn't said this.

"How much?"

"Nine hundred dollars."

My mother took a breath in. I may as well have said nine million. "Nine hundred?" She began breathing quickly. "No, you can't come. No, no, that's too much! You can't."

"But that was the cheapest fare," I said. "There just isn't anything else."

"No, you can wait. You can wait a few weeks for the advance purchase." Her voice was very strained now. "There's no rush to come out here!"

I didn't know what to say then. Why did I mention the money? I had thought I only wanted her to help pay for the ticket. Perhaps I wanted to express the urgency I was feeling, and money seemed the only way.

"And Paul has been here, too," she went on. My oldest brother had arranged a business trip to San Diego that week. "All these visitors— it's tiring him out!" she cried. "Carol was reading to him half the day and not letting him sleep. He was better last week. He needs rest!" She paused a minute, and then she said it: "And I don't want him to get the idea we think he's going to die."

"Something doesn't smell right," Megan said.

I stopped drying myself off. I had swum to the far cable and back once more. "It's just seaweed," I said, pointing. "Look, there's old seaweed all around." It was a salty, rotten sort of smell. Ragged, brownish shreds and little gray pieces of drift- wood were everywhere.

Megan didn't seem convinced.

I sat down, exhausted from my swim, sniffing the air every few minutes. The beach was not clean, it was true. "I think I swam too far," I said, trying to change the subject.

Just then we saw a Parks truck arrive and three men in green overalls get out a little ways down the beach. They took shovels from the back, conferred with one another about the spot, and began to dig.

"What are they doing?" I asked.

We watched as they dug a shallow hole. They put their shovels aside and stooped. In a moment we saw them pull at an animal's leg.

"Jesus," Megan cried, turning away. "It's a dead dog."

We both groaned and lay back on the blanket, shutting our eyes.

"Somebody must have buried their dog on the beach," I said. This was more appealing to me than the idea that it had somehow floated in—from the same water where I had just been swimming. There were a lot of old people living in the highrises along the boardwalk, I reasoned; I imagined one of them doing it—an old man—at night—burying his old dog that had died. "Well, at least they took care of it now," I cooed, speaking like a television mother. "It's all taken care of, dear."

Megan laughed sleepily. "All gone now."

Later, however, when we were leaving to go have dinner, we saw the whitish paw of the dog sticking out of the nearest trash can.

I hurried past, but Megan stopped, suddenly fascinated. "Ooh, I want to see," she said.

"Megan—" I held my nose dramatically. "Come on!"

She hesitated a moment, but then she shook her head and quickly caught up to me. We reached the boardwalk, and I hurried up the steps.

"No wonder it still smelled bad," I gasped. "Why would they put it there?"

Megan shrugged. "I guess they didn't feel like carrying it away."

2. A RANGER

In another beach town, in late July, Megan and I sat waiting for breakfast. The floor was dirty gray, the tables red and chipped. Behind the U-shaped counter were empty shelves with one or two doughnuts, it seemed not because all the others had been bought by eager customers, but because there had never been any to begin with.

Megan's deepset eyes gazed downward, her cheekbones looking especially pronounced. "Is this place depressing you?" I asked. We had planned to have a big breakfast together before the beach this week, and then we walked all the way through town from the station, and this was all we could find. Even now, on the periphery of my grieving, little things like that could bother me, make me feel doomed. "Should we go?" I asked.

But Megan only laughed. "No, it's fine." We turned together and looked at the video game in the corner, a big black booth with bright decals, the violent game scrolling past on the screen, making whizzing noises. "It's charming," she laughed.

The waitress, frazzled and middle-aged, foreign but not a hopeful kind of immigrant, returned to explain that she didn't have enough French toast batter for two. I accepted pancakes instead.

"You're very docile today," Megan said.

As usual I was trying to be cheerful and witty. I made a grotesquely docile expression and looked out the window blandly.

Shortly we began to talk about Glenn and Ramon. Megan had just entered therapy and was full of ideas. "It's like everything I do naturally is wrong," she said. "Everyone I've ever been involved with has been really crazy. I seem to respond to that!" She laughed. "It's like whatever my intuition tells me to do, I should do the opposite."

I sipped my bad coffee a minute. "I know. I feel like with Glenn—I should have seen it coming all along." I said I'd been thinking about a strange joke he once made. "I can't remember what we were talking about, but at some point he said to me, 'If I were your father, I don't think your childhood would have been much different.'"

Megan chuckled wryly. "And what if he was your mother?"

The food arrived, and I began telling Megan some news I had gotten a few days before, regarding exactly how and when Glenn had hooked up with his new boyfriend—and who else knew before I did. "It turns out this woman we know, Sue, introduced him to that guy," I said, quickly growing agitated. "And she's been sort of bragging about it."

Megan rolled her eyes. "That's really nice."

"I figured out she must have set them up quite awhile ago, too—like a month at least before Glenn told me about him." My lonely mind had gone to work on it like a puzzle, and I couldn't sleep all week. "I'm much calmer today," I lied. "Actually I'd like to hurl large pieces of furniture off rooftops. . . . I called him Friday to yell at him, but he wasn't home."

Megan sighed sympathetically, poking her French toast. "I haven't been able to reach mine either," she said. "I'm thinking of just going over there tonight. Is that stupid?"

I shrugged. Ramon, whom Megan knew from one of her teaching jobs, had just been fired and was refusing all help and advice. He had been on probation a long time for canceling too many classes, and finally the dean let him go. Now he went out drinking every night and wouldn't answer his phone.

"We can't control them," Megan said, speaking in a particular voice she uses, like a mad professor in a movie.

When I was 12, and my grandfather was dying, my mother went to visit him and told him she was in Chicago on some sort of business. This was a trip of more than 2,000 miles, by a part-time bookkeeper in a wig shop, who rarely flew anywhere and had never traveled before without her husband. Could my grandfather have believed her? He was Christian Scientist, and I remember my mother explaining how for him disease was, above all, a spiritual and mental struggle. My grandfather's outlook was important, she said, so she didn't want him to think he was dying.

"Mom," I said now. "When Carol called. . . ." I didn't know how to calm her down or change her mind about my coming. "Mom, Carol said—"

"Things just aren't that bad," my mother cried. Now that Carol had left, she seemed to have changed her mind. "There's plenty of time. The doctor said it could be six months! He's just very overtired right now."

I didn't know whom to believe. On the one hand, Carol had been quite clear that it was urgent for me to come. On the other, my mother had been staying with Ken for weeks, and she surely knew better than Carol, who had only been visiting, what his condition really was. Anyway, since my mother was the one responsible for his care, I felt I had to respect her wishes. But even now I wonder if I should have trusted my intuition and disobeyed her. "Mom," I persisted. "He said 'Come soon.' That's what Ken said to me Sunday. 'Come soon.'"

"He's not always coherent," she said quickly. "He could have thought you were in California already, or that you were back in college or something, or around the corner. You just don't know."

"But he said come soon. . . ."

My mother sighed. "He didn't know what he was saying."

It was incredibly bright, and hazy. We plodded along the dry, fine, peaked sand, until we began to pant. Megan changed course and we switched to the hard, wet surface near the water. "Oh, much better," Megan said. "There's that story that Einstein figured out why that is. He was at the beach one day and it came to him. Surface tension or something."

The tan, wet sand glistened under our feet.

"Here?" Megan asked.

We began unpacking. "I don't think you've adequately complimented me on my new bag," I said, trying to be carefree. I lifted it and set it down again, blue canvas with a big black strap. It was part of a self-improvement campaign. "I had expected you to be so proud of me." All summer Megan had told me I had to get a new shoulder bag. "Now I'm sure to find a new boyfriend."

"Appearances are important," she said dryly.

I began putting on sun block, which takes me a very long time. Megan sat patiently, waiting to put it on my back. I smoothed it on my shoulders, my collar bone, my chest. It was gooey and white, and it wouldn't quite rub in. I began on the tops of my legs.

"Jesus, are you ever going to finish?" Megan said at last.

I continued rubbing. "Megan, if I miss even one little spot, it will be bright red." I remembered having the same discussion once the summer before with Glenn, an awful vacation on Cape Cod.

"OK, OK," Megan said.

"No, really, it's happened before. I can't just dab a little here and there like you do. I'll have a spot the color of—" I looked around and saw the red markers down the beach, at the edge of the lifeguard area "—the color of that flag there."

Having decided not to go immediately, I tried to console myself that my sister had only panicked and there was, as my mother said, no hurry.

In fact, my mother was so sure of Ken's condition that she and my father left San Diego the following week and returned to San Jose. They had been away from home for two months and there were things that needed to be done. They left Ken in the care of the two home aides

*and planned to return in two weeks. It was agreed that I would come
visit after that.*

*But only after two days the aides began reporting bad news. Ken
was having more difficulty breathing, and he seemed to be in more
and more pain. My mother was constantly on the telephone trying to
understand what was going on. One of the aides—his name was
Clifford—was hard to deal with, and my mother said he was "slow."
He didn't explain things very well, and he didn't seem to listen to my
mother's instructions on the phone.*

*I had heard about this Clifford the week before. He could be very
patient with Ken, my mother said, but already there had been problems during Clifford's first week. He was qualified to give baths, cook
and do laundry, but he pretended to have medical knowledge that he
didn't have. "I've worked with AIDS patients many times before," he
told my mother, and in his careless, slow voice he lectured her on Ken's
condition, predicting what treatment would next be offered by the doctor. He saw himself as the one in charge, often telling the other home
aide what to do. My mother had had to admonish him not to make de-
cisions but to call her or the visiting nurse for advice.*

*My mother said Ken didn't seem to like Clifford, and I began to
harbor a fear that in his confusion Ken would somehow think that this
Clifford was me, finally come to visit. Clifford was like a nightmare
version of myself there in San Diego, caring for Ken when I couldn't,
talking to him in an idiot nurse's voice, blundering, officious, slow-
witted. . . .*

*One night Ken was especially lethargic when it was time to be
washed, and Clifford panicked. Without calling anyone, he sent for an
ambulance and had Ken taken to the emergency room. My mother was
furious. "I told Clifford no hospitals! Over and over, I told him.
That's what Ken kept saying when we checked him out last month."
She was breathing hard and she spoke with great emphasis, like one
defending herself against some unreasonable authority. "He doesn't
want to go into the hospital again!"*

*Ken was taken home, but he was soon put on morphine. He no
longer got out of bed at all, and his breathing grew worse. I think my
mother didn't want to see this as a crisis, which is why she didn't go
back down to San Diego immediately. Now it all seems clear, but at
the time, even the doctors didn't understand what these new developments meant—or if they did, no one told us. "I just don't know what
to do!" my mother kept saying.*

*"Do you want me to go to San Diego this weekend?" I asked. By
this time I had found a good charter flight. "It's only three hundred,"
I reassured her. "I could go this weekend."*

"What? Oh." I heard her breathing. "You could?"

In fact, I was terrified of going by myself, and I had no idea what I would do when I got there, what I would tell Clifford or anyone else to do. My brother was dying, and I had no idea how to help. "Yes," I said. "I could get a ticket tomorrow."

She sounded a little relieved. "All right, please. That would be a big help." She sighed. "There's only so much I can do from here. . . ."

That was Monday. I booked a flight for Friday. On Wednesday my mother called to tell me that Ken had died.

This was the beach Megan and I had wanted to try back in June. It was further out even than our usual beach since then, more pristine, less crowded, the sand a narrow and steep strip between green dunes and the water. It seemed almost wild, and there were wild roses all along the path to the concession area and the bus stop. Their petals were pink and floppy, and their odor was strong and sweet, like the air everywhere in San Diego the weekend of the memorial service.

Carefully I carried lemonade and hotdogs back to Megan. Just outside the picnic area I spotted one of the other two gay men I had seen earlier on the bus, shaking out his towel repeatedly on a small lawn. I watched his slender, surprisingly appealing body, feeling ridiculous that I was carrying a tray full of hotdogs. He turned, and we looked at one another with a strangely neutral curiosity.

I remembered the first time Glenn and I met, at a Valentine's Day party. He said he was a painter, and I told him about the orange and black cityscape from Woolworth's in my parents' family room. He nodded with twinkling attention, and I suspected that here was someone I could really talk to. We sat in a corner, and I watched his foot wiggle on his knee. He said, "My mother had a still life that was three dimensional. The bowl and the pieces of fruit were raised, like that was more realistic." He made a cupping gesture with his hand, and I reached down and untied his tennis shoe.

I entered the sandy path with the wild roses and began to argue with him in my head. "How could you be so dishonest? How could you lie to me like that?" He waited weeks to tell me he was seeing someone else. A forgivable crime in itself, but I had also figured out that before he told me, we had had dinner

with that woman Sue and two other new friends of ours—Susan
and Suzanne were their names. All of them must have known
about Glenn's new boyfriend. Over dessert he began running
his fingers through my hair as the three of them watched, mesmerized. I had wondered at the time why it was such a strange
evening.

He had left me to find out these things months after we had
already broken up, when it was too late for me to do anything
about it. Our parting had been fairly calm, but now I was never
so angry in my life. I walked along the beach, my head beginning to hurt in the particular way it had been hurting all week,
like a hangover. The lemonade sloshed and spilled. I thought
that if I could somehow construct the perfect argument, I
would at last be right in Glenn's eyes. I wanted to lay down the
law. "You fucking coward. What did you think, that this
wouldn't get back to me? Oh yeah, right."

Megan and I stayed into the early evening, until the light began to slant and the water grew velvety and molten. Megan sat
alone by the water's edge fingering the sand, slender in her
black suit, and I thought Ramon would come around soon if he
was smart. I went swimming one last time.

Unfortunately, the busses to the train station stopped running before the beach closed. We sat on the bench watching
cars go past for a half hour or more. "They're all laughing at
us," I said. "There's no bus coming." But it was getting not to
be a joke anymore.

At the park office, a young ranger, tubby and tall with thick
glasses, agreed to take us to the station. "You're lucky," he said,
opening the door of the squad car. "Anyone else on duty would
have made you call a cab."

I had to ride in back, behind the wire screen. Megan sat up
front. "This isn't so bad," I said, shutting the door uneasily. I
checked the handle and confirmed that it would not open from
the inside.

But though I expected claustrophobia, once we got rolling it
seemed to me not much different from riding alone in the back
of my parents' car after Ken went away to college—my parents'
high, tomblike headrests hiding their heads. I joked to myself,

"These wire screens could be a new product for parents to keep their children at bay."

We drove in silence for a few minutes toward the causeway, the radio squawking. *"Three white teenagers in a Ford van proceeding on the parkway in the wrong direction . . . . Alcohol involved. . . ."* I thought it would wise to make conversation with the ranger, since he had made it clear he was doing us such a favor. I introduced myself and Megan.

"I'm Chris," he replied gruffly.

"Oh, Chris," I blurted. "That's what people always call me by accident. Cliff, Chris."

In silence we climbed the long bridge in the fast lane. I watched the other cars on the road from the new perspective of the back of a police car.

"Now I know what it's like to be a perpetrator," I offered.

Chris seemed to loosen up then, handing Megan his nightstick. "You can poke at him with this if you want."

I chuckled loudly. I decided it was easier if he thought I was Megan's boyfriend.

"You two from Manhattan?" he asked.

"Brooklyn," Megan said.

Chris explained that he had grown up in Park Slope. "Eighth Avenue and Eighth Street. 552 Eighth Street. You can go look at the building. 552," he repeated.

"Huh," I said. The radio continued to squawk. "This must be a big change living out here by the ocean."

"Oh, I haven't lived in Brooklyn since I was eight," he replied. "We got out just in time."

As in a conversation with my father, I wondered if some racist commentary was coming next. Fortunately he fell silent and began fiddling with his radio.

We were just reaching the end of the bridge, and Chris began to accelerate rapidly. Shortly we were speeding along at about 85. "This is great," I thought to myself, feeling the movement of the heavy squad car. "I guess when you're a cop, you can go as fast as you want." We would reach the station in no time. Already I was thinking how I'd be home soon and I could try to call Glenn once more. "I can finally get this off my chest," I thought.

But then we were suddenly slowing down again, as if life

could never again allow me to get anywhere ahead of time. Chris turned to Megan, lifting one hand from the steering wheel in a kind of shrug, apologetic. "I was starting to pursue someone. But then I remembered you two were in the car with me, and I couldn't do that now."

3. THE FLIES

It was another two weeks before I reached Glenn. As it turned out, he was in Italy with his new boyfriend. This was the trip Glenn had once planned to take with me.

I thought I had cooled down, but as soon as I heard Glenn's voice my hands began to shake. I told him the things I had learned, how he had lied to me, how others knew before I did. I recalled our dinner with the three Sues.

"How could you do that to me, Glenn?" My voice was cracking, and I decided not to hide it.

"I'm sorry . . . I'm sorry," he sighed. He sounded genuinely upset, a rare thing for him. "I'm sorry about a lot of things."

I sat staring miserably at the phone cord, which for the past two years seemed to be the conduit for every kind of bad news and unhappiness.

"I'm sorry I went away with someone I didn't really care about," Glenn said at last. "I'm sorry I wasn't with you."

I looked sideways, as if this was some kind of trick. Somehow I had never imagined this answer. "Why are you saying that? Why are you telling me this, Glenn?"

"Because it's true." And he began to cry.

Megan and I trudged down the sand, past the slatted wood fences. The sun had come out as soon as we arrived. I looked up, and it seemed it was cloudy everywhere but right here. And though it was a Sunday, and this was the most popular beach, it was not at all crowded.

"Well, something had to go right this summer," Megan said. "I guess this is it."

The sand was firm and well packed from a week of rain. "We were presented with a choice, before we were ever born," I said.

"You can have love, or you can go to the beach this summer. We chose the beach."

We had, in fact, gone to the beach almost every weekend this season. Now it was nearly Labor Day. I stared at the peaks of sand below my feet. "Walking through sand. This is exactly what we needed to learn for our next life."

We reached a low, recently flooded area, strangely flat and grayish, wide and full of broken white shells, though the water was another 500 yards off at least. "Ouch," I cried. The shells cut my feet.

"It's like mud," Megan said. The sand was especially hard-packed here, unpeaked. "I wonder what Einstein would say about this."

The ground rose and grew soft and sandy again. We stood and viewed the ocean from the top of a small rise, below which a shallow trough had been created, two inches of water, and beyond that another strip of dry sand, and then the sea.

"Weird," Megan said. We had never seen it like that here before, and I thought of all the changes the week of hard rain had wrought.

I looked around—the new sun, which seemed to be here to stay, big white clouds retreating, light green grass on the dunes, bright sand, the water. "What an incredible day," I cried, turning, wishing that that was enough.

"Cute guys," Megan said, her tone surprisingly light.

A group of lifeguards was pushing a boat in from the waves.

"That was a new thing for Megan to say," I thought, unfurling the beach blanket. She had been too busy all summer fighting with Ramon to point out any lifeguards. Now things were going more smoothly, she had told me. Ramon had decided to go back to school for another degree. He had even come over and fixed her kitchen light this weekend, and then he stayed the night. "Maybe things will work out for them," I thought.

Meanwhile, Glenn and I were supposed to have dinner again that week, our second meeting. He had lied to me, it was true, and I didn't want to trust him, but something told me to try again. Maybe I could see things more clearly this time around, I thought. He and I had never even known each other before my brother was sick—it was one of the first things I told him about myself. Already I was grieving, anticipating the end; and then Ken died. For two years that disillusionment permeated and colored everything. But now I was coming out of it.

And then there was his dark, somber face before me in the restaurant—restored to me—his eyes bright and intent behind a new pair of glasses. . . .

Shortly I woke. "I'm going in!" I cried, and ran down the beach.

The water was light green and full of seaweed, very clean, and cold from the rain. More like June, I thought, not quite shivering. I waded in further. The waves were little and broke completely where the water was just at your waist. But they turned out to be perfect body-surfing waves, very gentle and very effective. You stood there waiting for them, not minding the shallow water, and seeing the water rise you took your opportunity as always, swam eagerly toward shore, and then they carried you in to just two or three inches of water. I swam for half an hour or more alongside one of the teenage guards, watching his thick back as he paddled around on a small board waiting for the next wave. He called out to me, "Best waves all year!"

"I'm glad it's almost fall," Megan said. Around her lay books and newspapers. Her efforts at Spanish had succeeded: by now she had graduated to *El Diario* and *One Hundred Years of Solitude*. "God, Cliff, what an awful summer."

It was true. "Well, even so, I don't want it to end," I said. I was almost disappointed that Glenn and I might get back together, because it meant this particular time was over. In retrospect the season seemed very pure.

"If you have a boyfriend again, you won't have so much time to see me," Megan said.

That was another thing about this summer I didn't want to end, these long days with Megan, time stretching unbounded in the sandy afternoons. "You'll be busy too," I replied, meaning recent developments with Ramon.

"Yeah, well, we'll see. . . ." She lay back amidst her Spanish books and closed her eyes.

The waves were particularly beautiful to watch today, sparkling at the break and foamy in the shallows. I began to feel sad. The fecund smell of fresh, wet seaweed was especially strong—the way it is in California.

After my brother went into the hospital the first time, we had Christmas that year in San Diego. One day we went out to the beach, and Ken and my parents and I walked tentatively along the water in the wind. I took his picture on the rocks. Though he had almost died in November, by Christmas he was recovering fairly well, and he would be back at work in a few weeks. It seemed all our hopes for his recovery were working. He was weak but he laughed easily that weekend—his high, cackling laugh, infectious and feeding itself in waves, always over something recklessly and elaborately imagined, the laugh I learned from him and remember from childhood.

But in the picture I took, Ken looks out from under his wide-brimmed hat doubtfully, his brow furrowed, trying to smile and succeeding only with a few teeth, his face gaunt—the clear winter sky and cold sea behind him.

> *Later my mother spoke to Ken's social worker. The woman explained that this kind of end was common: the primary caregiver leaves for some reason or another, and the patiently simply gives up. It wasn't my mother's fault, the social worker said. If she and my father had stayed, Ken might have gone on for two or three more months—on morphine, bedridden, his mind gone, barely breathing.*
>
> *I was at work when my mother had called. Mechanically I told my boss that my brother had died, and I went about preparing to leave the office. Glenn was working in his studio that day and he didn't have a phone, so I just got in a cab and went there. It was strange to be speeding down Broadway in the middle of the day, riding in a cab instead of on the subway, watching buildings go by. I imagine it was a Checker cab, though of course there were no more Checkers by then. But the space inside the cab seemed huge and dark, and the ride somehow timeless.*
>
> *I wasn't even positive I would find Glenn, and I remember the relief I felt when he opened his door. Behind him, the walls were hung crookedly with half-finished drawings. I told him the news, he held me, and I began to cry.*

I got up and went for a walk, staring down at the yellowish shallows, and the sand.

The marked child goes through the day. The orphan brain

sings to itself. Some hear the voice of their loved one, encouraging them. Sometimes I imagined that. But rarely, and neither did I try to speak to my brother in the middle of the night. Even now it's too hard to define the shape of what's been lost. Childhood; and as an adult, a succession of long-distance phone calls, occasional visits. My days were ostensibly no different now; we could simply have neglected to call one another all this time. He was like money I had left in the bank, and now it was gone.

I didn't feel my brother had died justly, or for a just cause, or in a manner having dignity, or that his suffering was of any use to him or anyone else, or even that he was in any sort of heaven that I could imagine. I only grew used to it all, and to the fact that none of the facts could have been changed: they simply began to take their place in a bigger world, and time filled in on the other side, like sand against a jetty. He was cremated and he has no grave, but I thought maybe the sky or the horizon could somehow know the moment and place of his death (a small house in San Diego, February 22, 1989), or that of my loss (my desk at work, later that day, phone in hand, listening to my mother's shaky voice)—that one small place; for me, a notch in the world.

By now I had walked quite a ways. I turned back down the beach toward Megan and the blanket. In a while I saw her there, sleeping. I had picked up shells on my way: a black, round fan, a white one the same shape, and a small, worn lozenge of mother-of-pearl, black around the edges. I left them for her on the blanket.

I lay back in the sun and sighed. Megan turned her head groggily. "Are you OK?"

I nodded. "I was just thinking." But I asked myself the same question, and listened carefully a moment, as if learning my own language. I didn't seem to need to talk, and just then I couldn't have explained my thoughts anyway. "I'm good," I decided.

Megan closed her eyes again. "All right," she said doubtfully.

I nestled into the hard sand and felt almost serene, and sleepy. In a moment I could hear the thuds of footsteps on the sand as people passed nearby.

* * *

The flies came in twos and threes at first. We thought that we were simply trapped in a small swarm of them, that they had for some reason picked us out, as gnats will. Soon there were more of them, landing on our legs, our ears, the blanket. They were somewhere between gnats and flies, and they would not shoo unless you actually pushed them off or killed them.

I watched one land near the blanket and nose into the sand blindly as if expecting food. Next to me, Megan sat slapping the air. The shells I had left her were scattered. Finally I stood up, swatting at my legs.

"Maybe it's the suntan lotion," she said.

"But you aren't even wearing any. Or hardly any at all."

"You didn't put any on either?" I shook my head. I was tan by now, and besides, we had come so late in the day that I didn't need any. "Look," Megan said, pointing.

All down the beach, people were flailing their arms, waving towels in the air.

"It's not just us," I said.

We looked back at the white blanket, where several were crawling now.

"God, get away!" I cried, swatting at them. "They don't fly away," I said.

"They're dying," Megan replied. "Look, they're weak. They can't get up."

More had landed on the blanket, long brownish bodies and gold, transparent wings, crawling listlessly as baby possums toward their milk. "No, they're just wimpy," I said. "You know how gnats can be really wimpy?" I recalled the tiny black gnats in the schoolyard, how Ken and I used to call them "Leonards," because you could simply bat at them right in the air and kill them.

"They came here to die," Megan said.

I pushed one off my arm, and it fell fluttering to the blanket. "This is a fucking plague of Egypt. I'm going swimming until they go away."

"That's right, leave me here."

I ran into the water, dunked myself, swam back and forth a few times. But the waves had gone and it was cold. I came back in.

"Is it any better?" I asked, shaking out my towel.

"No." Megan sat looking at her arms and legs to see if any had landed on her.

"Maybe we should ask the lifeguards," I said. "Maybe they'll know—"

"—if they're going to go away. Yeah," said Megan eagerly, getting up.

We walked down the beach to the high, white chair, where one guard sat and two others stood by.

"Hi," I said. "Are these going to go away soon?"

The one in the chair was older, and sat there swatting the air with his towel. He spoke like a scientist. "The wind shifted and blew them here against their will," he said. "They don't want to be here. They have no choice."

"Oh," I said, smiling at the younger guard who stood by, and catching sight then of his perfect chest and abdomen between the half-zipped sweatshirt. I looked away quickly, scanning the buggy air. "So this isn't going to stop?"

"It happens when the wind comes from the north," said the one in the chair. "Unless the wind shifts again, they're here to stay. Hey, you got any bug spray? Because if you do, give it to me, please." By now he had put the towel on his head. He was quite a comedian. "You two can leave. I can't." He batted at the air around his thigh. "You heard of 'The Birds.' This is 'The Flies.'"

I looked at Megan and shrugged.

We walked back to our blanket, the sun in our eyes. "And it was such a perfect day," I said in mock pettishness. We stood for a moment looking down the beach. In fact, by now nearly everyone had left. "I guess if they were going to go away, the guards would have said so."

Megan sighed. We had only been here an hour and a half.

"I guess we should go," I said. But I wasn't really unhappy; somehow the scourge of the flies had taken me out of myself, and I was glad for so small and so tangible a crisis.

We had to take everything out of our bags and shake them, because the bugs had crawled inside, between our clothes and books. At last we were packed up and headed toward the pale brick concession building, which stood in the sunshine like a great sand castle. A few people remained, sitting at the aluminum picnic tables, but they too were swatting their heads miserably, and after Megan and I had put on our shoes we turned down the path to the bus.

The light angled steeply before us, already like September. We saw the bugs clearly then, against the darkness of the trees, thousands upon thousands of them, swarming, lit by the yellow, late-afternoon sun.

We would come to the beach just a few more weekends that year. The bus's windshield was covered with specks, and the full load of beach survivors was strangely quiet as we traversed the water's causeway—quiet and relieved and expectant, as if we were a heroic and exiled people, driven by plagues into a new land.

A SEA OF DECAYING KISSES

• JUSTIN CHIN •

Anna May Wong is dead. Left on some ice float, lips unkissed. Anna May Wong and Mae West were the only two Hollywood leading ladies that never got to kiss their leading men. The studio brass thought that there was too much smoldering sexuality already without the smack of lip contact.

I used to date this Dutch man. The only thing I can remember about our time together is his saying *Suck my tongue, suck it hard*. I can't even remember his name, what he looked like, what his body or hair felt like in my hands, nothing. Nothing but that voice—probably not even his, but someone else's that I've replaced in my memory—telling me how to kiss him.

I have a friend who believes that the truth of love lies in the act of tongues. He refuses to kiss anyone unless he's positively sure that he's in love with that person. Once he's sure, he'd rather deep kiss than indulge in any fondling or anything ejaculatory. Once they kiss, once those lips touch, tongues slipped into the others' mouth, wham!, that's it, he wants the person to be his forever.

Aren't you placing an inordinate power in a tongue? I once asked him. An act? An organ that ceases to work if you can't smell, if your nasal passages are blocked by allergies or bad sinuses? But he doesn't hear me as he's busy thinking about someone he kissed four weeks ago. I hate to admit it, but sometimes I think he's right. When you kiss someone, it's the first taste of his mouth that will make or break your heart.

Acupuncturists believe that you can tell what ails the body by looking at the tongue. The coating of the tongue, how the tissue looks, how it hangs in your mouth, the cracks, the shape, how wet it is. Everything about the tongue all points to something in your body. Every part of your body has some causal connection with your tongue.

I'm on the plane looking at the man beside me. I'm looking at his hands. Big, rough. There's some downy black hair on the back of his hands, on the flesh of the back of the fingers. He picks up the small airline muffin from his food tray, cuts it into thirds with the plastic knife, smears some spread on it and brings it to his partner's mouth. He holds the piece between his thumb and middle finger, the second finger outstretched, ready to wipe the bit of crumb and butter off the side of his partner's lips. I stare at his hands through the whole trip. Two rings: a wedding band and a collegiate-looking pinkie ring, chunky with fake green gemstones looking like moss on gold. Hands, fingers to mouth, tongue. Along with a good smooch, I want a slice of tenderness.

"My love life (underline) (period) My love life is sometimes good (comma) sometimes bad (period) When it is good (comma) I am happy (period) When it is bad (comma) I feel sad (period)"

Inevitably, I find myself hanging out at Cafe Loveless, home of broken queer hearts. Warm coffee, warm soy milk and warm draft beer, first refills free. The fridge broke down in 1986, the half-and-half ran out three years ago and never got replaced. You get to choose your coffee: Bitter Black or Diabetic Shock. Don't bother asking for an ashtray, there aren't any. Just tip your cigarette over the edge of the table; flick your ashes to the floor. Use your shoe to wipe it into the ground. You can request tango music. Just ask the man behind the bar but nobody feels like dancing much at Cafe Loveless. Just want to sit on the hard plastic chairs and nurse a warm coffee or warm beer, ashes underfoot, wanting to lick the spill off someone's fingertips. All dreaming of hot Fabio-like romance while the jukebox racks up the compact disc of Linda Rondstadt's greatest hits. *That will be the day, when you say goodbye, that will be the day ...*

It's been so long since I've been in love with someone that is in love with me in return that I can't imagine the knowledge of knowing someone's body so intimately. How you can both be lying naked together on some lazy afternoon and you know where the soft and ticklish spots on the other body are, where the hard unfeeling parts crusted with dry dead skin are, where the hair is thick and luxurious, where it is soft and where it is a scant fuzz.

These days I'm only left to obsess about men that I chance across. An obsession is different from being smitten. One, you want to know every detail about the prey, the other, you just want to fill in the blanks with your fancy.

I'm trying to figure out what it is about this man that obsesses me. What it is that makes me think of him all the time, want to hear his voice, imagine him standing outside my door. I love the way he moves: how his whole body, compact and sinewy, cuts through the air, determined and hard. I love his body hair: the way the stray strands of chest hair carelessly wisp out of the top of his T-shirt and curls in the hollow of his neck; how the hairs on his forearms mat down out of his rolled-up shirt sleeves, looking soft and shivery. I love the way he holds his cigarette even though I am an avid non-smoker, I love the smell of stale cigarette smoke on his clothes. I love his tattoos. I love the way his ears feel. I love the way he leaves the smell of his body on my body, the taste of his tongue in my mouth.

Once, I fell in love with an architect simply because I loved the fact that he makes buildings. Great big buildings. That such a small man made these great structures out of steel and concrete that hold people and things up, pull them away from the ground and hold them up to the scrutiny of air, gravity and the elements.

I'm at the premiere of a really bad play that I co-wrote. It's another one of those funny coincidences that there were all these men that I have had affairs with, there with their little non-threatening boyfriends in tow. Well, I really wasn't having an affair with them, they were having an affair with me, which is a small but gaping difference. At any rate, they were all trying to ignore me or else be very cordial and brief with me. Something about boyfriend being jealous; something about protecting their happy homelives: the whole idea of the two-bedroom apartment one-joint-vacation a year let's-cook-together-darling lives. The red-light special at Relationships R' Us, open 24 hours 365 days a year.

During the intermission, I thought all their avoidance and their nervousness that I may say or do something to ruin their domestic bliss was quite funny. By the end of the play, and it was more dreadful than I thought it was, I began to see the pathetic nature of the whole setup.

Jealousy. They want to avoid the bugbear of jealousy. I'm sitting at a cafe when a man that I once had sex with (while he and his boyfriend were in the middle of a breakup), joins me. I haven't seen him in yonks and we chat a little, suggestions of a future tryst. He can't sit too long, boyfriend (they made up, apparently) may see us, he says, *jealousy*.

I thought you two had an open relationship, I said. His words were "modern relationship" or "modern couple," or something equally nauseatingly vague. Doesn't matter, he'll still get jealous, he tells me.

You only get jealous because you want to be all things to the person you're smitten by or you think you're smitten by. Doesn't matter if you're not that thing or don't ever want to be that thing, you just want your sweetie to think that you are. And that's when you end up wearing stupid little tank tops and little cutoff shorts simply because your sweetie found some tramp attractive in them, never mind you look like some twitting idiot outside of your regular T-shirt and jeans ensemble that he first fell in love with you in. It's worse when it's not something physical like clothes or hair or body. Suddenly, you find yourself laughing different, moving different, method acting. Yikes. The superior ones simply smack their sweeties on the head and develop an intense hatred towards their sweeties' obsessions. The inferior ones crumble.

Jealousy. All it takes is one chaste smooch to betray.

* * *

I used to date this man who was obsessed with the color of the water in his toilet bowl. Blue. He wanted it to be as blue as possible. To acheive this, he resorted to dumping two or three of those blue-dying toilet bowl cleansers into the cistern every week. Once, he even used dye, but that only stained the porcelain.

It really got to be an obsession. When he entered his house, the first thing he did was head straight for the bathroom and flush the bowl. He even brought the blue cleanser tablets when he went on a trip, just in case the hotel's toilet bowl didn't flush blue. Several times every night, he disentangled himself from our legs, arms and the twisted sheets to go and flush the toilet.

All this was fine, but I guess I knew the relationship wouldn't work out because I liked to piss in the bowl and watch the blue water in the toilet bowl turn green then yellow. I derived the same childish satisfaction as I did in all those years of high school chemistry laboratory where I delighted in watching the liquids in the test tubes gradually precipitate and change colors in a glorious chemical reaction. Suddenly, the most boring white powders would turn into a stunning cloudy crimson, or the bland milky liquid would hiss and spit gas and turn into a silver suspension floating in a thick greenish-yellow solution. Of course, I was supposed to be observing how the periodic table and the elements and compounds that make up this world we live in affect our lives, but damn, those colors!

Years later, I happened to see him on public access television. He had his own show about Psychic Powers. Come to think of it, he always did say he was psychic. He was talking about spirit guides, those proverbial "little voices in your head" and how they talked to you. He asked the viewers to ask their spirit guides to tell them what color he was thinking of in his head. I guessed blue. I was right.

Seeing him on that program and knowing that he was psychic made me feel so much better. At least now I know he knew that I wasn't going to return his phone calls. Still, in spite of his bizarre obsessions, he was really a rather sweet person. And in spite of everything, he's also the first man out of many that I wished I had kissed good-bye properly.

Then there was this other guy, every time he got aroused, his salivary glands kicked in and he would salviate like mad. This meant he always had to spit. He kept a little spittoon (it was a cheap waste basket, really) with tissues wadded on the bottom beside his bed for this purpose. You would think it was quite gross, but actually he was a damn good kisser.

I knew a man I was dating was far too sensitive for me when he locked himself in the bathroom after I came home with various parts of my body pierced.

"Oh honey," he said through the locked door, his voice in some kind of whimpering sob. "Piercing your body! But why? It's . . . it's such a random act of violence."

"Well, sweetie," I tried reasoning with him after I lured him out of the loo by lying about needing to shit real bad because of bad bacon. "It's hardly random. It's not like I was caught in a drive-by piercing."

Conventional wisdom has it that the most sensitive people are the best smoochers. This man was a horrid kisser actually, too much teeth, too little tongue, too much force. In this case, conventional wisdom and Newton's Second Law of equal opposite reactions seemed to have betrayed me.

I'm trying to remember my first kiss but I can't.

Obsessions are best kept that way. It's really not wise to try and bring them to you even if you desperately want to. Even if you're horny beyond belief.

I discovered this with another obsession of mine. I meet him quite by chance, the best way to meet anyone. For the week after our meeting, I kept saying his name over and over because I liked the way the syllables bump into each other in my mind. He works for a large chemical corporation, but tells people that he is a photographer and a video maker. He likes horror fiction, werewolves, vampires, that sort of thing. He writes short fiction and is on a gothic horror kick: Asylum doctor turns into an insect in a despicable plot by alien spiders trying to breed flies out of humans for consumption. He wants to take my picture, he tells me as we wait for the J-Church. He says I will end up looking Japanese when the picture comes out. I say *no*. He begs, says *please please, I'll do anything, anything*. I tell him no, *I don't like cameras*, I say. He walks to the edge of the platform, turns around and says *anything* one more time. He tells me how great the picture will look: half my face in shadows, half in a blinding light. He gives me some of his writing to read. I wish he didn't. I am not shocked by the writing at all. The improbability of it all does nothing to scare me. I tell him about Oliver Sacks's work, about how people are trapped for years inside a dead lifeless body, active minds stuck in a lifeless body, senses forced to watch everything change around them but powerless to feel or do anything. That's what scares me. He's unfamiliar with what I'm talking about. He gives me another piece. *It's unfinished*, he says, *help me find an ending*. Still, I love the way he says "I've got a brilliant idea" when something strikes his mind. I like the way I sound like him when I'm reading an unfamiliar text out loud. He's making a video about werewolves. On the streetcar, he touches my chin, rubs the unshaven bits of fuzz and asks me if that was intentional. I say it's not, I rub his scant goatee too and he laughs. He tells me that he just recently had to change his aftershave, something about allergies causing blotches, and I remember the smell of his aftershave days ago when I leaned in to hug him good-bye. The smell of his aftershave mixed with the grimy smell of a workday. I get off the streetcar, cross the road, try not to look at him, but as the streetcar speeds by I see him through the plate glass of the back door, he's sitting with his legs up on the seat. One night, I want to take him to Dolores Park, I want to sit him down in the middle of the park and I want to kiss him while the bats in the park are squealing because of the cold. Few people know that there are bats that live in Dolores Park. I've lived around the park for two years. I didn't know myself. One day, I was walking past the park late at night to go to his place to pick up some papers and I heard the distinctive squeal of bats. Bats usually don't scream like that, the reference book in the library says, it must be the cold, they must be suffering.

One day I invite him over. We end up in my bedroom where we start fooling around. It all would have been fine if I wasn't so conscious of the fact that I had carefully folded his manuscript of writing that he had given me to read into neat kindling and laid the entire script of thirty-odd pages in my fireplace. The unburnt manuscript-kindling resting under the packed-woodchip log just hidden from his view by the dark fireplace screen and my houseguest periodically knocking on my door asking me if I wanted a bacon and egg on white bread sandwich made the entire tryst quite unsettling. That and his deformed left nipple.

As sexually liberated as I try to be, deformed nipples scare the shit out of me. I don't mind the severely pierced keloided ones because I know they were manipulated into such a state; but the ones that slant off to strange tangents all by themselves, aureoles that cave into dark nipples that look like large blackheads, those give me the heebiejeebies.

Penises are a different matter though. I quite enjoy deformed penises. This is probably because the first penises that I was attracted to and spent hours staring at and masturbating to were those in my father's medical books that he stored under my brother's bed.

Following the page numbers in the index, I was led to little shriveled diseased penises rotting through to the urethra, hanging bulbous members bloated to look like a fleshy tennis ball and dangling members in semi-erection to show the world their horrible scabs and sores—all found in fabulous color.

Perhaps all this prepared me for the first pierced penis that I ever saw. It was at a jack-off party and somehow, it didn't faze me, in fact I found it quite erotic, and I thought it was a shame the bugger it was attached to was more interested in wanking off with someone else all evening. My companion, however, found the pierced dick quite unsettling and his balls immediately retracted into his body and he had to escape to the kitchen to recompose himself.

He later told me that he was unable to have a full erection for days after witnessing that penis.

Once, I had phone sex with this man. He had a very normal voice. Nothing exceptional. Tonal quality, inflection, phrasing—the kind of voice you hear on the street as you pass by two people chatting away or when the phone rings and it's someone you don't know, he gives you a name you don't ever remember and then tries to sell you investment information.

He wanted to be fucked in the arse without a condom, wanted to feel it, *been so long, man, really need to feel that hot cock in me*. I made him shoot his first load on my dick, then fucked him up his arse using his gism as lubricant. After I came, I put my hand under his arse, palm up, he squeezed our collective cum and anal mucus out of his rectum noiselessly onto my waiting palm then jacked off another load into my hand. He used his tongue and mixed the two, his watery gism and my denser congealed gism into a swirl and licked it off my hand, every single drop. When that was done, I wiped my hand on his face, pulled him to me and kissed him hard on the mouth sucking his tongue roughly.

I'm trying to remember my first good kiss but I can't.

I've had incredibly bad luck with demonic-looking men. Sure, I find them vastly attractive but somehow, they seem to be attracted to other demonic-looking men. I try to look demonic but it really doesn't work with me. The best I can do is look like the boy next door's younger brother who lives beside the most gorgeous demonic-looking bloke. The most erotic thing I have ever seen was this brilliantly demonic-looking man eating sushi with a metal fork. On anyone else, the sight would have been quite ridiculous, but on this one man, it was enough to make me want to cook him breakfast for the rest of my life.

In my search for a demonic-looking lover, I tried placing a classified ad in the local news weekly, but due to a typo, I was surprised to discover that there were quite a sizable number of actual Satanists in San Francisco.

The other day, as I was walking down the street, I discovered a new fetish: Men with tattoos on the back of their necks. The back of a man's neck has always been the favorite part of a man's body for me. This does get quite problematic as I will often find myself getting quite aroused when I'm sitting behind a particularly sinewy neck on the bus or when the lights from the cinema screen hit the side of a fuzzed neck in front of me.

Ah! The cinema. At a rescreening of Bertolucci's *The Sheltering Sky*, I participated in some heavy flirtation with this man. Throughout the movie, I gave up on Debra Winger's search for her sexual self for that man's neck and how it glowed in the flickering of the screen. After the screening, I was determined to try and pick him up. I tried to approach him but the crowds cut me off and when I did reach the foyer, all that was left of him was the tub of popcorn he was munching into and the Dixie cup of pop soda resting in the empty popcorn tub. One in the other resting on the edge of the trashbin. Suddenly I was gripped with the urge to grab his trash and lick the tip of the straw where his lips lingered during John Malkovich's tragic and pointless death. Fortunately, the cinema manager came by and tipped the cartons into the bin and stomped the trash down with his boot to flatten it, thus saving me from embarrassing myself from such indecently obsessive acts.

Now I find myself falling behind men on the streets who have these black squiggles peeking out the tops of the back of their shirts. And worse, I find myself longing to lean over and place my lips on that mark. Nothing else but lip to neck.

The act of kissing a person's neck is possibly the most sensual act known to humankind. The neck is the body's most vulnerable spot: muscle, nerves and veins built around a vertebral column. In the animal kingdom, the smart mammals have been known to protect their necks vehemently; they never ever expose their necks unnecessarily. If you watch docs on hunters and the hunted, that's where lions bite deer and where lions bite each other. Never mind the little bit of flesh over the heart, there're ribs that protect, but the neck, nothing.

The lips also are highly sensitive: something about all those blood vessels flowing so close to the surface and the close proximity to the tongue and all of its glands and sensory stuffs.

There is a proper way to kiss someone on the neck. First, you must always start on the back or the side. Second, and this is the most important thing, you must never, never touch the other person with any other part of your body. Only lip to neck, nothing else. Let the neck feel only the press of warm lips and the lips feel the vast flesh of neck. When this happens, the microscopic space between lip and neck heats up vastly because air is a poor conductor of heat. It's kind of like how a blanket or an animal fluffing its fur works. You may be in the middle of the Sahara and you will still feel that one intense spot of heat surging out of your lover's lips and through your neck.

Smooch music: Sam Cooke, Marvin Gaye, the Supremes, Dusty in Memphis, Ella doing Gershwin, Ella with Ellington.

It's late and I can't sleep. It's been raining like mad and the roof is leaking everywhere. There're drops of water that sneak down the fireplace and drop like flies on the dead ashes. I have to keep my curtains drawn to trap the heat. That's fine, but when the wind blows, the leaves and branches of the palm tree outside my window scrape against the pane. It makes a hideous sound. I know if I can see the smack of the frond on the pane, it'll all be okay. But the curtains are drawn, I'm lying under three blankets and a sleeping bag trying not to move or I'll wake the damn cat curled up at the foot of the bed. I'm still trying to remember that first good kiss and the last good kiss and what happened in between while Ella scats something fierce; and while my heart breaks again, Anna May Wong and Mae West are off somewhere holding each others' faces in their hands, teaching each other how to kiss.

FEARLESS

• JAMESON CURRIER •

Though he harbored a virus within his body that frightened so many people and so many more misunderstood, Barry did not think of himself as diseased or infected. He liked to consider that they, he and his virus, coexisted with one another, as many members of his support group preferred to define the relationship. So it always came as a surprise to Barry when someone found out he was HIV-positive and asked if he had any symptoms. "None," he always answered, though he would never vocally complete his thought, *none of your damn business.* And then he would feel the intensity of his interrogator's stare, as if to prove he was lying, scrutinizing him, possibly even thinking that the red bump on his cheek was something more than a blemish, something far, far more frightening. Or if nothing physical was detected, nothing, nothing at all, his interrogator would look deeper, right into his soul, hoping to discover the roots of depression by the way he carried his body. After years of questions, frowning eyes, and too-sincere embraces, Barry was still learning how to channel his anger. In his support group he was always yelling at everyone, "Don't you realize how much stronger you are than this virus?"

David, however, could not shake away his years and years of loss. For him the epidemic had been going on far too long. He had lost most of his friends, his coworkers, the men he knew at the gym or the bars or the clubs or the baths. He had even lost his job and his health benefits when his boss died and the company closed, a greeting card company that operated out of a Greenwich Village brownstone. In the early days of the epidemic David had volunteered, done fund-raising, worked as a buddy; later, he marched in demonstrations and buried even more friends. Things had changed for David. When he had first moved to the city he was light and campy; now he felt he was entirely too serious, solemn, and glum. He approached everything now with anxiety.

They met in the rain.

The night before the AIDS Walk had been a restless one for David. Two years ago he had walked with a group of twelve friends. Now, four were dead, one had gone to live with his parents, two had moved away from the city, two others were diagnosed. This year, everyone he knew who would walk was tired and burned out, bowing out graciously by explaining they would be out of town for the weekend. This year, the weatherman had predicted rain. In the morning when David got out of bed the rain fell so hard on the roof of his fifth-floor apartment it sounded like a subway car approaching but never arriving. It left him feeling impatient and uneasy, eager to settle on some sort of destination. Should he walk today? Would anyone walk? He called the weather line. Rain all day. He showered and dressed and sat by the window, watching the raindrops splatter puddles like boiling water. He waited and waited, changing his mind every minute, finally deciding that he would just go to the registration point in Central Park, turn in his pledges and contributions, and then leave. When David got to the park, he was surprised at the number of people who were already there. Pausing atop a rock that provided a view of the Great Lawn, he was astonished by the sight of thousands of umbrellas, moving in and out of large random patterns like the kaleidoscopes he used to hold up to his eye as a boy. How could he leave now when everyone else was staying?

So David remained and walked.

That same morning, when Barry woke up, he was curled around a guy with a goatee who snored through his mouth. He could not remember the guy's name, had no idea where he was in the city, even if he was still *in* the city; but he did remember they had met at a club near Avenue A last night when he had been waiting in the line for the restroom. When Barry slipped away from the guy, stood up beside the bed, he had felt the chill in the air and heard the taps of raindrops against the window, just as the heaviness in his head shifted toward a headache. As he slipped on his jeans, the guy with the goatee rolled over, opened his eyes and looked at Barry and studied his face, as if trying to memorize a criminal he would later have to identify, and then, without saying anything, closed his eyes and went back to sleep. On the street, Barry realized he was still in the East Village, and darted beneath awnings till he reached the corner of St. Mark's Place. Waiting for a cab on Lafayette, Barry noticed in a store window a poster for the AIDS Walk. He looked at his watch and then back at the poster. He knew he was too late. It had already started. And the rain made him feel really lousy. He hadn't planned on going anyway. Everyone at work had asked if he were participating. It was as if, because he was gay and positive and open about both, he was *expected* to participate. Barry hated that expectation, which is why, when he finally found a cab at the corner of 13th and Broadway, he decided, only at the late, last minute, he would go to the park. When the cab dropped him off, umbrellas were streaming out of the park onto Central Park West like a long, black river.

David, practical and worried about his health—as he was always catching cold—was dressed in layers. He wore a T-shirt underneath a long-sleeve T-shirt underneath a sweatshirt, a sweater and a denim jacket. He wore his chino pants because he felt they would dry out quickly, two pairs of socks and his heavy winter boots. Wes, David's friend who now lived in Los Angeles, would have wisecracked that David looked like a walking Gap ad. David carried the wide, oversized umbrella he normally hated using in the city because it meant dodging everyone else's umbrellas. By the time he had walked to 96th Street David's pants were soaked, his shirts and sweatshirt and sweater were damp, and he knew it was only a matter of time before he could feel the water seeping through his boots, chilling his toes. But he let none of this bother him. Around him everyone else was soaking wet, too; as people passed him, David noticed everyone was collectively laughing or moaning or singing or chanting—the ever-resourceful New Yorkers had turned towels and shopping bags and banners and plastic garbage bags into survival gear.

Barry had stopped into Woolworth's to buy a cap before joining the Walk. He was soaked after the first five minutes, the wind had started whipping the crowd, and not even the long windbreaker Barry always wore around the city could keep him dry. I'm such a jerk, Barry thought, and lifted his head up to the gray sky, thinking about a way out of this madness.

Barry first noticed David when the crowd reached Riverside Park and volunteers were distributing frozen yogurt in small plastic cups to give the walkers energy or optimism or both. David, who was trying to hold his umbrella, eat the yogurt with a plastic spoon, fight off the wind and rain, and walk—all at the same time—had gotten his legs tangled in a discarded plastic bag. It was this cartoonish lunacy that captured Barry's attention, the waif-like Chaplinesque figure struggling with the weather and the attacks of urban garbage. But what pulled Barry even closer, drew him like a magnet, was David's scrubbed, boyish face—the fair complexion highlighted by the dark, doe-like eyes and the thick brown hair that was weighted down into curls from the pressure of the rain. Barry followed David to an overflowing garbage can where David lightly tossed his uneaten yogurt onto the top of the pile and untangled the garbage bag that was twisted around his foot.

David first noticed Barry when he turned and headed back into the crowd to continue walking. He noticed him again a little later when he switched the umbrella from his right to left hand. But it wasn't until David thought he noticed Barry shiver that he moved in closer. Barry's clothes stretched heavily against his body, his sneakers left wet footprints behind him, even in the rain, and he had turned his cap backwards and now walked with his hands clasped behind him, like a penitent priest, his head bowed to meet the onslaught of the weather. David noticed the jeans ripped just above the knees, the dark hair of Barry's arms matted against his skin where Barry had pushed up the sleeves of the windbreaker, the left ear triple pierced, the pendant—a cracked heart—that bounced atop his black T-shirt, the neatly trimmed black beard that covered Barry's face, even the raindrops suspended on the surface of the hair.

David held his umbrella higher, not shielding his face, worrying that if he were wet and cold that Barry, so lightly dressed, must be freezing. Finally, out of so much genuine concern, David walked over to Barry and asked, "Do you want to get under?" at the same time lightly shaking his hand that carried the umbrella. Barry turned and looked at David as if for the first time, moved underneath the umbrella and said, "Do you want me to hold it?" The voice is what caught David—the pitch so deep and heavy, so unexpected from such a slender man— almost magisterial, David thought, like that of an old, over- weight English actor.

"No, I'm OK," David said, and then realized the height of Barry and lifted his hand, as if holding a torch, so Barry would not have to stoop. Barry moved in closer and draped his arm around David's shoulder.

The physicality did not strike David as odd. Everyone was huddled and twisted together beneath umbrellas. But what hap- pened as they walked and asked each other simple questions— "Are you from the city?" "Did you do the Walk last year?"—was that their eyes would lock as they looked down or up at one another and their touch would shift—David placed his arm around Barry's hip, Barry twisted his chilly fingers be- neath David's T-shirts for warmth. They walked this way, smil- ing and embracing, till they reached the Park again. By then, of course, the rain had stopped and what was left of it was a soupy drizzle. That was when Barry turned to David and kissed him. David, caught up in the moment—the Walk, the rain, the close- ness of Barry—lifted up onto his toes and leaned into Barry, feeling the water trapped within Barry's beard ribbon down his chin.

When they broke apart they looked awkwardly away from one another, till Barry took David's hand and led him to a bench. Barry sat on the top frame, his feet resting on the seat of the bench, and pulled a pack of cigarettes from the pocket of his windbreaker. He offered one to David, who stood beside the bench and shook his head no, then lit it with a lighter he pulled from the pocket of his jeans.

"You should know I'm positive," Barry said, blowing a stream of smoke into the air.

David's back stiffened. In less than an hour he had imagined falling in love. Now, in two seconds, he was breaking up. "We should dry out," David said. He looked around, wondering what to do, knowing he was being tempted and tested. "Come on," he said, and this was when he took Barry's hand. "I'm not far from here."

They caught a cab at Columbus Circle, holding hands till the driver dropped them off at Ninth Avenue.

"Welcome to the slums," David said, unlocking the street door of his apartment building. "It's a straight climb to the top."

"Straight?" Barry said, grinning, and turned and kissed David. David, now, was lightly embarrassed, wondering if passersby on the street could see them in the building vestibule.

Inside David's apartment, Barry again kissed David, testing him once more, wanting to see if there was any fear in his kiss. David pressed his tongue into Barry's mouth and Barry gasped for a moment, pulled back and slipped his hand beneath David's shirts.

Now David leaned back and removed the denim jacket he wore; it landed on the floor in a wet thlop. He led Barry through a tour of the apartment till they settled, standing, in front of the bed. Barry again kissed David, this time at the neck. David felt the bristles of Barry's beard, one moment prickly, then wet, then slick like an animal's fur. David slipped his hands along Barry's forearms, amazed at their leanness, the tendons and veins popping right up to the skin.

They continued to peel wet clothing from one another—jackets, sweaters, shirts—rubbing their hands along the dampness that remained on their bodies, warming and drying each other's skin with the friction of their touch. Barry stepped easily out of his sneakers. David sat on the edge of the bed and unlaced his boots, then Barry leaned down on top of him and lifted their bodies into the bed. As they removed the rest of their clothing—socks and briefs—Barry was amazed by the thick muscles of David's body—the heavy arms, the wide shoulders, the deep muscles of his back, like those of a wrestler or a high school coach; he had imagined David would have had a more lean, boyish physique. David was mesmerized by the dark hair that covered Barry's entire body—coarse and bristly about the legs, flat and silken as it traveled up his stomach and splayed across his chest. He was surprised, too, by the narrowness of Barry's bones at his shoulders and hips—so slender and precise

they appeared almost feline. He held on to Barry as they continued kissing; David was not really sure where his movements
were to carry him and he felt, instead of relaxing, his body tens-
ing. It had been a long time since David had allowed himself to
enjoy sex, a long time, too, since he had allowed himself the
touch of another man.

Barry was not frightened at all. He held on to David and
stroked him and kissed him. Sensing David's anxiety, Barry
straddled David's thighs, his knees pressed against the mattress,
next to David's hips. "Relax," Barry said, and David felt the
voice reverberate through his chest and he closed his eyes as
Barry stroked him till he came. Barry then lay down beside David, and David turned his body toward him, their eyes locking
as Barry then slowly jerked himself off.

David found a towel, dipped a washrag under the warm water, and returned to the bed, cleaning first himself and then
Barry. Barry stayed and fell asleep and David held him from behind and watched TV in the darkened room. Through his mind
ran the list of safe and unsafe guidelines. How safe was kissing?
Jerking off? A shared washrag? David knew he was being silly;
hadn't he done more dangerous things besides kissing? Hadn't
he cleaned Peter's catheter daily, washed shit off of Neal, wiped
up Glenn's vomit? Just when David himself had nodded off, he
realized Barry had gotten out of the bed, and he lifted his head
away from the pillow and heard the shower running. David lay
there until Barry came back into the room, a towel draped
around his waist. "Everything's still wet," Barry said.

"There's some T-shirts in the top drawer," David replied,
motioning to a bureau against the wall. "You can take one of
those. And there's a pair of sweatpants in the bottom. They're
probably too small, but they'll last till you get home."

"I'll give them back to you the next time I see you," Barry
said.

There was a profound pause between them, as if neither
wanted to say anything. "Will I see you again?" Barry asked.

"There's no reason why you shouldn't," David answered and
watched Barry get dressed.

By the next morning David had made up his mind that he
wouldn't see Barry again, that he had only been caught up in

the moment and that he and Barry weren't really compatible. Barry smoked, after all. And, though David would never admit it to anyone else, he was scared of becoming infected himself; this was something that could potentially lead to his own death. But there, in the newspaper, were photographs taken the day before of the Walk. At home, after work, there it was again on the news. All those people in the rain. Wouldn't David's fears about contracting the virus make him, in his own way, homophobic and bigoted? This was something he knew he had to confront. David called the number Barry had left, and when Barry answered, he asked how his day was, did he see the paper this morning, was he watching the news? Barry said he hadn't seen any of those things, but he had been thinking about David all day. They talked briefly about how wet they had been, wasn't it amazing, they laughed, David fully entranced by the sound of Barry's voice.

They made arrangements to see each other two days later.

They met for dinner at a crowded Mexican restaurant in Chelsea; Barry brought along the T-shirt and sweatpants he had borrowed from David. At a table in the back Barry ordered a margarita and lit a cigarette. This momentarily confused David; wouldn't someone who had tested positive give up smoking and drinking? "Is there a reason why your ear is pierced three times?" David asked instead.

The question surprised Barry. They knew, at this point, so little of one another, that this was, to him, such an odd question to ask.

"The first time was for myself," Barry said. "The second time I don't remember. The third time was to really piss off my boss."

Barry explained he worked at a bank on Wall Street where everyone tiptoed around the conservative executives. He hated the job, hated the hours—he was a night person, really—hated wearing suits. His grandmother had found him the job when he had left home because he could no longer get along with his father. His first week at the job he grew his beard. The second week he was promoted. He said, lighting another cigarette, he didn't understand any of it.

David said he had moved to the city fifteen years ago, after graduating college, to become an actor. This made Barry turn pale, and he stared at David, stopped his talking by placing his hand on top of David's.

"How old are you?" Barry asked.

"Probably older than you," David answered.

"How old do you think I am?" Barry was stunned, caught off guard.

"Probably close to your thirties."

"I'm twenty-two."

"*Twenty-two?*" This stunned David. How old had Barry been when he had tested positive? David wondered. David sat there, shocked, wanting to cry.

"I thought we were the same age," Barry said.

David felt his face turn a bright red. "I'm flattered, I think," he said, hearing his own voice turn high and thin. "But I've been through a lot."

It was then that Barry realized how little he knew of David, and now, sensing this gap, this difference in age, he felt his caution returning, not wanting himself to know any more details about David. Every time he had gotten close to someone he was always pushed away. The virus, the damn virus. He wasn't even sick. It was particularly harder, he had discovered, with the older men. Those that remembered what it was like before the epidemic began.

"How old are you *exactly?*" Barry asked.

"Exactly? Thirty-seven," David answered. "And seven months."

What saved Barry that night was David locking his stare into Barry's eyes. What does one say to a twenty-two-year-old? David had thought at that moment, and heard himself rambling into a monologue about how he had never been able to make it as an actor because he didn't have the self-confidence to make it through auditions. Then he began talking about the job he had lost, the friends who had become sick, and he realized he was dropping his cards and guts and baggage right there on the table, even sitting there saying how, at times, he just wished he were someone else. Barry ordered another margarita.

"Do I scare you?" Barry asked.

David knew exactly what he meant. "Yes," David answered.

It was then that Barry realized that he had been sitting there with an erection.

They spent the night together at David's apartment.

* * *

When he was alone David could not sleep. He kept worrying. Why was he doing this? His gums bled easily when he flossed, his hands were full of paper cuts, he always nicked himself when he was shaving. There were a million ways he could become infected. He would work himself up into such a state of frenzy that the only way he could become calm was to remind himself that no one really knew what was going on, no one *really* knew what was causing this craziness. Then he would think of all the positive men he had kissed or had sex with in his lifetime. But that would lead to a roll call of the dead and David, now near tears, would sit in bed shaking his head, wondering, why was he here—negative, healthy, and depressed? What was going on? Finally, he would turn on the TV or the radio, hoping the sound would keep him from thinking too much, and he would lie down again, curling into a tight fetal position, waiting, waiting for sleep to return.

Barry, too, had trouble sleeping; he had come to believe things were now divided into "Us," the infected, and "Them," the healthy. He knew too many guys who had been dumped because they were positive. But what kept Barry up at night was the worry of who would be there for him if he got sick. He had never been able to ask others for help, but then he had never, even, tried to get close to anyone, not even the members of his support group—when he reached a point of connecting or caring for someone he usually asked to be placed into another session. At night Barry would imagine himself sweating from a high fever in a hospital bed, totally dependent, and he would be seized with panic. He did not trust his doctor. But Barry knew, too, he had progressed beyond his fear of abandonment. He had pushed everyone away himself. He would get out of bed and walk around his darkened apartment, reminding himself it was not too late to find someone; he still had time. But it was important, he knew, not to get hurt. He had to protect himself, too.

They met again on Saturday to see a movie in the Village.
David was already at the corner of Bleecker Street when Barry arrived and greeted him with a kiss on the lips. David gave Barry a weak and embarrassed smile, and as they walked together to-

ward the theater, Barry took hold of David's hand. David, surprised, looked down at their hands, joined at his side, as if it were a scar or a blemish he were not supposed to acknowledge but *had* to inspect. David had never been comfortable with such open public affection between men, and he wondered now if Barry had misread him from their rainy walk from last week. He looked out at the people passing them on the sidewalk, hoping to spot another male couple holding hands, but all he saw were startled expressions, eyes focused in their direction, right at their hands. David moved their joined arms so that their hands fell behind his back as they walked, trying to rationalize his timidity and uneasiness. Wasn't Barry's public affection just another thing he had to overcome or adjust to, like his youth and smoking and sero-status? Weren't they, after all, walking in the *Village?* Wasn't this *their* part of town? Finally, however, worried by the stares they were still receiving, David just let go of Barry's hand, knowing it must *really* look queer to be *holding* hands and *hiding* them.

By now David had reached a foolish state of confusion. He had not dated anyone in over nine months, not since his blitz period—the period he had answered personal ads, joined a dating club, and started calling a phone line—the results of which were too many dates with too many wrong guys. But even in his younger days, even when he had been Barry's age, David had never been able to master the protocols of dating. He had never known when to be aggressive, when to wait for a phone call, when to flirt with someone or how to catch a stare on the street. In those days he had felt awkward and unattractive, always standing on the outside of gay life; even the clues and codes mystified him—what were all those keys and colored handkerchiefs *really* about anyway? But sex had always been obtainable for him—he was always approached at the bars or the baths; in fact, he went to those places to find reassurances that he was *not* awkward and unattractive. In those days dating to him meant having sex. Sex, sex, sex. It's why he got together with a guy for a second time. No matter what incompatibilities there were, sex was an action that made them compatible, even if only briefly.

Now, everything about Barry bewildered David—the touching, the holding hands in public, the fuzzy feelings David felt inside while they were together. But David also thought that with Barry he had not made any progress after all these years; what did they have in common with each other, really, besides their desire to have sex with one another? David had hoped that by now, at his age and having survived this far into the plague, he would have reached something *beyond* a sexual relationship. Was he merely using Barry as reassurance of his own attractiveness or was he instead simply smitten by the attentiveness? Was he afraid of falling in love or worse, falling in love and being abandoned, or even more worse, falling in love and watching someone die? Was the real issue Barry's sero-status? Or had David accepted that through the act of sex? Or was David simply *incapable* of a relationship? But David could even justify now that Barry wasn't physically even his *type*. Wasn't David, after all, attracted and more interested in guys his own height and age—those boyish, actorish friends, conservative and nonthreatening, who knew the same subjects he did, could talk in the same shorthand about the theater or books or movies? But even this was discouraging; somehow everyone David knew or met these days was already attached to someone richer or better looking or taller or smarter. Perhaps what David needed *was* someone younger, someone uninhibited and dauntless.

Though Barry was first drawn to David because of his boyish looks, Barry knew he and David were really not compatible. And it had nothing to do with David's age, nothing to do with David's reticence or overeducated response to everything. Emotionally Barry found himself drawn to men who were adventurous and willing to take risks, the reason why he was captivated by the spontaneity of the club crowd, those ready to just go out there and dance and sweat it out. But physically he was wildly attracted, too, to those macho-masculine men who were tall and unapproachable-looking, rough around the edges, the straight construction worker-cowboy types, the kind who presented as much danger as discipline. "In other words, someone unavailable," a woman in his support group had laughed the night Barry had explained this. That was the first group Barry had left. He had changed therapists for the same reason when, in a session, his doctor suggested that perhaps what he was searching for was a surrogate for the father he felt had abandoned him.

When Barry had brought the subject of David up at his support group meeting that week, Ken, an older man who believed he specialized in being dumped—even older than David—warned Barry to be prepared for the worst. "People don't change," Ken said. "If he hesitates now, he'll hesitate later." Justin, a year younger than Barry, yelled at Barry and said he should just forget about David. "It's his fault, anyway, man," Justin said. "They fucked around for years. Those kind of guys gave us AIDS." That prompted an argument within the group, angry cross-examinations and challenges displacing Barry's desire for advice.

Earlier that week, when David had phoned his friend Stuart and asked if he, Stuart, would ever date someone who was positive, there followed that notorious gap of silence. By the time Stuart spoke, David already knew his answer.

"You're putting your life at risk," Stuart said. "No one else. *You* have to make that choice."

When David pressed him harder, what would Stuart *do*, Stuart again avoided the question. "I have a lover," Stuart said. "I'm lucky I don't have to be out there."

David called his friend Wes in Los Angeles and asked him the same question. This time there was no hesitation. "No," Wes said bluntly. David and Wes had slept together years ago. Now Wes worked for an organization that raised funds for AIDS research. When David pressed Wes to explain his decision, Wes answered succinctly, "I can't work with it *and* live with it." Later, toward the end of their conversation, Wes asked David, "Do you feel something for him?"

"Yes," David answered honestly, but then he remembered he had also felt something for John-Boy on "The Waltons" and Michael on "thirtysomething."

David wished Barry was negative. Barry wished David was positive.

They held hands throughout the movie.

Afterwards, Barry took David home to his apartment on the Upper East Side.

David had not been aware of how much money Barry had; it was certainly not apparent in Barry's choice of clothing or restaurants, not even hinted at in his attitude. Barry's apartment was on the top floor of a Park Avenue building, decorated with dark, bulky wooden antiques and tapestries, large floor-to-ceiling windows providing a city skyline view. Barry explained that the furnishings and the apartment belonged to his grand-mother, though she had not used it in several years, since Barry had asked to move in; she now stayed at the house in Westchester.

"Do you want a drink?" Barry asked, and David, disappearing into the cushions of an overstuffed couch, shook his head and said, "No, I'm fine," and noticed as Barry opened the bar, the crystal ice bucket and glasses, the bar stocked with an assortment of foreign liqueurs.

For the last few years David had lived on the brink of poverty. David had payed for Neal's funeral with his own money, bought medication for Glenn, loaned Peter money he knew he would never see again. David had lost jobs, quit others, moved in and out of apartments so many times that he had now become so poor, so behind on all his loan payments and credit cards, that his creditors had taken to calling him periodically to check on his financial status—was he working, why were the payments late, could he send something in now, just a little? Sometimes David believed if it weren't for his regular collectors—Mr. Shaw from American Express, Mrs. Watson from Chemical MasterCard, Andrea from Citibank—his phone might not even ring at all. These financial problems had produced in David such a lack of self-esteem that he could no longer listen to his friends' vacations to Europe or trips to the Caribbean, no longer listen about the cars they were considering buying, no longer care, even, what new plays or restaurants or movies they had discovered—everything seemed so unattainable to him. Sometimes David tried to shrug it off with a joke, saying that he half expected one day to walk into a bank or a store and alarms would go off and security guards rush at him, yelling, "You owe us money! You owe us money!" But the truth was, David was worried that now no one would take him seriously; could anyone ever find him attractive living with such troubles? David had also come to believe, in that same light-hearted manner, that the only person who could fall in love with him now would have to be someone obscenely rich. Or would have to be either a doctor or a psychiatrist, someone who could talk David out of all of his neuroses.

He told none of this to Barry, of course. Rich, well-to-do Barry. Barry who drank and smoked too much. Barry who could march in the rain without even an umbrella for protection. Barry who was fifteen years younger than David but looked four years older. Barry with whom he had such a difficult time finding things to talk about, things they shared besides that crazy, intense chemical attraction of sex. Barry who was positive and seemed to now live, not with a joy or a fervor for life, but precariously, teetering on a ledge.

At the back of David's mind, of course, was Barry's status. What if Barry got sick? Would David take care of him? As he had done with the others? Could he *really* go through that again? David had never had a lover—a string of boyfriends, yes, but never a lover—and his closest, most intimate moments were the ones he had spent washing Peter when he was sick, helping Neal walk from the bed to the bathroom, feeding Glenn when he was too weak to do it himself. There was always the possibility that Barry *was* stronger than the virus; wasn't the news full of reports now of stories of weaker strains and longer life expectancies? But for David, there was always the possibility that he, himself, could slip across that line and become infected.

Barry was acutely aware of the division between himself and David because of the virus. It was an issue with every man he had met and dated since he had discovered his diagnosis. Barry refused to believe that sex was a moral or legal dilemma for him. The problem was unsafe sex. He knew the facts; he operated within the guidelines. But what upset Barry was the way gay men had become interested in safe men, not safe sex. Most negative men would not even consider dating a positive man; ironic, Barry thought, that in a community so passionate about civil rights, discrimination, and anti-bias legislation, there were still men who would walk away from him the moment he explained he was positive. Even the personal ads reeked of codes: healthy playmate seeks same, responsible man wanted, or, more blatantly, negatives only need reply. And now even the positives had made the division even wider: special bar nights for positives, dating clubs for positives, special newsletters and support groups and circle jerks for positives. All Barry really wanted was someone who would not be afraid of him. The concept of safe sex was that safe sex was for everybody, but HIV had now become more than an opponent for some men; it had become, in this disturbed and distorted fashion, the antagonist of love. For years Barry had never really wanted a lover; what he enjoyed about sex was the raw, physical anonymity of it. When Barry left home at sixteen he knew nothing about safe sex—his parents had created for him such a protected environment that the equation between sex and death was not even considered a probability. Barry believed that what had happened to him—his sero-conversion in the early period of his exploring his sexuality—was no different than what had happened to those in the early days of the epidemic. He could not blame himself any more than he could really blame his parents or his teachers for their lack of perception. He mentioned none of this to David, of course, but he joined him on the couch, placed his drink on a glass-topped coffee table and lit a cigarette.

David had given up smoking, had given up drinking and pot and recreational drugs. Sometimes David felt he had gone through every modern gay phase possible—the theater phase, the bar phase, the opera, baths, gym phases, the disco phase, even the twelve-step and activist phases. Sometimes all this history of himself just wore him down. What was left, David felt, was a hollow shell, waiting to be refilled. As David watched Barry take a deep, long drag off of his cigarette, he realized that of course Barry should smoke—it made sense—what did Barry really have left to lose? David reached out and touched Barry on the arm and it was here that Barry recognized, for the first time, that this was not a touch of sympathy or concern but one of understanding. Barry leaned over and kissed David, and David, at that moment, tasted everything—the cigarette, the alcohol, even the breath of passion of another man's life.

It was David who suggested they move to the bedroom; Barry led the way.

David spent the night tossing, unaccustomed to the bed and Barry beside him. David never liked sleeping over with someone; it always seemed to shift a relationship into a more intimate and awkward level. Barry woke up intermittently throughout the night, lifting himself out of sleep to remember who lay beside him; Barry seldom had overnight guests, preferring instead to absorb himself into someone else's life. Before them was a large window and a view of the night sky. David, waking, noticing the deep violet clouds, was reminded of those nights years ago when he would stumble out of a disco or the baths, his mind tinted by alcohol and drugs, and he would suddenly notice, upon turning a corner, a huge, wide pocket of the Manhattan sky. It always made him feel vivid and indestructible; not now, looking at it through his sleepy haze, it made him feel old and defeated. How could he deny or fault Barry for wanting that same illusion, the invincibility of youth? As the morning light began to outline the clouds like veins of marble, David reached out and drew Barry toward him. They made love again, and afterwards, David held Barry in his arms, Barry's head pressed against David's chest, David stroking his fingers through Barry's hair. They stayed that way, watching the morning sun bleed into the horizon and Barry felt, for the first time since discovering his diagnosis, something was attainable for him, a future was possible with another man. David felt he was capable of protecting Barry from every harm, helping him navigate the muddy river of youth.

Barry was the first to get out of bed. He dressed and went to the deli on Lexington Avenue and brought back the Sunday *Times*, bagels, and coffee. David sat at the grand piano and sight read a book of Jerome Kern songs.

It was a beautiful spring day and Barry opened the windows of the apartment, causing the light to break through in rays and the sheer curtains to billow and curl as they would in a movie. They showered and decided, each to himself, that they were not tired of one another nor ready to part, and they agreed to take a walk to Central Park, amazed that only a week ago it had been so rainy when they met.

On the way to the park Barry noticed young men everywhere, young men dressed in tank tops and shorts, young men carrying backpacks and gym bags, young men wearing caps and sunglasses and Walkmans. At one point they passed a young man and his girlfriend holding hands, a man Barry found so handsome that he upset Barry's balance, weakened his knees, made him momentarily lose his logic. Of course David had no-

ticed Barry's reaction; David had also noticed the girlfriend noticing Barry. Barry knew he had to find a way to handle this dis-
traction, knew that if he were to make a relationship with David
work he would have to channel his obsessions in other ways, or
at least *discuss* them and acknowledge them to David; David,
however, knew he had to accept Barry's preoccupations, wasn't
that, after all, a distinction of being both young and gay? Near
Fifth Avenue a gaunt man with a ragged beard crossed in front
of them and it was here that David recognized the man as
someone he had seen years ago in his gym. David averted his
eyes, embarrassed and upset, feeling guilty once again by sur-
viving, guilty for being alive and healthy and negative when so
many of his friends and lovers and boyfriends and tricks were
either positive, ill, dying, or dead. Barry, now realizing something had passed between David and the man, took David's
hand, and it was then that David gave it willingly, here realized
that one had to have such an immense courage to date these
days—to be fearless, really, to fall in love. At that point David
became immune to everyone's stares, existing blissfully in a moment of affection.

It was a perfect day for the park. They lay on the ground at
Sheep Meadow watching a boy and his father fly a kite, then
walked to the pond and watched the miniature sailboats, then
rented bikes and cycled around the horse-drawn carriages.
They ate hot dogs and ice cream from vendors. David felt as
young as Barry had imagined him to be. Barry moved everywhere with the lightness of hope in his step. They did not part
from one another until twilight, kissing unashamedly in front of
everyone at Columbus Circle, beneath a sky fading as brilliantly
as it had arrived.

That was the end of their first week together.

What happened was David got sick. A cold. A bad one. He
had a fever and deep pains in his chest, as if he had pulled a
muscle. Bad enough to cancel a date with Barry. Barry offered
to come over anyway, cook David something, though when
Barry heard himself saying that he thought it sounded false.
Cook what? he thought; he didn't know how to cook. "I'll bring
you some medicine. Or something," Barry said.

"No," David replied, not wanting to seem vulnerable. "I need to just shake this myself."

Barry was pissed when he hung up the phone; he felt David was using this as an excuse to push him away. David was not really *that* sick; the issue was once again that Barry was positive. Barry went out to a bar, then to a club, then home with a guy named Allen.

Barry was not home when David called later that night. David left a message on Barry's answering machine that some medicine would be nice, so would some company. Barry did not get the message till the following day when he got home from work. When Barry called David, David did not pick up the phone, thinking it was Mr. Shaw from American Express, calling to inquire about when another payment could be expected. Barry was so upset he could not leave a message on David's answering machine. Days passed. Barry went out to another club. David agonized over whether to call Barry again, then decided, impulsively, to visit a friend out of town.

Time passed between them.

Months later, sometime near Christmas, David spotted Barry through the window of a store on Christopher Street, his arm draped around another man. It was then that David crossed the street to the other side, not wanting to become upset, wanting only, instead, to survive.

LAND OF LOVE

• JOSHUA DAVID •

Winter is not pretty at the Land of Love Hotel. Snow falls
heavy and wet each day, freezing to a crust at night. The wishing well and heart-shaped swimming pool are sealed beneath a
glaze of ice. Stuart sometimes wonders if there is any other
place. He visits Boston from time to time and has been to New
York twice, but today it seems the kitchen window has framed
his entire world: the road he plows each morning, five stucco
guest wings with failing septic systems, and the dimly glowing
surface of the frozen lake.

   Stuart's father modeled Land of Love after the famous honeymoon resorts in the Poconos. He outfitted each room with a
heart-shaped bathtub, a round bed encircled by mirrors, and
red shag carpet on the floors, walls, and ceiling. His quarter-
page ads used to compete in bridal magazines against luxurious
four-color spreads from Cove Haven and Mount Airy Lodge,
but he pulled the ads two years ago, offended by the pouting
travel editor from *American Bride* who wore beetle-shaped sunglasses and had a manner when touring guest rooms of taking
prissy sniffs as if she smelled something repugnant. Now Stu
Senior relies on a blurb in the Mobil Guide to draw guests to
his "Little Piece of Paradise," twenty miles east of Pittsfield. It
doesn't hurt that roads in this area are poorly marked. A pair of
leaf peepers or antique hunters will sometimes stray down
Route 4, hoping for a scenic road back to the interstate, until
wearied by the curves, disheartened by so many bait shacks and

candle shops, they turn in at the gate, vulnerable in their exhaustion to the smiling promise of the concrete cupids that line the driveway.

Stuart stared down at the property he will one day inherit, his face as drained of color as the frozen snow. He has the same mystified expression that other nineteen-year-olds have when looking in a mirror. The slowly falling flakes exhaust him. It seems he is constantly shoveling out from under. Stu Senior never considered the harsh Massachusetts winters. He thought only of white sailboats on blue water, yellow flowers, and a gold course glowing green from a double dose of fertilizer. He skimped on construction. Now there are cracks in the cinderblocks, and moisture seeps inside, soaking the red shag rugs. When the ground freezes, it puts pressure on the septic lines. If Stuart does not make his weekly rounds with the honey truck, pumping out the system, sewage will bubble up the pipes into the heart-shaped bathtubs.

"Voilà," says Stu Senior. He slides a plate of brown scrambled eggs in front of Stuart. "Some Cointreau in this." Ever since Stuart's mother left when he was six, Stu Senior has been cooking his own special way: a can of this, a can of that, a splash of one liqueur or another.

"Eat, Stuart, please. Just coffee is no kind of breakfast."

"Pop, the *gas*." Stuart points at the stove's blue flame. "Twice last week, I came home and found the burner going."

"Not me."

"Yes, you."

"No." Stu Senior ignores the flame and bends for a scrap of lint on the carpet. His rear end is such a wide and vulnerable target. "If you just pick these up," he says, "then they're gone."

To see him now, it's hard to imagine Stu Senior once had the ambition and ability to build Land of Love. He disappears for hours each day. No one knows where he goes. Stuart thinks it's best not to ask. He has noticed something shaken in his father's eyes, a veiled desperation that was not there before. The staff has noticed it, too.

"Did you bait the traps?" Stuart says. "They're still calling about mice." He holds up the complaint form Jilly gave him. "Room 9. Scuffling, behind the wall."

Stu Senior's stare is glazed and slightly panicked. His mouth opens, closes, then opens again, but he says nothing.

"Forget it, Pop. I'll take care of it."

"*I'll* do it," says Stu Senior. "I said I would. So I will."

"Suit yourself." Stuart sets his cup in the sink. "As long as it gets done." He unhooks the key to the honey truck from the board.

"What's the rush? You've barely touched your eggs."

"Today is pump-out, Pop. I'm behind already."

Stu Senior nods, shakes a Carlton from his pack, and lights it by the window, staring at the snow-swept scene. "Another shitty day in Paradise," he says.

The honey truck is a scaled-down version of the trucks used to deliver heating oil. It has a white cab and a barrel-shaped tank, painted pink. Stu Senior got the pink paint cheap from Benny at the mill, but he only used one coat, so a shadow of the former slogan can still be read: *Roto Rooter that's the name. Away goes trouble down the drain.*

Stuart has rigged a snowplow to the front, so he can plow up to each wing and hook into the sewage bypass; while the truck pumps out the system, he inspects the rooms. Georgina, his girlfriend, says it's ridiculous how much work he does, but it has to be this way. They've laid off so many people. And even a re-pellent chore like pumping out doesn't diminish Stuart's feeling for the place. Beneath the snow, there is earth, and he knows every inch: where pipes run, where tulip bulbs are planted, where his dog lies buried. If at times Stuart imagines being in another town, living another life, he also knows that the daily routine of his father's hotel has become his routine, that the two things—place and person—have become decidedly entangled.

He plows the entry road, twisting through the woods to the gate. The highway has been salted; eighteen-wheelers rumble past, rocking Stuart on his springs. He turns the truck and plows back toward the main lodge, passing the driveway to their house, which sits at the edge of the snow-shrouded golf course. From this distance, the neocolonial ranch looks almost grand, with Stu Senior's red Buick warming in the driveway, chugging soft gray puffs. Stuart feels a sense of accomplishment as he wrestles with the steering wheel, stomps the gas and clutch.

The tire chains are clinking, and the plow lifts a gray curl of snow that tumbles on itself.

Ahead he sees a red parka. It's Boyd, trudging to the dining room from the employee parking lot. Boyd buses tables during lunch and bartends at the hotel's Heartthrob Bar at night. Stuart would like to toot the horn and pass right by, but he decides it's better to act normal. He'd stop for anyone else, so why not Boyd? With a foot on the brake, he leans across the seat and opens the door.

"Need a lift?"

Boyd's face is blotched purple from the cold. Stuart used to think that the moonlike quality of Boyd's eyes came from his generous, unaffected nature, but lately he's been thinking it might be a lack of intelligence. There's a red, sticky-looking spot under Boyd's nose and white crust at the corners of his mouth. Not attractive, Stuart tells himself. It won't happen again.

"Thanks, boss," says Boyd.

"Don't call me that."

Boyd looks at the floor.

They bounce along in the truck. As usual, Stuart can't think of anything to say. They graduated in the same high school class last year, but they weren't friends. Boyd was an athlete and socialized with other athletes.

"Busy up there last night?" Stuart finally manages. He knows it wasn't busy—he saw the receipts this morning. But silences with Boyd are dangerous: closed in a tight space with him, like in this truck, he feels a charge in the air, a droning buzz that needs to be covered.

"The couple from Providence," says Boyd. "They stayed till 1:30, dancing all alone."

"With you watching?"

"Didn't seem to care."

"I couldn't dance all alone," says Stuart, "with someone else, I mean, knowing I was being watched."

"Wouldn't be a problem for me," says Boyd, staring straight ahead.

Stuart feels a clenching in his throat. Something beneath the surface of Boyd's voice both pleases and repels him; he wants to change the subject. "Pretty, the lake. The patterns of snow on the ice."

"I like it better in summer."

"It is nice in summer," Stuart admits.

"At night, especially."

Heat rushes to Stuart's cheeks. Why did he even mention the lake? It was exactly the topic he should have avoided.

Last summer, when the lake was sparkling in the sun, some of the younger staff members posed as happy couples for the new brochure. Stuart posed with Georgina, and Boyd posed with a waitress named Diane. There were seven couples in all, grinning for the camera across heaping plates of polished fruits and sailing small boats with their legs and arms entwined. Nobody got paid; they did it for the free food and booze. The party started after the last shot at sunset and lasted well into the night. Sometime after midnight, Stuart and Boyd left the group to share a joint. They went down to the lake to do this.

A pull from Boyd's pale chest in the black water drew the men together until they touched. Stuart felt Boyd's hardness press his hip, amazed that such a secret would pass silently between them. They climbed onto the golf course and lay naked on the fresh-cut grass. Clippings stuck to Stuart's back, and the stubble on Boyd's face scratched. "Put it in me," Stuart said, and Boyd did. At first the tearing pain was awful, but that gave way, and Stuart was dizzied by the invasion deep inside. Then his nostrils flared at the scent of his own bowels, and he wriggled away before either of them came.

"I've never done that before," Stuart said. "I'm sorry."

"For what?"

"The smell."

"I don't care about that."

"I do," said Stuart.

"It's only natural," said Boyd, but Stuart was already running. He dove in the dark water and swam out to the center. He floated, staring at the stars, until he was sure that Boyd had put his clothes on and left. Emptiness twitched and stung where Boyd no longer filled him. But in the lake, at least, he felt cleaner. And older. "Never again," he said to himself. "Never again," over and over, until it melted into a meaningless chant: *ganeverra ganeverra, ganeverra. . . .*

"Here we go," Stuart says now, wheeling the truck to the service entrance.

"Thanks," says Boyd. He turns, stares; Stuart tries to shield himself but cannot. The coaxing in Boyd's eyes becomes a glower. He twists his mouth—is this a sneer? He climbs from the truck and slams the door.

Alone, Stuart sits gripping the wheel, staring over the hood, down the hill, which is so green in summer. A snow-glazed lump rises from a cleft in the slope. It's the wishing well where he posed with Georgina for the brochure. He keeps the photo in a gold frame on his desk. Georgina looks perfect in it, the sun lighting her blonde hair with a halo from behind. Stuart's arm is wrapped around her waist; a second before the shutter clicked, he squeezed the ticklish spot above her hip, so she has been caught laughing, her eyes alive, the way a person laughs when the greatest pleasure is still to come.

When Stuart plows up to Reception, a tall man in a black overcoat walks out and raises his hand. It's a small, controlled gesture, but it has power. Stuart stops.

"Are you in charge?" the man asks. He is balding with a well-trimmed beard, and slim. Stuart thinks he could be a senator or millionaire. He has that exclusive look of satisfaction. "Your receptionist won't give me a room. You must have a room."

"We're pretty-well booked," says Stuart. Actually, only three rooms are occupied, but Stu Senior says to claim a full house at all times. It keeps people from haggling over price.

"That's not what I was told. The girl said there was a room, then she wouldn't give it to me."

Stuart cocks his head.

"Because I'm alone."

"Ah," says Stuart. "Land of Love is a couples-only property."

The rule is designed to keep out trios, gays, and swingers. Stu Senior feels it's important for Land of Love to stay romantic, and for him that means couples: one man, one woman. He doesn't want it sleazy like the waterbed dives on the strip. But Stuart wonders if he should make an exception. This man obviously isn't with a group of swingers, and they could certainly use the business.

"Is that really what it's called? Land of Love?" He looks at the lodge, then back at Stuart, with a smile of amused distaste.

"You must have seen the sign driving in."

"I wasn't driving. The man from the Shell station dropped me. Alternator trouble. I'm trying to get back to Boston."

"From?"

"Wheatleigh."

Stuart nods. Wheatleigh is a posh hotel in Lenox. It costs three hundred dollars a night to stay there.

"I was hoping I might lie down. I'll be stuck here all day." He gives *stuck* just enough kick to make Stuart feel ridiculous.

"It's not so bad. Some people come hundreds of miles."

The man looks at him with frank disbelief.

"Honeymooners," Stuart says.

"Honeymooners!" The man is laughing at the sky now. Who does he think he is? A glint in his eyes makes Stuart feel bare. It seems he knows what Stuart thinks at night.

"So. You'll tell the girl to give me a room?"

"No," says Stuart. "We're a couples-only property, as I said before. But you're welcome at the restaurant, and in the bar."

"You're joking?"

"These are the rules."

"Land of Love. . . ." The man shakes his head; his mouth curls in a thin smile. "Just my luck."

Stuart laughs nervously. *Eat shit*, he wants to say.

As he hooks the pump to the sewage bypass at the Paradise Villa annex, Stuart finds himself wondering. The man said he was going to Boston, but his voice carried the lilt of someplace foreign. A place Stuart has never been and might never go. Stuart pictures him naked. His body would be pale, nearly blue, with dark hair on it. The thought makes him shiver.

The pump chugs smoothly, sucking waste from the septic tank buried beneath the parking lot. The motor spins when it's finished. Stuart holds his breath. He is amazed at how much stink can escape in the moment between unhooking the hose and capping the valve. His gloved hands fumble, and the cap falls in the snow. He digs frantically, holding his breath, until he finds the cap and screws it back on. He jogs away from the valve and takes deep gulps of air. Even at this distance, it smells rotten and sweet.

Georgina's cart, stacked with white towels, stands outside room number 9. On the ground there's a breakfast tray. A squirrel sniffs the tumbled plates and dirty napkins. The squirrel tries to eat the leftover eggs, but they're frozen to the plate.

Georgina glances up when he comes through the door, blowing a wisp from her eyes. She's kneeling on the platform at the center of the red-carpeted room, scrubbing the heart-shaped tub.

"Where are we today?" asks Stuart.

The TV flashes game cards on the screen, black kings and red queens, dropping to the green felt table. There's a man in a tuxedo, then a woman in diamonds, slipping into a fur coat.

"A spa in Germany," says Georgina. "Joan Collins goes there."

This is Georgina's favorite show. Each day it visits a different place, exotic and expensive, faraway. She makes fun of the host sometimes, mimicking his pretentious voice, but she also memorizes the names of the tropical islands and mountain resorts. She will occasionally surprise Stuart by saying, "Boca is so *boring*. Let's do St. Barth's this year," or, more wistfully, "Remember Val d'Isère?"

She stops scrubbing to watch a TV skier feather his way down a powdery slope. The volume is muted, and Stuart can hear the pull of her breath. Something shines in her eyes, a glimmer left over from the high school production of "Carousel," when she sang, "This Was a Real Nice Clambake, We're Mighty Glad We Came." Stuart can never forget the way the spotlight shone on her mugging face that night. She kicked her black Capezios under her petticoats, and he was amazed by the sparks from her eyes. It seemed so right that lights should shine on her, that she should reflect them back at him.

"They've got everything in this place," she says, pointing at the TV, where a blonde woman swims beneath an indoor waterfall. It unnerves Stuart that she watches these gilded flickerings so intently. In high school, she used to talk about leaving, about going to New York or Los Angeles, to act and wait tables. She had her bags packed. She'd saved up from working summers. Right after graduation, she said. Then her father had half his

lung removed. Now she won't leave until it's over. Stuart sometimes hopes that all the doctors consulted and the sickmeals
prepared will make her forget about leaving. He resents how
the TV wakes the old ideas.

On the screen, an orange-faced playboy sprawls on a marble
slab. A hefty woman dressed in nurse's whites slaps brown mud
on his face. "Really," says Georgina. "There isn't anything you
can't have there."

"Heart-shaped tubs?" Stuart asks.

"No heart-shaped tubs," she admits, spritzing cleaning fluid,
wiping around the drain. "Although. . . ." She flips the sponge
to peel away a black circle of matted hair, imprinted by the
drain mesh. The kinky weave is clumped with jellied semen. "I
think I could live without heart-shaped tubs for a while." She
tucks the hair into a limp, green garbage bag.

"Uck," says Stuart.

"You should have seen their sheets."

"That's what a honeymoon is all about, I guess."

"It's not their honeymoon," says Georgina. "I heard him on
the phone making kissy-kissy to his wife. The woman comes
out of the bathroom and gives him this sly look. No shame.
They didn't even care I saw."

"Maybe you misunderstood."

"I know by this room," she says. "It's never the honeymooners who have so much sex. It's the people having affairs."

It disturbs Stuart that she has thought about the subject and
come to this conclusion. What else does she know? They've
never made love, though there's been plenty of fumbled kissing
and fondling. Does she guess why he stops short? Sometimes
Stuart thinks she does, that she continues their relationship
only out of pity.

Georgina pushes to her feet, slowly. Her knees seem unwill-
ing to straighten. She grimaces, pressing her hand to her spine.
"I get so stiff sometimes."

Stuart hates to see this. "I wish I could pull Jilly off reception
and put you there," he says.

She smiles—for his benefit, it seems—and says, "I'm fine."

He looks at her and thinks of the years ahead, how those
years should be organized around her. He wants that so badly.
He pulls her close and kisses her neck, the place behind her ear,

down to her collarbone. He concentrates on her skin beneath his lips, the soapy smell of it, but he can't keep images of Boyd's face, Boyd's body, from flashing in his head. He stares at her, into her eyes. He concentrates on the darkness of her pupils, trying to narrow his gaze so it fits like a pin into the black openings. He tugs her collar and slides his hand over her breast.

"No," she says. "Your hands are too cold."

His stare doesn't waver. He feels her stiffen and he grips her arm tighter.

"Why are you looking at me that way?" she says. "You look spooky. Stop."

He doesn't stop.

She says it again, louder, "*Stop*," then pulls free, glaring. "Suave, baby, Real suave."

He slumps to the carpet. "I'm sorry." He lies back and stares at the mirrors on the ceiling. The perspective is disorienting. It feels like there's no floor. He sees himself sprawled on the raft of his green parka, floating on a red shag sea.

"It's this place," Georgina says. "We have to get out of here."

It surprises Stuart, and pleases him, that she has said *we*. He allows himself to imagine opening night on Broadway, Georgina taking her curtain call, shooting a special glance down to him in the velvet plush of the orchestra.

"I have to stay," he says. "Dad can't do it anymore."

"You underestimate him. He'll manage fine."

Stuart shakes his head. "It would crumble. The whole place would fall into the ground."

"That will happen anyway. Sooner or later. It's inevitable."

It bothers and excites Stuart that she has ideas like this. There's glamour in her pessimism. It's the shadow that makes her whole.

"Can't you see?" she says.

But this sounds more tired than glamorous.

He points out the window to the lake, covered with flat, gray ice. "That's what I see."

He feels the gulf yawning between them. He tries to hug her, but she isn't hugging back. He runs his hands down her arms, refusing to let go of her fingers. He holds them by the tips, as if she's playing London Bridge with him.

"Look," he says, pointing with his chin to the mirrored ceiling, where they're reflected from above, joined at the fingertips. "Don't we look good together?"

She squints up at the mirrors, her nose wrinkled. Her mouth opens slowly, but she does not comment.

"We've always looked good together," he says.

He wishes she was right, that the hotel could run without him. But it can't. This problem with mice, for example. Stu Senior will keep on forgetting. Soon people will find droppings in their beds if Stuart doesn't bait the traps himself.

It takes a moment for his eyes to adjust. The utility passage is dark, a tunnel of pipes and wires running behind the wing; it smells musty, like sawdust and old smoke. Between wooden studs, numbers are painted on the wallboard to tell which room is on the other side. 13, 12. . . . Each has its own water shutoff, circuit breakers, and Jacuzzi override. The beam from Stuart's flashlight glides along the floor. He doesn't see any mousetraps, baited or not. Stu Senior probably never even bought any.

He stops behind room 9 and presses his hand to the splintered wallboard. He wonders if Georgina is still cleaning on the other side. The idea of them separated by such a wall pleases him: red shag on her side, bare plywood on his. What if she's thinking about him right now, at the same time that he thinks about her? That would mean they're destined for each other. Walls are so symbolic, he thinks.

He feels something loose on the plywood and sees a glint he's never noticed, a thin, tin disc, the size of a nickel. It swings on a nail. He pushed it aside and presses close. He's dizzied by the fish-eyed view of the red-carpeted room, distorting at the edges. When Georgina walks to take a fresh bedsheet from her cart, she shrinks to a tiny speck. When she returns to center, she's large and oddly bloated. She shakes the sheet, and it floats, a swell of white, to cover the brown-stained mattress.

He steps back and shines the flashlight at the wall. There's no sign of recent drilling. The hole appears to have been there always.

He leans forward to look through again. Georgina is bent over the bed, tucking sheets. Then, for no apparent reason, she stops in the middle of doing this. It's like she has seen something, but there's nothing—nothing he can see. She sits on the edge of the mattress, covering her mouth with three fingers. She doesn't move, but something is happening. It's happening behind her eyes. One of her dark thoughts, Stuart guesses, the source of which he has never understood. Stuart can feel it pulling her away from him. She slowly stands, shaking herself free of a shudder. She slips pillows into white cases and plumps them on the bed.

It amazes Stuart that by spying on her this way, he gains access to a secret moment, and all he learns is how little he can know. He feels humbled by the thought of such mysteries contained in other people. He leans his head to the wall and looks at his feet. Three cigarette butts lie stubbed on the floor. He bends for one and rolls it in his fingers.

His stomach cramps, squeezing the acid of his gut into his throat. The red letters around the filter spell *Carlton.*

He looks through again. The bed, he now understands, sits at the center of the lens, in the zone of least distortion. He pictures a naked man and women wrestling on it, the couple Georgina described earlier, having so much sex. Is there something special Stu Senior would like to watch them do? Is it so particular that he has to smoke three Carltons before it happens? Maybe the cigarettes mark three separate occasions, smoked after separate pleasures. Stuart tries to form a picture of his father peeping through, tugging at himself, but he has never even seen his father naked; the imagined scene lacks a crucial dimension.

He isn't angry. He can't even dredge up sadness. What he feels, more than anything else, is small. Small to be cramped in the tiny passage, standing on this precise dot in the world, while outside, the boundless, snow-covered landscape spreads for miles.

The Eve wing still needs to be pumped, but the honey truck is full. Sewage slops and pings behind Stuart's head. He must gently pulse the brakes, because the load has its own momentum; it will send him careening across the slick if he tries to stop too suddenly. He's thankful for the cold, at least, which keeps the odor down to a pungent wisp.

He wheels out to the main road, heading for the treatment plant. The ride is all uphill, and he can't accelerate quickly. Cars start passing him, sending slaps of slush against his windshield.

An eighteen-wheeler slides in front of him and he feels a strange reversal in his gut, as if he were actually slipping backwards, down the hill, toward the musty space he just left, between those two dark walls.

The road levels, and the chains clink faster in a whine against the salty paving. He passes the sweater mill, the liquor barn, the shoe outlet before he gets to the turnoff for the treatment plant. Usually, he'll drive down the dirt road to the pumping station, and while the truck gets emptied, he'll sign the account book and bullshit with Skeeter. Today, though, there's a chain across the road. He climbs down to open it. It's padlocked on both sides. He looks at his watch: five-fifteen. This is a county plant. It closes at five. And today is Friday; they'll be closed all weekend.

"Shit," he says.

It occurs to him, driving back: Why not the empty the honey truck down at Love for Life? Nobody ever stays there, so that septic tank will be nearly empty.

Love for Life is Stu Senior's timeshare venture, separated from the hotel by twenty acres of woods. He started it during the boom, but his money ran out. In the drawings, there were three rows of 20 connected units, modeled after Swiss chalets, with shiny cars in the driveways and slim couples smiling on pleasure boats tied up to the docks. Only a single model unit was ever completed. The rest is a jumble of half-finished foundations, skeletal timber and pipes, and crudely bulldozed lots at the lake's edge.

Is that when it began? Stuart wonders. When the money ran out on Love for Life? He cannot remember a time before that failure when his father looked as defeated as he sometimes does now.

Stuart drives beneath the weatherbeaten sign: *One Week of Love for the Rest of Your Life. Starting at $3,999*. He's surprised to see tire tracks leading down the road before him. He wonders if high school kids have gone down to get stoned. But when he gets to the site, he sees Stu Senior's red Buick parked next to the model unit.

"What are you doing?" Stu Senior shouts from the doorway. He's wearing a blue smock.

"Emptying it in here." Stuart hooks the hose to the septic pipe, which juts up from the rubble.

"Don't!"

"I have to."

"Stuart! I said *no.*" He stands with his hands on his hips. Stuart has seen a similar expression on the faces of children in the supermarket: the threat of tantrum.

"Why not?"

"Because."

Stuart hesitates. This could be the tiny twig which, to pull, will bring the whole pile crashing down. The years of acquiescence weigh on him; when he unhooks the hose, he feels even heavier. He drags his feet through puddles, crossing the debris-strewn lot.

It's been a year since he was last inside the model unit. The rust-upholstered furniture has not changed, but the paintings are new, leaning against walls, propped on chairs, stacked in corners. Each canvas shows a similar scene: a lake backed by mountains and snow-capped trees. It's not the lake outside the picture window, though. The tree trunks are too straight, the mountain peaks too perfectly pointed.

"I've been learning off TV," says Stu Senior. He gestures with his brush to the screen, where a man wearing a black beret demonstrates how to use the sponge to make real-looking clouds. A pipe cleaner, he says, can be used to make real-looking birds. "This lesson's the best," says Stu Senior. "I've got it on tape."

"Why not paint our lake?" Stuart asks.

"This one is prettier. We don't have such good mountains. The colors are better, too."

Stuart looks closer at the canvas; the paints are unmixed, straight from the tubes. His father loves these bright blues, greens, and whites so much.

"I'm making one for each unit," Stu Senior says.

Stuart sees the red-and-white pack of cigarettes poking from his breast pocket, the saucer full of butts. He feels queasy and sad. He wants to mention the peephole, but he looks at the floor instead. The rust-colored carpet is coming loose. He remembers once when the shag came loose in a guest room. He lifted it and saw a nest of shiny, black earwigs underneath, scurrying for cover. He will not look under this carpet. He will bring some tacks and nail it back down.

"Listen, Pop. . . ." he starts, trying to explain why he needs the septic tank at Love for Life. If he does not pump the Eve wing, there could be trouble over the weekend. "Remember last time?" he says.

"That wasn't so bad."

"You didn't have to clean it," says Stuart. "And those people. They'll never come back."

"They never do anyway."

This is true, Stuart thinks. None of them ever come back.

"That's why I wanted the timeshares," says Stu Senior.

They stand together, contemplating what has not happened. Nobody has ever lived in the model unit, and already the furniture looks shabby, out of date.

"I don't get it," says Stuart. "It's just for the weekend."

"Once you start using it that way, it's never the same."

"What?"

Stu Senior gestures with his hands, meaning *this*, the room, but also something larger: the hotel, the timeshares. Everything.

Stuart sometimes forgets that the heart-shaped swimming pool, the champagne waterfall, and the suites with red shag on the walls are his father's creations. Having grown up here, it's easy to think these things always existed.

He tries to imagine Stu Senior bringing his young wife, Stuart's mother, to this property before there were buildings on it. How would he have described his plans? Was she moved? Did she think it was a tribute? And when exactly did she see it for what it was? Because one day she did. Maybe she found out that Stu Senior was peeping through the walls, or she took up with the lifeguard, or she simply realized how long she'd been in this one place. Whatever the truth was, it was not one she shared with her son. Stuart has not spoken with her since the day she left. She made no effort to contact him during the first years, and it was too late, as far as he was concerned, when the cheerful letters started to arrive; he never wrote back. Now she just sends a card on his birthday. *XXOO, Mother.* Her return address in Arizona is printed on a label she sticks in the corner. Stuart tells himself that he doesn't want to see her, but he wonders what she looks like. The last he remembers, he was diving from the dock, calling, *Watch me*. He still sees her wide-brimmed hat, her big sunglasses, the way she sat in the chaise, ankles crossed, flipping through the pages of a travel magazine. She drank Tab from a can wrapped in a napkin, and when Stuart called, *Watch me, watch me one more time*, she gave him a fluttering wave with her fingers before he dove into the cool, clean water.

"It really was beautiful," Stu Senior says.

"What?"

Stu Senior shakes his head.

Everybody has these visions, Stuart thinks. Only a few people try to make them real.

"Please," his father says. "Just don't empty the truck down here."

Stuart feels drained. It takes so much energy to make things stay the same.

Stu Senior lifts his brush and says, "Meet me tonight. We'll deal with it then." He dabs yellow on the canvas, following the painter on TV. The TV painter says that's how sun looks when it shines on a lake. A smear of yellow down the middle.

It's dark when Stuart gets back to the hotel, and cold. He goes to the Heartthrob Bar to warm up. Gas jets flicker in the fireplace, casting a burnished glow over the room. Tiny white lights outline mirrors shaped like hearts.

Boyd looks at home behind the bar, a fixture in the room. When a waitress hands him an order from the dining room, he reaches for bottles without looking at their labels. Stuart marvels at the complexity of the human body, that Boyd's hips wiggle when he stirs a martini.

Boyd's mouth tasted sour when they kissed that night, like milk that's about to turn. It wasn't a pleasant flavor, but Stuart wants the taste again.

"Since we're alone. . . ." he begins, not sure what comes next.

"We're not," says Boyd. He points to the back of the room.

Stuart sees shadows in the booth. He recognizes the curve of Georgina's neck, a waver in her voice, a flutter like a hummingbird's, determined to stay aloft.

"Who's that with her?"

"Don't know. Car trouble, I think. He's been hanging around all day."

Stuart remembers the bearded man from earlier, now reaching forward, over the table, to touch Georgina's hand. He can't hear what the man says, but he hears Georgina laugh. At first Stuart takes pleasure from her laughter. A weight has fallen away; she hasn't laughed this deeply, so heartily, since the drunken parties, the delirious nights after the high school play.

But it's not Stuart that she laughs for.

"Stuart, this is Dr. Simon," she says. She does not seem aware that pink has flushed her cheeks. "He used to live in New York. He knows an agent I could meet."

It's unfair: agents in New York. . . . Stuart can't compete. He tries to stare the doctor down, but this man has an eye for weakness. He knows that Stuart has imagined him naked.

"Stuart?" Georgina says, half a question, half a warning.

She must see in his face the choices he's considering: He could kick the doctor out. He could scold her for socializing with a guest. He could punch the doctor, start a brawl of some sort. This last choice would be totally out of character, which gives it added appeal.

"Honestly," says Georgina. "We're just talking." She squints toward the bar. "Boyd," she calls. "Tell Stuart how we've just been talking, Dr. Simon and me."

Boyd shrugs. He will not get involved.

"I'm afraid I don't understand," says the doctor.

He does understand. He knows that Stuart would kneel in front of him. Stuart hates him for that.

"Stuart is acting strangely," says Georgina. "He's had a long day."

It only makes Stuart feel more pathetic that she looks at him affectionately. All at once, he sees the stains on the ceiling, the burnmarks on the tables, the rips in the banquettes, repaired with colored tape. Even with the dim lighting, it's so obvious. What's the point of fighting anymore? And yet he feels the need to behave jealously, like a character from a soap opera. In the melodrama he dreams up, he screams at them both, *Get the FUCK out of here*, throwing everything into this one word, *FUCK*.

"Maybe I should go," says the doctor. He turns to shake Georgina's hand.

"Maybe you should," says Stuart. He stares at the doctor's hand as it folds around hers. The fingers are well-tended, as if he's had a manicure. He can do things with these hands that Stuart will never know.

"You were very rude," Georgina says, after he has left.

Stuart stares at her blankly. How many times have they shared dinner? How many times have they kissed? He tries to think sweet, sad thoughts about her nursing her dying father, but this stirs nothing for him. He tries to think lurid thoughts of her strapped into frilly lingerie, but he can't even strike the spark that would light the flame of such a fantasy. He saw it between the doctor and Georgina, though—the sharp, blue crack of something real.

"What's the matter?" she asks. "I wish you'd tell me."

He stalks back to his barstool.

"Stuart?"

He can hear her breath, she's standing right behind him, waiting, and yet he says nothing. He stares at the bartop, focusing on the silver flecks in the pink Formica, until Boyd tells him, "She's gone."

He will never be able to tell her. It will end, horribly, with silence.

"Turn on the piano."

Boyd puts the cassette into the machine behind the bar. The keys of the white piano depress themselves mechanically. They use this machine in winter when there aren't enough customers to pay for a piano player. The phantom baby grand tinkles in the empty lounge. Boyd stands straight before Stuart, a barcloth draped over his arm.

"Make me a drink," Stuart says. "Something exotic."

"With an umbrella?"

"Please."

While Boyd chops pineapple and puts banana in the blender, Stuart traces his fingers on the bar and tries to imagine, drawing the lines in his head, his trail today, the path that led him to this seat. He wants to drink, to be light, to float.

"Another," he says, after draining the bamboo cup. "Stronger. Not so sweet."

The mechanical piano plays a Christmas song—at least Stuart thinks it's a Christmas song. He tries to remember the words. Oh Christ let us. . . . No, that's not it. Oh come. . . . yes, oh come. *Oh come let us adore him, oh come let us adore him.* That's how it goes.

Boyd slides the next drink across the bar. This one is served in a plastic volcano with red plastic lava dribbling down the slopes. A straw pokes out the crater, and Stuart sips. It tastes like bitter medicine. He looks at Boyd. He wants to find the details to describe him accurately, but when he searches Boyd's half-smile, he only sees lips and teeth, reminders of biology class: incisors are for ripping meat. On the surface, Boyd is a textbook example, unexceptional in most ways. Yet confronted with the moon of his face, Stuart remembers the awe he felt as a child, mezmerized by a speck of dust, wondering if it might contain a secret universe. Glimmers of smoky light fleck the corners of Boyd's eyes, where the folds of lid join like a wishbone. These corners of Boyd's eyes are terrifyingly inviting places. The ghostly piano climbs to a crescendo, *Oh come let us a DOOR him. Come let us a DOOR-OR him. . . .* Why did Stuart pull away that night? It seems now like a terrible mistake, the worst he's ever made.

The snow comes down hard. Roads that Stuart plowed earlier are under two inches. It falls faster and faster. Snowflakes touch like spiders on his cheeks.

He climbs into the honey truck and starts the motor for some heat. While he waits for his father, he nips from the bottle of brandy he took from the Heartthrob Bar. He doesn't exactly decide to start plowing the parking lot. It just sort of happens. And he's plowed three wobbly rows when the Shell truck pulls in. Following it is a black Mercedes: Dr. Simon's car. The mechanics park it in a corner and drive off in the truck. White flakes drift down to the black roof. Stuart continues plowing. The doctor is nowhere in sight. Eating dinner, most likely. Stuart smiles at the thought of him shoveling—his fashionable overcoat, his manicured hands in soft leather gloves. Four passes in the truck and Stuart plows the Mercedes in on all sides. This happens surprisingly quickly, as if time were sucked out from between each of Stuart's movements.

He swigs again from the bottle. When he slipped behind the bar to get it, his thighs brushed Boyd's, and Boyd looked over his shoulder. If only these silences could be translated. So many embarrassments would be avoided. Like the way he dared to let his hand settle lightly on Boyd's waist. All Boyd said was, *Don't.* It seemed, at that moment, that Boyd meant, 'not now,' but reverberations of the word have penetrated, and Stuart now fears, with a withering in his chest, that it was a *Don't* of greater proportions.

The chains chink crazily. Through the glaring snow, Stu Senior waves at him. Stuart sits high in the seat, and his father looks so small, standing in front of the snow bank. The honey truck's headlights shine on his face. He is still waving—waving at Stuart. The plow scrapes and sparks the asphalt.

Plow Stu Senior into the snowbank, Stuart thinks. Just plow him in. He would see the lights bearing down. He would know his son was driving. He would be sure the truck would stop at the last minute. But Stuart wouldn't stop. A foot of snow would be plowed on top of him, and by the time it melted, Stuart would be gone.

Stuart is amazed by his capacity to produce such a vision. He is further amazed that the barrier that keeps his vision from becoming reality is so thin, and so weak. His foot trembles on the accelerator. Just a membrane, really, separating him from that dark possibility.

"Why you must have plowed that lot seven times," says Stu Senior, wheezing to climb into the truck. "You drive this thing so fast. For a second there. . . ." He does not finish this thought, but lights a Carlton. He tells Stuart to drive to the lake.

The darkened woods seem vast. All that exists is contained in the truck's cab and in the funnel of headlights that pulls them over the snowslicked road. They say nothing. Both stare straight ahead. If Stuart didn't know the limit of these woods— that a mile in any direction would bring them to an outlet center—he could be fooled into thinking he and his father were explorers. But he knows the land has been scouted. If the boom had continued, it would have been developed. The woods have been left behind only because the money ran out.

The ice looks smooth from a distance, but as they approach, the headlights show the pockmarks left by thaws and rain. Still it's very pretty, Stuart thinks. "What a night," he says, thinking more of summer, the water slipping up his ankles.

"Back up over there," says Stu Senior. He points to a narrow peninsula beyond the boat ramp, jutting into the lake. "You've got to get the tank right to the edge."

"You can't be serious." Stuart grips the wheel, his foot on the brake. He throws the shift to neutral.

"Come on," says Stu Senior.

"I won't."

"What, you won't?"

"Pop. It's the lake. For God's sake."

"You never noticed before."

"Before?" says Stuart. "You've done this before?"

"It's a very deep lake."

Stuart slumps in his seat.

"Don't give me that face."

Stuart cuts the motor, pulls the key, and jumps from the truck. He tries to run, but it's black in the woods and the snow comes halfway up his thighs. The cold scours his throat and lungs; he feels miserably sober. He pulls the bottle from his pocket, takes another swig, and looks back through the trees.

There's a pocket of yellow glowing inside the cab. Stu Senior fumbles with his jailer's ring and bends to the steering column. He must try several keys before he finds the right one, because there's a long silence, with just the snow falling through the beam of headlights, before the engine turns over. Billows of smoke puff above the roof, and Stu Senior leans out the door, hanging from the wheel. He looks backward as he reverses onto the point. Now the headlights shine through the woods. Stu Senior threads the hose over a low branch. Once the pump is rumbling, he steps away from the truck. The hood of his fat parka sags over his brow.

The stewing sewage creates its own heat; Stuart can barely see the sludge through all the steam. Even at this distance, with such cold, the smell gives him spasms between his stomach and his throat. He has to swallow bile to keep from puking.

The ice bed creaks and pops. Each time the sludge threatens to grow into a pile, it collapses and spreads wider. As the steam beings to clear, Stuart can see the dark stain spread. The pump motor spins furiously. It seems the tank is empty—nothing more comes out—until a hundred gallons spew all at once. A crack splinters into the lake, and a groan echoes across and back. Stu Senior turns off the pump. It's silent after that.

Stuart wades out from the trees. He clambers over the icy roads to stand beside his father. "Everyone will see," he says. "It'll sit there, right on top."

But it doesn't. It sinks, gurgling, beneath the split and melting ice. Snow continues to fall, at first turning dark on contact, but then staying white and sticking.

"At the edge," says Stu Senior, "the ice isn't as thick as you think."

A ghostly stench hangs in the air. The scent is rotten, yes, but there's an underlying sweetness, too, barely detectable, rich like frying liver. Stuart hasn't eaten all day. His nausea wavers beneath a much greater hunger. He has not felt such gaping emptiness since that night last summer, the first spasmodic quivers when Boyd slid out from his gut.

OUT THERE

• WESLEY GIBSON •

Billy hadn't wanted to break up with Mitchell, or anyone for that matter, in a pancake house: blueberry syrup, hairballs of whipped butter: it lacked; it was homely. A year and a half ago his friend Brett had died during a margarine commercial. T.V. light the color of blue flame had shuddered over the darkened hospital walls, over the I.V. drip and the barely nibbled chocolates, over the unopened roses that had arrived that morning. They'd thought he'd get better again, like the last time, and the time before that; but he'd hemorrhaged suddenly while the voice-over had nattered on cheerfully about less fat, low calories, long life: it wasn't even butter.

"What do you mean?" Mitchell repeated. The slightest rivulet of brown syrup nested in the corner of his mouth. It looked like glue, like a mouth badly mended. Billy pushed aside the impulse to wipe the syrup away. Even to mention it seemed too intimate.

"I think we need a break," he said. Mitchell was beautiful and bright and funny and Billy didn't love him.

"What do you mean?" Mitchell said for the fourth time.

"I think we shouldn't see each other for a while."

"What do you mean?"

Five hours later, on the porch off his third floor walk-up, dawn cascading through the sky in great red and yellow gusts, it was Billy's turn for repetition. He hit his forehead against the faux Greek columns dotted with cool morning dew. The discrete, clear pearls of water were smashed into blotches, into small amorphous lakes too transient and insignificant to bother charting—there weren't maps for this—and he said, "I don't know, I don't know, I don't know."

Mitchell didn't cry. They had known one another for eight months.

Nine?

Billy had said it first. "I love you." After the condom broke. They had both tested negative months before, independent of one another; but the accident had renewed the earlier relief, the disbelief at his luck; and he had mistaken the flood of his gratitude for love.

It was the morning of their break-up. God, the sky was beautiful.

The Grill was a dusty vegetarian place that served beer and had a bulletin board for posters with detachable phone numbers. The posters, muddy Xeroxes, some in lime greens and hot pinks, advertised for roommates. Non-smoking lesbian allergic to cats. The descriptions emphasized what they didn't want. These people had been burned; sharing had made them cranky. They probably accounted for the other posters selling inner peace and tickets to bands called Kitty Litter. Billy wrote down the number of an AIDS volunteer group with the bartender's pen.

He waited for Clare, whose sculpture had opened at the gallery down the street. The one serious gallery in town. Everyone agreed. Clare sculpted in hardened lava and coral, materials that cut; and though she wore industrial strength gloves while she worked, her hands were always nicked and bandaged and stippled with the white nebulae of tiny scars, her reason for giving up sex. "I couldn't even beat him off," she'd say, modelling her damaged hands. Clare liked cats and green lipstick and cheap beer and sadomasochistic pornography. In that order. Billy couldn't explain it, but her sculpture looked like that.

Her entourage was small tonight: two men.

She wore combat boots, fishnets, cut-offs and a red silk blouse with a huge bow. Her torso looked like a wrapped present. The blouse and her green lips gave her a sinister, Christmassy air. St. Nicked, Billy thought, glancing at her gifted hands. Her hair was twisted around a large plastic bone.

They kissed.

"How was it?" she asked.

She had refused to go to the opening. "I know what they look like."

"Great," Billy said. "Mobbed. One woman caught her dress on Theories of Dominance 1, and some guy in the meanest-looking leather vest in the world scraped his elbow on Theories of Dominance 5. Or was it 6?"

"6, probably," Clare said. "The coral I used in that cut you if you looked at it wrong."

"Poor Mike was running around looking for a Band-Aid and sweating and you could see visions of lawsuits dancing in his gallery-owner's head. Leather vest ended up with a wad of toilet paper stuck to his arm."

"Like shaving," one of the men said.

"People should be more careful," Clare said. "Did the cut guy have a tattoo?"

"No," Billy said, "not even an earring, just that mean vest."

"I'm John," one of the men said, holding out his hand.

"Me too," the other said, also holding out his hand.

Billy shook both their hands with both of his and said, "Me too."

"No he's not," Clare said. "He's a Billy-Goat." She was big on pet names.

"I could tell you weren't," one of the Johns said. "You don't look like one."

Billy wondered what a John looked like. From the evidence before him, he couldn't begin to guess. These Johns were Night and Day. John Night was packaged into thick, black ponytailed hair, a dangle earring, a red sweater tucked into jeans which were tucked into combat boots that were the identical twins of Clare's. He was tall and lean. He had the half-smile of a practiced ironist and his deep, brown eyes were almost too moist, like someone tearing from a sudden, sharp wind.

John Day was stocky. His head was misted with short, blonde hair and he was wearing the kind of large glasses Billy associated with old men whittling into rain barrels. He was also in red: a preposterous, paisley shirt and hip huggers circa 1972. Captain Kirk boots; chain mail belt: a dandy. His face was boyish, innocent even; though Billy knew Day couldn't be either: all four of them were in their thirties. Clare was divorced. Billy had moved back from New York a year and a half ago after a decade that seemed, in retrospect, like a line from a poem he couldn't quite remember, something about hurly-burly and the buckshot of grief.

"Who's buying me a beer?" Clare asked.

"Me," Billy said.

"This is the only place in town where you can get a decent beer," she said.

"Black Label?"

"With a lime and a straw, please."

She smiled, her lips like plump crescents of honeydew.

Billy's mother tried. At lunch she said, "I saw two men on Oprah last week who wanted to get married." Helen tried to understand her son's life vicariously, communally, through the sub-plots of nighttime soaps, through Ted Koppel's blunt interrogations. She mentioned her latest tidbits offhandedly, her eyes skittering over his face for signs that, at last, she had stumbled across a clue.

"In-laws," Billy said. "Ugh."

Helen's mostly uneaten sandwich lay in a nest of crinkled aluminum on her tray. She lit another cigarette. Her idea of lunch was four Pall Malls and one Diet Coke with two squeezes of lemon: food was a formality.

"Have you sold any of your furniture?" she asked.

"Not a stick," he said.

Couches elaborately inlaid with antique pocket watches; complex chandeliers constructed from copper pipes; bookshelves assembled from glass bricks, firewood, and tinted with ice pink fingernail polish: Billy's furniture; unsold; in various stages of development. A director's chair made of beach ball and salmon-tinted plastic rods stood at Duchampian attention on the unused gas stove. Three-foot-long granite conch shells, some vague idea about a love seat forming, stacked by the bathroom. Sawdust and glass beads. Reams of fabric. Levels, lengths of chain. Everything found: alongside interstates, in abandoned diners, in junkyards and junkshops, rusting in streams. He

called himself an archaeologist of the recent past. Helen called
him a waiter.

"I think I'm going to start dyeing my hair again," she said.
Helen had just turned fifty and had responded to it by alter-
nately discussing plastic surgery and trips to the Bahamas, neither of which she could afford. She also continually revised the
litany of people to be excised from her will. Billy's sister, a thin
chain-smoker like her mother, currently topped the list.

"You look great either way," he said.

"Your sister said I looked old," she said.

So that was it.

"Hi Billy. This is Mitchell. Trying to be friends. I don't think
it's working. Give a call anyway. Do you have my Janet Jackson
tape or my Edmund White book?"

"Hey Bill. Steve here. Tuesday afternoon. Been thinking
about you a lot. Call me this week. Collect if you want. Well.
Bye."

"Billy-Goat. I have something to tell yooouuu . . ."

He decided to call Clare first. She was the only one of the
three he hadn't slept with. He found the phone under his bed
and didn't know what it was doing there. In his twenties, he'd
never been able to find his keys. Now, he always knew where
his keys were but he sometimes found books in the refrigerator.
If the shaving cream wasn't in the medicine cabinet, it might be
in the silverware drawer. He had to look everywhere for anything. Living with himself in the past couple of years had become like living with a mischievous child. It no longer surprised
him when he found the iron in the sock drawer, any more than
picking up the phone to hear of the deaths of friends surprised
him. He'd taken to saying, "Oh dear," when the calls came; re-
flexively; and he'd stopped trying to stop himself from blurting
it out because he supposed it helped him dull the blow in some
way. He'd lost a friend to anger after a couple of Oh Dears. He
now understood how people became distant, eccentric, bitter.
Each time you came up from the undertow of grief, you were
a little farther from a shore it seemed less and less desirable to
return to.

He could still smell french fries from lunch with Helen on
his fingers and on his breath as he held the receiver to his face.

"Hi Clare."

"Billy-Goat," she squealed. Clare thought squealing lent excitement to almost any encounter.

"Are you working?"

"Hardly. It's only three o'clock. I've just had my first cup of coffee."

"I just had lunch with my mother."

"Well, I have just the thing to pick you up."

"It wasn't bad. We talked about her hair color."

"Creepy."

"What's your pick-me-up?"

"Funny you should put it that way. Well . . . hold on; let me get a cigarette."

He could hear Clare's soaps in the background. She was an addict. Something crashed and she said, "Bad Monsoon." Monsoon was the moody, eighteen-pound Maine Coon her other cats steered clear of. Billy bit off a fingernail and spit it into the ashtray. It tasted like french fry.

"Anyways," Clare said, "you have a choice."

"I do?"

"John or John."

"Somehow that doesn't sound like a choice even if I knew what I was choosing."

Suddenly Eastern-European and breathy, enough like Garbo or Dietrich for Billy to get the drift, she said, "Zhey vant jou."

"You mean vant-me vant me?"

"Like they think you're really cute and may the best man win. I've been designated as their spokesmodel."

"This is weird."

"You could be excited."

"Is that the same thing as frightened?"

They were trying to be friends. They met at Marie's, which was near the campus where Mitchell was studying architecture. Students in Walkmen bobbed their heads over cups of coffee. They talked excitedly, fingering earrings, slapping the table for emphasis. They sullenly read fat books by Germans while eating tuna fish sandwiches. Billy knew he had drunk coffee, slapped tables and eaten tuna fish; but it seemed more like a fact he had retained from BIO 101 about mitochondria or cellular reproduction than a real memory.

He was late. Mitchell was halfway through his salad. They were meeting for lunch, which happened in daylight and had none of night's implications.

"You'll never change," Mitchell said.

It seemed impertinent from someone whom Billy had gone out with six months, or was it seven; particularly when there were thirty-one years or so preceding their affair during which he had changed considerably. He'd changed from diapers to long pants, from women to men, from cheerful pessimism to this, whatever it was. Mitchell was always on time and never put books in the refrigerator. He was also six years younger and he was right: Billy had always been late. Billy could have taken this from Steve: they'd been together for eight years. They'd blown their twenties together. Steve could say always. This boy had no right. Billy's body count was higher.

Billy shrugged and smiled apologetically. He ordered coffee. Maybe he'd slap the table.

"How's school?" he asked like an uncle at a funeral.

"Hairy?" Mitchell paused. "Yes, hairy. Wild and wooly and about to eat me alive."

"Sounds like school."

"How's your furniture?"

"Unsold."

"Sounds like your furniture."

"You used to like my furniture."

"I guess I lied."

"What about that coffee table I made you?"

"I threw it out."

The waitress set down Billy's coffee. It was too black and had spilled; the half-and-halfs were soggy and brown. Billy opened one—it spurted on the table—poured what was left into his too-black coffee; and downed it in one, long drink.

"Nice to see you again," he said.

"I'm sorry," Mitchell said.

"Don't be."

"I didn't really throw the coffee table out."

"You don't have to like my furniture."

"But I do. I think if you really tried you could sell it."

"I do try."

"One day when I'm successful I'll help you."

Billy could picture it: Mitchell being successful and buying a footstool one year, a floor lamp a few years later. To his lover, Mitchell would say, "I used to date him"; and as the lover, suddenly swollen with the brief panic that he was not loved enough, looked over to Mitchell from the corner where they were trying out the lamp, Mitchell would say, "It was a long time ago." *Architectural Digest* would be thrown across Billy's coffee table, the one Mitchell hadn't thrown out. The shaving cream would be in the medicine cabinet. They would never die.

Billy decided to date. He consulted Clare.

"Do you think it's alright?" he asked. "I mean to date more than one person at the same time?"

"Of course. Straight people do it all the time."

"Did you ever date?"

"You mean more than one person at a time?"

"Yeah."

"I cheated on my husband."

"Technically, I don't think that counts."

"So no, I never technically dated; but I'm not exactly a bell-wether. Lots of people do it."

"I either fucked or fell in love, no in-between."

"Lucky you. I always only fell in love. I could never get it into my head that this person you were doing this thing with could be someone you didn't love. It was too, too, too, too, too, too intimate."

"And I mean real dates with going to the movies and kisses goodnight and no sex."

"Good luck."

"You don't think I can do it?" It irritated him but not in the way that Mitchell had. Clare had held his hand when he was scared and run up curtains for his apartment when he'd moved back from New York. She was allowed. He mistrusted friends who didn't have a sense of his limitations.

"I think you can do anything you put your mind to," she said.

"Now if only I can get my dick to listen."

It wouldn't. He and John Day slept together after the first date. It started when John Day spilled beer on his shirt, another preposterous paisley number, this one in refrigerator green. They didn't make it to the movies. Billy tried: "I don't think we should sleep together on the first date," feeling like Linda Lovelace disguised as Sandra Dee. John Day was not put off by Billy's disguise. He'd said, "Why not?" smiling and pulling Billy gently towards him by the collar. John Day had a sly, giddy smile that had disarmed Sandra Dees from time immemorial. He kissed warm and tough. He'd tested negative. It was good-bye Troy Donahue and volleyball on the beach. It was hello Deep Throat. It was hello darkness.

They kept losing their erections.

Beach ball didn't work: it was too flimsy; it wouldn't take weight. So Billy was coloring canvas faux-beach-ball, only not so realistic, only more gestural, only it wasn't going so well. He used warm crayon which had a nice waxy smell and a wonderful texture; but he didn't think it would last. Actually, he liked the fact that it wouldn't last. He liked materials to announce their impermanence. Anything else was a trick. Most people who bought furniture didn't share his aesthetic. He realized that. Still, if he ever opened a store, he would call it Gone Tomorrow; and it probably would be.

The phone rang.

"Hey Bill."

"Steve."

"How's tricks?"

"Tricks were for the seventies. Are you still a dope dealer?"

Steve had been a futures trader until his CEO had made the *Post* with his multiple indictments. The company had bellied-up. These days, Steve sold X-tasy in discos and babysat for rich people. It was an uneven living. He sold the Porsche. He said he was happier though Billy didn't see how that was possible: Steve had seemed plenty happy before; nothing fazed him. He had fallen drunkenly into the Hudson and almost drowned after their break-up, but that had been an accident. He'd blamed Billy for it.

"Same old Bill," Steve said. "Always taking the dimmest view possible of things."

"I used to be very lighthearted."

"You were never really lighthearted, just younger."

"How's our apartment?"

"The same."

"Do you know that sometimes I have the impulse to tell people that I used to have a great apartment in the West Village? It seems like my finest achievement."

"When are you moving back?"

"Never."

"Love?"

"More like trouble. I'm dating."

"What's that?"

"It's like sleeping around, only without the sleeping around part."

"What's that leave?"

"Dates."

Billy called and invited John Two, who did not wear preposterous paisley shirts, out for a movie and a bite to eat. This was going to be a date-date.

"Gee, I don't know," John Two said. "I'll have to ask my Mom."

"Is that a yes or a no, wiseguy?"

"When?"

"Saturday."

"I know a couple of parties we can go to."

"I don't want to go to parties. I want to go to a movie, then out for a bite to eat. This is my date. I called."

"You don't have to sound so ferocious."

"If you don't follow the dating guidelines to the letter, it turns into sleeping around before you know it."

"Tell you what. Let's go to a movie, then to a party. I think parties are approved by the Council on Dating."

"I think it's too early in our relationship to compromise."

First. The bank machines were down and Billy was cash-poor. John Two gallantly offered to pay, "even though this is your date." Then. They were ten minutes late and Billy was one of those people who couldn't miss so much as a preview. They stood in the parking lot, John Two leaning against his motorcycle with his arms and legs crossed. "He's too cute for me," Billy thought. It was cold. Billy hadn't worn a sweater. He hadn't wanted to look bulky. He concentrated on not shivering. John Two had offered him a sweater before they left; and Billy had said, no, it's such a nice night; and John Two had said it would be pretty cold on the bike; and Billy had said, smiling, that's alright, he was tough. The wind hadn't been cold blocked by John Two's sweatered body. Now, Billy was freezing. Not-shivering required a kind of rigor-mortis and he was afraid if he relaxed an inch, he'd convulse.

The world was going to the movies. The world was on a date. Couples held hands. Boys fumbled through their pockets for money while girls looked discreetly away. Boys handed girls their tickets. Boys guided girls into the multiplex cinema by the crook of their sweatered arm. Everyone was wearing sweaters. Everyone was sensible. Billy was tempted to blow John Two right there between the freshly painted yellow parking lot lines as a revolutionary act.

"Did I hallucinate the women's movement?" he asked.

"The way I see it," John Two said, "we have two choices. We can go to parties where we'll probably feel even more uncomfortable than we do now; or we can go to my place where I have food, wine, and cable; and where we might feel awkward but at least I'll be home."

"We could make it another night." Billy was glad his face was frozen or he was sure it would be doing something undignified and beyond his control, like pouting.

"Is that really an option?"

John Two's apartment was warm. Ten points. He picked up a CD from one of the haphazard stacks by the player and put it in. He threw his leather jacket over an armchair already loaded with jackets and jeans and socks and a rumpled cloth that might have been the flag of an exotic nation. Haiti, maybe.

"I hope you like country music," he said.

"I like k.d. lang but I'm not sure that counts."

"It's a start."

John Day's apartment had been cluttered with toys that did unexpected things like vomit, and postcards from Europe, and Mexican-looking things, and dozens of Polaroids he'd taken of men, women, and children all got up in the same tatty ballgown, and lunchboxes—shelves of them—embossed with everything from the Challenger to Teenage Mutant Ninja Turtles. Mitchell's studio had been humble and spare and clean with mismatched, slightly shoddy furniture and a few silver-framed architectural line drawings on pearl grey walls—a student place. Steve, in an orgy of newly made money, had stuffed their apartment with flashy, black leather furniture that devoured the place, and investments. A Schnabel drawing bought only because it was a Schnabel drawing. Steve loved to admit that it had no other merit. The I-am-a-cynical-stockbroker phase. This was when he found beauty sentimental. "You know what's beautiful?" he'd say. "Money is beautiful. And you wanna know why? Because it's perfectly abstract." A futures trader had to believe that. As an X-peddler, Steve had rediscovered beauty. He'd burnt the Schnabel and kept the ashes in a little sealed jar, the former home of marinated artichoke hearts. "Hear that?" he'd sometimes say when he called Billy. He'd be shaking the jar of ashes at the phone like a witch doctor. You couldn't hear anything. "That's the eighties," he'd say.

If someone had asked him to describe John Two's apartment, Billy would have paused and stammered and finally said, "I guess it's ordinary." It was so ordinary, it was odd. The living room furniture was a set. It matched. The kind of stuff you waited for a sale to buy. It wasn't bad. It looked like it had been made from very large rain barrels. Very new rain barrels that had never seen rain. Billy guessed it would have been described as rustic. He also guessed it would have been described as masculine, if by masculine you meant no frills, not one. There were prints of ducks and prints of old mills and photographs of badly dressed, earnestly smiling people—relatives. The walls were off-white. There was a television and a VCR. A half-filled glass of something watery and brown sat on an end table. On the floor by the couch, a cycling magazine was opened to an article, "Ten Speeds: Why and When." There were lots of meticulously cared-for plants, a veritable greenhouse by one window.

"Wanna beer?" John asked.

"Do you still have that wine?"

"It's been in there a while. I'd go with beer if I were you."

"You lured me here under false pretexts."

"It's good beer."

They sat on the couch, careful not to touch, not even knees. John closed the magazine and put it on the coffee table. It was addressed to him. A subscriber.

"Do you bicycle too?" Billy asked.

"Nah," he said. "Too much peddling. I just like the pictures."

John worked for a landscape architect.

"What do you do for him?" Billy asked.

"The dirty work."

John had dropped out of college after three years. He'd been a Horticulture major. His mother was dead. That was her in the picture. His father was retired. His sister was a married nurse. His long black braid was beautiful. He'd met Clare when he was dating another friend of hers, Wayne, did Billy know him? Nice guy. Kind of crazy. But nice. The amethyst in John's ear, his beard, that beautiful black braid. There was something wild and serious about him. A pirate. That was it. He was glad they hadn't gone to the movies. He'd had a long day. He'd worried that he'd fall asleep. He took off his shoes, boxer's boots. No, he didn't box either. He just thought they were cool. His white socks were smudged black from them. Last night he'd dreamed he was a tree and he'd hated it, not moving and fall coming on. He'd wakened in a sweat. Not that kind of sweat, he said quickly. God, his eyes, black as his hair. He'd also lied about food. There were some chips and some tuna fish. Did Billy want another beer? John stretched before he went to the kitchen, longer and leaner than ever. Not possible. He's too cute for me, Billy thought. John did have cable but really, that was a lie too. All that was on it was bad movies, worse game shows, stuff in Spanish. Did Billy know Spanish? John had had three semesters in college and thought he could ask his way to a bathroom if he had to. At one point he'd wanted to save the rain forests of Brazil. But that was a long time ago. Though he still might. You never could tell.

God, his eyes.

The VCR clicked.

"That's *Twin Peaks*," he said. "I'm taping it."

"I'm the only person I know who hasn't seen it."

"I could explain it as we went along."

Twin Peaks turned out to be very complicated and the only thing Billy knew by the long middle commercial break was that Laura Palmer was dead, which was what he knew before John's explanation.

"It's great, isn't it?" John said.

"Yeah," Billy said.

"Wan' another beer?"

"Sure. And some tuna fish."

They ate it out of the can with teaspoons. All his forks were dirty. When John put his arm around him, Billy realized they were leaning back, that nearness had sneaked up on them (on him at least); and he wondered when it had happened; and the pleasure of it was like a forgotten language he wasn't sure he wanted to remember.

At eleven o'clock, John took out the tape—he had a complete library of *Twin Peaks*—and said, "OK. Date's over."

In spite of himself, Billy said, "It's early."

"But I had a long day and have an even longer one tomorrow because the moron I work for overloaded us again. Besides, all good daters should be in bed by midnight or they turn into crabgrass. I hate crabgrass."

At the door, after it had been established that Billy's was close and he preferred to walk, after he'd asked for the name of the CD he'd barely listened to, after he'd asked what a particularly sinister-looking plant was and had gotten the Latin name, after he'd thanked John for the beer and the tuna and the history of *Twin Peaks*, after he'd patted himself for the keys he never forgot anymore, John held out his hand and said, "May I have the pleasure of your company sometime this week?"

"Do we get to kiss?" Billy asked.

"You're a fast one," he said, planting one on the top of Billy's head like Billy was ten and sexless and always would be.

The news was on in the living room. Helen had changed into the sweatsuit she wore most evenings and was swirling the top third of a hard fan of spaghetti into the boiling pot. Steam gusted around her. A cigarette in an ashtray on the counter was one long worm of grey ash and a lipsticked filter. Her other hand rested near it, the one with the wedding ring, though the divorce had been several years ago. Three? Four.

"Why can't they make spaghetti that fits?" she said.

"You could break it in half," Billy suggested.

"Then it's too small. There's nothing to wrap around your fork."

Billy was cutting tomatoes for salad. Helen had redone her kitchen recently but Billy really couldn't see the difference. Or rather, he'd known it was different, but still felt like he could have been in any kitchen, anywhere. He'd stopped offering her pieces of his furniture.

The sauce simmering in the crock pot ladled the air with garlic. Billy closed his eyes to smell it better and didn't see Helen when she walked over. She pushed his bangs from his forehead and startled him. He cut himself. A crack of blood welled up on his finger.

"I'm sorry," she said. "Go run it under some cold water. I hope there's still a Band-Aid in the medicine cabinet."

There wasn't.

"I don't know," she said. "I guess I stopped buying them when your sister moved out."

"It's OK. It's tiny. I'll just use a paper towel."

"I don't think I've ever cut myself. Isn't that weird? Everybody cuts themself."

"You're blessed among women."

They ate in the living room and watched *Jeopardy*. Billy couldn't answer questions much past the $200 range but Helen did well in Potpourri. The computer analyst from Santa Clara was mopping the floor with the other contestants. He knew everything: Sports Cars, Medical History, Medieval Literature. The spaghetti was good: Helen's sauce was the one thing that hadn't failed her. The crushed carnation of paper towel around Billy's finger brushed at his face while he ate. A small starburst of blood had seeped through.

"Something's burning," he said.

"The garlic bread," Helen said and walked with a what's-done-is-done casualness to the kitchen.

The broiler, which always stuck, rattled as she wrestled with it. Blue-grey smoke lazed into the living room. Billy was suddenly full and tired. He hated the computer analyst from Santa Clara and all his useless knowledge. Did he know why they couldn't make spaghetti right? Did anybody?

Helen gave him a ride home. She fiddled with the radio; nothing seemed to satisfy her. Billy stared out the window. Lights were on in all the houses and nobody was on the streets. The pine tree deodorizer swinging from the rear view mirror had gone flat and the car was stale. Billy cracked the window. His heart throbbed in his finger. Little tufts of paper towel whiskered the clotted blood.

"It's a little cold," Helen said.

"It's a little ashtray-smelling in here."

"'It's very cold."

"I'm getting out in a minute."

A few seconds later, she said, "You were just friends with that boy in New York, right?"

"Which boy?"

"His name started with a B like yours."

"Brett."

"Brett. A friend, right? Not like that other boy."

"Steve?"

"Steve. He was something else, right?"

"You can say that again."

John Day showed up bearing a battered lunch box with Boy George on it. The paint had scuffed away from Boy's raised aluminum hat and plaits, surrounding his face with a small map in bas relief of an indecipherable mountain range, the Pyrenees, the Alps. It was a bad likeness. He looked like someone you thought you knew, an old buddy's kid sister who'd started using makeup.

"I already had one," John Day said. "It's kind of beat-up, but it was such a great price, and I thought you might get a kick out of it." He went thrift-shopping every day, to yard sales and flea markets every weekend.

"I overestimated his audience," Billy said.

"I liked Boy George."

"I liked the idea of him."

"Isn't that the same thing?"

"I suppose. Have a seat."

"Where?"

John Day had a point. For all of Billy's furniture, there wasn't a place to sit unless it was on that pile of books, or the giant granite conch shells which didn't look very comfortable, or on the floor if you cleared a space. Everything was unfinished or stacked on top of each other. As Billy looked at it through John Day's eyes, he realized that it looked like nobody lived there, like it had been abandoned for years.

"Come sit on the bed while I change."

"I don't think we'll make it to the movies if you take your clothes off in front of me."

They didn't. They also couldn't come. After an hour or so, they subsided into caresses, Billy rubbing little circles on John Day's belly, John Day kneading the back of Billy's neck until the massage drifted away to the tips of his warm fingers barely touched to Billy's hair, and small snores rippling through his nose. A block of moonlight fell through the window, bleaching out a rectangle of the bedroom's darkness. Outside it, things had become their shadows and did not imply themselves—dressers, vanities, mantelpieces—but primitive groupings to ward off evil. John Day smelled of the sweet-sour of his own dried sweat. Very soon, Billy would kiss him on the ear and wake him. Billy would not tell him tonight. Billy would suggest dinner at the Grill. John Day was a vegetarian, a lapsed microbioticer. They would know people there, probably join someone. Billy would be home by midnight. When John Day suggested that they spend the night together, Billy would say he was tired. When John Day tried to kiss him goodnight, Billy would shake his hand. If John Day called next week, Billy would be busy. It was all so unreasonable.

"Hi Billy, this is Mitchell. Listen, you can have the Janet Jackson and the Edmund White. I don't like being your friend. I know we haven't talked in a few weeks but I don't want you walking around thinking we're friends because we're not."

Clare invited Billy to a *Twin Peaks* party in D.C.

"I don't want to drive up there by myself," she said. "My car's been acting up."

"Can John come?"

"Which one?"

"The dark one."

"That's funny. I would have thought the other one was more your type."

"So would I."

"So are you an item?"

"We've had a few dates."

"Semi-item."

It was a two-hour drive. John sat in the back. He kept reaching around to pinch Billy's thigh. Clare smoked and drank her extra-large 7-11 coffee and free-associated about her childhood. Occasionally, she'd veer out of her lane and say, "Whoopsie." She'd come as Laura Palmer. She looked exactly the way she always did but she'd painted her face a deathly white and kohled her eyes. John, in a plain blue suit pinned with a toy sheriff's badge, was supposed to be Detective something-or-other. His hair was slicked over to the side and his braid was hidden under the jacket. Billy wasn't anybody.

The interstate was long and deserted except for a few eighteen-wheelers and cars with one person in them. The broken white lines dividing the highway shot under the car like logs down a flume. The car was messy: crumpled cigarette packs, crumpled coffee cups, bits of coral and lava, cat hair everywhere. The speedometer was broken.

"How do you know how fast we're going?" Billy asked.

"I just know," she said.

"This feels like the right speed," John said.

"Thank you, Detective," she said.

Clare lived by instinct, Billy by fear. It was too early to tell what John lived by. Reason, probably. He liked to know how much was left of anything: time, pairs of socks, milk in a carton. He looked at his watch during movies.

Three quarters of the way there, the Toyota began hiccuping and lurching. A few minutes later a sound like one food processor devouring another ground from under the hood; the headlights and the dashboard failed; and they were rolling silently through darkness. The trees on the side of the highway were flat, black silhouettes of trees and the moon was missing. Clare pulled over into the emergency lane.

"Uh-oh," she said.

She tried the ignition. It clicked hollowly.

"Do you have any flares?" John asked.

"Clare?" Billy laughed.

"Yes, I do," she said, turning towards Billy and sticking out her tongue, a trademark gesture.

"I'm shocked," he said.

"I like the color. I've been trying to think of a way to use them in a piece."

The flares sputtered out hot pink sparks and cast a surpris-

ingly bright light, given the gigantic and resolute black of the
night. Billy wriggled his nose against the whiffs of sulphur.
He'd forgotten to eat before they left and his stomach twisted
and yawned. He and Clare leaned against the trunk, their hands
hidden from the cold under their crossed arms. John was bent
under the lifted hood, though Clare had told him not to bother.

"Find anything?" she said.

"Nothing. No oil, no transmission fluid, no water in the ra-
diator."

"Whoopsie."

Trucks passed and a Toyota the same year and make as
Clare's slowed down, reconsidered, then sped off. One of the
flares died unexpectedly and Clare replaced it. Billy wondered if
he looked mad when John gave him a reassuring squeeze on the
back of the neck and a peck on the temple.

"OK," Clare said. "Drastic measures."

She put her satin ballet slippers on the roof of the dead car
and peeled off her striped woolen leggings.

"You're not," Billy said.

"I am."

She hiked her black mini-dress up another indecent inch and
modelled her left leg at what there was of the traffic. It was a
beautiful leg, long and shapely; and Billy was sure you couldn't
see the unshaven down of it at sixty miles an hour. She added
vixenish tosses of her hair and Ann-Margrety, pre-serious-
actress heaves of her bosom when truckers began tooting their
applause. When they didn't stop she blew them kisses and said,
"Pigs." Billy didn't think she'd last long, but she didn't have to.
A Lincoln actually stopped.

She pulled the hem of the dress down as far as it would go,
mid-thigh, and ran over barefoot, saying, "If he asks for a
blowjob, I'll send for one of you guys."

He was older, Asian, called Sam, and lectured Clare on who
might have pulled over.

"I had my bodyguards," she said, smiling into the large backseat where John and Billy sat.

God, it was warm; and the car glided along on something
that felt like assurance. Clare's leggings were tied around her
shoulders like a sweater. The Lincoln still had its new smell.

The E-Z listening was actually soothing and frightened Billy. Something must have happened to his taste in the cold.

"Fantastic," Clare said when they passed a batch of interstate signs in Arlington, "my parents live off the next exit. Do you mind, Sam," she said, touching his shoulder.

Sam scowled paternally. His silver hair had the iridescence of a fish under the dashboard's low, green glow. "If you were my daughter," he said, "I'd have to spank your bottom every other day."

Clare laughed but she cut her eyes to Billy. He knew what she meant. It had given him the slight creeps, too.

He couldn't say why, but he was surprised that Clare lived in such a neighborhood. It was disorienting to think that she hadn't always been Clare, a sculptor with a thing for cats and S-M pornography, that she'd had a bedtime and maybe acne. God knows she had talked about her childhood; but those stories had happened a long, gotten-over time ago. Worse things had happened since then. A rotten marriage and therapy for the rotten marriage. The deaths of friends.

Clare offered to send Sam a sculpture but he didn't like art. She shook his hand instead.

A light was on in the living room of her parents' ranch house and smoke puffed from the chimney. John popped something into his mouth. Billy wanted to ask what it was, but if it was drugs he didn't want to know. Their breath came out in clouds.

The Lacys were in their seventies. They'd been going through wallpaper books. An indifferent black cat was curled up on a stereo speaker. Billy, starving, wanted to grab a handful of caramels from the cut glass bowl on the coffee table.

"What have you done to your face?" her father asked.

"It's a party thing. OK. So, listen. This is my friend Billy, and this is my friend John, and we were headed to this *Twin Peaks* party when my car broke down."

"Oh, Clare," Mrs. Lacy said.

"So we need to borrow your car."

"To get back home?" Mr. Lacy asked.

"No, to the party."

"What about your car?" Mrs. Lacy asked.

"It's dead. I'll rent something tomorrow."

"Oh, Clare," Mrs. Lacy said.

They took a modular-looking, many-seated thing with rounded edges painted the most sensible red Billy had ever seen. The Lacys claimed it was a van but Billy knew vans were not painted sensible colors and only had two seats, one for the driver, another for his girlfriend. Everybody else sat in the back on the floor and smoked pot. There might be a makeshift cot to fuck on, a cooler for beer, some shag carpet on the walls. Futuristic landscapes were sprayed across the sliding doors. Billy had not seen what he thought of as a van since the late seventies; but this kind of radical mutation took generations. The Lacys thought they had a van but what they really had was a small bus to take disabled people shopping in.

The Lacys listened to the same E-Z listening as Sam, saviour and possible pervert. Billy clicked it off but John picked up the tune—a funereal version of "Like A Virgin"—right where it had left off. He whistled it. He had a nice whistle: rich, resonant, varied. Clare sang along, heartfelt and out of tune, substituting her obscene lyrics for Madonna's coy ones. Clare loved Madonna. She knew every verse. Billy harmonized on the chorus, if you could call the tuneless collision of their voices harmony. Singing helped his hunger. When they were done, Clare rolled down the window and lit a cigarette.

"It's freezing," Billy said.

"My parents would die if they knew I smoked."

"For God's sake, you're an adult. You're divorced."

"I know, I know; but everybody in our family dies of cancer. It would kill them."

They got to the party just before eleven. It was packed. Half of the guests had come as Laura Palmer. Clare disappeared immediately to look for the woman who had invited her and to run into gallery owners who had previously expressed an interest in her work. Billy remembered when parties had been smokey, when he had smoked, when the difference between carefree and careless had been negligible. Now the only people who smoked were Clare and his family. "I've given up too much already," Clare would say when he nagged her about it. He didn't nag his mother. Smoking was her life.

He wished they hadn't come. Except for the Laura Palmers, he didn't know who anybody was supposed to be. He hadn't been to a party in several years. He couldn't remember how you had fun at them. Three different men reminded him of Brett. It was this one's hair, that one's mole, the way another cocked his head as he listened. Brett had owned a complete collection of Anita Bryant records. He'd written a monograph on mannerist painting. He'd made perfect fried chicken. Every Christmas he'd bought his mother a half ounce of Chanel No. 5 so he could have the bottle when she was done with it. He'd been vain and funny and exasperating and generous and right now Billy would have traded everyone he knew for one of Brett's whispered and withering asides about the Laura Palmers. Brett would have known what to do with this party.

John said, "I think I see the bar."

He guided Billy by the arm through the crowd. People were spilling drinks left and right. The air was a riot of hair mousses. Billy wished people still smoked. He wasn't hungry anymore, but when they passed a vegetable tray he scooped up the last few forlorn florets of broccoli. They still had a nice crunch. At the bar there were half a bottle of Campari and cases of ginger ale left.

"There's beer in the fridge," a Laura Palmer said.

"You wanna beer?" John asked.

"I don't know," Billy said.

John turned Billy around by the shoulders and kissed him. "You alright?" he said.

"I think people are staring at us."

John embraced him and whispered in his ear, "That's because we're young, we're beautiful, and we're in love. They're jealous." A joke.

John was positive. He'd told Billy over dinner last week after the waiter had taken their order. Billy had looked away to the handful of pink carnations in the vase of an empty Perrier bottle. He'd wanted to sip his wine, but it had seemed imperative not to move; to wait; to see. "Does it make a difference?" John had said.

"No," Billy had said. He could have been lying. He didn't know.

Love. Even as a joke, it kicked up a dust of confusion. There was a time when Billy could have said, "This is love. This is grief. Here's one of me having fun." But now all his loves were streaked with grief; and all his griefs shot through with a terrible love. This borderless place he'd been shoved into was identical to the place before, but the old maps were useless, the language was subtly different; and he stumbled over the future tense of its verbs. Across the room Clare was laughing with some other Laura Palmers, and it amazed him, and he laughed; one short laugh that was almost a cough. John would think it was for him, for his joke. They were still hugging, and Billy patted John on the back, a gesture, he knew, that was still a sign of solace.

SPIRIT HOUSE

• GARY GLICKMAN •

Where I used to live, behind the little house I lived in with a man I used to love, lived a rich man with many dogs, whom he loved, and though he loved men more, or at least desired them more, he had never loved one, never had one to love. That is perhaps why, after all, when his dogs killed our kitten, our first after years of dog-happy contempt for feline habits, he merely threw the white and orange corpse into the thicket over the fence and shrugged his shoulders in supposed confusion while I hunted for the creature in the overgrown field we both coveted—its old owners were about to die—calling out its name from one end to the other in the cold, spring dusk.

He had left us alone, our first few years there. We had come from the city, believing, in our hopeful youth, that we had found what we wanted and could take it away with us, to treasure it and isolate and protect it like Rapunzel locked in her tower. Instead, like her we languished at our windows, wondering why we were bereft. We had our love. We had our work and our fireplace, and our little but energetic dog. What then had we left behind, in that plague-beseiged city? What had we given up, those dark December afternoons when the house was finally repaired, beautiful and cozy, and we wandered, one upstairs, one down, wishing it were not so cold beyond the windows, that we might escape?

We didn't know. I hid upstairs at my desk, typing a word or

two hopelessly, pulling at my hair, while the man I loved typed away furiously just below, not, as it seemed to me then, articles that everyone back in the city would read, nor stories that would fill books that would line his study and be translated farther and farther into the world. Instead he was typing into a world he had recently discovered called CompuSex, which anyone with a computer and a telephone connection-device could join for a monthly fee and several dollars for each hour "on the line." There were several such electronic communities, but the one my friend joined, the one he helped create by typing so many words into the constantly "scrolling" dialogue, was called Gayline. Anyone could type in, but only the truly interested persisted for long. What appeared on screens across the country was a playscript, constant and extemporaneous, in which the players all used pseudonyms, but soon recognized fellow enthusiasts and looked impatiently for each other to sign on again after periods of screen silence.

Big Balls: Hey there, Norfolk Slave-Master, Where ya been?

Slave-Master: Hey, BB! I was out with my lover's parents last weekend. What's been happ'nin out in Iowa?

BB: That's Idaho. Not too much. I've been hanging out on the computer. . . .

Occasionally the conversations became more pointed toward titillation, and you could arrange, by typing in a special code, to "go private" with an interlocutor of your choice. Evidently many keyboards were splashed with semen, but mostly the titillation was in writing or seeing things written that hardly anyone would dare write if his face were known, or his real name. Of course, people often exchanged phone numbers, too, if a particular dialogue seemed interesting enough to risk the much more personal sound of the voice. Often I heard the door close downstairs when the furious typing ceased, and though I never picked up the phone during those times, I sometimes wandered downstairs for a glass of juice, or a walk to the village, and heard the murmurs, from down the hall, that only jealous lovers understand.

At night, when the other houses on our street were already dark and the village had been deserted for hours, we often watched movies rented from the bookstore in town. Afterwards, often, I would go upstairs, but my friend would stay in the dark, watching a sex video he had rented as well, from the other store, the one just beyond the village. *Too Big To Handle, Bigger Than Huge, Beyond Your Wildest Dreams.* Sometimes I would come downstairs again. Remote control in one hand, boxer shorts around his knees, he would look at me, or else not look at me, as we negotiated embarrassment and resentment, defiance, permission, generosity, longing, gratitude and regret. I stood there mesmerized as I always was even by soap commercials, let alone the primitive icons dancing before us, phallus disappearing into flesh, idolized and transformed, rods of power and submission, seminating finally, like a priest's shake of holy water, onto faces, buttocks, backs, smooth-skinned, muscley bellies.

I didn't touch him, at first, I couldn't, it felt false as prostitution, using my touch merely as accoutrement to the image. But then, sitting down near him, I'd touch myself, throw off my clothes, abandon myself as simply as possible, and be done almost always before him. He had rented the tape, and wanted to see it to the end. By the time he climbed into bed I was asleep, or too tired to talk, or touch beyond a snuggle I longed for but couldn't bring myself to initiate.

We met just before Christmas, the year his mother died, and he brought me home as if he already knew it would be the last Christmas for that family, held together mostly by a few last threads of anxiety and guilt: that she was doomed but lingering, that the waiting was hard, an imposition no matter how you pretended, and that her husband had another love, far away but patient. We lied, we said we'd been together a while already, not just the few weeks which seemed, anyway, because of our excitement, like a substantial time. He wanted her to see me, and to approve, perhaps, but also he wanted my witness for this first season of his life that was already dimming to shadow. The family house, across the country from where we lived, was like a paradise to me, hummingbirds at the feeder, geraniums still blooming in December beneath the redwood trees, bright persimmons hanging on like holiday ornaments to leafless branches.

At first, she wouldn't talk to me. She was polite, even generous, a liberal mother, but the drama in that quiet house, that
quiet garden, was already into its last act, and you couldn't in-
troduce too many new tensions or even ideas without confusing
every other. Still, I helped her set the table, dry the dishes, and
was up early a few mornings when she was in a good mood,
feeding her dogs and the old cat who slept all day but still, after
twenty-one years, would get up one more time if you kicked it,
or opened up a can of fish. Eventually she wanted to talk to me,
to tell me something or give me something, in that season of
giving, though she didn't at first know what. A sandwich, beautifully made. A sweater she had knitted for someone else, a size
too small. A family outing to the sea lions on the coast, which
meant, I believe, that I had been accepted as a member. For a
long time she wouldn't look me in the eye, however, and I think
it was because, despite our many differences, she had seen
something right away I didn't understand until years later, a
similarity in our eyes or in whatever place the eyes reveal, that
disconcerted her, in this the end of her own life, seeing the
choice her son had made, beginning his own.

We looked for a house of our own, that year, as if my friend
knew his mother would soon be dead; soon after she died we
found one and bought it. Perhaps that death was the sadness
and fear and isolation we were swimming through, the high
waves we couldn't see beyond. As if fearing a kind of drowning,
he seldom left the house and almost never the village, though
I was teaching and had to travel into the city every week. The
village library and bookstore were just a walk away, and there he
would go briefly each day, our dog on a long leash, returning in
time to watch the afternoon soap operas. Somewhere in between, he wrote his books. Maybe the days I was gone he was
able to work, able to put aside all the shields and diversions
which, when I came home, sprang up each time to protect him,
TV and videos and computer games and laundry and vacu-
uming the rug, though the life we had envisioned sharing was
everything else. At sunset he took the car to the A&P, and came
home to cook, turkey tetrazini, macaroni and cheese, and other
dishes from his childhood, but mostly pasta with different kinds

of sauce, huge bowls of it, which we ate watching the television far across the room, game shows, evening comedy serials, the news with its long strings of commercials.

I sat with my back to the screen. Sometimes I would light candles, make a salad. I would turn the lights down, the new fancy lights with a dimmer switch, until the candlelight was just brighter, and our little scene reflected romantically—though only I could see it—in the dark windows all across one wall. In the dim light the windows looked onto the back garden, abandoned during the winter months, revealing it to be, without its summer profusion, just a few paces of mud and weeds and buckling brick. Like Dorian Gray's portrait, it seemed to reveal too much about us, about our home, our life together, and we didn't like to go out there.

"Can we turn up the light just a little bit?" my friend often asked, unless he was feeling guilty about the television and his own unimpeded desires. Almost always I complied, there being no romance for one, it seemed, at least not in company.

And so we decided to get the cat.

"I think the dog's depressed," one of us must have observed. Yes, it was true. She was hardly more than a puppy, then, from an ancient terrier race that is among the bravest and least introverted among all the family of dogs. At six weeks she was the shyest of the litter, tentatively padding over to us after her more boisterous brothers had already run up to the edge of the pen, fighting for the chance to be petted.

("Who'll take her if you two split up?" the woman asked us, and we smiled, and shook our heads knowingly.)

At seven weeks the dog was timid for half an hour only, already pleased to be free from the competition. At ten weeks she learned to bark, an enormous, outsize bark for such a little dog, the bark of wildness, of serious work as hunter or shepherd, and by three months she won most arguments.

But she had taken to curling up, evenings, in the dark guest room far down the hall. During the day, too, she retreated there, unless she heard a sigh or a shuffle and divined, always correctly, that it meant we would be opening the door, going somewhere, anywhere. She took to standing guard outside, just in case one of us might try to leave secretly. She learned to jump into the car, if the window was open, and if not, then she would sit, shivering on the roof or the hood, looking back through the kitchen window for us with accusing eyes, impatient to forgive, and to be on our journey whatever it would be. As a result we took her everywhere we could, carrying her into stores when necessary, tying her up outside the A&P, the bank, the coffee shop, the library. In thunderstorms, when the sound scared her into a frenzy and we were sometimes not at home, she would often escape and run through the village, crossing busy streets, looking for us up and down the aisles of the supermarket, or the farmer's market, or the bookstore, the library, the bank.

"Yeah, she was in here," said the check-out lady. "Over by the vegetables."

"I saw her," said the man at the shoe store. "Came in by the front door, left by the back."

Her fear, however, made her docile, and she would climb into anyone's car who let her, and someone always called us to say she was safe and very well fed. And now, these cold months, with two men home most of the time for company, she was curled up all day long on the sofa, surer sign than either of us would admit that a poor dog who absorbed even subtle tensions and distant thunder could not help but show what we ourselves were hiding.

Company, we said, was what she needed, so we went to the pound to look. And though every orphaned creature knew us before we knew them, we shook our heads finally against another dog. What did we know even then? That we could not bear the burden even of our little house, our simple life together, our one canine responsibility, and that another would be the end of it all? And so, even sneezing and wheezing, we went in to play with the cats, and found the smartest one, the most trusting and affectionate one, that would cheer up our cat-loving dog. If our dog became cheerful with us and our life again, maybe we could become that way too, maybe what we knew and saw and felt so deeply was not after all the only truth. Reconciliation, starting again and again, putting off knowing. That cat was our love, so fragile and naive and tentative, and we were happy again for a while. We didn't let it out of the house.

* * *

"Oh neighbor! Neighbor!" The voice was sing-song but suspect, like the tricky, humiliating tone of girls in kindergarten calling out some boy's name. We were out in the back garden, admiring the new roof and the new windows in the early dusk, when the winter sun was just setting behind the little white church across the field. At the fence, squeezed in beside the rhododendrons, stood our neighbor, just where he had stood the few other times he came to deliver us a message: that our *bitch*, as he always insisted on specifying, had once again climbed under the fence and was cavorting with his Airedales, which would have been alright, he sometimes added, were it not for the not-yet-inoculated litter, who were thus obviously still vulnerable to foreign bacteria. That was how he put it, about our dog. Thank you, we would usually say, and run over to collect her.

"Oh neighbor, neighbor!" he called this time, with the same mocking disdain. We turned around, caught too close to the fence to run inside pretending we hadn't heard. Whenever he came to the shared fence he was only twenty paces from our house, looking in like a farmer at his livestock. When we looked through the fence we were still two acres from his windows. We looked around for the dog.

"No," he said. "Your bitch has not graced us this time with the pleasure of her—let us say, not-too-subtly sexual antics. I saw you two out here on this dark December twilight, looking so prettily domestic, and I realized that I have been remiss in my duties as neighbor." He was dressed all in red, red cotton stockings, red sweatshirt and red cotton cap, like one of Santa's elves except for the green padded army jacket.

"Excuse me?" my friend asked, already moving toward the house. "Excuse me, I think I hear the phone ringing." He ran inside.

"I hope it wasn't anything I said!" our neighbor said in a muted version of that mocking whine, as if there were no possibility it could have been anything he said.

"Oh, no," I said. "I'm sure the phone was really ringing."

"Well, what I was saying to you both—and now I'll have to say to you alone—I have been remiss in my duties as neighbor, and I would like to invite you boys to my not-so-humble abode for a drink. Tomorrow night, for example. At six."

I told him that would be very nice, and that I would ask my friend. I myself had been curious to see the inside of that big house we could see from our new bedroom windows on the second floor. Also, I was having trouble writing. Words would not come to me, passion, the sound of my own voice. Stories would not come to me, and here, suddenly, it seemed that one had, if only I would recognize it. For that I wanted to risk the possibility of a moment's boorishness and boredom.

"I wouldn't set foot in that guy's house for all his money," my friend said. "What did you tell him?"

"I told him I'd go, but that I'd have to ask you."

"Tell him I'm sick. Tell him I have the flu. Anything. I'm not going."

When I climbed over the fence and walked across those frozen acres to his Christmas lights and French doors, I practiced the casual lie to my escort of his five dogs, practiced saying it lightly and thus believably. Instead, when he asked, I told him that my friend had wanted to come, but that he had been up most of the night vomiting and all day sweating through a fever, and thus was feeling too weak.

"That's a shame!" my neighbor said, and pushed me down into a low rocker by the fireplace, where a section of tree trunk was burning. "Now this is how to make a fire!" he said, and filled my large brandy snifter to the brim with champagne. He held up a large tray as well, covered with salmon mousse and vegetable pâté, crackers carefully sorted out into the shape of a fan. "Drink the champagne while it's potent," he said. "I've got an entire jeraboam you've got to finish." He held up the huge bottle, still more than half full.

"At last," he said, sitting back in his own rocker, and petting one of the five dogs who had settled all around us, two of them with their muzzles in his lap. "He's my favorite, this one, the father of them all. He was a real stud in his day, let me tell you. Twice a national champion. We understand each other, I think. Don't we, Percival?"

The dog looked unblinkingly up into his face.

"I've never loved anyone as I love this old dog. And no one has ever loved— But you must tell me everything about yourself. I was in the Vietnam War, you know. You were probably a child at the time. I have many stories I could tell you, no doubt

you would find them interesting. My family goes back to the
first American Saint. You've heard of her, of course."

I told him I hadn't, that I was Jewish and we didn't keep good
track of saints.

"A Jew! Not surprising, you know more and more there are
many Jews in this area. My own family has been here—
summering, I mean—at least five generations, when it was just
a few families, and we all knew each other. Now, of course, it's
different, but so be it, I've gotten to meet *you*. Otherwise we are
from Newark, New Jersey, and, then, since the turn of the century, the New Jersey countryside, a quiet village called
Bernardsville, near Lewiston—"

"That's funny!" I said. "*My* family comes from Newark, too,
and they moved to Lewiston about the same time!"

"Bernardsville is a very different place from *Lewiston*," said
my neighbor. "I doubt very much our families would have
met."

He told me about the saint, whose named he shared, and the
many wealthy and important ancestors who had carried the
name before him. He told me his neighbor wanted to buy his
house, she wanted to expand her grounds. She was from a very
old family, too, a liquor heiress, she said—naming the
company—and could offer him any price. "Madame," he told
me he said. "I am a direct descendent of the first American
Saint. Has your family been here longer than that? And I'd like
to make you the same offer for your own home. I've been
thinking I need a little guest cottage for summer company."

I laughed, rocking with enjoyment, and he poured me another beakerful of champagne.

"Let me read to you," he said, and sliding his rocking chair
closer, pulled onto his lap a large book. "Do you know Corin-
thians? You should."

The passage he read aloud, I soon realized, was about the
shame of sinning.

"Do you know what his sin was?" my neighbor asked, turning, and with a strong breath looked into my eyes.

"No," I said, grinning drunk. Then I stopped grinning and
said I had to get back to my friend, who needed me to make
him soup.

"Let me give you a tour of the house first. I'm sure that

would interest someone of such culture as yourself." He pulled me by the arm, steadying himself with a tight grip, and we walked, almost ran through several rooms, in which he vaguely pointed out some antiques in passing. "Some things were stolen," he said. "Once by a young man I knew, superficially— perhaps I'll tell you more about that later on—and once by a stranger."

In a moment we were in the middle of the bedroom, where finally he stopped, still holding my arm. "And this is the master bedroom, with its original Queen Anne canopy and bed," he said. "Which I hope you'll be getting to know quite a bit more intimately."

I was pleased to have someone say such a silly thing to me, it was flattering and also I'd always wanted to know if people really spoke like that.

"What's down there?" I asked, grinning again and turning away to point down the hall.

He pulled me around and had his tongue in my mouth before I could speak.

"Oh, oh!" I said, like the heroine of a melodrama, and tried to push him away, my hands on his chest. "I don't think we should be doing this," I said, trying to match the calm elegance of good breeding with which he was evidently used to bullying people. "You know what they say about good fences making good neighbors!"

"Yes, well your little bitch knows how to climb over for what she wants." He grabbed at me again but this time I twisted away.

I thanked him for the champagne, grabbed my coat and scarf and ran back through the night to our house.

"Well?" asked my friend, and I stood in his study a while, shaking my head, feeling guilty, laughing but unable to describe what had happened. Still I tried, and we both laughed, and when our friends came over the next day for tea, he had me repeat the story for them . . . "And look what I found in the mail this morning!" said my friend, bringing out the ribbon-tied, hand-written scroll we had found in the early morning, a get-well card from our neighbor.

"Sounds crazy," said our friend, the husband, who was a doctor.

"Rambo elf," said his wife.

We all laughed, until we heard the familiar call.

"Oh neighbor! Neighbor!"

We thought it was only the halucinatory echo of a good story, my own impersonation. But the voice came again, and I walked out into the dark. At the fence was our neighbor again.

"Hi," I said, squinting to see him.

"How is your friend?" he asked, jogging in place, hugging himself for warmth. He was still in his red winter costume.

"Oh, much better, thank you. The fever's down."

"I just came out to see if perhaps there wasn't something I could do."

"Oh, no thanks."

"I see you're having a party." Through the big new windows we could plainly see my friend at the table with our two guests, laughing and laughing over tea and slices of cake.

"No, no," I said. "Not really. Some friends just came over to visit."

"Wouldn't you consider it mere neighborly consideration to reciprocate an invitation with an invitation?"

"Excuse me? Oh, would you like to come inside for some tea?"

He said he would, and climbed, like an enthusiastic but overgrown elf, over the fence.

Our friends were surprised to be sitting at the table with the man we had all just been laughing about. As I handed him some tea I introduced him, however, as if they had never heard his name. When he heard my friends' name he suddenly smiled.

"Oh, well, with your Irish name you'll no doubt appreciate my family genealogy, which leads back directly, as you can tell from my own name, to the first American Saint, with whom you must, no doubt, be familiar. . . ."

It was the same story I had been paraphrasing five minutes before, the same character in the same red costume, the same condescending inflections and pretentious words. It was as if, with the power of my imaginative skills, I had summoned him up before us, and our friends were not bored but rather tempted to laugh, plainly showing it on their faces as if it were not a real man sitting there reciting to us but just the image of one, a Disney robot that would repeat his life-like performance

every twenty minutes. He jumped into several other stories before anyone could interrupt, somehow also eating his piece of
cake and then another. The last anecdote was about some andirons he had found in the shape of Airedales, which he had
bought from a Jewish antiquarian for an outrageous price. "My
hosts will appreciate this story," he said, without looking at us,
"the ancient Hebrews having been well acquainted with the sin
of avarice."

"Well, gotta go—" said our doctor friend.

"*Really* nice to meet you!" said his wife. And they fled.

I thought we would never see them again. We were left
standing up in the middle of the room, clapping our hands once
or twice in a show of finality.

"Very nice that you came by," I said.

"I've got to get back to work," said my friend and walked
out, but we followed him into his study, which was already lined
with foreign editions of his books.

"Oh," said our neighbor. "Are you a writer too?"

"Yes," said my friend, his back to us. When we left him I
heard nothing for a while, then frantic typing.

"I'm afraid I've hurt his feelings," said our neighbor, who was
standing next to the fireplace, warming his hands over the weak
flame and not moving for his coat.

"Would you like to see the rest of the house before you
leave?" I asked.

"You need andirons!" he said. "How can you have a fireplace
and no andirons? You'll have a fire, you'll burn your house
down. After our little tour, I'll go back to my place and then I'll
come back here with some andirons you can borrow for as long
as you need them."

"That's okay," I said, without much hope.

As we climbed the stairs, he touched his hand to my back.
When I shook my head he stopped.

In the bedroom he went immediately to look out the window.
"This is what I wanted to see," he said. "I was wondering if you
could see my house from here. I see you can't see very well. It's
strange, I can see these windows so clearly. So now I'll go back
for a brief minute, and then I'll return right away with the andirons."

I thanked him and declined his offer, but he insisted yet again.

"Well," I said, "I'll go back with you and get them. That way—" I was going to say that that way he wouldn't come back here. Instead I said, "That way it'll be less trouble."

"Oh, no trouble."

"Oh, yes! I'll have to be getting to work myself."

"You two work all the time, I take it."

"Pretty much," I said.

The next day I went to the city, where I was teaching a class of students who were new to reading and writing. One of the assignments was a How-To essay, and the best one was called, "How To Frame An Innocent Person For Kicks."

How To Frame An Innocent Person For Kicks

We were hanging out with my friend Nicky, and he asks us if we want to know how to frame an innocent person for kicks. We told him yeah.

First you go to a bank. You take a withdrawal slip, and write on the back of it, "This is a stick-up. Give me all your money." Then you put it on the top of the pile and go wait in a corner.

In a little while a little old lady comes in, fills out the form, and goes over to the teller, who turns the ticket over to stamp it. "Is this a joke?" the teller asks, and the little old lady says "No, this is not a joke. Give me my money!"

Then bells ring, and the cops come in. It's a kick.

Speaking of this same Nicky, he tried the same thing a while later and got caught.

The End

In the middle of the night, my friend called me.

"I'm scared," he said. "I don't know what to do. I called my brother in Toronto, he thinks I should call the police."

"What's wrong?" I asked. I was used to certain exaggerations. Out in the country, the world can get very small, you can hear your own heartbeat again but sometimes you forget to remember all the others. Alone at night, a bruise becomes a sarcoma, a cough the first onslaught of pneumonia. My friend was not exaggerating his fear.

"He was at the fence again today. I was working at the dining room table, thinking what a nice afternoon it was, how nice to have the silence, when I heard—you know his call. I looked up and there he was, watching me. It was too late to drop the blinds, so I went to the door, and asked him what he wanted.

"The Lord has arranged that I should be locked out of my house and home," our neighbor told him.

"Excuse me?" asked my friend, like me unused to such language. "You locked yourself out of your house?"

"No. I did not lock myself out of my house. The *Lord,*" he reiterated, "has seen fit to lock me out of my house and home."

"Did you lose your keys?"

"I have not lost my keys."

"Do you need a screwdriver or something?"

"I have a screwdriver."

"Do you need to call a locksmith?"

"No, the *Lord* has seen fit to keep me from my hearth, and offer myself up to the kindness of strangers."

"Well," said my friend. "If you have a screwdriver, and don't want to call anyone, there's really nothing I can do to help you." And with that he closed the door and stood behind it a long time, until, peeking out the window, he saw our neighbor had retreated.

"So why are you scared?" I asked him. It was nearly three in the morning.

"Because he just called again. I let the machine answer, but then I thought it might be you, and I went down to listen. He was very drunk. 'I'm so, so sorry for what I've done,' he said. 'I hope you'll forgive me, and I want to make amends. It's ten—no, two o'clock, rather late, I realize, but I want you to know you're welcome to come over at any time. I want to make amends. And your way will be lighted by the lights of the Christmas trees.'

"All the little lights are still lighted in his backyard," said my friend. "I've locked all the doors, but I'm afraid he'll try to get in."

I suggested he take some aspirin and go back to bed. By the time I traveled home at the end of the week, there had been nothing more from across the fence, except once, when our dog escaped and came home again, a little red ball and some tinsel had been attached, emphatically, to her collar.

After midnight, the doorbell rang. We were reading in bed, warm and intimate again, protected from the snowstorm outside. The dog barked in the guest room and ran to the door, still shouting the alarm.

"Don't answer it," my friend said, hiding under the covers.

I put on a robe and went downstairs. When I opened the door there he was, in his martial elf suit, covered with snow.

"The Lord has directed me to throw myself upon the kindness of strangers," he said, and, flinging out his arms, stepped inside, falling onto me, pulling me into an embrace. "Take me, I'm yours. I've never told anyone before that I was—that I am—" For a while he sobbed on my shoulders, as I struggled under his weight and liquor breath and the snow melting into my robe. The dog slunk back to bed.

"Why don't you sit down a while," I said. "I'll make us some tea. You can put another log on the fire."

"Who is it?" my friend called from upstairs. "It's too late, he should go home!"

When I came back with the tea a huge fire was blazing, five or six big logs that would burn until dawn. I gave him his mug of tea, and sat down across from him in the dark, in the rocking chair where my father used to rock me on his lap when I couldn't sleep. After a long time he started to speak, in a quiet, simple voice I hadn't heard before. It was the story of his life he had never told anyone, not the genealogy but the alcoholic parents, the boarding school violence, the army, the secret desires he had never revealed, except with extreme contempt and the exchange of money.

From upstairs, my friend called my name. "It's too late, he should go home."

"I'll be up in a little bit," I called to him.

The story was coming to its natural end, although its narrator was taking every detour, Sheherazade afraid for her life. "I've never done this before. Never talked to anyone. I don't have real friends. How would I meet someone, I mean, another—man? I'm sure I'm too old, an old, old dog. I don't know how," he said, sounding more and more awkward, a person with a soul. Pinocchio must have sounded so sad, feeling for the first time his bruisable limbs. Or Frankenstein's monster, resurrected and betrayed. But this man was no monster, no doll. I gave him the unmiraculous answer of a few telephone numbers, hugged him firmly, sexlessly, and opened the door to the snow and the night. Without a word of thanks, he turned and left.

The cat trick worked. The dog was excited and very busy, shepherding the tiny but robust creature from room to room and chasing it whenever it leapt off the furniture onto the floor. She curled up at night exhausted and woke us up early in the morning with renewed enthusiasm. Our house was too busy and noisy for melancholy, and we were reunited in the husbandry of creatures needing our simple attention. We were indulgent with them, smiling when the kitten jumped up to explore the dinner table crowded with pasta and salad, laughing when a lamp crashed down in the wake of a late-night steeplechase. And because indulgence is catching, we were generous again with each other.

With the first warm days of spring I hurried to turn over the heavy earth in the garden and plant the first seeds, parsley and lettuce and cabbage, sweetpeas and radishes and carrots. I dug up squares of sod to expand the vegetable patch, bought half-barrel tubs for geraniums and a hammock to put between the two trees where we could lie together in the shade when the weather warmed up. I was so busy I didn't notice the typing so much, neither when it started nor when it stopped. My friend had finished a book, and then another, and was not so afraid to go out anymore. In fact, when he wasn't typing he was mostly going out. I was trying to be too busy to notice; the warm weather was coming, and in the garden there was a lot to do.

The other thing I didn't notice was our kitten growing adventurous and bold. He flashed out into the garden sometimes when we opened the door for the dog. He knew, from our dog, that if you hunch down a dog won't really hurt you at last, what seems a beast will shake you by the scruff a little but then lick your ears and your eyes, somewhere between interspecies revenge and mothering. He liked to watch those five neighbor dogs through the fence, much larger versions of our dog, and sometimes to swat at their big Airedale noses through the chain link. They hovered around on the other side, panting and smiling that animal smile that has intelligence but no humanity. One day I heard a catlike scream and the busy, victorious growl of a big dog. I listened a while, but heard nothing more, and thought it was just another of those endless fights between natural antagonists, after which both creatures run away, licking their wounds but feeling victorious.

"Where's the cat?" my friend asked me, hours later.

I told him, "Somewhere inside, I imagine."

But he wasn't inside.

"Have you seen a kitten?" we asked our neighbor, who hadn't called or come up to the fence again since that winter night. On Valentine's Day there'd been a grotesque valentine hand-delivered in the box, picturing an old, ugly transvestite holding up a bloody heart as if it were his own. Except for that, he had left us alone.

"No, I have not seen your little *kitten*," he said. "Although I don't imagine it's wise to let an inexperienced creature out of the house. My dog Percival once had an unfortunate incident with a feline combatant, and has been awaiting an opportunity for vengeance ever since."

"Well, if you see one—"

"Yes, yes," he said. "I shall carefully deliver the creature back to your loving arms."

That day and again the next I spent looking around the neighborhood, hunting back and forth with my dog through the overgrown field next door. When I found the corpse, with its soft flank ripped open revealing ribs and guts, I didn't say anything, didn't call out, didn't accuse our neighbor of his obvious cowardice or worse. I didn't want to disturb my friend, whose frantic typing I could hear all the way out in the field, and who had a harder time than I with death and bloody nature. I buried it in a deep hole just on our side of the fence, under the trees and old leaves, hesitant to cover up the pretty white and orange fur, which, even bloody, still seemed something delicate, something to pet and cherish. But it was getting on to dusk, and I knew I had to bury it deep, or some creature would dig it up again.

They had a beautiful house, my friend's parents, but like us they traveled often and far, as if beautiful things were always only far away, or as if their own house itself was only beautiful from great distance, the thought of it. On her last trip before she died, my friend's mother brought back a miniature pagoda, a doll-sized house with a red sloping roof and intricately painted panels, which was fastened to the top of a post like a birdhouse and fixed to the terrace outside her bedroom.

"It's a spirit house," she said to me, soon before her death, standing in her white terry bathrobe as we drank a mug of coffee together in one of the few moments we were ever to be alone. We would be leaving soon, her son and I, and, wanting to show me kindness, she had offered to point out some of the various fruit trees they had planted over the years, some of the many garden miracles of living in California, which, even moving three thousand miles for, from the cold East, had somehow not made them happy, and now it was the end. "They put them up in their yards, and hope good spirits will come to live in them," she said. "And they put out all kinds of food to entice them, and little gifts. You should see it. Usually I think that stuff's all crap, but this one caught my attention."

We stared at the empty little house a while, and then she wiped her eye that was always tearing; even when she cried for real she sometimes pretended it was just the disease.

"You know, it's funny, once or twice I've put a strawberry in there, or a piece of bread. I haven't told anyone, but the next day, it's always gone. I just don't know what to think. Maybe it's the cat. Hard to believe, though, about that cat. Still alive. Outliving me, even."

"I don't know about that," I said, stupidly.

"Oh yes," she said. "Probably. Some cats don't die, you know. They just go on and on, way after their time, until one day they just disappear. I suppose they go off and die alone. It's not a bad idea."

"Yours seems to be hanging on," I said.

"Would you like it?" she asked. "The house, I mean, not the cat?" She shook the post a little, trying to uproot it.

I laughed and said we'd have no place to put it, in our one-room city apartment.

"Oh well," she said, leaving off, and rubbing her hands from the effort. "Just thought I'd ask." And she clapped, calling to her dogs, it was time to feed them.

* * *

Not long after the cat was killed, my friend and I decided not to live in our house anymore, and then not to live together at all. It wasn't decided at once, clearly, but slowly, after traveling far away, and staying on, and coming back always briefly only to pack again. We laughed about our neighbor and worried about his returning, but he left us alone, and never even called to us again from over the fence. When he saw us in our yard he never came close. Another spring came and nothing got planted, the flowers that opened were flowers from other seasons, other years, from when it seemed we would be there for a long time together, season after season. I live now with very little I had in that house, a few favorite cups, a set of sheets and some books I take with me wherever I go. Sometimes I watch a video myself, rather than go stand around wasting time, making up lies about what's worthwhile. It makes me nostalgic and want to explain to someone, as if there were a private joke no one else has remembered.

Once, it seemed we would long outlive our neighbor in that place, and now it seems that, despite our intentions, we are the ones who will have been chased away, perhaps to better places. I used to think that kitten had been a visiting friendly spirit, brief emblem of our good fortune until its untimely demise. Then sometimes I've thought our neighbor was a spirit of confusion and envy we didn't know enough to keep, at all costs, out of our house; and that I should have said right away yes! to the totem my friend's mother offered me, that symbolic home she was trying to believe in even at her last. If I had said yes . . . would we have been happy? Would she have felt better perhaps even a few minutes, during that year that was her last? Maybe there isn't good or bad, just visitations along the way, enabling the future to come. Like that I can still dare to say yes when no seems the only comfort. Like that I can raise my eyes from disappointments, imprudent intrusions, confused attraction, envy and contempt like our neighbor's quiet enmity once he had revealed his secrets, and not been right away rewarded. He didn't actually kill our kitten, I try to remember. He may even have helped us, a benign spirit after all, though unconscious as most must be.

Only recently have I come to see that our own little house, abutting the much larger property, might have been someone else's totem and we merely its visiting spirits, all of us coming together to send each other on our way. Who knows, maybe that's why we were summoned to that house, and afterwards there was nothing more to keep us. You never know who the good spirits are, whose spirit you may be.

BOYS ON FIRE

• RAPHAEL KADUSHIN •

David first sees the photo in Marco's apartment. It's printed on a dog-eared page torn from a book and it has the grainy look of something obscene, so before David makes out the image he knows he doesn't want to. Instead he looks at the caption. "Mr. Morris Epps," but there's no man in the photo. All David finds, peering closer, is a small pair of empty shoes sitting side by side, on a flowered carpet, looking forlorn.

"Kind of a short man," David says.

"What?" Marco calls from the kitchen.

"Morris Epps. Where's the rest of him?"

Marco sticks his head around the wall, stares for a minute and laughs. "Oh that. Look in the shoes."

David, already feeling panicked, squints down at the photo. He sees a little pile of ashes spilling over the lip of the left shoe, like a sad punchline.

"That's the guy after he exploded," Marco yells. "What do they call it? It happens all the time; people just shoot up in flames, you know, all those people who go out to get a pack of cigarettes and never come back."

David pictures Michigan Avenue lined with smoking pairs of shoes, big black holes of heat, and when he gets in bed that night, pulling up against Marco, he waits to combust. A twister of steam will come winding out of his ears, a long plume of fire will barrel down his nostrils and in the morning his charred imprint will be etched against the sheets like a sheepish shroud of Turin.

"Marco?" he says watching the man who's flat on his back snoring slightly. "I'm too big for my bed," Marco had said last month, the first night they slept together, and now David sees the man's feet splayed over the edge of the mattress, the spade-shaped toes spread wide. "Marco," he says again, to himself, fanning his small, inflammable fingers across the sleeping chest. Somewhere a siren goes off. David gets up to look, drawing the curtain open, and watches a shadow streaking past, down Marco's fire escape. "It's me," he says, turning back to the bed, "your little tinderbox," but Marco only flips over onto his belly, the white strip of his back glowing in the moonlight like a large, corporeal thing that's indifferent to every danger.

In the morning David gets into his car and speeds all the way north up Lake Shore Drive, watching the tall buildings slowly shrink down into suburban bungalows. When he reaches the driveway of his house he sees Bobby aiming a garden hose at a bed of flowers. The water arches high in the air, like a cartoon rainbow.

"How was the conference?" Bobby asks. He comes over to the car and bends his head through the car window, giving David a quick kiss on the cheek. David tries to remember his story but all he sees are Marco's toes. "He's too big for his bed," he thinks.

"The usual?" Bobby helps.

"Yeah. Just me and eggheads. The hotel room looked out on a brick wall."

"You should have just driven home."

"It was too late. I didn't even get a dinner break. What's new here?"

Bobby takes him around to the back where their little garden is filled with newly turned plots, like a cemetery. "Here," Bobby says, "I've got the hydrangea bushes. They're going to be banked by tiger lilies and some begonia but I haven't decided about the shady part. Probably just impatiens, though I really want to stick to the perennials. Oh, and here's the big news: the painter's coming back tomorrow to fasten the grates."

"Get out the party hats," David says, staring back at the squat house that looks blinded, its windows glazed by a cataract of sunlight. "It's what we need now," Bobby had said, when they moved from San Francisco to Chicago, after they spent a blistering summer on North Clark Street, and at first David had agreed. The tree-lined street in Evanston was a calm backwater and their big bedroom under the alcove seemed like a hammock strung above the hedge rows out back. Bobby, who was tired, felt at home. Sometimes David found him looking at the old photos—pictures of shaggy, long-haired boys long gone. Sometimes he tried to picture Bobby's life before they met. He imagined the loft in the Mission filled with big, smoking bongs and loose-limbed men twirling in circles with their eyes closed, spinning out some sort of hippie dance that involved silky scarves and barking dogs. It was all before his time. When he came to San Francisco everyone was in mourning, wistful for their raucous pasts. "You're a nice boy," people told him, as he smiled like an icy madonna, and he knew he'd already been cheated out of something. Now, he thinks, he has a garden of his own.

"Smell this," Bobby says, bending over a big yellow bloom.

"They all smell the same," David says, running a finger down Bobby's cheek, slightly flushed and softly curved as a child's. He goes into the house and calls Marco, watching Bobby through the kitchen window. The phone rings twice and then Marco's machine clicks on.

"Leave a message if you want," Marco says, his words muffled by something he's eating. David hears him swallow hard and he pictures the big Adam's apple bobbing up and down. "Wait for the beep," Marco says, ripping off something with his teeth, but all David hears is the recorder whirring.

"What are you eating?" he asks the machine and then when he realizes there won't be a beep he whispers softly into the phone. "Marco, it's me." He listens as the tinny trace of his voice disappears, like something folding in on itself or a joke that no one understands.

That night David watches Bobby in bed; his curls are damp against his forehead and he moans softly when he rolls onto his side, pulling his long legs up against his chest.

"I'm still awake," David says, getting up and visiting all the places he tries to sleep. There's the couch in the guest room and the futon mat he sometimes unrolls in the hall; there's the pile of chair cushions he spreads against the floor of the bathtub, concocting his own cold cradle. The house, he knows, is conspiring against him and he tests each floorboard carefully, looking for the trap plank that will send him plummeting through space like a dumb skydiver. He goes outside and sits on their front stoop. A pitted half moon hangs behind the trees.

"What are you looking at?" David asks. He gets up, goes back inside, and leaves a note for Bobby. "Went for cigarettes," it says. Then he climbs in the car and starts driving. When he reaches the lake he unrolls the windows and watches himself in the rearview mirror; he likes to see his bangs wrap across his eyes. He lights a cigarette and blows smoke out his nose. "I'm a French boy," he says to himself, "I'm a frenchfried boy." The Chicago skyline is a sheet of lights. He smells perfume in the air and he sees a woman running out of an apartment, the strap of her black dress falling down over one bare shoulder. "Call me Pierre," David says. The radio is playing an old song: "and then," a man sings, "your heart will fly away."

On Marco's block he brakes in front of a fire hydrant and checks himself in the mirror again. "I likes what I sees," he says to himself, making his eyes go heavy-lidded and steely, remembering the leather boys on Halsted Street. Marco's door is locked but the lights are on and when he hammers on the door he's relieved when he sees the shadow of a head rearing up against the glass. "It's too small," he suddenly realizes but the man is already opening the screen door with one hand and pushing his red hair off a sweaty forehead with the other.

"Looking for Marco?" the stranger says, sounding resigned.

"Yes," David says.

The man shrugs and then laughs. "We're all waiting for Marco, we're lined up around the block, a whole conga line of us, driving by his window, checking to see if the lights are on. But who cares?" He looks hard at David. Then he does a double take, like someone playing to an audience, and cups the boy's face in his hand. "Oh la," he says, "you look like the first man I fell in love with."

Inside Marco's kitchen David sees the answering machine blinking, gorged with calls. "Where did he go?" he asks.

"Me," the man says, "I'm Oskar. I don't know where he went; out with someone, he's a busy man." He does a little pirouette and goes over to the kitchen table, grabbing a smoking joint. "Who cares though? Huh? I've got all night myself. I'm just careening through life."

David pictures a horde of men hammering at Marco's door, waiting for the beep, leaving silvery, breathless messages on the broken answering machine, listening to Marco rip off something with his teeth.

"And you?" the man asks.

"And me what?" David says. He looks at Oskar's chest. The man's black vest scoops under his pectorals like a bustier; his nipples look rough-eyed and raw. "What accent is that?" he asks, hearing something guttural in Oskar's throat.

"OK, I get it," Oskar says. "I'll let you do the interview. It's German, East German. Touché for you though, most people don't hear it." He stubs the joint and starts rifling through Marco's refrigerator, pulling out a can of juice. "I left when I was a kid. My aunt, who's still there, just sent me a photo. She's holding a big chunk of the wall in one hand like some freedom fighter, though she was the biggest commie commissar in town."

David pictures Oskar crawling over the ruins of the cracked wall, free at last to wear black leather. He crosses his eyes.

"What's the problem?" Oskar asks, pouring juice into a cup.

David looks in the man's eyes; he thinks they may be hazel but it's hard to see past the dilated pupils. "I had German relatives, too," he says. "Meet my grandmother the lampshade."

"Oh," Oskar says again. "In Germany they call it the catastrophe, like it's something fate had in mind."

David smiles. "Sure. The big faux pas. The what-were-we-thinking decades."

Oskar looks mournful. "Listen," he says, reaching over and putting his hand on the back of David's neck, like an apology. The juice in his other hand sloshes up over the rim of the cup. "You're in over your head here. You're probably a nice boy but you don't know Marco. You're not really even his type. Where did you meet him?"

"It was a freak accident," David says.

"And we know who the freak was." Oskar sits down at the kitchen table and starts drinking. "You're welcome to wait if you want. We'll wait together." David, standing just inside the door, deciding what to do, watches Oskar's hands circling the wet glass. What he notices are two purple nails. Is that fingernail polish, he wonders, and then he suddenly realizes that the nails are bruised black and blue, ready to peel off like scabs.

"Watch your fingers," he tells Oskar, turning toward the street and slamming the door hard behind him.

In the morning David sits in his tiny office, in the publishing company where he works as an assistant editor. He scratches at a manuscript page, adding the little carets and flags that he thinks of as a private code. He pictures himself hunched over the drafting table, a wizard in a pointed cap, someone trying to keep an old flame lit.

"I see you all in white," a psychic once told him. "You were a vestal virgin and then an oracle at Delphi. I see you leading the Jews out of Egypt."

"I was Moses?" he asked.

"No," she laughed. "You got lost somewhere in the desert. You're a nice boy."

When he picks up the phone to call Marco he knows he won't be there. The tape, though, is a new one. "This is Marco," Marco says but now he's drinking something, gulping it down hungrily, so that his words sound liquid. "Leave a message or don't."

Think cheerful, off-handed, devil-may-care, David tells himself. "How's every faggy thing?" he asks the machine. "This lambada's for you."

When he tries the number again that afternoon someone answers. "Hello," Oskar says. David hangs up, scared now. He remembers how Marco's lashes lie in a dark, spidery fringe against his cheeks when he sleeps and the way his veins glaze the underbelly of his arms, as delicate as the raised hairlines that web old porcelain. He thinks about the way the man slowly unbuttons his shirt, with one practiced hand, opening up his whole big body like someone who is too generous, or just careless, and how his thick fingers rake the black bangs back from his low forehead. Before David leaves work he tries again but now there is no answer and when he gets home the line is busy.

"Hi hun," Bobby says, coming in, his pants smeared with garden dirt. David grabs him and holds his face against Bobby's neck; he feels a pulsing vein and he sees them as two orphan boys, draped around each other in the hallway of the strange house. "I feel at home here," Bobby had said, when they debated the move and David, a cautious boy, understood him. At first he liked lying in their big bed, looking out at the tree tops, wrapped in sheets, pulling the whole house around him like a blanket. He would stand in the door of Bobby's studio, watching the man drawing pictures of dead friends and sunny landscapes, surrounded by pastels, lying in a nest of candy colors; he would stare at the happy Bobby who whistled softly as he drew the time before David, when he lived out of a shoulder bag and left lovers framed in windows, watching his nonchalant back trail a whiff of patchouli up and down Russian Hill. Now, David thought, we're safe. But then the house slowly turned on him. It watched him, sloe-eyed, when he walked up the front path and it buckled at night, so that David, lying in bed, listened to the place trying to shed its own skin.

When he tries Marco, again, after dinner, he decides to take what he gets. "Hullo?" Oskar answers.

"Where is he?" David asks, feeling tired.

"Who?"

"Marco, where's Marco. This is David, the one who came by last night."

"Oh," Oskar says, sighing. David pictures Marco handcuffed to a bedpost, a muzzle stuck in his red mouth. "The thing is, well, this is the thing," Oskar says, his voice fading away so that David realizes the man is crying. "The thing is he's gone."

David sees Bobby coming in through the back door, holding a big can of bug spray.

"I'm coming over now," he tells the phone, feeling all of his features slide over to one side of his face. When he opens his mouth he hears his head say something but it feels as tightly hinged as one of those talking hands, a bunched fist.

In the car David starts driving fast. He thinks of Bobby standing in the doorway, yelling something, and he lights a cigarette, watching the match flame up with a little sputter. He tries to remember something about Marco, a moment to save. What he remembers is the first time he saw the man, the time he expected to die. He was watching Marco's face in the window of a van that was barrelling down the road; he was fixed on the brown eyes in the windshield as he waited to be flattened in the middle of Fullerton Street.

"God," Marco had said, breaking in front of David's spellbound body and jumping out of the van. "You came out of nowhere."

David saw the long black bangs sticking out of the baseball cap and smelled the dope on the man's breath; he saw the soft dark hairs running up the bunched length of Marco's arms and a long tendon shooting into his shirtsleeves, like something racing to get somewhere.

"Are you OK?" Marco asked, holding him so that David felt puny.

"I need to sit down," he had said. When they got to Marco's apartment he knew what was going to happen. Marco's lips brushed against his and his tongue rimmed the inside of David's mouth. When it was over David thought this is the accident. He saw his heart flopping around on the floor like a grounded fish, bug-eyed and begging for air.

"I'd let you stay," Marco said, "but I'm too big for my bed."

"I'm fine," David said, running to his car, watching himself in the mirror, pushing his bangs out of his eyes, speeding down the street past the spot where he staged his own sacrifice, looking to see what he left behind.

The other things he remembers are just little pieces. He remembers the hot August evening they went out to a bar on Halsted Street. "Keep an eye on this," Marco told the bartender, tapping his glass of beer, a sweet bully; when he smiled he looked like a boy afraid of losing something. Two men in a corner whispered and laughed, pointing over to Marco.

"What do you do?" David asked him. "I mean for a living?"

Marco had shrugged, smiling again. This, David thought, is the smile you see on foreigners' faces. When they walked out onto the humid street two boys were kissing.

"Dangerous," Marco said, grinning. Back in the apartment Marco stuck his face under the kitchen faucet and hurled his wet head back, so drops went flying against the wall. "Oh man," he said, "that feels good." David had walked over and rubbed his lips against Marco's closed eyes, licking the lashes, and then he took the man's whole big tongue in his mouth. Now, David thought, I can't talk. Marco groaned a little. "You can't fake that," David had told himself, pushing his hair out of his face, wondering how he looked, thinking of himself as something unglued and very brave, as someone who wasn't afraid to die.

When David brakes in front of Marco's apartment he sees Oskar sitting on the front stoop, beside an overstuffed shoulder bag. His head is crowned by a big panama hat.

"Where is he?" David asks, calling from the car.

Oskar pushes the hat off his forehead and walks up to the curb. His red-rimmed eyes look glazed and one of them swells over a faint blue bruise.

"He had to get out of town, one of those deals that went bad. He's at his sister's, in St. Louis, and you're going to take me there. Right? Because I'm not in the mood to argue; we'll just get in the car and go. Right?"

David stares at Oskar's eye and tries to focus. A deal that went bad, he thinks, one of those deals.

"What's the address?" he asks.

"Oh sure," Oskar laughs. "The thing is you're not going to find him without me, I'm the only one with the treasure map. It's a group tour."

"Fine," David says, opening the car door. Oskar gets in and stretches his legs out in front of him. He wears big khaki shorts and his knees look as bony as an old man's.

"Listen," Oskar says, "neither one of us needs this but we're both in it now so let's not argue."

David shrugs. He stares back at Marco's apartment and he pictures the answering machine blinking, like one of those little black boxes people find in plane wrecks and play over again and again, listening for clues.

When they get outside Chicago they start passing through little towns. There are siloes and junkyards by the side of the road and sometimes clusters of trailers.

"I lived in one of those once," Oskar says. David stares straight ahead, following the yellow line in the middle of the road. Oskar prods his bruised eye with a finger. "I lived in a trailer in California," he says, "on the beach, with a man who once played Big Bird. In the Ice Capades. When I knew him, though, he was between jobs and a little cranky but when he got on skates you'd watch him cut up the ice and you'd see this other side of him. When he got sick he lay in the hospital bed with his bird drag on, propping cigarettes in the big beak, moulting like crazy. There was a layer of feathers flying around his bed when they wheeled him away. A real cutup."

"I'll bet," David says.

"Yeah. Me and Big Bird. Who knows? Before I met Marco I was seeing this kid in New York, a sixteen-year-old kid. We'd fuck in the front seat of his junked car, in the Bronx, and his mama would be hanging her head out of the apartment window above us, screaming 'Joey, dinner's ready.' Actually his mom was fine. We met and got along but I figured we'd end up side by side in the window ringing our hands, scanning the block for Joey, screaming for him to come home."

David looks at Oskar. He sees him wrapped around a boy, his snakey arms and legs pinning little Joey down, a rubbery octopus.

"What about Marco?" Oskar asks. "Did he ever kiss you?"

David sighs. "So we're gonna have like a slumber party?" he says. "Swap beauty secrets and stuff?" He remembers the way Marco's tongue nestled in his mouth, still as a pact. "Yes. He kissed me."

"Oh. Because he doesn't just kiss anyone. He's very picky about that, almost squeamish. He works up to his kisses and then he leaves you for dead. After he kissed me the first time everything else seemed pointless. I'd spend days thinking only about that kiss, thinking how could I keep going until the next one. I'd watch people on the street, going to their jobs or out to get groceries, and I'd wonder how they survived without that kiss."

"Yikes," David says. "Maybe just settle for a handshake next time." He thinks if he watches the road closely it will become a mantra, something soothing.

"The heart's gonna do what the heart's gonna do."

"Mine's attached to a brain."

"You're a chilly one," Oskar says. "Mr. Flipper. Really, though, you're just scared. Really you're a bigger poof than me."

David feels tired. He wonders if Oskar is improvising their route and he pictures them flying blindly down the dark highway, pitching headlong into a country he doesn't know. "I need to stretch," he says, pulling the car over to the side of the road and getting out. He sees a farmhouse lit up down the road; there's a clothesline strung with long dresses hanging like wraiths, empty and spineless. He hears Oskar crunching on the gravel road behind him and he suddenly feels cold; he imagines himself trussed by the side of the highway. He starts walking quietly toward the house.

"You know," Oskar calls behind him, "you have a right to be scared. But I don't have the time. I just hold my nose and dive in."

"Leave me alone," David yells back, jogging slowly toward the house now. He thinks he sees two people silhouetted in a window, bending toward each other, whispering something.

"You're not going to shake me," Oskar says, his voice sounding winded. When he pulls up to David, by the side of the house, he grabs the boy hard. David is surprised by how muscular the man suddenly feels. In the light from the window Oskar's face looks skeletal and fierce. "Want to hear a secret?"

"No," David says. He looks up at the window but he can't see the people inside. He wonders if they've gone off to eat dinner. They're spooning pot roast into each other's mouths, he thinks. Afterwards one will wash and one will dry, that's the kind of couple they are.

"I take Marco inside me without anything," Oskar says. "We don't use any condo-mints so I can feel his big dick all the way up me." David tries to pull away but Oskar has him pinned against the wall of the house. "I feel him shoot inside me until he fills me up, to the top. Here's the other secret. I myself will fuck anything but he will too." David turns his head so it's pressed against brick. The house is cold he thinks as he sees Oskar's face close in on his. When the man's lips crash against his own, grinding into him hard, he feels like something being branded.

Back in the car David drives fast.

"I'm sorry," Oskar says. "It's the ecstasy, it pumps you up until you blow."

David shrugs. "Forget it," he says, because now he knows what he is going to do. He watches the darkness outside the car window, looking for clues, but all he sees are patches of soupy fog that mass in front of the headlights and then disappear. Sometimes there's the outline of a tree, or another silo. Oskar sits with his hands tensed in his lap. "You don't know where we're going, do you?" David says.

"Sure I do. We're getting close, I can smell him." Oskar puts his hat back on his head, like someone preparing to arrive. "You know what makes him so attractive? Marco?"

"You remind me of someone," David says. "Maybe the Ancient Mariner, a man with one story."

"Whatever. It's the fact that he's so big. There's this thing about big dudes. You know they can kill you and it's an act of simple generosity that they don't."

"Uh-huh," David says, suddenly gripping the wheel hard. He sees a sudden spray of neon lights and a Mobil sign. "I'm getting some soda," he tells Oskar, parking by a gas pump and climbing out of the car again.

"I'm right behind you," Oskar says, following him into the brightly lit station. There's a tall man standing behind the counter and when he turns around David sees an American flag stretched across the front of his T-shirt. There's something written underneath it. "Try burning this, asshole," David reads.

Oskar props himself against the counter and looks at the T-shirt. "Got a match?" he asks David. The attendant stares at the two of them, like someone deciding what to do.

"You with stupid?" he asks David.

"No," David says. He stares at the wall of cigarettes stacked behind the man and then he turns around and walks outside, back toward the car. A fat man is pumping gas next to his car.

"You know how I got this big?" he asks David. "Too many English muffins with butter."

"English muffins," David echoes. He slides into his car and closes the door. He looks back at the station and sees Oskar talking to the attendant. He sees the attendant's mouth opening wide but he can't tell if he's laughing or shouting. This, he thinks, is what I'm going to do. He starts the car and guns the motor. Oskar is still standing with his back to the car, talking. David puts the car in drive, pulls away from the pump, and then he honks, so he sees Oskar's face turning toward him, caught in its moment of surprise.

When he gets home David finds some flowers lying on the front porch, their ripped roots trailing behind like tangled hair. The house is quiet, happy to have him alone. He climbs up the steep staircase and crawls into bed. "Now," he thinks, "I'll pretend to sleep." He stacks two pillows under his head and lies flat on his back. Something creaks. "Bobby?" he calls. He can see the moon through the window, staring back at him. For a moment he almost dozes but then he sits up in bed. "Is this," he thinks, "what I saw? Is this what I remember?"

He gets out of bed and walks back downstairs, onto the front stoop. He looks at the outline of the car, sitting in the driveway, and he sees Oskar's face turning toward him, shouting something. This, he knows, is what I saw. He gets back into the car and starts driving, heading up along the lake, watching the reflection of the blazing buildings in the water. He parks the car and walks toward the lake. The grey tide laps sluggishly against the gravely sand; David bends down and dips his hand into the water's mouth. He can see the dead moon looking at itself and he remembers Oskar running toward him. What I saw, he thinks, is the man's arms stretched out toward the car, and a little flicker of flames that started fanning out across the span of Oskar's fingers. They had sputtered like ten birthday candles and then started spurting, running down the length of his arms, shooting along the roadmap of his veins, engulfing him. He had watched Oskar's legs burning up slowly, trailing smoke as they tried to run, and he saw the man's head surrounded by a ring of fire, like a leaping wreath. When he ran out of the car, toward Oskar, everything was blazing. He thought that's all there is but suddenly the fire dipped down, and he found his friend's face again. "Oskar," he had called, "Oskar." The man tried to say something but David didn't hear. All he saw was Oskar's glowing face framed by big plumes, shining through its circle of fire, so for a moment he looked happy, like someone inventing his own shimmering new life.

HOT CHOCOLATE DRIPS

• BRIAN KIRKPATRICK •

When I proposed a feast for Valentine's Day, Colin flinched.
Nothing exotic, he said. None of your mother's recipes. No
curried garbanzo beans, no tamarind chutney. I did not realize
he paid attention to the things I served. I remember how he
pushed aside all the wonderful foods and piled his plate with
plain, dull rice, and how he gulped down pots of orange spice
tea. But it was to be our first Valentine's Day together, and I
promised I would keep in mind his sensitive Irish stomach.

During the three and a half months we dated, I waited patiently for Colin to invite me for dinner, and while I waited, I
tried to imagine what culinary skills Irish-American mothers
taught their sons. I had vague ideas about Irish cooking, but I
wanted to penetrate the food secrets Colin picked up. What
delicacies Colin's mother made when he was sick. He wanted to
talk about his '54 Buick Skylark, not food, and when I pressed
him, he told me he was American . . . not Irish. This insulted
me as if my mother and I were some kind of boat people. We
were Americans . . . we were from Oakland.

I began my shopping a month before the feast. The day I
drove Colin to Marin County, I had a mild fever just anticipating the scent of chocolate. I could never plan my trips to the
candy-making shop—they had to be spontaneous and carried
out with haste, otherwise my body would begin to shake and
could be calmed only by a mouthful of crystallized ginger, a
candy my mother made and packed for me in waxed-paper

wrappers. The thought of massive slabs of chocolate from Holland, Brussels, and Milan was too much to endure for more than a couple of hours.

I felt the same tension in my muscles that day as I did the time I raced home with Mr. Lapis on the seat beside me. He glared up from the cover of *Mandate* with his lapis lazuli eyes, and I almost hit a streetcar. I never mentioned a word of this passion to Colin.

At the candy shop, I leaned my hand on the glass case to cool my palm. I bought a rum raisin truffle. Colin asked if I needed to sit down and he slumped into an iron scroll chair. The salesgirl, assuming that one truffle was the limit of my purchase, shifted her attention to Colin, and she came out from behind the counter with a menu.

While Colin ordered his scone and tea, I began stacking ten-pound slabs of chocolate by the register. I grabbed two tins of Dutch processed cocoa. With my car key, I pried open one of the lids. I moistened my finger.

"Sir!" the salesgirl said.

"It's OK," I answered, "I'm buying it." Then I glanced at Colin. "We have so few safe pleasures left."

I dusted a large bottle of Indonesian vanilla extract on my Levi's, then opened it to sniff.

"Please," she said, "I will get in trouble."

"Colin, smell this . . . better than poppers ever were."

To ease her mind, I handed the girl my credit card. "And if you'll bag me two pounds of hazelnuts and a pound of pecans. . . ."

I settled into a chair opposite Colin. Pecans, I thought. "Make it two pounds." I could get my mother to make up a batch of hot spiced pecans. I guess I sat there for a while. Colin munched on his scone and I daydreamed about my mother making candy.

Before I entered kindergarten, my mother told me I had curry in my blood, and so, every time I had a cut on my finger or knee, I would lick and suck the wound waiting for my tongue to burn. I told her my blood was red—not yellow like the curries she mixed in her tiny marble bowl. She told me that if my blood were yellow, I'd have a temper no one could squelch. No, my little chili pepper, she said, you have the far rarer red curry like your father. All men in our family do. You want to taste everything, and your tongue will get you in trouble someday. Mother warned me. She said I'd frighten potential lovers, but that kind of talk to a four-year-old didn't mean much.

Colin's first words, or the first words I remember, came when he helped me load the car. "Who's going to eat all this stuff?" I closed the tailgate of my Honda Civic and cupped my hands around his ear. "You," I whispered. "You asked for chocolates for Valentine's Day." He tried to pull away, but I managed to plant a kiss on his neck. "What we don't have room for, I'll take over to the AIDS hospice. Nothing will go to waste. Don't worry. Now, do you want one more hit of vanilla before we start back?"

I wanted Valentine's Day to be perfect, and so I took a tablecloth to my mother to be dyed. She claimed that she was the best batik artist in the Bay Area. Better than any of those anorexic, blond Anglos. Well, that could have been true. I did know that her talent for creating colors far surpassed anyone at my local paint store.

When I arrived at her garage studio, I found that she had already spread out various red, orange, and purple powders on a worktable, and that she had mixed a few sample combinations. She wore a virgin pair of white overalls and a white T-shirt. Her silky black hair, with which she used to swat my father's chest when they were married, remained under her T-shirt and next to her caramel skin.

As a child, I would sit on a stool with my file of magazine pictures, and without a word between us, I would point to a bird, and she would mix colors. After a while, she'd look up and I would move the picture next to her mixing jar. We would shake our heads, and she would begin again. We did this for hours at a time, and not once did we name a color as if a word might have broken the spell.

That afternoon gray clouds slid over the garage skylights. I knew by the heat of the spotlights that she had been working some time. We nodded, and after the most fleeting hug, I pulled the tablecloth and my tropical flower book from a shopping bag.

"And did you bring his picture?" she asked.

How like my mother, so aware of the mood color sets in motion, to want our faces, Colin's and mine, near her mixing jar so that the tablecloth would be perfect.

I pulled a snapshot of Colin from my flower book.

She shook her head. "Bet he hasn't even tried the hair conditioner I gave him. Look at that orange, wiry mess."

But the mess, as my mother called it, I found erotic and hot. I like Colin's wildness. Sometimes I pleaded with him to give up his deodorant just for a weekend; however, the suggestion startled Colin, maybe repelled him a bit.

"I want that," I said with my finger on an epiphyllum, an orange-red blossom with an overlay of magenta that gave it a purple sheen.

"This is not going to be easy," she responded.

". . . and that . . . and that," I said as I flipped pages. After I had pointed to each and every color I wanted, and inserted markers, I slid the book between the jars and went off to a chair she kept in the corner. There was a small bookcase next to the chair and on the middle shelf, just where I had left it, my familiar copy of M.F.K. Fisher's *How to Cook a Wolf*.

Once, in the middle of her experiments, she turned and said, "Chandy, I hope you realize you owe me a ride to the candy shop."

Some time passed, and then she was finished. I knew that when I looked up and saw her pulling her black hair out from under her T-shirt. "Come see," she said as she brushed her hair.

Indeed, my mother had outperformed nature.

"Now," I said, "you'll want some quantity of those dyes." I dug down into the shopping bag. "These should be done, too," I added and produced packages of white sheets and pillowcases.

"Chandy, Chandy," she said. "Are you sure your boyfriend wants red passion sheets?"

"Father did," I answered. Both of us paused and remembered the time Father came home from a business trip and had Mother, despite the midnight hour, remove the bed sheets and replace them with red silk ones he pulled from his suitcase.

"Your father was not an American . . . he was a tropical bird. Tell me, what color sheets does Colin use? Blue is more what I picture."

"He hasn't invited me to see," I said.

"Oh," she murmured. "The affair is, what do they say, unconsummated."

"Mother, don't use that word."

"Yes, my sweet chili pepper, unconsummated."

Colin asked when the chocolates would be ready and I knew, finally, I had ignited a pilot light. I resisted asking how he and his lover, the one who had died the year before, celebrated the day of romance. A few times I noticed Colin wearing socks with teddy bears and hearts, and I knew enough to keep quiet.

"So, did you do any shopping yet?" I asked. "Did you notice how cards are getting sleazy again? Fewer safe sex cards this year . . . it might be a trend or a sign they used up everything funny about safe sex." I rambled on, filled the chilly air with words, and with them, hoped to cover over my original question about his getting me a gift.

Colin stopped, and he slipped the folded newspaper under his dog. He squatted next to the animal.

"I'm making you something," he said. "But it won't be anything to eat. And," he added, "it doesn't involve my mother."

"I want to make love so bad," I said and while Colin was still squatting, I moved around behind him and rubbed my crotch against the upper part of his back.

Colin stood quickly, and if I had not swung my head back, he would have smashed up against my chin. Then he turned to face me.

"Chandy, you're something. You want to do it in the street like a dog." He swooped into my face and left a kiss.

"More!" I demanded. "More!"

"Hell, no," Colin said. "We're on the street."

"Then let's go into this furniture store."

I thought of unspeakable pleasures on the mattresses and sofas and what we could do with our clothes still on. My tongue quivered, and I reached inside my pocket for a piece of crystallized ginger. I sucked hard on the candy until my spirits were calm again.

"What size ring do you wear?" I asked.

"Chandy, no jewelry, please. You shouldn't spend so much money."

"Silly, I'm going to make chocolate rings."

Later, in front of my apartment house, Colin and I hosed down my car. This was a weekly ritual ever since my mother told Colin that if he wanted to keep me, he should force me to exercise. She recommended tennis. Mother kept no secrets and she confessed to Colin that if she had been more diligent, if she had made a point of reserving tennis courts, Father would not have wandered off.

So, my six-year-old car got washed once a week. When it rained, we put on our slickers and threw the soapy sponges at each other. The poor car became the object of our displaced sexual energies. We scrubbed, we waxed, we buffed.

Most people, I suppose, obsessed with car maintenance think of their vehicle as a hobby or a lover. My Honda was transportation. Colin, on the other hand, was so involved in his white Skylark convertible that he did not even trust *himself*—he sent the car to an auto detailing place and paid big bucks to have it cleaned with toothbrushes.

"Your mother," Colin yelled above the vacuum cleaner, "called me and asked me about sheets."

I switched off the machine. "Can we quit yet?"

Colin untied the bandana he used for a headband and stuffed it in his pocket. "Tell her I don't need any."

"She's lonely, Colin. Don't you and your mother ever talk about bed linens? I hope you weren't abrupt."

"What's there to say about sheets? Oh, and she asked me if I could help her get you off—those were her words—*get you off* the ginger candies. She's convinced they aggravate your problem."

"Well, you can tell her next time she calls. . . ." I paused, and decided not to reveal any more of myself, or the ways Mother tried to manipulate me.

Mother imagined all kinds of problems. She thought I was too exotic to be popular with my peers. I can't explain just why she picked on the ginger candies at that point. She had made them for twenty-eight years, and she told me that even before I ate solid food, she was stuffing little chips of the candy in my mouth.

The Asian passions were in me—I could not help it. Mother, on the other hand, flaunted her American tastes for Colin's benefit. She invited us for an American celebration, Ground Hog

Day, a date, no doubt, she noticed on the calendar. She cooked bloody steaks on the grill, then smothered them with ketchup. Of course, if she had really been an American, she would have pulled up the coriander and turmeric she grew in the yard, and she would not have needed air freshener to mask the odor of cumin seeds in her kitchen. Colin seemed to appreciate her foray into American cuisine, her potato salad and frozen broccoli. He remembered to bring her flowers and she cooed through the meal like a teenager.

I was annoyed by the way Mother tried to seduce my boyfriend. The beef blood, the commercial mayonnaise, it was all so crude. She, of course, barely touched the flesh on her plate preferring, instead, the purity of a dry, boiled potato. Through the meal, I watched her as she moved her potato away from the trickle of blood until, eventually, she built a little dam with broccoli chunks.

I ignored the meat and potato salad, and I concentrated on the broccoli. I went back for seconds and thirds. Mother's campaign to prove how normal we were seemed a disaster, though from the way Colin looked at my mother, I knew she had stirred something sexual. He ate his steak as well as the one from her plate. Colin's green eyes glistened.

I had to consider the possibility that my spicy cooking was killing Colin's libido. The way Colin hugged my mother when we left—the way his hands moved ever so gently along her spine—proved that I hadn't imagined the evening. I needed to bring his attention back to me, to *my* spine, and so, shortly after that meal, I changed course and planned an Irish feast for my Colin.

I threw myself into the project with all the care I normally give to green chilies. I went to the library and took out books on Irish cooking. What a queer island. I had no idea what the things would taste like, and so I picked recipes by their names. Kidneys in their Overcoats. Boxty. Soused herrings. Brotchan Foltchep (a leek and oatmeal soup).

I took three days off from work, and spent one of them combing San Francisco for ingredients. Have you ever shopped for lamb kidneys? Not beef, *lamb*. Or held them in your hand? I rushed home and squeezed them. Then, I stuffed all the food into the refrigerator and shifted my attention to chocolate truffles. By midnight, Valentine's Eve, my nose, my elbows, even my beard had smudges of chocolate. I showered and went to bed.

The first thing I did the next morning was eat half a platter of chocolates. Then I got out of bed. The sun was halfway across the sky already, and on my answering machine I found two messages, Valentine greetings from Colin and someone selling life insurance.

The afternoon disappeared. I played a tape of Irish fiddle music, both sides twice, while I scrubbed potatoes and pounded out my Boxty bread. Irish whiskey, I discovered, was not for sissies. I kept a glass of it on the counter, and every time I tasted something, a slice of raw leek or a herring or a piece of potato peel, I washed it down with the whiskey.

Mother arrived finally. "What's that smell?" she said, holding the shopping bag with my tablecloth and sheets, heading straight for the oven.

"Kidneys in overcoats." I turned and waited for a compliment.

"You look pale like one of those pink Anglos." She ripped off a paper towel, held it under the faucet, and dabbed my forehead. Her hand gripped my jaw. "Let me see your tongue."

I escaped. I guess, by that point, I was not surprised she had cast aside my instructions and had used green and blue dyes for the tablecloth and sheets.

"Why can't you be normal?" she said. "You make kidneys for a romantic dinner. Your father, he ate light. All he wanted was an apricot and a few nuts and he could go on for hours." These last words she called from the bedroom where she put on the new sheets.

She was about to set the table, too, when I handed her a small box of chocolates. I nudged a rose water truffle into her mouth, then I pushed her out the door. She resisted. I pushed harder. Had she stayed a minute longer I would have confessed severe stomach cramps. A half hour before she arrived, the mass of chocolates, Irish whiskey, herring, raw potatoes and leeks had begun to roil in my gut.

I remembered not to place the chain on the door—Colin was

due in an hour—in fact, I left the door open a crack, then sidled over to the sofa.

I knew how I wanted to lay—in a fetal position on my side—and yet, I couldn't, not the way I was dressed in my silk shirt with the monkeys and my snug linen trousers. I would be a mess of wrinkles in minutes. So I eased myself down, stiff, flat on my back. I tugged my shirt and trousers until there were no folds of cloth under me. There I stayed, five minutes, ten minutes, twenty minutes. Ready, I kept telling myself, to jump up and begin the seduction I had planned for three months.

My stomach, my intestines, whatever it was that would not quiet down, got worse, and when Colin slipped through the door, I lost all vanity and I curled into a ball.

"Something's burning," he said and raced to the kitchen.

"No. Me!" I groaned.

My body shook when he leaned over and grazed my cheekbone and beard. He was so erotic. So maternal. He asked what he could do and I told him to get the silver tray with the chocolate rings out on the kitchen counter and to turn off the oven. He set the tray on the floor below me. And when I moved my head, I saw that the chocolate had melted. Colin picked up one of the red pin cushions and hot chocolate drips fell to the tray.

The whiskey in my stomach dissolved another herring and I clutched my knees. "I'm sorry the kidneys burned," I said.

But Colin had abandoned me and I realized he was on the telephone talking to Mother. No, he did not want her to come over. He said that several times. Firmly.

"Got a pen?" he asked.

I pointed to the top of the television.

I heard him repeat the names of various herbs and oils and ask her to spell them.

Colin cupped his hand over the speaking end. "She says it's serious." Then he jotted down a few more things and hung up.

"She wants me to make a paste," he said as he tried to unfurl me and spread my legs along the sofa.

"What paste?"

He told me to rest. He would need a few minutes. In my agony, I watched him pass between the kitchen and the bathroom, I saw him with small brown bottles, the ones my mother left in my medicine cabinet. I smelled camphor, valerian, rosemary. An odd combination, good enough to repel moths, perhaps. I began to wonder if Colin had gotten the names straight. How would he ever get the proportions right?

"I am not going to drink that stuff," I yelled out.

But Colin and Mother had other plans. He came back to the sofa with it in a dish, not a cup. He unbuttoned my shirt and unfastened my belt, pulled the trousers to my thighs.

"See? It's an ointment," he said. He dripped a small amount of the goo just below my ribs and began, with very cautious fingers, to massage the skin. He worked his way to my navel, then back up again. This went on for several minutes, back and forth, more goo each time.

My mother, for an unexplained reason, had prescribed a placebo. This, I was sure. Not that I was ready to ask Colin to stop. While his fingers had no effect on the toxic Irish food in my stomach, they did not make it worse, and had the fingers not been soaked in camphor oil, I might have leaned forward and kissed them.

"Better?" he asked forgetting where his fingers had been and pushing back the red hair on his forehead.

I would have lied right then if I had to.

"Not at all," I answered.

But instead of applying more ointment, he started to get up off his knees. He held his fingers up and looked around, and I guess because he couldn't find a towel, he rubbed them vigorously against my ribs.

Another call to Mother. With the receiver cradled against his neck, Colin returned. He dipped his fingers in the dish and started the massage again, this time with more pressure.

He described to her where he was. She gave him instructions and he moved below the navel.

"Lower, still?" he asked.

I knew her game. This had nothing to do with my cramps. Mother saw her chance to push the romance, and she acted quickly, no doubt, fearing that if Colin tasted the food, he, too would become an invalid. She probably regretted that we had not gotten to the bed, but at the same time, proud that at least one of us was without clothes. If only the herring and potatoes had not been fermenting in my bowels, if only I were in a romantic mood.

"I can't go much lower," Colin said, and I could well imagine Mother whispering into the phone, in her most sensuous voice, "Lower, lower."

CLUB FEET

• ADAM KLEIN •

My mother and I were both born with club feet. For thirteen years she wore a cast on her left leg, and I imagine the current stiffness in her gait is what she learned from wearing the cumbersome iron. Advances in surgery, and perhaps even in the casts themselves, enabled me to overcome my deformity in only three years of my childhood. I don't remember the stories my mother recalls of how I used my cast to bust open the door of my parents' bedroom, or how I loved to climb anything, and how I could swing that cast over any piece of furniture, always leaving a tear in upholstery, or scratches in the wood. I really don't remember it at all until I look down at my bare feet—a difference of three sizes between them. They're not handsome feet, but neither are they impaired in any way.

And I only mention the feet because no matter what other features I share in common with my mother, it is our feet, with the aberrations now corrected, that seem to express our bond most adequately. I remember rubbing calamine lotion into the cracked bottoms of her feet while she lay in bed watching Red Buttons or "The Honeymooners." She would say, "My son, the podiatrist."

Maybe I could have found some interest in that occupation if all the feet I encountered were as bad as hers, because I did enjoy bending back each of her claw-like toes, and pulling off the dead skin from her heels, and watching the cracked skin fill in with calamine. But her feet were particularly ravaged, not simply because of the long years they were bound in casts, but also because she never wore a closed shoe, wearing instead Dr. Scholl's sandals during the years of her compulsive gardening.

After the first surgery on my feet, the doctors explained to my parents that I might not ever walk with grace, that dancing was just about out of the question. I'm still unsure of whose determination, my mother's or my own, enables me to dance as gracefully as I do today. I suppose I'm lucky; there has always been a strong determination to conform in my family. There is always the possibility that my dancing has really nothing to do with determination, that it was merely the improved technology around club feet that is responsible for the miracle. Maybe, as my mother would come to accuse me, it all came too easy, I never had to suffer the way she did.

I'm afraid I've already misrepresented her. She would claim that, in fact, she had never suffered, that thirteen years of wearing that cast on her teenage leg that would never share the shapeliness of the other, were survival years, not years of vanity. The stories she told of her childhood were scarce as the food she had in her house. Her father had committed suicide during the Depression years; she was born a month after they'd found his body on a railroad track. She was born into a family with an older sister and three older brothers. All of the children were forced to help their mother provide.

When my mother tells a story, she tells it to make a point. Her stories are used to exemplify what she considers to be a suitable response to the inevitable difficulties of life. They are like the spotlit moments when a character in the Bible converses with God or an angel, and though she is not a religious woman, the analogy still fits—her stories always advance a moral. They are not stories that are told to engage the imagination; rather, they are used to correct what might have been imagined incorrectly.

So I am hesitant to talk about her past, to reiterate the few moments of her adolescence that she shared with me, enormously confident that her stories would not suffer by interpretation. Already I have betrayed her, but not without some justification. Betrayal, like our club feet, has always been a bond between us. But also, I believe that her stories are a part of my past.

Nevertheless, I will begin with a story of my own. I was fifteen years old, tall and too thin, with a horrible complexion, but still hoping that I might be considered beautiful by someone besides my mother. Even my parents shared this dream, and bought me clothes that I am now sure were out of their reach. My thirst for love was a challenge undertaken by the whole family, and my mother always had the name of one young girl or another who might fulfill the task of loving me. But at fifteen I was already striking out on my own.

We were living in Miami at the time, where my parents had moved just after my father had come back from the Korean War. He was a war photographer who kept his personal records of the carnage in old scrap books with rubber bands holding them closed. In Miami, they bought a house spacious enough to hide the army lockers he couldn't quite part with. These and his photographs were stored in the crawlspace with the hurricane supplies.

Their quiet residential experience wasn't mine. A flotilla escalated changes that had for years been occurring in Miami. By the time I was fifteen, my entire circle of friends was Cuban. We shared an obsession for clothes, social life, and for freedom. Throughout the city, warehouses were opened up as large dance clubs. There were always *quinces* to attend, coming out parties for fifteen-year-old Cuban girls, staged with more daring and more money than I'd ever seen at a bar mitzvah. Once I saw a girl lowered to the stage in a spacecraft, while a group of Cuban boys danced with glow-in-the-dark stars. Even the YMHA, where my parents had taught me to swim (I was four years old when they threw me into the pool), was converted to a Cuban nightclub.

It was at one of these clubs one night that I met Phil Marie. I saw him drawing a car on a napkin at the bar. He wore a Batman T-shirt under a jacket. He was beautiful and I walked up to him and I spoke to him. He was an artist whose concern was "the deception of the image." He was very straightforward in his work about deception; he cut Styrofoam to look like stones: slate, limestone, coral even. He would cover their surfaces with glue and pour sand over the cut mold. Then he would paint the forms. They always looked like new rocks. He was tied up when I met him, waiting to speak to the owner of the bar about an installation. He was hoping to install a faux waterfall. This was going to be a challenge, he told me, as he'd never created fake water before.

I let him charm me with the sketches he penned and passed to me, evaluating each one and tucking it away in my shirt pocket. "You'd make a great illustrator," I told him, but he took offense.

"My commercial work is rocks, but my drawings and paintings are fine art," he said firmly.

He'd gotten drunk waiting for the owner to emerge out of some back room, and had gone through a stack of napkins. The bartender finally suggested he try back again the following day. Reluctantly, he turned to me and asked me if I'd like to leave with him. Outside was the red Studebaker he drove. He told me he had no money except for that car. He loved that car. There were roses he'd left under the windshield wipers.

He was renting a small cottage in Coconut Grove. There was a dark path that led to it, and I remember thinking it was perfect for him, a real hideaway. He opened the screen door for me and we were on the porch under a torn, paper lantern. I remember him blindly kissing over my face and tearing the buttons on my shirt, and how, blindly, I kissed him back.

When we went inside, there was only a mattress and a couple of boxes he was using as a table. "Once I get some work in this city I'll be able to set this place up," he said. "In the meantime, it's just you and me and a bed."

"I don't need anything else," I told him, but of course I did.

I started to spend all my time with him. I brought him lunches, dinners, things he needed around the house. I thought nothing at the time about taking things from my parents' storage space. When they weren't home, I'd go into the crawlspace and blow the dust off their wedding gifts. There were lamps and pots and pans still in boxes, even the stereo my sister had left when she'd gone off to college. The night I brought that over, we listened to an album I'd found up there, *Music for Lovers*, compiled by Jackie Gleason. We danced together on the porch, and in the silence between songs we could hear the lizards scrambling through the dead leaves that had accumulated there.

Phil could stay in all day working on his paintings. I couldn't help it, to me they looked like illustrations. He took them directly from young boys' magazines. Paintings of fire trucks, sports cars, and airplanes. I'd walk in and find him with his work scattered in front of him, and he looked just like a boy himself. I was startled when he told me he was forty-one.

I would be sixteen in two weeks. When he suggested a party at the cottage, I was thrilled by the idea. "Invite your friends," he suggested.

Three days before the party, he told me, casually, that he of course had no money, but that he would make me something special. I financed the party by theft. I took liquor from my parents' bar, money from my mother's purse. I wanted all my friends to see how he'd gone all out for me. There were cheese spreads, crackers, breads, wine, pâté. I took a string of lights from my parents' storage and hung them from the trees in the yard. By the time the guests began to arrive, I was exhausted.

Phil did all the entertaining. He made sure glasses were filled. It didn't matter that he never bothered to refill my glass. I wasn't a guest. I was certainly independent enough to keep my own glass full.

The party seemed to be going on without me, and I was drunk enough to consider the possibility that that may have been happening all the time. No one seemed to notice when I laid down on the grass and fell asleep.

When I woke up, the lights I'd strung in the trees were turned off. The party had dispersed. I staggered up to the cottage and let myself in. Phil was naked on the bed with my friend Raul. They had a candle burning and the *Music for Lovers* record playing on the stolen stereo. I'd hoped for the comic moment when they'd both scramble for clothes, or tell me I was drunk and misinterpreting what I was seeing. But neither of them moved, except to turn and look at me, as though I was a maid who hadn't noticed the Do Not Disturb sign.

I guess I thought, if they're not going to be the spectacle I'll just have to do that, too. I started to grab up everything I'd stolen and brought to Phil. I pulled out the stereo and gathered up the bedside lamp, blankets, and chairs. And when it dawned on me that I could never carry it out of there, I left it all in the corner of the room like a surrogate me, an imposing totem of my generosity and their indebtedness.

When I lost my patience with Phil, I lost it for my parents and home life as well. It wasn't innocence, but some kind of faith I'd lost. I let my parents know I was miserable, but I kept my reasons from them. I told my friends the whole story, except the parts about my stealing all that stuff. I guess I didn't trust them with that blackmail material. No doubt, my mother would have trusted any source who claimed to know the truth about her fine china, missing then for at least a week.

My mother proffered comfort with one of her own stories, and I believe it was told with a number of intents, some of which she was unaware of. In retrospect, it seems her sharing this story was the way she tried to induce me to share mine. But I think she was skeptical that it would work, and so her story, by the end of her telling it, became something of a parable on the self-indulgence of suffering.

She began by claiming that she never felt pretty or desired by anyone. She was fifteen, and the cast on her leg had become more of a cage in which she lived.

It was her older sister, Evie, who first began to adorn herself with makeup and jewelry, and whose figure could make the plain dresses she wore receive undue attention. They were living in New York during World War II, and though men in uniform were a common sight, my mother thought of them all as young heroes, and she described a line of white-suited sailors with their perfect black shoes standing along the piers like a contingent of angels. She and Evie walked past them with a bag of groceries they were bringing home, and the men circled around Evie and took the bag from her hands, and with her burden lifted, they coaxed her down to the beach.

Three of the sailors, the most handsome of them, wanted to walk with Evie along the shore. My mother, with her iron cast, could barely manage to walk across the sand, and Evie asked her to stand by the rocks. The sailor with the grocery bag placed it down beside her and told my mother to keep her eye on it, then winked at her before he ran off to join the others at the surf.

She watched them disappear under the piers, and it was a long while before they returned. I can't imagine what she thought about while they were gone, perhaps that they had taken her sister to heaven. But when they returned, more than an hour later, she was still standing where they'd left her. There was sand on the men's uniforms and in her sister's hair, and after trudging up the beach, they were out of breath.

Before the sailor gathered up the sack of groceries to carry back to the house, he made an attempt to lift my mother up and spin her around. But while my mother had stood in the sun, the cast had grown searing hot, and when the sailor touched it, it scalded his hand. The others laughed as he clutched his hand between his legs, cursing and whining.

That same year, Evie got pregnant and disclosed to my mother that she wasn't sure who the father was and if it was the man she suspected it was, he was probably at sea. They went to my grandmother who found someone to perform the abortion and though Evie hemorrhaged, she eventually healed, but could not have children again.

My mother's embarrassment and suffering was temporary, like a hand withdrawn from a flame. But Evie's misery was like a cast for life, and made my mother's cast seem like a small inconvenience. In fact, my mother claimed her cast had protected her from devils disguised as angels.

I don't claim to have told the story the way she did. She was much more frugal with words. But I've told it the way I remembered it. I remember it as a story she benefited from by telling, and that is what makes me doubt she ever told it truthfully.

At the time, I certainly doubted that all misfortune has its benefits. I didn't think that my friend Raul might also be betrayed by my lover, and that would somehow compensate for my humiliation. I doubted, also, that every story deserves another story. My mother sat back with her arms folded across her stomach and waited. When she discovered my story was not forthcoming, she finally asked me why I had become so morbid. That was the term she used, not depressed, which was a word she would not fathom. That was a word for shrinks and people who depended on them.

I don't think it was in the spirit of rebellion that I concealed it from her. I think I believed then, as I do now, that some stories are our own, and that by telling them too soon, we limit their effect on us. I admit, I wanted to experience the full, protracted suffering I associated with the loss of a lover. I was also sure that my mother was not interested in understanding, but in remedying my problem. We sat at a deadlock; she urging my divulgence, me denying her, until she became exasperated and went in to bed.

My mother once said, "A mother knows everything." She meant for me to understand that that was her responsibility. I'll tell you how I luridly imagined what happened as a result of this precept: frustrated by my silence, she must have lain awake long after my father had fallen asleep, and some inkling of intuition or suspicion led her to believe that I possessed something that would answer her questions.

She waited until I had left the house before she began a thorough cleaning of my room. She found what she was looking for in my dresser, but she must have turned over several pungent jock straps, none of which were mine (at the time I had weekend employment at a Jewish country club where I was as able a locker room attendant as my mother was a housecleaner). In either case, I am still disturbed today by her oversight. Had she recognized the usage I made of those jocks, she might have been embarrassed from further inquiry. But rummaging further, she found the letter and it was the letter that enabled her to launch her inquisition without her having to imagine a thing.

She was setting the table for a game of mah-jongg. Her friends would be arriving in a couple of hours. She was filling ceramic bowls with candy and nuts. When I arrived home, she looked up as though she was startled, and perhaps she was; I'm sure she could not help but to have seen me differently.

But I saw something had changed in her, too. It was a look of shame that had irrepressibly risen to her surface. It was the shame she had denied by her storytelling.

"Do you want to tell me something?" she asked finally.

She came around the table and squeezed my arm. "You don't need to tell me," she said, and pulled the letter from an apron pocket.

I could easily re-create the argument that ensued, with both of us playing defensively, because arguments around the issue of privacy have never ceased for me, nor have the strategies changed. What I found most compelling was my mother's insistence that one must "fit in," that if I chose the life of a homosexual, I would be ostracized, singled out, kept apart.

And I imagined myself sitting alone on a beach somewhere,

sharing my mother's unvoiced humiliation while a muscle-bound cartoon kicked sand in my face. And I said to her, "Perhaps I will have to learn about devils disguised as angels."

Curfews were instituted in the belief that homosexuality existed only when practiced. These were desperate measures that I couldn't be bound by, and I remember pulling up in a car full of friends when the sun was coming up. My mother would be preparing my breakfast and about to wake me up when I would come in the front door, just ready to fall asleep. There were the tedious arguments that never broadened our understanding of each other. And then grudging silences.

You may wonder what my father's reaction to all this was. He was an imposing presence wearing massive suits from Big and Tall shops, but beneath the Mafia looks and dark glasses, he was really terrified by conflict. He wept when my mother showed him the letter, but refused her suggestion that he have a little talk with me. He was a traveling salesman and I never saw much of him. One day the phone rang. "How are you, Dad?" I asked. His voice was shaky and finally broke on the other end. He asked to speak to my mother. I remember sitting in the kitchen while she spoke to him on the phone.

"You did what?" I heard her asking. "What are we going to do now?" And finally I heard her say, "Then make an appointment with a psychiatrist and explain to your boss that you can still work while you see him."

"Your father's had a nervous breakdown," she said, "he walked out of a store with the equipment he'd just sold them."

His boss had already suspended him from further work until he was fully evaluated by a psychiatrist. I think we all sensed that there was no specific amount of time implied by this and, in fact, my father never did resume work for that company.

Not that he didn't conform to the wishes of his boss—he did seek out the counsel of a psychiatrist, and after each session defended himself against my mother's ire. For her, the whole thing was an embarrassment and I believe she felt that there was an analogy between a twisted mind and a twisted limb, and that a therapy should be first and foremost corrective.

"And what did you discover today?" she would ask him. "How much longer?"

And despite the fact that my father grew sullen and timid in response to these questions, his withdrawal and vagueness only assured her that his sessions were not working. It was only a month before she demanded his return to work. I heard them talking about it late one night after I had arrived home, silently unlocking the door, taking off my shoes, and drifting past their bedroom. I heard him sobbing, and stopped to listen.

"What can I say to Epstein?" I heard him ask, "I have nothing conclusive to bring him."

"Use that," she said, "tell him the therapy isn't working. Explain to him what was on your mind when you did it, not in detail, but tell him that your son is having problems and that you collapsed under the stress."

Their voices lowered and I could no longer hear them, even with my ear pressed to the door, but my mind was full of talk, and I urged myself to believe that I wasn't at the root of my father's collapse. For the first time I began to pity my father, fearing that he would lose the one opportunity he had to understand the real source of his anxiety, but I could not trust my pity, fearing that my mother may have clarified his problem in the clear terms that are characteristic of her stories.

I slept fretfully and was up when they awoke the next morning. My mother was laying out the clothes my father was to wear to his interview. He smiled at me, pitifully, from their bedroom doorway, then closed the door before he began putting on the prescribed suit. My mother was busy cutting grapefruits in the kitchen, and sprinkling sugar on each half.

I sat with them at the breakfast table. My mother tucked a bib over my father's shirt and tie. She complimented his barber who had trimmed his hair just a few days before. After he had eaten his grapefruit, and stood away from the table, she came up close to him and straightened his tie and held out the jacket for him to slip on. I hadn't seen that doting tenderness in years, and I felt strangely moved and terrified at the same time.

She came back to the table to clear away our dishes and her mood had already darkened. I waited to see if she would mention the interview, but she did not. Instead, she began talking about the neighbors whose homes she'd watch through the mirrored window in the living room. I already recognized that her stories about the neighbors were her roundabout way of confronting me. She asked me about the good-for-nothing son of

Mrs. Rosenbloom, who was growing pot plants along the side of their house. She'd watch his comings and goings with keen interest.

Finally she said, "The days of entertaining our neighbors are long gone. Every time Ruth speaks to me she wants to know about your father and you; she acts as though we're some kind of TV show—there for her entertainment."

For as long as I could remember, Ruth Rosenbloom had been the bane of my mother's existence. She'd once told me about the horrible affront Ruth had committed on the day of my bris. At the time, my parents had been friendly with the neighbors. They had just moved into their home. There are photographs of my parents entertaining the neighbors on the lawn, all of them with drinks in their hands and a grill smoking in the background. The neighbors had returned the gestures by helping with house repairs, and throughout my mother's pregnancy, they had urged her to take a less active role in the construction of a fence around their property. It was only in the middle of her eighth month that my mother could be convinced to put down her hammer and take on the role of supervisor. She remains proud of the fact that she saw the fence completed in her first two hours of labor pains; it was only then that she allowed my father to rush her to the hospital, with the neighbors in a caravan behind.

She claims that I was born without hesitancy, which surprises me even to this day. But then, my birth has been so mythologized by her, it seems more likely that this "anxiousness to enter the world" was merely a response to my early complaints at having been born at all. She has admitted, however, that I was an ugly baby, and that it was with horror that she recognized my turned feet.

The neighbors gathered outside the glass window to watch me, while my mother wept to my father that she was responsible for my deformity.

She remained inconsolable until my father sought a doctor's intervention. He assured her of the commonness of my condition, and that modern medicine had led us away from the primitive measures she had endured as a child, and though he doubted I would dance, he consoled her that my childhood would be normal and happy. His authority soothed her, and she was soon able to accept the congratulations from the neighbors who filed in around her bedside.

So of course, by the time of my circumcision, my neighbors were all fully aware of the fact that I was a child awaiting two surgeries, my penis and later my foot, and certainly they knew that I would wear a cast on my foot long before I wore a pair of baby shoes. And that is how Ruth made her grave mistake. She brought to the bris, as a gift, a pair of plain, white baby shoes.

Did this gift signify her hope for the future when my feet would no longer turn away from each other? My mother chose not to believe so, and from that point forward, she kept a firm distance from Ruth, and almost all the neighbors, as though they each possessed the same potential for ignorant or intentional malice, which she equated.

Her isolationism might have worked while I was younger, but while my father was unemployed and I was climbing out of my window in the middle of the night, my mother was certain the neighbors were collecting the information, waiting to humiliate her yet again. She suddenly had both of us to attend to, which took some of her attention off me and enabled me to resume a private life that had been prematurely, and far too brightly, illuminated. After all, I was no more rebellious than my peers, just more committed.

I discovered a drag club on Miami Beach that flaunted its tacky exoticism. The performers were either overweight or anorexic and desperately untalented. But I could watch them for hours, one after the other making a show of their failures, their alcoholism, and their bad attitudes. One could expect the bouncers to have to remove Lola from the stage; her numbers had the tendency to become an assault on the audience, baiting them to get up on stage and do a better job than she if they thought they could. And she would only leave the stage when the bartender or someone in the audience promised to buy her a drink.

I marveled at how they lived. As much as I doubted my parents' values, I imagined that at some point I would be forced to share them. It was these amateur drag shows that made me realize just how vast the world was. The drag queens challenged everything, not simply gender, but propriety as well. If they sensed they were being laughed at, they laughed along before the joke got too old.

I planned a party for a weekend when my parents were leaving town. It was my mother's prescription of a "rest cure" for my father. Though many of the guests had attended my birthday party at the cottage, the spirit of this party was radically different. I chose my parents' bedroom to act as an orgy room, replacing their reading lights with red bulbs. I moved the stereo from my bedroom into the living room and cleared the shelves of my mother's Kewpie collection and my father's Norman Rockwell ingots. I invited the guests to come in drag, to bring drugs and alcohol, and to bring pajamas if they wanted to sleep over.

I remember being tentative about the music and the noise, but my friends' assurances overrode my concern, at least temporarily. A once smoke-free environment had my eyes watering in just a few hours. Before I knew it, friends had invaded my parents' bar and medicine cabinet, traipsing around drunk and on Valium, dressing each other up and undressing each other in every corner of every room. I wandered around like a good hostess in one of my mother's aprons, offering cocktails to the guests and urging couples in various states of undress to use my parents' bedroom for the unholy acts.

Things died down by the early morning. Many of the guests had gone home, some were sleeping on the couches and floor and I found myself cleaning up bottles and overturned ashtrays, stray articles of clothing, and even some of my mother's makeup that someone had drawn from her bag in the bathroom. I was suddenly engulfed with anxiety, with fantasies of them arriving home early, and the facts of the bottles missing from their bar, their bedding wet with semen and spilled champagne, the smoke that seemed to linger even with the windows and doors open.

A friend of mine, Armando, held the trash bag open as we moved among the bodies. For each of my worries he offered tender assurances, and when the last bottle had been picked up, he led me toward my bedroom and urged me to sleep with him. When we turned on the bedroom light, some moans issued up from beneath the blankets.

"Let's try your parents' bed," he suggested. He took off his clothes and crawled over the filthy sheets. I joined him, naked, on their bed. There was a tremendous erotic charge in my final act of defilement. Our mouths and our chests came together, and I felt my feet digging into the velour spread piled at the foot of their bed. I looked into the eyes of the framed photograph of my mother; at the bottom of it she inscribed her dedication to my father and I whispered it in Armando's ear, "All my love to you, Baby."

I'd never walked in on my parents having sex, nor had I heard them. Sometimes I would find them in the morning asleep with the television still on and a pizza box with some leftover slices between them. My father expressed his affection through telling dirty jokes which my mother would respond to with feigned shock even though she would often have to remind him of the punch line. Having sex in their bed was not exciting because of any of their activity. If anything, I felt I was originating the "primal scene," and my excitement was generated from the idea of them walking in on me.

It is assuredly this erotic fixation with being discovered that prevented my housecleaning of the following day from perfectly masking the events of the night before. Certainly, I'd come close. I mopped and dusted, put everything back where it belonged, washed sheets and towels, and even went so far as to replace some of the bottles of alcohol in the bar. The rest, I hoped, would go unnoticed.

What I'd neglected, of course, was the makeup. Nothing was mentioned, however, until my father returned from his interview, visibly distraught as though he himself had been caught in some perverse act. He stood for a moment unsure in the doorway. If my mother hadn't been so quick to greet him, I suspect he would have quietly turned and fled.

"How did it go?" she demanded, her hands on her waist, as though she was defending something behind her.

"They've asked me not to come back," he said quietly. Then, in a moment I wish I hadn't observed, he looked at her tearfully and asked her, "Do you want me to leave?"

Even my mother looked awkward, her mouth searching out an expression comforting but firm.

"Come in," she said.

I snuck back into my bedroom while they talked in the

kitchen. Though I didn't want to hear them, I couldn't bring myself to drown them out completely with my records. I cannot claim surprise at hearing my name spoken in the exasperated and angry tone that by now seemed inherent in the name itself. It had been two weeks after the party and I had, to some extent, been waiting to be invoked. The fact that it was an unrelated matter, my father's unaccountable theft and its repercussions, did not surprise me either. By that time, it was impossible to localize a problem or blame. Nothing any of us did was discrete anymore.

I went to the record player and shut it off; I'd come to the last disc of Berg's *Lulu* and worried that its cacophonous climax might fuel their accusations of me. My mother had come a way in her assessment of my antisocial behavior; where I'd once been the flawed product of their conscientious upbringing, I now had taken on the dramatic proportions of a stranger, a boarder at whose mercy they had found themselves.

I overheard her assurances to my father that he was not to blame, he was not mad. It was I who needed help. If they continued to allow me to go on the way that I was going, the family (and this she pronounced like a curse) would rot from within. Perhaps my new position as a sort of stranger within the family made my parents naturally superstitious of me. It was this superstition that had suddenly driven my mother to believe in something she had never had faith in before: psychiatry.

True, she had gone along with my father's recommended therapy but the fact that it had failed to produce results for him supports my opinion that it was a leap of faith, the calling in of the witch doctor or exorcist, that my mother resorted to while scheduling an appointment for me. I was summoned to the kitchen where she offered me the time and date from a Post-it stuck to the tip of her finger. In another clinical gesture, she dangled her makeup bag before me and asked, "Do you want to tell me about this?"

"No," I answered, as there really was nothing to tell. Had she taken the jock straps from my drawer, I might have blushed. She had, in this case, allowed her imagination to fill in the gaps. The missing makeup and apparent return of some gouged and mutilated lipsticks and eyeshadows were the basis for her assumption that I had gone on to the next step of homosexual development: the inevitable renunciation of my gender. This theory went along with another of her theories, that using her makeup was an attempt on my part to mimic a heterosexual lifestyle. I'm still unsure as to whether she considered that hopeful.

As ludicrous as the accusations were, any attempt at refuting them on my part were viewed as understandable lies in the face of such shameful behavior. And so I tempered my responses, which were initially quite negative, and consented to their suggestion that I see the psychiatrist. After all, what could it hurt? And, I reminded myself, it was my mother and not I who had had such doubts about them.

One thing I was certain of was that my mother and I had gone as far as we could talking with each other. Everything we said seemed to have some other meaning beneath it, and in the same way that my mother walks with that stiffness from so many years in casts, I seem to maintain an inhibition in my language, finding in it an inherent, or possibly inherited quality of concealment.

I didn't believe that it was communication we were both attempting. It has taken this much time to recognize that we did not so much want to discover each other's secrets, but to find a way to reveal ourselves. I am sure now that we were both trapped in one of the great and painful deceits of language: an illusion of its transparency. It was this dream of nakedness that drove my mother to the most drastic, literal acts.

I began seeing the psychiatrist, a middle-aged Jewish woman with whom I felt immediately at home. And it was in her office with its dark wood and draperies, its shelf of leather-bound books including the complete standard edition of Freud's works, that I began to understand the significance of our club feet.

I was withdrawn from therapy at the crucial juncture when the conflict with my mother seemed best handled with her at one of the sessions. The therapist had asked both my parents to come to the session so as not to put my mother on the defensive. But from the moment I broached the news to them that Miriam and I felt we could accomplish a great deal if they would join me for just one session, my mother began to fear a setup.

"Why should I go?" she asked. "It's your problem."

Well, at one point it was my problem, then it was my father's problem, and now it's the witch doctor's problem, I thought. Anyway, with much resistance, she and my father drove me to her office and decided they would come in for a short while.

Before my mother sat down, she asked, "Have you made any progress with him?"

It was the first time that I saw my therapist caught off guard, but I had warned her. She urged them to sit down, and took a seat herself. She regained her composure then, asking my mother in a volley, what kind of progress she had expected.

While my mother turned uncomfortably in her chair, Miriam began speaking verbatim, as though a copy of Freud's famous letter to the mother of a homosexual son had been freshly drawn from its envelope. All the great lines were there: "it cannot be classified as an illness . . . a variation of the sexual function . . . many highly respected individuals of ancient and modern times . . ." But her most impressive performance came when, quoting Freud, she directed his appeal to my mother as though they were her words. "By asking me if I can help you, you mean, I suppose, if I can abolish homosexuality and make normal heterosexuality take its place. . . ." She shook her head sadly, explaining that my sexual preference was not the source of my conflicts. It is the family, she began to assert.

My mother was enraged. "You want to tell me what's normal?" she asked, her voice painfully restrained. "I suppose you regard it as normal the fact that he dresses like a woman? That he steals his father's underwear?"

I turned to watch my father as he drew a handkerchief from his pocket and wiped his eyes under his glasses. He reached out and took my mother's arm. "Let's go, honey," he said sniffling. She pulled away from him as though she was disgusted with everyone in the room.

"And what kind of role model do you think you are?" she asked my father scornfully, "sitting there crying. You've never had a moment of strength in your life."

"That's not fair," I interjected.

She gathered her purse and coat and stood up.

"What's not fair?" she asked. "All I wanted was for you to have a chance at a normal life. They'll never accept you. It's like you've chosen to be deformed. Why would anyone choose that for themselves?" I wanted to answer her, but she and my father were already at the door. "We won't be needing your services anymore," she informed Miriam, then slammed the door behind them. My heart was pounding with anger.

"She can't get over that foot of hers," I managed. And I told Miriam about her cast and how she'd never been able to admit how it had humiliated her and set her apart.

Miriam made the generous offer of seeing me again, free of charge. I told her I appreciated the offer, but didn't feel right about it, and when I left her office a half hour later I was surprised by the feeling of friendship that gripped my throat and made it hard to say goodbye.

I expected tension when I arrived home, but was surprised to find my parents dressing to go out for dinner. They urged me to dress quickly and join them. I thought, maybe Miriam had made an impression, maybe my mother was sorry for what she'd said or just felt better for saying it. But I thought, in the spirit of coexistence, it was better to accept and make concessions, or at least, not disturb the respite.

I was startled by my parents' suggestion that we order drinks before dinner, and more startled still when we continued drinking throughout the meal. An unfamiliar and desperate intimacy found its way into our nostalgia. My mother brought up the time when my father had come back from the Korean War, his body mottled with boils, and how she would have to force him to get undressed in front of her, and how she'd use a washcloth on his back but she couldn't be gentle enough. He would try to hide the fact that he was crying, but his whole body was shaking with his sobs. And he said to her that he was crying not because of the pain, but because no one had ever shown him so much care.

And my mother asked if I remembered the time I was in elementary school and I wanted a pair of platform shoes like the teacher, Mr. Gutierrez, wore and how she'd taken me out to get a pair even though she worried it would be bad for my feet. And I reminded her how my teacher, Mrs. O'Connor, Southern trash that she was, had asked me to model them for the whole class while she told them only fairies wore shoes like that. My mother had stood up to Mrs. O'Connor then and I was transferred to another class by the end of the day.

We told these stories as if to practice their success, to re-hearse the feelings of resolve they each provided. One of us would take up the threads the other had thrown out, and so it was like an intangible weaving that transpired between us, like the sewing up of a fabric that had been unraveling. And by the time we had eaten our desserts and my father had assured us he could drive the few blocks back home, I had forgotten along with them the ugliness of the afternoon, and the months that had led up to it, and I told my mother that she looked more beautiful than I had remembered her ever looking.

Late that evening, I sat listening to records in my room, feel-ing vaguely disquieted by our excursion to the restaurant, al-ready thinking about how I would tell Miriam if I were to see her again. In some way, our levity and nostalgia felt like a be-trayal of Miriam, as though the cloth we were weaving was to be put over our heads, blinding and deafening ourselves to what she had tried to say to my parents earlier that day.

I heard a quiet knocking at my door and my mother came into the room wearing her nightgown and slippers. She sat down next to me on the bed and took my hand in hers.

"You know," she said, "I just don't understand what it is you don't like about women." I pulled my hand from hers and sighed exasperatedly.

"Is it breasts?" she persisted, and this time I noticed her touching her own through the thin nightgown. "Are you wor-ried that you couldn't please a woman? I've seen you in the shower—now don't be shy with me—you have a nice body, there are a lot of women out there who would be happy to have a man like you."

I felt trapped suddenly, and she took my hand again.

"What could I have done to make you fear women so much?" And with her other hand she dropped the strap of her nightgown and began to pull my hand toward her. I stared at her breast first with disbelief, then revulsion.

I twisted my hand from hers, saying very slowly and clearly, "Please get out of here."

When I'd pulled my hand from hers, she seemed almost to awaken and her expression was awkward and confused. She pulled the strap up on her nightgown and padded silently from the room, and I, shaking, locked the door behind her.

* * *

Months later, I was back to my same old tricks. My parents had discontinued their curfews and inquiries. My father had opened his own business and both he and my mother were concentrated on that. I was left to pursue my own pleasures.

One night, there was a large drag party planned at one of the clubs and I'd decided to dress for the event. That afternoon, while my parents were at work at the store, I went through my mother's closet. I thought it would be amusing and a little perverse to go as my mother. I found what had to be one of the ugliest dresses in her wardrobe, some synthetic green and white checkered dress with gold decorative buttons up the front. I was carefully going through her drawers for underwear and stockings when I discovered a plastic bag with something inside it. I sat on the floor before her dresser and opened the bag up on my lap. There, as new as the day they were delivered, were the plain, white baby shoes Mrs. Rosenbloom had brought to my bris. I felt suddenly stricken, shocked that she had kept them all these years. I put the shoes back in their bag and into the dresser, and then, sadly, I hung the dress back on the rack.

DELIVERY

• MICHAEL LOWENTHAL •

Jason's sister is having a baby, and she wants him to deliver it for her. Becka is having a baby, and she's only eleven years old. Jason just turned eight himself, and he is sick of being the doctor. He is sick of not even being allowed into the fort until the last minute, and then having to reach up inside his sister. Jason wishes he could be the one having the baby.

Becka says he can't because he's a boy. Boys grow up to be doctors, she says. Then shouldn't the *father* be a boy, too? Jason wants to ask. Couldn't he at least be the father? But he knows he'll never get to because that's what Janine always plays. She's Becka's best friend and she gets whatever she wants.

Jason asks questions, trying to get out of his job. "Why do you need a doctor anyway?" he says.

"You always need a doctor, dummy," Becka says, from lying on her back on the blankets. Her brand new, cupcake-sized boobs point straight up into the air. "Otherwise the baby might not be safe."

Janine looks at him cross-eyed. "Yeah, dummy."

Jason hates it when Janine talks to him that way. *She's* the dummy, and she's just a year older than him. She hardly even has any boobs yet.

"It's just a stupid ping-pong ball," he says to get back at her.

"It's *not* a ping-pong ball," Becka insists, "it's a baby." She props herself up on her elbows and stares at him with narrowed eyes.

"Is not," Jason sneers.

"Is so."

"Is not."

Janine pushes him hard on the shoulder. "Is too so. It's a baby and we're gonna name him Patrick."

Jason laughs through his nose. "Patrick the ping-pong ball!" It's the stupidest thing he's ever heard. Then he sings, squeezing the words into the tune of "Rudolf the Red-nosed Reindeer": "Pa-trick, the ping-pong ball, was a stupid nothing but a ping-pong ball."

He's about to start another chorus when he sees Janine ready to smack him. He shuts up and concentrates on biting a hangnail from his pinkie.

"Fine, leave if you want," Becka says. "But you don't *ever* get to watch us make the babies again. Now get out." With that, she lies back flat on the blankets, and Janine crawls up beside her. They're both pretending he doesn't exist.

Jason just sits there without moving. He's trying to figure out if Becka's serious about not letting him watch them. Sometimes she just says stuff like that. You've got to test her, make her live up to her word.

Becka lifts up her head and peeks past Janine's shoulder. "I said, *get out!*"

She's serious, Jason decides. Too serious. He scrunches backwards out of the fort as quickly as he can. Outside, he sits on the carpet and sulks. He hates it when Becka gets mean. Now he won't have anything to do for the rest of the afternoon. Jason lies down flat on his stomach and stares through the forest of shaggy beige carpet fibers. It's not a forest, he decides, it's a field—neat rows of carpet plants ready for harvest. He bites off the end of one thread with his front teeth. It's dusty and strawlike. He spits it out.

Jason flips onto his back and stares at the ceiling. He can see the cracks where the sections of drywall come together, where the plaster has split and made the paint peel away. The cracks seem to pull wider every day. Jason thinks a lot about cracks: these ones, the ones girls have, the one Becka wants him to reach inside.

Jason wishes he understood more about girls and stuff. Becka keeps promising to explain but she's never going to get around to it. She spends all of her time now with Janine.

Jason can hear the girls moving around in the fort. Janine is talking in a low voice, trying to sound like a man, saying things like "Go faster now. Faster." She doesn't even know how to do it right, Jason thinks. No matter how low she makes her voice she still sounds like Janine. Like a girl.

It's too much for Jason to take. He pokes his head back under the wall of the fort. "OK. OK. I'll do it," he says. "I'll be the doctor. But only if I can still watch you make the babies first."

Janine rolls off of Becka and shrugs her shoulders meanly, as if to say too late, we don't want you now. But before she can open her mouth, Becka says, "It's a deal. But hurry up. We're almost done with the first part."

This is how they make the babies: Becka and Janine crawl into the fort. It's not a real fort, just their dad's poker table pushed into the corner of the family room, and a couple of chairs added on to make it longer. There are sheets and a big yellow tablecloth draped over so you can't see what's happening inside. Becka and Janine crawl in, one at a time because the entrance is between the legs of one of the chairs. It's so small that you have to lie down with your arms at your sides and scrunch you knees up and down like an inchworm.

Inside the fort, Becka and Janine manage to get all their clothes off, and they lie there next to each other. They lie there pressed against each other with no clothes on, just their skin everywhere. Jason is more used to it now, but in the beginning it was almost more than he could handle. Not the boobs so much, which look about the same naked as they do through a T-shirt. But between the legs, that's what Jason couldn't quite believe. Nothing but a line, that line that looked like a wrinkle at first, then opened up like his grandmother's toothless smile. And the hair. He still wonders how Janine can have curly hair there, when the stuff on her head is so straight. There's only a little of it, a wispy tuft on each side of the line, but it's darker than her bangs, darker than it should be.

Jason can't ask about these things. He's not allowed to talk while they're doing it. He can't even go all the way inside the fort during this part. They only let him lift up a corner of the tablecloth and stick his head underneath. Sometimes he's not sure he'd want to be any closer.

Becka begins by clenching and unclenching her fists, making soft little oohs and aahs like the sounds Jason hears sometimes from Mom and Dad's bedroom early on Sunday mornings. She squeezes her fists and her eyes at the same time, and her breathing gets deeper and deeper. When Becka's breathing is so deep that it sounds like she's sleeping, Janine rolls over and climbs on top of her. Janine climbs onto Becka like she's a saddle, sits on top and rubs her stomach on Becka's stomach. Or maybe the place below her stomach. Janine rubs up and back, then wriggles side to side. After just a few seconds she starts to sweat. She looks serious, almost angry, but Becka is still smiling.

Jason wonders where they learned how to do this. Who will tell him what *he's* supposed to do?

Then they kick Jason out. They say he has to do his own job: watching out for adults. Becka tries to convince him that it's a really important job, just as important as actually making babies, because if adults come everything is ruined. Jason knows they just want him out of the fort.

Jason sits on the daybed. They've made him leave for the good part as usual. He sits on the daybed and traces the flower patterns in the fabric with his fingers. He thinks about making up the flower pattern and how long it would take to paint it over and over and over onto the fabric. He wonders if they use this as a punishment, like writing on the blackboard after school: I will not chew gum I will not chew gum I will not. Maybe the fabric is made in the girls' jail, the way the men have to paint license plates.

Jason gets bored with the flower patterns and looks around the family room. There's Mom's exercise bike, Dad's paperweight collection. There are records by the stereo, mostly opera and other stupid stuff. The magazine rack, the TV set. Becka's Nintendo games and her abandoned dollhouse. It's supposed to be the family room, but not a single thing there belongs to him.

He looks at the flower pattern again but then he remembers how bored it just made him. He grabs the remote from the coffee table and thinks about turning on the TV. It must be almost time for Oprah. But Becka told him he couldn't watch TV. She said with all that sound he wouldn't be able to hear somebody coming down the stairs. Jason wonders what he would do if Mom or Dad walked down right this instant. Maybe nothing. Just let them come down. After all, *he* wouldn't get in trouble for just sitting there. Becka and Janine would be the ones to get caught. But he knows if they got caught, they could never play fort again. Then he would never find out what they do in the second part.

Becka and Janine are making noises inside the fort. Jason can't tell what they're talking about, but he thinks Becka is asking questions because Janine is saying something like "oh maybe, maybe." The tablecloth bulges out in the shape of a head and then collapses back to normal. They're moving around so much they might knock down the fort. Jason tries not to listen to them, tries to stop imagining what they do in there when he can't watch. Becka says they just keep rubbing, exactly like the part they let him see, but Jason knows there's something more. He's seen Hector try to climb on other dogs, and someone told him it's kind of like that.

There's a hand in Jason's lap. Between his legs, a hand squeezing on his wiener. It's his own hand. He didn't even mean to put it there, but now it's rubbing back and forth, up and down, in rhythm with the word Janine keeps repeating: maybe, maybe. "Maybe I *can* make babies," Jason is thinking. "Maybe I can teach myself how." His pants are down now and he is rubbing, rubbing, thinking this must be part of how you're supposed to do it.

Jason sees a ping-pong ball. It's rolled off the table and fallen to the carpet. He tries to look away but the ball is staring at him, watching him from the floor. He swears the ball is an eye looking at his own. Or not an eye, a head. A bald baby's head. Maybe Becka and Janine were right all along. It's not a ping-pong ball, it's a baby, a little baby that he could bring into this world.

Jason is shuffling across the family room, taking jerky steps with his pants around his ankles. He's moving as fast as he can and still stay quiet, moving toward his baby on the floor. When he picks it up, it is smooth in his fingers. It is round and smooth and new as a little egg. And it's in his mouth filling one cheek and then the other, in his mouth and all around his tongue. It is big, almost too big for his mouth, so big it fills him and makes his jaw stretch too far. His jawbones hurt but it feels good. Jason wants to stretch, wants to open up all the way.

It takes a few tries, and some poking with his middle finger. Some probing and some spreading of the rubbery skin. The ball is covered with spit and that helps him push it in. It makes him gasp at first and he loses all his breath. But then it's inside and he can feel it living in there. The ball is in Jason's crack, the crack where babies come from.

Jason shuffles back across the floor to the fort. He has to move carefully to keep the baby inside of him. He wants to show Becka and Janine that he was right, he can have a baby. He wants Becka to be the doctor, to deliver it. She owes it to him to trade parts this time.

He lies on his back and squirms his way between the chair legs, wriggles his shoulders until he's halfway inside the fort. Janine is kneeling down by Becka's stomach. Her hands are doing something but when she sees him she jumps away.

"Hey! Get out of here," Janine yells. She kicks her leg at him. "We're not ready yet. You're not allowed until we call."

Jason dodges her kick and squirms further inside the dark fort. "But *I'm* ready. I'm going to have *my* baby."

"You can't have a baby," Becka says. "You're a boy."

"I can so," Jason says. "I can so, and you know it. You have to deliver it."

He spreads his legs and grabs her hand and puts it down there. He grabs her hand and tries to push her fingers inside.

"Gross! Let go! You're being disgusting." Becka yanks her arm away and slaps his leg. "I'm going to tell on you. I'm going to tell Mom and Dad what you did."

"You will not!" Jason yells. "Or I'll tell them what *you* did. What you and Janine do every afternoon after school."

Becka slaps him again, harder this time. Jason kicks back at her, and then Janine gets in between them. All three are thrashing around, hitting each other. Thrashing around and getting tangled in the sheets. Something rips and suddenly it gets lighter inside the fort. One of the chairs topples over and lands on Jason's head. He starts to cry but it's not because his head hurts. He is crying because the baby has popped out of his hole. He tried, but he couldn't keep it inside. He's just a boy, that's what he'll always be. He shakes and sobs, thinking of everything he can never do.

There is no fort left now, just a table. Just a poker table and a pile of crumpled sheets. Becka and Janine have put their clothes back on, and picked up the chairs that had fallen over. They're standing over Jason, kicking him in the ribs to try to get him up.

"Come on stupid," Janine says. She kicks him again, lower, in the soft flesh of his stomach. "Get up and get dressed. Your parents might come down any second."

Becka stomps her foot. "Stop crying and get up or you'll get us all in trouble."

Jason lies there, curled in a fetal heap, holding his stomach so it doesn't hurt so much. He doesn't want to stop crying, doesn't want to pull up his pants. He wishes he could close his eyes and disappear.

"I'm going home," Janine announces. "I'm not going to let your dumb brother get me into trouble."

Becka grabs Janine's arm. "No. Wait."

"Let go!" Janine yanks free and starts walking to the utility room, to the back door. "You're as dumb as he is. Why'd you have to let him play?"

"Janine," Becka pleads. But Janine marches out the door and disappears.

Becka clenches her fists, helpless, kicks her shoes at the carpet. "I hate you," she yells, and Jason doesn't know if she's talking to him or to Janine.

Then she collapses onto the floor by the wrecked fort. At first she won't look at Jason, pretends he's not even there. She stares at the door where Janine left. She wrings her hands in the useless heap of sheets.

A door bangs somewhere upstairs. It's just the wind, but it startles Becka. She inches over and kneels on the rug alongside her brother. "Jason, come on," she says. "Jason, really. You have to get up." She puts her hand on his shoulder and shakes him. Then a second time, more gently.

He still doesn't move so she starts rubbing the shoulder, squeezing the muscles that curve the way up to his neck. It's been a long time since they've sat together, just the two of them, alone. She squeezes his small shoulders, massages them until Jason's sobs slow down to almost nothing. Becka uses her hand like a magic wand, makes it hover in circles just above his skin, tickling the soft blond down until he is covered with small goose bumps.

Jason likes the feeling, he likes being with his sister. It's Janine who always messes things up.

Jason stops crying altogether. He reaches for his pants and pulls them up to his waist, shimmies into them without lifting off the floor. There's a lump in his underwear, something hard and wet. It's the baby, the ball. It must have gotten caught in the fabric when it fell out.

Jason tugs the pants as high as they will go and buttons them, wedging the ball up against his crack. It is close to him now, near his skin, as close as it will ever get.

He lifts his head into Becka's lap, facing in towards her stomach. He reaches up and places his small hand inside her shirt, just below her belly button. The same place where Janine kicked him, where the spreading bruise now aches. Jason begins to rub Becka's stomach in circles, tiny at first and then growing larger, wishing he could make his own pain go away.

THE DAY CARMEN MAURA KISSED ME

• JAIME MANRIQUE •

I was on my way to the Algonquin Hotel to have a drink with my friend Luis whom I hadn't seen in several years. It was 4 P.M. in mid-June, and looking up the vertical canyons of midtown Manhattan, I saw a lead-colored, spooky mist engulfing the tops of the skyscrapers, threatening rain. As I passed Sardi's, my eyes snapped a group composition made of three men, TV cameras, and a woman. Living as I do in Times Square, I've become used to TV crews filming in the neighborhood around the clock. But the reason I slowed down my pace was that there were no curious people hanging around this particular TV crew. The four people were not students, either—they were people my age. I noticed, too, they spoke in Spanish, from Spain. Then, to my utter astonishment, I saw her: *la divina* Carmen Maura, as my friends and I called her. Almodóvar's superstar diva was taping a program with these men outside Sardi's. It's not like I'm not used to seeing movie stars in the flesh. O'Donnell's Bar, downstairs from where I live, rents frequently as a movie set. Just last week, coming home, I ran into Al Pacino filming in the cavernous watering hole. You could say I'm starstruck, though; and I'm the first to admit it was my love of the movies that lured me to America. But after ten years on Eighth Avenue and 43rd Street, I'm a jaded dude.

Carmen Maura, however, was something else. She was my favorite contemporary actress. I looked forward to her roles with the avidity of someone whose unadventurous life needs the vicarious thrills of the movies in order to feel fully alive. I adored her as Tina, the transsexual stage actress in *Law of Desire*. But what immortalized her in my pantheon of the divine was that moment in *Women on the Verge* when, putting on a perfectly straight Buster Keaton-face, she orders the girl with the cubist profile to serve spiked gazpacho to everyone in her living room. After I saw the movie, I fantasized carrying with me a thermos of gazpacho to offer a cup to (and put out of circulation) all the boring and obnoxious people I encountered in my humdrum routines.

Carmen stood on the sidewalk, under the restaurant's awning, speaking into a microphone, while the cameraman framed her face and Sardi's sign above her head.

Riveted, I stood to the side of the men and diagonally from the star, forming a triangle. For a moment, I fantasized I was directing the shoot. What's more, I felt jealous and resentful of the technicians working with Carmen. To me, they seemed common, unglamorous, undeserving of existing within range of the star's aura. I stayed there, soaking in her presence, thinking of my friends' reactions when I shared the news with them. Momentarily there was a break in the shooting and, getting brazen, I felt compelled to talk to her. The fact that I was dressed up to meet Luis at the Algonquin helped my confidence. I was wearing what I call my golf shoes, a white jacket, a green Hawaiian shirt and a white baseball cap that says Florida and shows two macaws kissing. Therefore, Carmen was unlikely to mistake me for a street bum.

As I took two tentative steps in her direction, I removed my sunglasses so that she could read all the emotions painted on my face. I smiled. Carmen's eyes were so huge, liquid and fiery, that the rest of the world ceased to exist. For an instant, I felt I existed alone in her tunnel vision. I saw her tense up, and an expression of bewilderment, unlike any I had seen her affect in the movies, showed in her face. Carmen exchanged looks with her men, who became very alert, ready to defend their star from any danger or awkwardness.

"Carmen," I popped, in Spanish. "I love your movies. You've given me so much happiness and I want to thank you for it."

The star's full-toothed smile took me aback. Her men smiled, too, and went back to loading their camera or whatever they were doing.

"We're taping a show for Spanish television," Carmen said. She was wearing a short white skirt, and a turquoise silk blouse and red pumps, and her Lulu hair was just like in *Women on the Verge*, except a bit longer. Her lips and fingernails were painted an intense red, and her face was very powdered. Extremely fine blonde fuzz added a feline touch to her long, sleek cheeks. "This is where *Women on the Verge* received an award," she was saying as I landed back on earth.

A momentary silence ensued, and we stood face to face, inches away from each other. Her poise and her ease and her friendliness were totally disarming, but suddenly I couldn't help feeling anxious. I decided to finish the encounter before I did something silly or made her yawn. It seemed ridiculous to ask her for an autograph so, as a goodbye, I babbled, "You're the greatest actress in the contemporary cinema." That somehow wasn't enough, did not convey the depth of my emotions. So I added, "You're the most sublime creature that ever walked the face of the earth."

Any reserve she may have had left, melted. Diamond beams flashed in her coal-black eyes, which were huge pearls into which I could read volumes.

"*Ala!*" she exclaimed, an expression that means everything and nothing. Before I realized what was happening, Carmen glided toward me, grabbed my chin and kissed me on the cheek, to the left of my lips.

I bowed, Japanese style (Heaven knows why!) and sprinted down the street. At the corner of Broadway and 44th, I turned around and saw that Carmen and her men had resumed their taping. My heart wanted to burst through my chest. I was out of breath, almost hyperventilating. I felt strangely elated. Aware of the imbecilic smile I must have had painted on my face, I put on my sunglasses. Although the Don't Walk sign was on, I crossed the street. A speeding taxi missed me by half an inch, but I didn't care—at that moment I would have sat smiling on the electric chair. Standing at the island in the middle of Broadway and Seventh Avenue, I had to stop for a moment to recollect where I was going and why.

"Wait till Luis hears about this," I thought.

My friend Luis is a filmmaker and a movie nut; it was our
love of the movies that had brought us together. He had been
educated in the States, where he graduated in filmmaking at
UCLA. We had met in Bogotá, in the early '70s. I made my living at that time reviewing movies and lecturing about the history of the cinema at the Colombian Cinémathèque. Luis, who
was wealthy and didn't have to work, published a film magazine
and made documentaries. We were leftists (although we both
despised the Moscow-oriented Stalinist Colombian left),
smoked a lot of Santa Marta Gold, ate pounds of mushrooms,
and it wasn't unusual for us to see three or four movies a
day. We were the angry young men of the Colombian cinema;
we had declared war on the older generation of Colombian
film-makers whom we considered utterly mediocre and bour-
geois. I'm speaking, in other words, of my youth. Later I moved
to Europe and even later to New York where I now made a living as a college professor. Nowadays I'm haunted by the Argen-
tinean refrain: "In their youth they throw bombs; in their
forties, they become firefighters." Luis, on the other hand, had
remained in Colombia where he continued making documentaries and feature films that were distributed in Latin America but
had never been released in the States. Slowly, we had drifted
apart. He never called me anymore when he was in New York.
But this morning, when I had heard his voice, the years in between had been obliterated in one blow and I had joyously accepted his invitation to meet for drinks at the Algonquin like we
used to do in the old times when we dressed in jackets and ties
so we could sit in the bar and watch the film critics, movie directors, and stars whom we idolized and who frequented the
place at that time.

It began to sprinkle heavily when I was about a couple of
hundred yards from the hotel's awning. I broke into a fast sprint
in order not to mess up my jacket and shoes.

The last time I had been in the Algonquin had been to meet
Luis. I felt like I was walking into a scene of the past. Maybe
the crimson carpet was new, but the rest of the place was just
as dark and quaintly plush, as I remembered it. I told the waiter
I was meeting a friend for drinks. There were a few people in
the vast room. I scanned the faces looking for Luis. The times
had changed, indeed: I saw a couple of kids in shorts and

T-shirts drinking beer and munching peanuts. But I couldn't find Luis. I was about to ask for a table when a woman waved at me. I waved back as a polite reflex. When she smiled, I recognized her: it was Luis, I mean Luisa, as he was called in drag. I forgot to mention that even though Luis is heterosexual and has lived with a girlfriend for a long time, he is a militant drag artist.

Blushing, I said to the waiter, "That's my party."

Luisa offered me her hand, which I judged would be inappropriate to shake, so I bowed, kissing the long fingers which reminded me of porcelain pencils.

"You look like a Florida tourist in Disneyland," Luisa said in English, the language in which we communicated in the States. In this regard we were like the nineteenth-century Russians who spoke French among themselves.

"Guess who I just met," I said, taking the other chair.

"Let me guess. You have stars in your eyes—the ghost of D. W. Griffith."

"You're as close as from here to the moon," I said noticing the waiter standing between us. We both ordered Classic Cokes and this, too, was a sign of how much we and the times had changed. I told him.

"Was Almodóvar with her?" Luisa asked, reaching for a peanut.

Of course neither Luis nor Luisa would have been thrilled by my encounter. I remembered they both worshipped film directors; whereas for me, the star was everything. I felt disappointed. In my short memory, I had thought running into Carmen Maura was the most fortuitous coincidence that could have happened before meeting my old friend.

I shook my head fully exasperated. "She was taping a program with some guys for Spanish television." I desperately wanted to change the subject. Luisa chewed the peanut interminably. There was nothing effeminate about Luis when he was in drag. I can easily spot transvestites because of their theatricality and ultra-feminine gestures. But Luisa behaved like Luis: reserved, parsimonious in gesture, and with exquisite aristocratic elegance. She wore brown alligator boots, a long banana-colored skirt, a wide black snake belt around the small waist, and a long-sleeved blouse that closed at the neck with an eighteenth-century school of Quito silver brooch. The chestnut mane of hair was long and flowed all the way to her fake bust. It helped that Luis was extremely skinny and that his features were delicate and that he had a marvelously rosy complexion. His jade-colored eyes, framed by profuse pale lashes, were utterly beguiling. Luisa could have been mistaken for a structrualist pre-Columbian expert, or an Amazonian anthropologist, or a lady photo-journalist who photographed ancient cities in Yemen or some place like that. It took me a few seconds to remember the dynamics of our friendship: Luis and Luisa were the passive ones, the listeners who laughed at my jokes. I was their court jester.

Obviously I had gotten out of the Carmen Maura incident all the mileage I was going to get. I was rescued from my predicament by the waiter who set the Cokes down, asked us whether we wanted anything else, and left mortified by our drinking habits.

Instead of asking about our friends in common back in Colombia, I began with the most generalized question I could think of, "So what's the gossip?"

"I can't go back to Colombia," Luisa said with a twinge of sadness in her voice. She sipped her Coke to give me time to digest the news. "I had to get out of there in a hurry. I was in the middle of shooting a movie. Can you imagine the timing of these people!" Luisa reached for her big straw pocketbook and pulled out a small wooden box. It looked like one of those boxes where guava wedges wrapped in banana leaves are packed for export, except that it was painted black. She set the box between our glasses.

"It's a box for *bocadillos*. Is it for me?" I asked.

"No, it's for me. But open it," she prodded me.

Suddenly the box looked creepy, weirding me out. "What is it? A bomb?"

Luisa teased my curiosity cruelly, with her characteristic gothic humor. "You're not even warm. Just open it."

"No, you open it," I said, thinking she was about to play one of her nasty jokes on me.

"Okay," Luisa acquiesced, removing the top of the box.

Inside the box there was a crudely made replica of Luisa. Now I got it: it was supposed to be a small coffin, and something like dried ketchup was generously splashed over the little doll.

"That's real blood," Luisa said pointing at the red stuff.

"What the fuck is that supposed to mean?" I asked, horrified.

"Have you become such a gringo that you don't know what's going on in Colombia?" Luisa wanted to know.

"I read the papers," I said, shrugging. "I know paramilitary groups are killing prominent members of the opposition. Furthermore," I continued with my recitation to show Luisa I was still a Colombian through and through, "I know they're killing left-wing sympathizers and outspoken liberals. I keep in touch," I said, as if to absolve myself of all guilt. And yet, it just blew my mind to even think that Luisa might have become a leftist. If we had resisted the temptation back in the early '70s when the pressure had been intense, I refused to accept that twenty years later Luisa had finally succumbed to Marxism-Leninism. On the other hand, I had heard of people in Colombia who had become socialists just out of exasperation with the telephone company.

"First they call you. And they say something like, 'We saw your wife yesterday in the supermarket.' Or, 'we know at what time your little son comes home from school.' That's the first warning. Then they send you a blank telegram. And finally, you receive this little coffin, which means you have forty-eight hours to get the hell out before they pop you," she explained.

I felt nauseous. "Do you mind?" I asked, taking the top of the box and covering it. Next I gulped down half of my Coke. I looked around: Kathleen Turner was now seated at the table nearest to us. She was accompanied by an equally famous journalist. In the past, we would have been dizzy at the proximity of these luminaries; we would have sat there eyeing them, imagining their conversation, reviewing what we knew about them.

"But why did they send this . . . thing to you? Have you become a member of the Party?"

"I hope never to sink that low," Luisa smirked.

"Then why?"

"Those creeps are our moral majority. They hate communists, liberals, non-conformists, and homosexuals."

"But you're no gay."

"Of course not. But you tell them that. You try to explain to them that I dress in drag because of . . . artistic necessity. Just like Duchamp did. And Chaplin."

"I hear Muammar Qaddafi loves to dress in drag," I said, realizing immediately how inappropriate my remark was.

Luisa smiled. "He must do it for religious reasons, or something like that."

"So what are you going to do?"

"I'm going to Spain for a while. I'll look up Carmen Maura and say hello for you when I'm in Madrid," he teased me. "Sylvia will meet me there in a few weeks," he added, referring to his longtime girlfriend. "She had to stay behind to wrap up my affairs. Then we'll wait a year or two until the situation blows over. I don't think I could live permanently abroad. Colombia is home for me."

Becoming defensive, I said, "But you can't blame me for not living there. It sounds like I would have been one of their first targets, don't you think? I'd rather be a homeless artist than a dead hero."

Luisa sighed before she took a long sip. "Tell me about you. Are you happy? What have you been up to all these years?"

"You'll have to wait until I write my autobiography," I joked. Becoming serious, I thought: How could I make her understand my present life? A life so different, so far removed from all that stuff? She probably could see for herself that New York had become a third-world capital, like Bogotá; and America a class society, like Colombia. But how could I explain my new interests nowadays: body-building, a vegetarian diet, abstinence from sex, nicotine, and most mood altering substances? How could I explain that my current friends were not into revolution, not into changing the world, but into bioenergetics, rebirthing, Zen, Buddhism, healing groups, Quaker meetings, *santeria*, witchcraft studies, neo-paganism, and other New Age phenomena?

We did go on to lighter subjects as we consumed a few Classic Cokes. We gossiped about old acquaintances and friends in common, the Colombian film industry, the despised enemies of the past, and our favorite new movies. We agreed to meet for a farewell movie before Luisa left for Europe.

It was past six o'clock when we left the Algonquin, which by then was abuzz with all kinds of artistic and quasi-artistic people talking deals.

It has stopped raining, and the rain had washed away the layers of dust and papers that had accumulated since the last summer shower. The oppressive mist had lifted, too, and the worst of the dreaded rush hour was over so that although Manhattan was alive with the promise of night's splendors, the atmosphere felt almost relaxed. Or maybe it was just my mood.

At the corner of Avenue of the Americas, we hailed a cab. I kissed Luisa on both cheeks, closed her door, and waved goodbye as her taxi disappeared in the uptown direction. I felt rejuvenated. It cheered me to realize that the affection for my friend was intact and that we'd probably go on meeting for many more years. I meandered across town, enjoying the nippy air, and the pinkish glow of the bald sky over the metropolis. The sun must have hovered someplace over the Hudson, but night seemed to be pushing not far behind it. The lighted buildings and billboards blazed like a high-tech aurora borealis. As I passed Sardi's, I noticed its emerald green sign, and mailbox next to which I had stood watching Carmen, and the lamppost next to it, which now projected a circular beam of red-gold light under which I bathed, basting. I was about to continue on my way when, looking across the street, I spotted Carmen and her men still shooting their program. I stood still, becoming aware of the street separating us and the cars streaming by, and the slick Manhattanites, and the pristine tourists hanging in front of the theaters that lined 44th Street. And none of these people were interested in *my* Carmen. It was as if on the screen she had been created for all people, all over the world, but in the streets of Manhattan she was visible only to my eyes. I also knew that the magic of the moment when we first met was past; that it would have been inappropriate to interrupt her now, or to say hello, or to remind her that just a couple of hours ago she had kissed me. As if to snap the picture forever, I closed my eyes upon the scene and then I started walking toward home, without once looking back.

I crossed Eighth Avenue. As I passed in front of Paradise Alley, the porno palace next door to O'Donnell's Bar, the score or so of crack addicts hanging out in front of my place of residence were no longer hideous to me. This evening I accepted them as

the evil spirits necessary in all fairy tales. Pity arose in
for them. In their dead angry eyes, I heard their hop
and suddenly they seemed as doomed and tragic as th
who were being wiped out back home. The man and the
woman smoking crack in front of my door moved reluctantly as
I opened it and leaped over the puddle of piss that the rain had
not washed away. Taking the steps two at a time, I felt happy
and sad in the same breath. It was a new sensation, this happy/
sad feeling I experienced. It was sadness for all that was sad in
this wide, mysterious world we tread upon; and it was the unreasonable happiness produced by the tinsel gleam of the glamorous dreams that had brought me to America and for which I
had had to wait for many years before briefly, heart-breaking in
their fleetingness, they became real.

SOME THREADS THROUGH THE MEDINA

• RICHARD MCCANN •

When I left home, I made up this lie: I told everyone my father was French.

Français.

I said he was the son of a prominent French family which, for obscure reasons, had settled itself in Rabat, Morocco. *Une famille du haut monde. Une famille de fortune aisée.*

I said I was born in Rabat, too, although of course we all fled when the revolution began. *Dans un temps où tout était perdu. Une époque douloureux.*

If people asked about my mother, I said she was a divorced socialite, an American, whom my father had met and married during a sojourn in New York City. Her name was Maria Dolores, which, translated, means "Mother of Sorrows." She had what people called "Spanish eyes," like Gene Tierney in *Leave Her to Heaven. C'est amusant, n'est-ce-pas?*

I have never been to Rabat.

But I have been to Ceuta, although by then my father had been dead ten years. He died in a car crash near Johnstown, Pennsylvania, where he had gone to sell machine parts to a zipper factory. By then, my mother had taken to her room, where she devoted herself to the lyrical mysteries of the big band music that issued endlessly from her bedside radio. When she drank, even the silence around her said *Save me.*

As for me, I sat in the dining nook of that suburban house,

practicing a foreign language—*Je voudrais . . . je suis . . . je suis. . . .*

One night, I was playing Edith Piaf records in the basement. When I came upstairs, I found my mother in the living room, sitting in front of the TV, watching an argument on *The David Frost Show.*

"Good lord," she said, looking up at me. "Do you have to play those records?"

She reached for her drink. "Just promise me one thing," she said. "Promise me you won't become a homosexual."

In retrospect, of course, I see that I had already begun sounding like a homosexual, even though I hated them.

Ten years later, I was in a bar in Torremolinos, where the drunk German beside me kept repeating, *The self is a house you carry with you, The self is a house you carry to the moon. . . .*

I thought, *Sure.* That's when I hitched a ride to Algeciras, even though my mother was dead by then, because I wanted to prove that I could leave home.

I took the ferry to Ceuta. And the next morning, from Ceuta, I traveled onward in a broken-down Mercedes taxi, the driver smuggling Dior bed sheets beneath the backseat, to Tetuan and Tangiers. *Would the gentleman care to stop for tea?* the driver kept inquiring as we passed through villages deserted to sheep. *Would the gentleman care. . . .* We passed three women on the roadside, squatting over an opened suitcase, arguing over a hand mirror. We crossed a bridge where two soldiers with machine guns were guarding a man who was standing with his white caftan lifted to his waist, peeing into the river. When we stopped for gas, children besieged us. *Would the gentleman care . . . Would the gentleman care. . . .*

By the time we reached Tangiers, I was so fatigued by the assault of newness that I knew I could not fend off the Arab guides who seemed to loiter everywhere—bus stations, markets, hotel lobbies—hoping to catch the eyes of befuddled and frightened tourists, to whom they then bound themselves for days, and so, the second I stepped from the taxi, I allowed myself to be taken up at once by one of them, who, in what seemed a quick moment of cunning, grabbed my suitcase from my hand, vowed his loyalty and his services, and walked promptly up an alleyway dead-ending at a shabby pink stucco palace, the Hôtel du Roi. I followed.

His name was Mohammed. He was eighteen.

He showed me through the medina. "Does one enjoy the taste of these?" he asked, gravely touching a garland of figs. "Does one have an interest in local crafts? In Roman mosaics?" "Does one admire songbirds?" He showed me how carpet weavers unspooled their coarse bright threads and strung them through eyelets affixed to old planks and stone walls, so that they ran shoulder-high from stall to stall through all the twisting passages of the medina. "One might imagine this red thread traveling to the market's heart," he said, touching its taut circuit along the wall. Then he touched himself lightly on the chest, as if the thread were somehow secured there, knotted to his own heart, although whether he was its origin or its destination, I could not tell. "Perhaps if one were lost, one could follow this blue thread," he said. "If one were lost, that is. . . ."

Then he turned and he was suddenly standing by a gaudy stall, sorting through racks and racks of tape cassettes. He motioned for me to join him. "Do you like *Abbey Road*," he asked, "or this one called *Mellow Yellow*?" He said that if he were simply choosing for himself, he imagined he might particularly enjoy four or five cassettes featuring the melodies of Oum Khoutom of Egypt.

So that's the pitch, I thought. Perhaps, if he had more time to give, he might particularly enjoy new shoes as well. When I left, I assured him I had my bearings.

But the next morning, when I emerged from the hotel, I found him sitting at the curb, as though he'd been waiting since daybreak. Whether his patience derived from his promised loyalty, or whether he was leery that I was trying to ditch him, I did not know. "Today we will tour Tangiers," he said. "Today we will start with the ramparts."

For hours, as we walked, first ascending steep stone steps, then coming down through dark passageways that opened onto crowded sunstruck boulevards, he kept telling me how much he hoped to visit New York City, and how much he liked the Motown Sound, especially the songs by James Brown. Once, when I stopped to price some postcards, I thought I glimpsed him crossing the busy plaza, his bright blue T-shirt fluttering like a flag, and when I looked up to check, I saw he'd joined some Arab boys who were standing in a doorway, sharing a cigarette and laughing. "Those were my brothers," he later explained, although I knew that wasn't so, since he'd already told me that his family lived far south, below Tafraoute.

He proposed that we eat lunch. While we finished a chicken stewed in a brine of olives, he showed me the half-dozen letters he'd received from German and American tourists he had guided around Tangiers. They were short letters, written on aerogrammes and onionskin paper, and in a simple and hesitant language that hinted at the stilted syntax they had used with him, their authors assured him of the quality of his company, telling him how in their fond hearts it was he, Mohammed, dearest Mohammed, who stood for the soul of Morocco. Sometimes, there were snapshots enclosed—a heavy German blonde in a crocheted pink bikini, posed by an emptied pool; an angular, pock-marked man standing on a sun-bleached concrete driveway, holding a chihuahua.

"I am hoping," Mohammed said, carefully refolding a sheet of fragile blue paper, "that one day you shall write me such a letter."

The waiter cleared our dishes. I asked for a bottle of water.

In this way, we went on for hours. We looked at a mosque encircled by an iron fence of spears. We sat on a bench in an unkempt garden. "I could tell you the names of flowers in Arabic," he said.

Then, when it was dark, he steered me back through the narrow streets of the medina toward the Hôtel du Roi, where, for a moment, there was an awkward silence at the door. *And now what?* I thought—*Would the gentleman care . . . ?* Seen from a distance—by the veiled woman I saw glancing at us from an upstairs window, perhaps—we must have looked like strangers pausing to give the time or to buy hashish, or like paramours shyly parting.

"You are really so tired?" Mohammed asked, standing half within the building's shadow, desultorily picking at the pink stucco wall until paint chips fell to his sandals. Then he touched me lightly on the elbow, as though he meant to take my arm, the way Moroccan men did when they walked with one another, and his touch so exhilarated me—*He is beautiful*, I thought, *and nothing like me*—that I instantly imagined its possible intention as being some ludicrously sad contrivance of my own. Certainly he was simply attempting to negotiate whether or not I'd value his presence at the hotel door the next morning. But why should he?—certainly his presence was a fait accompli, for if there was one thing people said of all these guides, it was that they simply couldn't be shaken.

In this way, the debate I conducted within myself wore down my own desire. "Good night," I said. "I'm very tired. Very tired." Truly, I could not figure how to tell him just how tired I was.

That is, I could not figure how to tell him I wanted him to come to my room. My room was preposterously simple, if not in its execution, then in its mentality. On the right was a plasticized orange valet chair, presumably for *monsieur.* On the left was a bidet concealed behind a tattered green curtain, presumably for *madame.* In the middle was a sagging bed, presumably for pleasure. *Une chambre très bon confort. Un hôtel très agréable.* In retrospect, of course, I see Mohammed would have fucked me, if that was what I really wanted, or, perhaps, he might even have allowed himself to be fucked, after modestly preparing himself in the bidet behind the tattered curtain. In retrospect I see there was a way of telling him what I wanted, and doing so quite simply—words, for instance, or money, preferably in dollars or deutsche marks, although, if necessary, pesetas might certainly have been accepted.

In retrospect I even see that Mohammed himself had wanted this—I don't mean just the money—for on my fifth day in Tangiers, we argued, and he stormed off like an angry lover, abandoning me in the medina.

That morning, we had gone to a beach outside the city. For two days, we had been rehearsing the details of this excursion. For two days, I had been imagining us as we would be—lying side by side in the sun. I had imagined how the heat would calm us and how the cold water would startle us to life.

But the public bus was crowded, and the ride went on forever, through miles of industrial sites. When at last the beach was visible along one side of the highway, it looked mean and narrow, strung with heavy power lines. Where the road ran out, the bus stopped, near a Quonset hut where an old man was selling fireworks and oranges.

At first, we tried to lie on the small blanket we'd brought with us. But the wind drove us to take shelter by a concrete wall beside a culvert. In the distance, I could see a small girl dragging a rope through a pool of stagnant water. Nearby, a boy was slashing old tires with a knife.

"This is a terrible place," Mohammed said. "You can't like it here. It is terrible."

I wondered if really he had ever been here before. Back in Tangiers, he'd claimed to love the beach. He'd claimed to love it more than anywhere. He had said he'd spent whole days swimming in the ocean and that he'd spent evenings dancing at discothèques where he had met amusing people.

But now he looked simply worn and tired. He sat beside me, brushing sand from his bare ankles, then smoothing the legs of his trousers. He had brought neither a swimsuit nor a change of clothes.

He stood up. "I will get us something to eat," he said.

He crossed a small stretch of sand and climbed onto the shoulder of the road. He started down the blacktop, toward the Quonset hut. After a while he returned, carrying a bag of oranges.

He held the bag aloft. "I am bringing us these suns!" he shouted. "I am bringing us a whole bag of them! More suns than we can use!" As he came down the beach toward me, he made a small dance, jumping from one foot to the other, and then hoisting the bag of oranges into the air. When he stopped, he rotated the bag around his head, as if the oranges were orbiting there.

"It's cold," I said.

He sat down against the concrete wall and pressed an orange to his mouth. "You should eat something," he said, pushing the bag of oranges toward me.

But I said nothing. I watched him as he devoured the one orange and then another.

Then he gathered the rinds into a pile. When he looked up, he suggested we return to the city. "I know where you can get some very nice shoes," he said, resuming his old theme. "I know a man who sells nice shoes. All very nice. All handmade.

Completely leather." Then he pointed to his plastic sandals. "Not like these," he added. "These are terrible."

He began to enumerate the many places he knew where one could buy an inlaid box or a discount watch or even a dozen calfskin wallets. "Have you seen the ceramics of Fes?" he asked. And soon we were passing through the lower gate of the medina, following the weaver's blue thread, for I had allowed that I might be interested in something woven, if it were small enough to take along—like a prayer rug, perhaps. We passed cages of pigeons beating their wings. We passed an open hearth where a Berber was tempering knives. The whole way, Mohammed kept saying, "I know you will like this merchant. I know you will admire the things he arranges to sell."

When he saw Mohammed, the merchant rose from his stool to greet us. "*Salaamu'aleikum,*" he said, shaking my hand. Then he busied himself, unbinding a dozen small carpets and arranging them around his stall. "*Le monsieur, qu'est-qui'il préfére?*" he asked Mohammed. "*Le tapis rouge? Le gris? Le bleu?*"

When at last I chose a small rug, Mohammed said he would haggle in Arabic on my behalf. He carried the rug into the sunlight to assess its imperfections. He slowly examined each knot of its fringe.

The merchant followed him into the light. "*Que vous êtes fou!*" the merchant shouted, quite instantly irritated. "*Imshee!* Go away!"

Then Mohammed turned the rug over to count its threads. "*Na'am!*" said the merchant. And Mohammed said, "*Lah!*" They haggled for half an hour. They haggled for so long that I began to imagine that the beach had never been anything more than a detour that was calculated to carry me down the narrowing passages that led finally to the blind alley where I now stood. They haggled so long that I wanted to go.

Then they settled upon a price.

But I thought I saw Mohammed and the merchant smile, as if in concert.

Mohammed turned toward me to inquire, "A good value?" I hesitated—"*Well. . . .*"

And in that instant Mohammed saw that I feared that I was being cheated.

At first he looked embarrassed, as if he held himself responsible for having invented some affection he had imagined to be mutual. Then he looked at me directly, as if seeking some confirmation—or, more precisely, some denial—of the reality my hesitation had created.

But I looked away: After all, there was certainly no reason for him to be upset. After all, my caution was hardly personal.

He was furious.

He picked up the bag of oranges he himself had bought and shoved his way past me into the street. Then he turned and threw the oranges to the ground, and the bag split, and the fruit ruptured, and its bright juice puddled on the cobblestones. He shouted that I should keep them, they were his gift, *un souvenir très symbolique*, surely I could appreciate *that*, even if there was little else about him I seemed to understand. *"Évidemment, monsieur,"* he said, *"vous ne savez rien de Maroc. Ni des hommes. Ni de moi."*

My god, I thought as he walked away, *he's practically flouncing*.

Then I saw the merchants were watching me, and I imagined they found me at fault, as if I'd made some untoward suggestion which Mohammed had naturally rebuffed in the clearest and most necessary manner, and to show how unperturbed I was—it was nothing, *nothing* like they imagined—I turned toward one of them, the one who seemed the least successful, the most wretched and most needy, and I said, "I *assume* your rugs are handmade. I *assume* they are *originals*."

I made my way back to the Hôtel du Roi—to the lobby with its dirty banquettes and its caged reception desk, where the concierge presided over the room keys as though they were racks of pawnshop watches. I hated the concierge: each night when I came in, leaving Mohammed at the curb, I hated finding him in his steel cage, regarding me steadily as he sipped his mint tea; I hated asking him for my room key, whose number by then he surely must have memorized; I hated the way he dropped the key onto the counter, as if it were something he were selling to me, an undiscerning customer, who had chosen an utterly unattractive item of the very poorest quality, and I hated the way, as he pushed it forward, he smiled unctuously, as though to tell me my bad choice would surely cost me, but if that was what I wanted, then, *alors*, what could he do but oblige me?—*Caveat emptor.* That is, each night after I left Mohammed at the curb, I imagined the concierge had witnessed my desire, and then he'd disapproved of it, and of me, and of all my kind—*My kind! What kind was that?*—although, in retrospect, I see that if he was angry it was probably because I'd denied him the small bribe it would have taken to get Mohammed past his desk.

"*Peut-être monsieur désire autres choses?* Perhaps monsieur desires a newspaper? A nightcap? Anything at all?"

"*Non,*" I said, "*monsieur ne désire rien.*" Nothing, that is, except to get past you, past you and into that elevator that will lift me upward, shaking on its loose cables as it rises.

I went to my room and lay down. It was then I thought to go to Rabat. After all, I thought, it might be amusing to visit Rabat, since I'd talked so much about it once upon a time; and of course, Rabat had a reputation quite different from Tangiers. In the scheme of Morocco, in fact, Rabat was often considered somewhat quiet and even disappointing, although such opinions tended toward the highly touristic, formed by those least well equipped to get the feel of a place. But when it came right down to it, Tangiers was really a bit more like Tijuana than anywhere. One could hardly judge a whole country by its borders.

This was a good plan. But first I would get a good sleep—a very good sleep—and when I got up, I would probably find Mohammed sitting at the curb outside the hotel, as I always did, and I would explain that I was headed to Rabat, and, if he liked and had the time, I would be pleased if he'd be my guest for a glass of tea before I headed for the station. While we had the tea, I'd find an inoffensive way to settle up, for he had as yet received no money, which was quite unfair, since, after all, he had shown me around the entire city, and had done so quite intelligently. Not that it was rare, the thing about the money. Indeed, it was the custom—or so I'd heard—to present the money at the parting, so that it seemed like more of what it was, a deeply felt and well-intentioned gift, and not a series of demeaning tips awarded for specific services performed.

But of course when I came down the next morning, there was no Mohammed.

There was only the concierge—and beside him, also locked within the metal cage, was an Arab child, a boy. The boy was crying. The concierge was punishing him. I could not make out the offense. What carries us to places which express us better than we might express ourselves, so that were someone to ask, "What's the matter?" we might point mutely—"This . . ."

The concierge looked up at me. "There's no message from your friend," he said, "if that's what you're waiting for. . . ."

By then I don't think I expected a message from Mohammed.

The concierge unlocked the cage and pushed the boy, still crying, through the door. "Go on," he said. "Get out of here."

The boy hurried into the street. Then the concierge busied himself, copying sums from one black ledger into another. I simply stood there. I was trying to make up my mind. There was a hydrofoil leaving for the Spanish coast at 11:00 A.M.

The concierge put down his pencil. "Is there something else?" he asked, annoyed. "Look, if it's about the kid, he'll come back. He always does. He's my son."

So, he was his son.

And then I was crossing the Spanish frontier at Tarifa, its beach lined with army tanks. And then I was in Torremolinos, and from Torremolinos I hitched a ride with a drunken countess—"*Le Roi est mort!*" she kept shouting from her Fiat's open window—to Alicante, where she lived, and from Alicante I took a bus to Barcelona, and from Barcelona I boarded a train for the border at Port Bou. And at midnight in Port Bou, waiting on the concrete quay for the Paris Express, a blonde woman kept staring at me, as if I were familiar, until at last she asked, "*Sind Sie auch Deutsch?*"

"No, I'm not German," I said. "I'm something else." But I was thinking: *There's really quite a word for what I am.*

And then I was drunk, and I was in Paris, and I was at the Cinema Marotte, on rue Vivienne, sitting beside a Chinese man who rubbed my crotch as we stared in silence at a movie of two men fucking, one with his legs raised, slavish and demanding, and the other, mounting him, brutal and apologetic. The two men were muscled like Americans. "*C'est amusant, n'est-ce pas?*" the Chinese man whispered; he smelled faintly of the restaurant he must have worked in. Then he withdrew a handkerchief, which he fluttered briefly in the dark before dropping it to my lap, where he held it—"*Vite, ça viens*"—as I came. On screen the actors exchanged rôles, and the one who'd been on the bottom became wildly angry, unbelievably so, like a furious cartoon character, or maybe the movie itself changed, I don't remember—*Séances continuelles.*

And then I was alone again, and drunker still, and standing on the pavement, staring into a shop window filled with dusty stuffed iguanas and dying cacti, and in the rear of the shop, I could see five small lighted clocks that told the time in major cities around the world, and beneath them a banner: *Agence de voyages. Traversez par tôut l'univers.* In New York, it was late; in Paris, later still.

I hailed a taxi.

And then I realized that I could go anywhere, turn right, turn left, drive dead-on for a million miles, *traversez par tôut l'univers,* and I threw my cigarette to the gutter, for at that moment I realized I could give up anything, even smoking, I had no more dependencies.

A taxi stopped and I climbed in. The driver was a corpulent, middle-aged woman with her German shepherd sitting on the front seat beside her.

"*Hôtel Saint-Séverin,*" I said, although this wasn't really what I wanted. I simply didn't know how to direct her to drive on forever. Where was a phrase book, an emergency lexicon?— *Farther, farther, just get me out of here. . . .*

I must have scared her with my drunkenness, for as she drove she watched me in her rearview mirror. She studied me so long and so intently, in fact, that I began talking. I talked so much I couldn't stop. "I have always wanted to be in Paris," I told her. "It is all I have ever wanted. My whole life, since I was a teenager speaking French—well, for most of my life then. Since hearing Edith Piaf."

When I said *Piaf,* the driver eyed me in the mirror yet more narrowly. She sped up.

"When I was a child," I rattled on, "I listened to Piaf. I listened to Piaf in the basement rec room. '*Mon dieu,*' '*La Vie en rose,*' '*Je ne regrette rien.*' I unscrewed the shade from the floor lamp and stood in front of it as if it were my spotlight. Then I lip-synched to her records—*Ladies and gentlemen, I give you Edith Piaf! Tonight, the Little Sparrow!* I have always wanted to be in Paris. It is all I ever wanted. In *Paris.* All that time."

We were crossing Pont Neuf when the driver slammed on her brakes. Her German sherpherd was pitched against the dashboard, and suddenly we were stopped in the middle of the bridge.

The driver turned to face me. "*Mais monsieur,*" she said, "*vous êtes à Paris. Voilà, Nôtre Dame!*" And indeed, when I looked to my left, there it was, Nôtre Dame.

I felt sober.

How long had I been traveling? And how far away? And from what fixed point outside myself? There had been the club in Berlin where I'd watched the American soldier dancing with himself in a mirror, and the pensione in Budapest where I'd seen the old man sitting at his vanity, slowly applying pancake makeup to his face—"Shall you come in?" he'd asked, when he looked up and found me standing at his doorway. There had been the field at night along the river in Trier, and the abandoned Luna Park near Vicenza, and the public washroom of the train station in Zürich.

But I had gone nowhere. Nowhere at all. I was sitting in a taxi stopped on a bridge, watching the driver pet her German shepherd. For a moment, I wondered if the Tuileries Gardens were nearby. I had heard what men did there at night, by the back gate that led to the Orangerie.

Then the drunk feeling started again, the feeling that would last for years.

I wanted to say something to the driver. I thought she might understand. "My father always said he hoped that I'd see Nôtre Dame," I began.

But she was looking out her window. *All right,* I thought. *Just look away then—I suppose you think you're the soul of France. . . .*

"We lived in Morocco," I continued. "In the days before the independence, before the Moroccans made themselves into such a mob of Abduls and Mohammeds." When I leaned forward, I could see myself in the rearview mirror. I could see a part of my face and my mouth moving as I spoke.

ALL WHO ARE OUT ARE IN FREE

• JOHN L. MYERS •

CLIVE RUFFIN SPEAKING
OCTOBER 1992

"At there's where it happened." My first cousin JoNeil stepped down through the soft dirt of the field behind the Big House. A long, cool October wind kissed the tops of the sawgrass covering the field that grew cotton, years ago, back in the days when the place was a working farm. Now, it was ten acres of rough weeds and grass, with little pine saplings coming up—the first toehold of the creeping woods beyond that would soon come and reclaim the land. As JoNeil spoke, the same wind picked at her hair—it was blond this month—and whipped the tail of her skirt around her knees until she almost could not walk across the soft uneven ground.

Out, just in front of us, was the trampled-down spot in the grass, and two sets of tire tracks from where the ambulance crew had driven in and then driven out.

"I don't know what would have caused him to wander away from the house like that." She held tightly onto my arm as we walked closer to the spot. One hand gripped a crumpled tissue that she had not put down since Uncle Carrol died three days ago. "I mean, after the stroke last year, Diddy could hardly get himself to the bathroom anymore." We stopped on a small mound and looked down at the trampled grass. JoNeil stopped breathing for just a second, sucking in one long breath of air and biting down hard on her lip.

"I think he knowed," she said, stopping at that point, and refusing to walk any closer to the point where her father had died. I looked down at the spot and then my eyes wandered out to the edge of the woods beyond. I searched the tops of the trees, trying to remember if they had been that close to the Big House when I visited there as a child. I tried to remember if the open field—brightly speckled with yellow and blue morning glory vines the last time I saw it—had really been as small as it looked now. Those had been times when ten acres seemed like half the world to me.

JoNeil looked out across the land, the wind slapping her hair around and almost making her stumble where she stood. She looked away from me. "You know . . . it's almost as if he knew the Lord was calling him home. Don't you think?"

"Honey, I don't know." I stood back, scanning my eyes around behind us, back toward the house where the long pack of the cars of all our relatives was starting to thin. At the crest of the hill, I could just make out the front end of my car—the new white one. The wind blew a sudden break in the clouds and a bright ray of sun glinted off the headlights, as if someone up there had flashed them at me. "You know, Uncle Carrol was a mighty strong man when he wanted to be. And maybe he just took a notion to come out of the house and take a walk. . . ."

"But why would he have come out here to this old field?" She jerked her hands away from me. "There ain't nothing down here now but a bunch of old scrubs, and a couple of rabbits living under the stumps."

I heard two short beeps from my car horn. It was late, and we had to get back to Vander before dark.

"There isn't anything down here," I said, turning to look back, deep into the woods that grew dark with approaching night. "There's nothing down there but. . . ."

I didn't say the next words, and I didn't hear her say them, either, but I could see JoNeil's lips move, and I knew the words she said were, "the Tromping Grounds." The tops of the trees stirred with a rustling wind that rose up from the black woods beyond. And then a stillness settled around us. It was so quiet out there, I heard my heart beating in my chest. Behind us, up at the house, I could hear the screen door on the back porch hammer shut against its wood frame.

"There's no reason he would want to go down there," I said to her.

"No reason but the devil himself." She turned her back to the woods as a cold shiver pulled her arms tight around her waist, cuddling her breasts inside the thin cotton sweater she wore. Without speaking another word of the Tromping Grounds or looking back, my first cousin JoNeil directed me back up the hill, toward the house where Richard Alan waited by the car, talking loudly to Aunt Maude as he loaded our good china bowls into the back seat. And the extra two dozen clear glass salad plates we brought along, just in case they were needed. Richard Alan was always in his element at weddings and funerals.

Now, he patted Aunt Maude's hands as she turned and toddled away from him, heading back into the house. She still acted as though the idea of Uncle Carrol's being dead hadn't quite sunk in: she had strung her best white Battenburg lace apron around her black dress, and was shooed out of the kitchen when she fell into washing up all the dirty dishes with the cousins. Richard Alan turned toward us and shielded his eyes from the setting sun. I could tell, even from that far away, he turned a smile toward us.

"Y'all can come on back and visit us, now, anytime you feel like it." JoNeil stumbled as I offered her my hand to step up the last hillock and onto the farthest fringe of the back lawn. "I mean, now that Diddy's gone and all, you don't have to worry about him and . . ." Her voice trailed as her eyes looked up at Richard Alan for a second, and then back at me. "Poor old Mommie don't know the difference now, anyway." She mopped the wadded-up tissue under her nose, biting down on her lower lip as we walked across the lawn.

Halfway back to the car I stopped her, trying to have the last of her attention before she went back into the house, back to the ministrations of our weepy cousins, most of whom were putting on the big show, hoping to pick up a few extra dollars or a hundred acres or so from Uncle Carrol's will. Everybody just knew that since Carrol was gone, Aunt Maude probably wouldn't live to see the spring thaw.

"I thank you for saying that." I took her hands in mine. JoNeil's fingers were cold and damp, and hung loose in my grip. Not at all like the feeling of holding Richard Alan's thick manly hands in mine as we often did while watching movies on the television. "Richard Alan likes you a lot, and he likes the kids. Especially now that Marcus has run off." Her eyes filled as I said, "We'll be back. Soon. For the weekend."

JoNeil pulled me tight and kissed me once on the cheek, and as she did, I heard the silent sound of air pressing out of her. I knew that was the only crying she would do around the cousins; she trusted me enough to cry in front of me, and know that I would not make a big scene of it. I kissed her back, and headed toward the car as she walked on up to the house.

Behind me, down across the field, I could again see the mashed-down grass where Uncle Carrol had died, and the two sets of tire tracks. My eyes went straight across the landscape, in a line from there down to the woods, to where I knew the devil lived. I knew, because I had seen him there myself.

CARROL LINWOOD SPEAKING
JULY 1942

THE START OF IT

This here's my 4-F. I got it in the mail. As soon as I told Mamma about it, she fell down on her knees in the dirt right there in front of the Big House, pulling her skirts up to cover her face, and she cried. I wasn't sure or not if it was because she was happy for me to be staying at home and maybe living out this war, or if it was because she was ashamed of me not going. All six of my brothers have long since shipped out—gone all over the world to fight. But me, I have a bad heart and they told me I couldn't go.

Arlen got his papers last week. He was all ready for the two of us to go over there and shoot some Nazis and get on home, but you should have seen the way his face fell when I told him I couldn't go. I could tell he was disappointed, but he couldn't let on in front of Mamma because she had started crying that afternoon I got the letter, and she still gets real misty about it yet. Only she has stopped putting her hands together like she's praying, and she's stopped beating them on the ground so much. Some say Mamma has the second sight, and maybe she knew that if I was to go over there, I wouldn't come back. She won't say nothing to me about Arlen, though. And I am most afraid to ask her what she sees.

He's not one of us, you know. By that I mean the passel of cousins and such that lives here on the farm. Granddaddy and Grammaw are the ones that actually own the place. But all their boys is off to the war, them that's not too old. I have six uncles gone. There aren't any men left much to speak of, except Granddaddy and my uncle Tet who is almost seventy years old. He's starting to look feeble to me, and I bet he couldn't even pick up a gun if they was to put one in his hands. All the wives are here, though, and the kids. My daddy is the third from the oldest of his brothers, and I am the youngest of mine. I will be nineteen years old my next birthday, if I live to see May.

But Arlen. He's not part of them. He lives across the way from here, and he comes out through them woods yonder behind the house most every day. When we was younger, we used to play in them woods a lot. But now as we've got too old to be playing like that, he'll come over here of a night. We'll sit out on the back porch and I'll watch him smoke a pipe, listening to the sounds of the river around us. Sometimes we move Granddaddy's old Atwater-Kent radio out onto the back porch and listen for an hour or two. At night, we can get a station all the way from Cincinnati to come in real clear. Even better than we can get WBT down in Charlotte, which is maybe sixty miles away.

Thinking back, me and Arlen met the night we watched the heat lightning up on Settler's Rise, the high spot on our land from where you can see everything. He come sneaking up behind me one day as I was walking down through the woods, and just as pretty as you please said to me, "Hey, boy." We were both about fourteen at the time. I said, "Hey," right back.

I remember that time just like it was today: him standing there, one eye all squinted up as he looked into the sun, his hand shielding his eyes from the light. He looked like a little blond-headed heathen standing there, wearing little shorts that didn't half cover nothing, carrying a long walking stick that was so green the sap still bled from where he'd tore off the branches. I had never seen a white-haired boy up until that time because all of my cousins were dark-headed, but I have seen a few since, I might say. And he had these eyes that would look right through you, and down deep into your soul. They were the darkest brown eyes I had ever seen, and as he looked at me, I swear I saw a little laugh in them.

"What's the matter, boy, cat got your tongue?" He started toward me, swiping that stick around the underbrush as he stepped over the rocks and briars with his bare feet. I wondered if he had come all the way across the sawgrass field like that, and, if he had, did it not hurt to walk. He stepped right up close to me then and took my hand and pulled me on away with him. His fingers were hard and warm against mine, and I felt something surge into my arm for a second, as if he was a hot wire I'd grabbed ahold of. And then, as he skittered away, our fingers parted. I knew that I had no choice but to follow after him. Just like that. Not so much as a "how do you do?" or anything. And I knew right then that I would follow Arlen Longworth Lee off the edge of the earth if I had to, even though at the time I didn't even know that was his name.

That night we went up to Settler's Rise, which is the high spot of land on the farm. A hundred years ago, that was where my great-great granddaddy built his first cabin, which has now pretty much fallen into ruin. There's naught left of it now but a couple of pieces of old log ends, and a couple of chunks of scrap iron that are rusting away to dirt. When it was still standing, it was what my family called the Old House, and they lived there until there was enough money to build the Big House, down next to the Catawba River, where we all live now.

So we sat up there on Settler's Rise that night and watched as, off in the distance, we could see the heat lightning come toward us over the hills. The light flashed between the clouds and it reminded me of all them stories I'd read about the gods sitting up in the stars throwing spears and scepters at each other. The horizon was all red across the bottom and faded away to blue as the sun dipped away and we finely sat in darkness.

"Where are you from, anyway?" I asked him as he sat on the rock, with his knees pulled up to his chest, watching the lights in the sky. Before he answered, the night became all quiet, and the most you could hear was the sounds of the crickets all around us in the trees, and what you could see was the flashing of the lightning bugs in the air around our heads. Sitting up high on that ridge like that with those bugs lighting up the air was a little bit like sitting in the middle of the stars themselves. I wanted to reach out and grab one or two and give them to him for a present.

He turned to me at last and leaned back, resting his head against my stomach (for I was lying down across the rocks, watching the sky at the moment), and he said, "I'm from across that road yonder." He sort of nodded in one direction with his head without ever losing touch with my stomach. "But I'm here now," he said. "And here is where I figure on staying."

"You mean out here in the woods?" I said. I felt a little flinch in my fingers just then, like all I wanted to do was to touch that golden hair of his just once, to see if it was at all like mine, which is all black and curly. It felt like soft silk as his hair fluttered against my stomach, like a thousand tiny fingers tickling me. Only then, I didn't know to laugh.

"No, fool." He sat up on one elbow and leaned over so that he was right above my face. In a flash of the lightning, I could see those brown eyes looking deep into mine. The first roll of thunder started, far away in the hills: The storm must have been miles away, because it was a few seconds before the sound of the thunder came to us. And as that rumble came into my ears, he leaned over and planted this little kiss right on my lips that I will never forget if I live to be a hundred. No one had ever kissed me like that before and I just lay there paralyzed, feeling those tiny, hard lips pressed against mine, breathing in the smell of him—of a boy running through the woods on a hot summer day. And I had to close my eyes, afraid if I looked out, he would be gone.

I reached for him with my free hand, and just as I did, I grabbed a handful of air. Before I could open my eyes, Arlen had done scrambled down off that rock and let off through the woods, laughing to beat the devil.

"Hey, you!" I called out into the darkness to the sound of his laughing voice, disappearing deeper down into the woods—down into the part where we were told never to go. "Come back here," I said, but by then it was too late. All I could hear was the sound of his voice echoing in my ears, and all I could feel was the touch of his wild lips on mine in the darkness. He had run straight off into the brush into what my people had always called the Devil's Tromping Ground—a round spot in the middle of the woods, right in the midst of the trees, where nothing would grow. It was a perfect circle of hard-packed red dirt with a little pothole in the middle that never filled up and never smoothed over. Some said the devil popped up out of that hole every night and danced around in the circle until daylight. And if you ever got caught by him while he was a-dancing, you were forever his own.

I sat there on Settler's Rise that night, maybe an hour more, listening to see if I could hear the sound of Arlen coming back through the woods, but he was gone. All he left behind was that green stick he had carried. Whatever storm there was in the air that night, it rolled right on by without even rustling the leaves on the trees, and after the lightning stopped, it was just as quiet and hot as it had been before.

As I picked up the stick and started home, I wondered if Arlen might have been the devil's boy.

GOING INTO THE CIRCLE

Of course, I came to learn later that Arlen wasn't the devil's boy at all, though I must admit that first introduction to him left me to wonder. He had moved here from Burlington, which is way out east from here. Up until I was fourteen years old, I had never even been off the farm, not even to go to school. There was enough cousins on the place that a teacher was brought in for us. And none of us was allowed to go into town until we turned sixteen.

So having this strange boy who came from far away to live across the road from us was a most unusual treat, and, to tell you the truth, I think Arlen enjoyed the idea of being a curiosity. Pretty soon, we were as thick as thieves, and he spent as much time around our supper table for the next year and a half as he did around his own mamma's.

But I was invited over there a lot, too. The shortcut to their place was to go down the hill and across the back field, through the Dark Woods, as Daddy called them. Back there was the main highway that ran from Charlotte to Asheville. His family bought Doc MacFall's old house (a right mansion itself) and moved in. Come to find out, though, the "family" weren't but his mamma and him. Just the two of them, living in that big house at the edge of the woods. I later learned that his daddy, who used to be an overseer in a mill, had died in an accident with a carding machine.

We ran the woods together those summers, learning every square inch of land between the Big House and the river. We spent days and days hiding down in the woods, and running across the fields at night—two dark shadows across the landscape, skulking along by the light of the moon. Everything we did then was a great secret that only he and I shared. When somebody would ask me, "What do you two do down there in them woods all day and night?" I would answer back, "I don't know. Nothing, I guess." For, to tell you now, I can't remember a single bit of it, except that whatever it was we did, it was always together.

But for all that running around, there was one place I would never allow that we go, and that was the Tromping Grounds. He never tired of asking about it, usually late of a night as we sat around a fire in the old study. My granddaddy smoked these long briar pipes filled with rich tobacco that smelled of cherrywood and apples. And the more the cold wind beat up against the windowpanes, or leaked around the sashes to move the curtains, the more Arlen wanted to hear about haints in those woods, or the tales Granddaddy always had of all sorts of boogers living right outside our house. Out yonder, in the dark.

Arlen asked my granddaddy once why he didn't fence the Tromping Grounds off if it was so bad, and my granddaddy asked him to his face how it was possible that a man could fence in the devil. Some had tried to put up fences around the place to keep little boys from falling to their dooms down that hidey-hole, but them that tried only found the fences kicked down

and splintered the next morning, with the stub ends of the pick-
ets burnt off here and there. Probably, my granddaddy said,
from the touch of the devil's own hands. He said this was because where the devil touched you, it left a mark for all to see:
a burned-in scar that would spoil you for all your days and
would mark you as his. And that, my granddaddy said, was why
boys should never go near the Tromping Grounds: they would
be marked by the devil and spoilt for life.

Well, telling that story to Arlen was just the same as if you
gave him a written invitation to run down there and have dinner with old Beelzebub in person. This wild look came to
Arlen's eyes and I knew he wanted to go down there and see it
for hisself. Arlen never was one to be satisfied with what somebody told him. He decided that as soon as it was warm enough
to stay out all night, me and him was going to sneak off down
there, spend the night in the circle, and see this devilment for
ourselves.

That time came the spring we both turned fifteen years old.
He showed up on the back porch one evening late, with this
gunny sack under his arm, saying, "We're off on an adventure,
Fool," for that was what he always called me by then. "Go on,"
he gave my left arm a squeeze and turned me back to the house,
"run up the back stairs and get you a quilt and let's take off for
the night."

Now, Mamma was used to this after all these years of me
running off with Arlen and not showing up again for a day or
two, just as I was used to him dragging me off to God knows
where in the middle of the night. I never even once stopped to
question where we were going, because, ever since that first
night up on the Rise, he could have asked me to go off with
him to China, and I would have pulled a quilt out of the cedar
closet, stole a wedge of cold cornbread, and off I would have
gone. Arlen was just that kind of a boy.

So I pulled together what food I could scrounge up from the
safe and bundled it up inside a old blanket, and off we hit. He
grabbed me by the hand, and we ran together across the back
field, through the fresh plowed furrows waiting for cotton to go
in. I held on to his hand and ran along, thinking how much
larger and stronger that hand had become since that first night,
what seemed so long ago.

We stopped once, just at the edge of the woods, both of us gasping for breath for we had run flat out as hard as we could to get away from the house.

"Where's the fire?" I stumbled backward, loosing my footing in the loose ground.

He turned around and peeled off his shirt, his bare chest glistening in the moonlight. He was still working hard to breathe as he took my hand, placed it in the middle of his chest and held it firm there. "It's here." He pulled me closer, until I almost rubbed up against him.

Then, he took my hand and put it to his mouth and kissed his own sweat from my palm, and I almost fell down again. But that time it was because I felt all of a sudden weak to my knees.

"My beautiful Fool." He gently touched his salty lips to mine, dropping the rucksack and pulling me so close that I could not get away.

His hair was damp with the strain of running, I remember that now. I stood there, pressed up against him, and all I could think of then was the feeling of his beautiful soft hair rubbing against my fingers. And then, just as quick, he pulled away, picked up the sack and his shirt, pulled me by the hand, and run like wildfire. "We're not there yet," he called behind.

Of course, it didn't take all that long going down into the woods before I figured out where he was taking me. But by then, as I stumbled along, running my tongue over my lips, remembering the taste of him, my mind was too weak to argue. I knew that if we went to that place and saw the devil dancing in his circle, we would both die. But I figured after standing there in the dark and feeling Arlen kiss the palm of my hand in the moonlight, there won't be much more in life I would miss.

The closer we got to the circle, though, the more afraid I became. I believed all them stories I'd heard about the Tromping Grounds, and I knew there was a reason why nobody had stepped in there in the past hundred years.

At the edge of the circle, the moonlight shone down through the break in the trees, and it looked like a giant light up above shone down right there on the circle. At first, I was even afraid to look inside, for fear I'd see the old man dancing around. But

Arlen pulled on, tugging me by the arm, until we were right up against the edge. "See," he said, "there's nothing here to be afraid of."

Trusting him, I opened up my eyes and saw that the circle was empty. "We're going inside," he said. I felt the blood freeze inside me.

Then, before we could take another step, I heard this rustling in the leaves by us, and the fear overtook me so bad that I couldn't've run then if I'd had to. But it wouldn't do no good to run, because I already knew that no matter how hard you tried to get away, the devil could run faster than boys . . . even Arlen, who was used to running across rocks and briars in his bare feet.

Arlen must have been just a little bit scared, too, because I felt his hand all of a sudden go cold in mine.

"We're done for." I squeezed down on his fingers as hard as I could. If I was going to get snatched down the hidey-hole, at least I wanted to hold on to Arlen for as long as I could.

Just then, a little guinea hen came wandering out of the brush. She stopped when she seen us two, cocking her head to one side to get a better look. There we were—three sets of terrified eyes staring each other down in the darkness of that night. She scratched her feet a few times in the brambles and waddled away. She walked right toward the circle, got to the edge and stopped, and then wandered off into the woods in the other direction. Just like my granddaddy said: Even the animals of the ground and the birds of the air won't cross that land. For they know if they go in, they are gone.

Arlen just laughed as he watched that hen wander off, and he said, "See yonder, scardey cat, it was just a old guinea, and you about to pee your pants, thinking it was old Satan!" He laughed some more until I felt my heart start to beat again. And with one quick jerk of my arm, he pulled us both into the circle where a boy was never supposed to go; and there I stood, waiting for the clap of doom.

Nothing happened. Nothing at all. The place was as quiet as a tomb, as if all the air had been sucked out and left just an empty spot there. The ground felt warm to my feet (even though I was wearing shoes) and I couldn't hear the sound of the wind in the trees around us.

"Here's where we're going to stay," Arlen said, "and wait and see what happens next." He dropped his sack and pulled out an old quilt that used to be spread across his bed. His mamma would have strapped him if she'd known he'd taken it out and spread it on the ground like that. "Right here," he said, patting the ground beside him on the quilt as he sat down. It looked like he was spreading out a picnic or something. The way he looked at me with his eyes just then, I could not say no to him. Even if it meant that I was sinking down to Hell itself, which I knew we would be. "Come here, Fool," he said, and before I could resist, I was there on the quilt beside him.

I don't remember much of that night in the circle except that it never really got cold the way it does when you sleep outside under the stars all night. Before I knew it, he had pulled my shirt away, and was kissing across my chest, repeating my name over and over. And then, he was above me and holding my head in place with both of his hands as he kissed me hard on the lips. I remember gasping for breath and thinking how hot it was out there that night. And I remember grabbing ahold of Arlen's belt and trying my best to pull him up against me until you couldn't tell where one boy ended and the other began.

I remember his mouth by my ear, and the ragged sound of his breathing as I raked my fingernails down his back. And then the soft murmurs of his voice humming, crooning in my ear. "Oh, my darling Fool," he said.

Somehow, with a tangle of shirts and shoes, we were both naked out there on the quilt. As my clothes went away, I could feel the air growing hot against my skin.

Arlen was lying full-length against me, and I could feel all of his smooth body against mine as my legs wound around his. "I can't breathe." I tried to push away and pull him close at the same time. The air was stifling around me, and the more Arlen touched me, the more I wanted. Without answering, he looked up at me, and this glazed-over look come to his eyes. Without saying a word, he sat back and pulled up my knees to his face, gently kissing down the sides of my thighs until I thought I was going to die. No words would come out of me then as I was gasping to catch my breath and moaning at the touch of his fingers and lips against my skin.

Now, Arlen does not agree with me on what happened next,

for he says it was nothing at all except the two of us in that circle that night, and what would I know anyway, since I was out of my head. It was the first time I had ever had anybody do that to me, and I would never let anyone but Arlen do it to me again, for I tell you now I know what it is that my mamma calls the pain of love. And Arlen had never done it to anybody before that night, and he tells me he will never do it to another except for me.

But just as he was sitting there over me, and my hands stretched out and wiped away the sweat from his chest, he stood up on his knees and pushed my legs back, stretching them just about back to my head. He leaned over and pushed it into me, and I have never felt such a pain in my life as that. But the scream I let out was not for the feeling that I was being torn in two, but that I was as close as I would ever get to being as one with him. I grabbed him by the waist and pulled him as close as I could until he slammed up against me and leaned over, kissing me hard on the mouth, his sweat dripping down into my face.

I knew what was about to happen, because even though I could hold out for as long as I wanted to Arlen has no control down there, erupting like a volcano if you look at him wrong. He closed his eyes and reared back, giving it a few quick strokes, moving faster and faster—this intent look on his face like he was hard at work. And that is when I saw it.

Just as I knew he was about to collapse, I saw this hand come out of the darkness and grab Arlen by the shoulder. It was the longest, boniest looking thing that I have ever seen in my life, with long, dirty fingernails that snapped at me as they took him by the shoulder. I screamed at the sight of it and Arlen let out this loud gasp as I felt him emptying inside me. I don't remember much else, though, because the sight of that old hand grabbing him must have made me faint dead away. I woke up some time later and Arlen was asleep, curled up against me with his sweaty back stuck up against my front. I wrapped my arms around him, thinking that the air was as warm as a summer day, and fell off to sleep. So, even though Arlen claims that he did not see the devil that night, I know that I did.

That was the summer we moved out of our house and spent the whole time camping out on Settler's Rise. At night he slept next to me under the stars, climbing down in the morning to go off to eat and work the farm, returning again at night. My people would ask, "What do you two do up there on that ridge all the time?" and I would answer, "I don't know," for other than feeling the blessed pain of love every night in his arms, I really did not.

Three years have passed since that summer, and I suppose it is all over now, what with Arlen running off to the army. That war's just another booger story that he won't believe until he sees it hisself. He tells me he'll be home directly. Now I'm left at home with Mamma and all the cousins. I wonder, still, if my family is going to be able to tell that I am now the devil's own boy. If there is a burn mark on me, it is somewhere that I cannot see it.

JANUARY 1945

THE WAR

I got overseas letters from Arlen quite often. But he was never able to say too much about where he was or what he was doing. There was this code we used to say what we wanted to say without anybody else being able to read it in the letters. Even then, after he had gone off to the war, everything we did together was just as much a secret. "I remember that first summer when we were kids," he wrote. "I remember seeing the lightning for the first time." When he said that, I knew he was doing okay and that he would be home again soon.

Sometimes, the letters he sent looked like a slice of Swiss cheese they had so many holes in them, cut out by the censors. Last year, I got a letter from him saying that he was going off somewhere and he didn't know where, but that he would write again as soon as he could. "Be good, Fool," he wrote at the end.

I showed the letter to his mamma as there was nothing shameful in it that she would see, and I caught the worry in her eyes as she read Arlen's lines. I didn't know then, but it was mainly because she saw that the letters that he wrote to me were a lot longer than the ones he wrote to her.

But she had me down to her house whenever I wanted, and

she would have me to supper all the time. She kept a little banner stuck up in the front room window that the War Department had give her. It was a little red flag with a gold star in the center, and hung from a gold stick. That was the sign that "I have a boy that's serving over there." She was just as proud of that little flag as she was of him.

Then, right after Christmas, I was heading over there to visit, and just as I came into the yard, I noticed that the little red and gold flag was gone. The curtains was all pulled on the house, and there was a fresh poesy of white carnations and baby's breath tacked to the door.

I had to sit down right then, because my legs wouldn't hold me up to stand. My Arlen, I thought as I fell. I knew then that he was never coming back.

Without going any closer, I turned around and ran back through the Dark Woods, across the back field. The only place I knew to go right then was up to Settler's Rise, as there was something inside of me screaming to come out: It was a rage and a fear I'd never felt before, because I knew just as sure as I knew myself that Arlen was gone. And with him, so was my life.

I made it across that field without even knowing how I did it, and up the bank toward the Big House. My daddy seen me coming from the woods and he dashed out of the house.

"Carrol," he called out as he took off running toward me, "Carrol Linwood!"

He seen the look on my face and I know it must have shook him because he run down and grabbed me by the shoulders, knocking me down to the ground, with me all crying and throwing my fists in the air.

"What you running for, boy?" He fought to get my arms down to my sides.

"Because I can't fly, Daddy," I said. "Because I can't fly."

CLIVE RUFFIN SPEAKING
HALLOWEEN, 1966

DOING MEN'S THINGS

I was six years old the year they broadcast "The War of the
Worlds" on television. We drove over from Conover, me and
Mamma and Daddy, to watch on Uncle Carrol's set. He was the
only one in the family that had color. The movie was boring to
me, and what I really wanted to do was go back home and do
Trick or Treat, but Mamma and Daddy wanted to go over there
to see the color television.

About half past ten that night, the men started getting restless with the movie, and got to talking about the Tromping
Grounds.

Mamma didn't approve of that kind of talk, and said it gave
children nightmares. Never bothered me, though. I can sit
through a whole Frankenstein movie now and not have to put
my hands over my eyes once.

But the more those men talked about it, the more some of
them wanted to go down to see the circle for themselves. All of
them, that is, but my Uncle Carrol who said he knew better
than to go, because he saw the old man once when he was a
boy, and didn't want to pay a return visit. When he said that,
Mamma was about to clap her hands over my ears, but I
jumped away too fast and she missed. She said that Uncle Carrol shouldn't go around telling tales because somebody might
believe him. Aunt Maude leaned back in her rocking chair and
grinned at me and didn't say anything. She knew then that Uncle Carrol was telling the truth. I saw it in her eyes.

So, nothing do the men but run down there and take a look
to see if Satan was at the Tromping Grounds that night, or if
he was out in the woods looking for little boys to steal. I cried
until they took me along, too. Got to ride along in the open
back of Tet Junior's old pickup truck, something Mamma would
never allow, except Daddy was back there with me this time.
Daddy told Mamma that he wouldn't let me fall out, and he
would hold on real tight if we ran into Bells'bub out in the
woods. Mamma gave Daddy a whack on the arm, and we were
off down the road into the darkness.

Tet Junior pulled the old pickup off the side of the road, and up the old tractor path as far as we could go before the trees got too thick. I remember somebody pulling out the staves on the sides of the truck and flapping down the tailgate. Me and Daddy and the other men all jumped out the back.

It was starting to get cold by then, and I was glad Mamma made me wear my sweater. I didn't want to get stuck in the cab of the truck to keep warm when the adventure was just about to begin! So, we all started walking down into the woods toward the spot where Uncle Carrol said the devil pops up out of the ground. Somehow I got in the middle of the group, so all I could see was a lot of overall coats and big thick hands waving around in front of my face. I was about to stumble, and reached up to take a hand to keep from falling down and realized it was not my daddy. But Tet Junior, he took my hand just the same, and said, "You come along now, little Cooter, and don't you be afraid none."

I told him there wasn't nothing to be afraid of, as it was just some old woods and a bunch of crazy men out running the roads looking for a ghost. Some of them laughed when I said that, and I felt one of the hands pat me on the head.

Then, whoever was in front just stopped dead. I was mashed in among the legs and arms, and was trying to herd my way out when I heard this sound like somebody saying "Huuuuh." Only it was too loud to be somebody saying it. And then, it was like a flashlight shone right in my face as this bright light came on me, and the next thing I knew, we were running back toward the truck. There wasn't a thing to see but the ground passing under my feet, and a million brogans all around me flying and throwing dirt in the air as we ran back. We didn't even stop to latch up the tailgate on the truck as everybody held on for dear life while Tet Junior spun that old truck around and skittered it back onto the road, headed back to the Big House.

Somebody looked over at my daddy, whose face was covered with sweat, and said, "Lindy, I've never seen you bolt like that. I swan, your face was the color of cotton."

My daddy looked back at him and said, "How would you know what my face looked like, Elrod? All I could see was the soles of your shoes flapping in the breeze!"

Everybody was laughing by the time we got back to the

house, but Daddy told me not to tell Mamma what we saw down there, or she might never let us come back. When I looked at Uncle Carrol, though, I could tell he knew. There's never any lying to Uncle Carrol.

JULY 1976

SEEING THE DEVIL

This is the summer that I turn sixteen, and I am glad to see it come. My little brother Linwood is nine years old this year, and Daddy got him a shotgun for Christmas last year which he likes better than food or sleep. Everywhere that we go, that blamed gun has to go with us. Mamma makes him ride it in the trunk of the car, though, as she won't allow it up front with us.

One night we went visiting the Big House for supper, and after, Linwood wanted to go out walking in the woods to see if he could find a rabbit or squirrel to shoot. Mamma told me to go along with him to make sure he didn't shoot himself in the foot. That night, it was real hot, and everybody was sitting out in the backyard of the Big House, as it was cooler outside than in. I remember hearing their conversations fading into the sounds of night as Linwood and I walked further away from the house, across the old silage field, and toward the woods. Linwood spoke to me without turning around and said, "You know where I want to go, don't you?"

"Daddy said we weren't supposed to go down there, and you know what'll happen if he finds out."

"He's not going to find out," Linwood said. "And besides, we've got the gun with us . . . just in case."

I walked along behind him, wondering just how much good his little shotgun was going to be against the prince of darkness, but I decided to humor him, since I knew there wasn't anything down there to see but the woods, and a bit of stamped-down red dirt.

The night had begun to cool down as we walked through the trees. The leaves and scrubs left the bottoms of my jeans damp as I brushed by because the dew had already fallen. We stopped once so I could light a cigarette, and then crossed over the little creek, taking the long way around the farm. There was no use to hurry, as the old folks would sit out there and talk in the backyard until the sun came up if they were of a mind. Sometimes I wonder what it is that old people find so interesting to talk about all the time.

Finally, we came to a clearing in the woods that looked as if a hole had been cut out. Up above, the night sky shone through the canopy of leaves over our heads, and the moon lit the spot of ground that was completely barren of any life. "That's it," Linwood said, "it's gotta be."

"That's it." I nudged him along. Linwood might have been afraid to go on into the circle. Maybe just seeing it was enough. But when he saw me stub out my cigarette and go in, he followed right behind. All the time he kept the shotgun raised and resting against his shoulder. Just in case.

There wasn't much to say, for once inside that circle, you don't feel much like talking. Everything went all quiet and the two of us looked straight up through the hole in the sky and saw stars, and little wisps of clouds floating over the moon. I heard a rustle in the trees and then a quick snap. I sucked in my breath real fast and turned around.

"It's just a rabbit," my brother said.

"Do you. . . ." I had to stop and try talking again as that fright had made my voice sound high-pitched and peculiar. "Do you think we'll see it . . . him . . . tonight?"

"Doubt it." Linwood kept walking, around and around that circle.

"You don't believe those old stories they all tell about this place, do you?" I looked down as one of his fingers twitched around the trigger of the gun. "I mean, all that bull about him coming up and stealing boys and all. There's no way. . . ."

"Have you ever watched Uncle Carrol's eyes when he tells that story?" Linwood asked. "*He* believes it. You don't reckon that Uncle Carrol was. . . ."

"He'd *never* come down here," I said. "He won't leave that backyard any more, much less come down here to the. . . ."

"Maybe that's *why* he won't come down here," Linwood said. "Maybe he knows that if he does, the old man is going to snatch him back down the hole." Linwood turned, and I saw his eyes shining like two dark coals. "Maybe Uncle Carrol *has* seen the devil."

I turned quickly in the other direction, my finger fidgeting through my secret packet of Salems, trying to pull another one out. My fingers wouldn't work right. "I don't think we'll see anything tonight."

Clouds blew over the moon and we stood in heavy darkness. Around me, I felt the edges of the circle closing in, and something inside me wanted to run back to the open field. The air was hot around my head, and I was beginning to feel as if I couldn't breathe. Linwood just paced, holding the shotgun to his shoulder.

"We'd better get back home." I spun Linwood around by his shoulder. "It's getting late and Daddy's going to want to start back soon."

We turned to cross the circle and go back, and, as I turned, I was hit with a jolt of fear that made my knees buckle. Cotton filled my ears, and all I could sense for just a second was the sound of my own fear tingling in them.

Directly in front of us floated this big ball of light that hovered in the air. It looked like some sort of a glowing white mist that was circular, as best as I could tell, about the size of a car tire, and not more than five feet away from us.

I couldn't move. All of my joints froze where I stood. Linwood could have been in another world then for all I knew, because I couldn't take my eyes from the light. All I could think to do just then was scream, and that's what I did. When the sound started coming out of me, I was so scared that I couldn't stop screaming, even as I clawed for breath to scream some more. The air around me was hot, and I could feel it scald my lungs as I pulled in air and yelled it right back out.

Linwood lifted the gun and emptied both barrels into the light, but the shot went on through and into the trees beyond. I took off running out of there, not caring if my little brother was behind me or not, crying and screaming all the way. It's more than two miles from that spot up to the Big House, and let me tell you, I ran every step.

As we came up over the hill from the silage field and across the yard, Mamma and Daddy were there with Uncle Carrol and

Aunt Maude and their girl JoNeil, all wondering what the shooting and hollering was about. Linwood and me, we stood there in the dark, trying to choke out what had happened—that we had been to the Tromping Grounds and we had seen the devil in person. Mamma's fists balled up and I knew we were in for it then.

But before Mamma could say anything, the back of the house lit up with a white flash. Not the trees or the people standing in the yard, but just the house itself. It was the same light I had seen before, the one burned into my memory on that long run back home. The light was there, and just as quickly and without a sound, it was gone. The devil had chased us up from the woods, looking for something in the house. I tried to find a tree to hide behind, just in case I was the one he had come up there to see.

The chatter of the people in the yard quieted, and they all stood silent, looking down toward the trees beyond the field. The only sound I remember was Linwood and me panting for breath, and the secret, far-away sound of a soft breeze through the pines.

OCTOBER 1992

AFTER THE FUNERAL,
HEADED HOME

Even though Richard Alan and I have our own house down east in Vander where the cousins can forget that I'm still alive and a shame to the family, I still wake up with a start some nights, thinking I've seen that flash of light against the bedroom wall. Richard Alan will stir and wake when I jump, and say that it's just traffic outside, headlights shining in through the window. But there's a feeling in me now, as we head down the old highway, a feeling like when you push one end of a magnet hard up against another of a like pole. Maybe it's just Uncle Carrol's funeral on my mind. That, and the cloying mortuary smell of eucalyptus and cut roses still in my lungs.

"This is where it is." I leaned forward, searching, as I slowed the car. I knew Richard Alan was in a hurry to get back home. We had a long drive, down past Fayetteville, and the sun was already starting to go down.

I looked over at Richard Alan, who had already come out of his coat and tie during the two-mile drive from the Big House down the old highway by the river. Nobody much uses the old road now, and the trees droop over the roadway, occasionally scraping across the top of the car as we went down the sharply banked and curved road. "You wouldn't believe the stories my great-grandfather used to tell about this place." I pulled off the side of the road as far as the car would go into the undergrowth. "He said it was where the devil popped up to the earth at night, and danced until daylight."

Richard Alan, who liked to hear all the old stories my family told, perked up his ears and looked out the side window, pressing his nose up against the glass.

"I've read about this place in books," he said. "And I've always wanted to come down here to take a look at it." The car bumped along and stopped in the grass beside the road, and I put it in Park. "But I have to tell you," he said, "I think I'd rather see it by light of day." He turned to me, his eyes large and beguiling. He was only half kidding about going into the haunted woods with me in the dark. "Tell me again," he said, pulling up on the door handle and lighting up the inside of the car, "about the night you and Linwood saw the devil down here."

I looked at him and smiled as we stepped out of the car. "You think there's some truth to my great-granddaddy's story that if you see the devil out there, you'll belong to him?"

"Maybe." He wrapped one arm around my waist and pulled me close. "And maybe not. I won't say."

The place had changed a lot since I had been there last as a boy. The land was all taken over with gangly weeds and scrub pines that popped up any place a spare bit of sunlight came through the trees. But maybe a hundred yards away from the road, all that gave way, and we stood in the middle of a bald clearing. Looking straight up, I saw the darkening sky above us as the enveloping trees around us cut off the sound from outside.

I knelt down in the center of the circle as Richard Alan walked the perimeter, looking, I suppose, for the hoofprints of the devil. It was the kind of place that made you want to whisper, like you were in church.

"And great-granddaddy said this is the hole where the fallen angel pops out at night." I felt along the rim of the small indentation. The soil under my hands was warm to the touch, and I imagined I could see little wisps of steam rising from the hard-packed red clay. "He comes out and dances around in a circle here, happy for the ones he's pulled to sin that day." My fingers played across the hole where they tell me fresh dirt will not even fill it in. It looks the same to me as it did when I first saw it myself, sixteen years ago.

"And they tell me that if a foolish boy were to come down here at night and see the devil do his dance, the boy will be lost forever, snatched down this hole to roast on the coals of Hell."

A little whisper of a breeze played around my head as I rubbed my fingers against the warm ground beneath them. And in that breeze, I swear I could hear the sound of somebody laughing. A young boy, I thought. Laughing and then running away through the woods around us. And then I heard a second boy's laughter mixing with the first, as they both faded into the darkness that came all around us.

As I leaned closer to the pothole, a hand grabbed my shoulder, causing me to jump. I pulled away to leave Richard Alan's hand grasping at me as I fell backward on my haunches.

"Careful, there, you. I wouldn't want you to fall in and never come back." He caught the frightened look on my face and reached down to help me up. I felt foolish as he brushed the hair away from my eyes and said, "I always did like a romantic man who believes in witches and ghosts."

His kiss was a comfort to my lips after a long day of funeral talk and that house that smelled of mice and old women.

"You taste of JoNeil's awful double-chocolate pound cake," he said. "Let's hit the road."

We walked together up to the car and crawled back inside. Richard Alan started fidgeting with the radio to find a station, and I did a U-turn to get us back out to the interstate.

As I pulled away, in the red taillights of the car, I saw a quick flash of light come up behind us. And then the devil and his boys were gone.

[Deep in a dark patch of woods in Catawba County, North Carolina, there really exists a bald spot on the earth called the Devil's Tramping Ground. I know, because I have seen it. Parts of this story are true and parts are fiction, but I'm not telling which is which—j.l.m.]

SAGRADA FAMILIA

• DAVID RAKOFF •

When she sees her son get off the bus, Ellen chokes a little bit, suddenly. A discrete fistful of air comes up and punches her in the mouth, although the windows of the car are all closed. She has last seen him at Memorial Day and now, mid-July, she can see how much weight he has lost. In fact, she can scarcely believe he has made the trip alone from New York to Truro. These two-month gaps in contact serve only to shock and mortify her.

Leo stirs from his nest of newspapers in the driver's seat and says, affectlessly, "There's Marcus. He looks good."

Ellen turns in her seat to look at him. Who is this interloper in her family car? Is she the only one who sees this wraith-like creature moving across the parking lot on his spindly legs? The slight breeze outside is blowing his jeans as if they were made of the flimsiest silk.

Leo has relinquished his anguish and worry in favor of powerlessness. When Marcus was first diagnosed, they both got on the phone and screamed, literally screamed at the tops of their lungs into the receiver, that Marcus should move home to Cambridge. Marcus calmly told them (he had clearly rehearsed this scene many times before calling them) that his life was now in New York with Tom.

"So stay with Tom! Die and go to your grave in New York with Tom!" Leo yelled and smashed down the phone, the force of his anger pulling the whole unit out of the kitchen wall. The next day, Ellen went out and bought a table model and plastered the hole. She hung a small framed print over the unpainted spot. Three years later, Leo is resigned—almost punch drunk with impotent anxiety. Now, when they get off the phone with Marcus, Leo nods off immediately, like that film clip of the narcoleptic puppy who frolics around on the grass only to crash to the ground like a fallen stone, having fallen asleep mid-leap. Ellen doesn't sleep. She either cooks or drafts at her desk. Sleep has become an untrustworthy friend these last few years. Like being slipped an un-Mickey Finn, Ellen finds herself suckered each night into bed by the promise of rest only to be up and in the kitchen not two hours later.

Ellen watches her son through the windshield and thinks of his lover, Tom, and is reminded of a story about an anthropologist who proposed an eternal, unsolvable dilemma to some people in Micronesia. In an attempt to gauge their feelings of loyalty, kinship and fealty before and after marriage, he asked them, "If your mother and your wife were both drowning, who would you save?" What he amassed, instead, was extensive data attesting to the utter absence in the lexicon of a hypothetical case, as almost everyone answered, "But they are not drowning. They are alive. There they are."

"He is not drowning. There he is," she whispers, glancing back at him in the sun-shade mirror.

Marcus opens the back door of the car. He falls back against the seat, tired out from his short walk from the bus. He looks from Ellen to Leo, gulps a smiling breathless "hello," closes his eyes and leans his head back, allowing his father to drive.

Ellen talks at her son animatedly from the front seat. These first few minutes of reunion are always hardest for her. Until she can recover those Marcus characteristics, she barely recognizes this generic, cadaverous man. She tries to elicit facial reactions from him: arching eyebrows, a smile, a considered frown, anything that will motivate this sunken, drum-tight skull into some identifiable trait of her boy.

Marcus is exhausted and asleep in the backseat. She cannot stand to look long at his shallow-breathing head with its rattling snore. She is sure his soul is dissipating out of his slightly gaping mouth like the plume of fog from an opened bottle of champagne. When he was a child, she used to thrill to see him asleep, he was so beautiful. Thinking back on it, Ellen feels that it is the only time in her life when she has been calm, or at least stopped while conscious. She now wants to clap and shout and shake him out of sleep before death takes him, before his pigeon chest just gives up and folds in upon itself. She fiddles with the radio, looks out the window, presses her forehead against the sun-heated glass, trying to fry her skin.

Their summer house was always too big for just the three of them. At least when they were younger and Marcus just a little boy, there was a vital community around and the house a hub of sorts. There were the inevitable Cambridge therapist/architect couples like themselves, scientists from the Wood's Hole Institute, artists. They used to congregate on the wide, wraparound verandah, Ellen would cook elaborate meals that would be washed down with too much liquor. The same jokes would be told, the same wit trundled out. It seemed that Ellen was forever punctuating some pronouncement of Leo's by saying to the group, "What you must all realize is that Leo is at an advantage. In addition to being an Adolescent Psychiatrist, he is an adolescent psychiatrist," to much laughter and drunken cries of "touché," and then, invariably, the guitar would be brought out and they would sing the work songs of their pre-affluent days until the final, staggering march at 3 A.M. down to the beach for a group nude swim, and perhaps some furtive, unproductive, extramarital gropings in the beach grass.

Ellen was lots of fun back then; heightened, bright, edgy. Years later, she recognizes that her quick wit, her ease with the verbal barb is the only way she knows how to react anymore. She is burning too brightly. When she sees her friends lately, she silently agrees with herself beforehand that she will shut up, but there she is, maniacally interjecting, filling up the tiniest silences with her voice. Friends tell her of the deaths of other friends and she cannot resist—she says:

"Well, she was the meanest woman who ever lived and I say that with no fear of contradiction." Then she laughs her short silvery laugh, sharp and thin as water from a pistol.

People move away, summers are spent elsewhere, marriages break up, and Ellen and Leo rattle around in this extravagant house. This luxury makes Ellen feel guilty, but she is actively pursuing her materialistic impulses lately. She found herself downtown the other day buying black marble figs, cast iron snail paperweights, alabaster eggs; small useless things with heft that she can try unsuccessfully to crush in her hands. Her knuckles can go white and her teeth can ache with the effort.

The house has a main staircase inside with a gentle curve and a cool, dark underside. The bedrooms all face the sea, all have sloping ceilings. The kitchen was done up by the original owners like Monet's at Giverny—all periwinkle blue and saffron tile with an open hearth—with glass-fronted cupboards now full of haphazard stacks of Ellen's expensive multi-colored dishes. In preparation for Marcus' arrival, she went out and bought so much food that, even if he were well, there is no way he could eat any significant portion of it. She woke at three in the morning and began cooking. There is a leek soup chilling like a green ocean in a tureen in the fridge. She has arrayed the kitchen table like a circus: three perfect peaches in a blue bowl, black grapes on a yellow plate, six greengage plums, each in a separate teacup. She went down to the beach in the middle of the night and brought up bowls full of sand, which she has piled up in little hills between the dishes. She tore the buds of garlic from their braid and placed them around, too. The rest of the surface she has festooned with whole and cut fruit. It looks like an aerial photograph of a carnival. She will just have to keep her husband and her son out of the kitchen until she is finished. She might not even show them her handiwork at all.

"It's a Roman Jewish dish," Ellen says of the cold sliced tongue marinated in vinegar with golden raisins. They are eating on the verandah.

"The acid is a bit much for me. I have some lesions in my mouth."

"The last time we were together you wanted concentrated flavors. 'Concentrated flavors' you said. Hard salami, cranberry juice, plums. I thought this would be nice for you."

"I have some lesions in my mouth. I'm sorry. Actually, I'd love something nice and bland, like a potato, if you have one. I'll make it."

"Don't get up." Ellen cuts off his access to the kitchen. "I'll be right back."

Of course Ellen has potatoes, all kinds. She will make him every potato in the house in every way. She will press them up against him still warm, covering him in potato armor. She will work them under his skin. She will make him fat.

She finds some small purple ones lying here and there around a sand pile and some strawberries. The fragrance rising from the soft fruit in the display is warm and sweet with the incipient promise of a vinegary sharpness. The watermelon she had sliced up is no longer so wet, now more syrupy. She boils the potatoes, removes their black jackets and mashes up the violet flesh. She puts them in a yellow bowl and takes them out to Marcus.

"There. You can watch the sea while you eat."

Marcus looks up at her and screws his mouth sideways in an apology.

"I'm sorry. I can't eat anything right now. I really must have a nap." He gets up and slowly walks into the house. Ellen can hear his soft footfalls negotiating the stairs. The bowl of potatoes is warm in her palm. She watches the waves for a while, thinking of nothing. Feeling the warmth in her hand, watching the waves, hearing Leo snore under his blanket of newspapers on the swinging sofa. She comes to, puts the bowl down and goes up to see how Marcus is getting on.

In these past few minutes, he has only just made it to his room and undone two buttons on his shirt. Without a word, Ellen turns down the covers on the bed and helps her son undress.

He is indeed thirty-seven, she sees. In addition to being sick, he is no longer a young man. His hair is sparser now than ever and there is a lot of gray. It tufts out of his ears and falls out of his head and grows in isolated regions on his back like his father's. She can see the short tube of his Hickman underneath his undershirt. He no longer needs to be infused for hours at a time but Ellen has neglected to ask him when he stopped or why this is so. When he undoes his belt, his trousers fall all the way down, the keys in his pocket clanking loudly on the floor. He puts his hands on her shoulders as he steps out of his pants. His underwear and socks gape at the tops and bottoms of his skinny legs. She pats his rear end. She can feel his tailbones.

"You've lost your ass, Marcus. We're going to have to fatten you up."

Marcus says nothing. He smiles a little bit and gets into bed, facing out the window, away from her. She pulls the covers over him. He makes almost no bump in the blankets at all except for his hip-bone, which sticks up like a jagged rock or a shark's fin.

He is asleep before she leaves the room. She is glad to have this time alone with Leo and Marcus both asleep. She no longer sees her son's character. Marcus, once so verbal and engaging, is now so deadened and tired all the time. She does not know if this is dementia or the result of constant pain and starvation. Whatever the cause, although she knows the alternative will be much worse when it comes, she does not find Marcus to be good company anymore—something he most profoundly used to be. For a moment, she wants to go back into his room and shake him awake by the hip-bone and tell him so, "You are not good company anymore, Marcus," the way she used to discipline him when he was younger: "Stop showing off, Marcus," or "Show a little stoicism."

She walks downstairs, passes by the kitchen and surveys her landscape from the doorway. The whole room is smelling green and hot, as if she were baking the houseplants. She takes the tureen of soup out of the fridge and places it in the center of the table—it is a high mountain lake.

She stands in the shadow under the staircase for a while, feeling the wood. She walks outside. Leo sleeps still. She walks around the verandah on tiptoe, placing the balls of her feet on each narrow floorboard all the way around the house. She goes down to the beach, piles up wet sand and begins to carve away at it with a mussel shell. She is extremely adept at making sand buildings. She once made a near-perfect replica of Gaudí's cathedral in Barcelona, *Sagrada Familia*, using corn-cobs rolled in sand for the towers. When he was young, Marcus, as might be expected of a little boy, made piles of wet, dripped sand as his castles. "That's wrong, Marcus," is what she said to him. What she really wanted to express was that, although his structures resembled Gaudí's, they lacked an underlying logic or structure; a controlled anarchy of form. She knew that it was too harsh, but she had always felt so strongly about architecture. Marcus reacted by creating even more juvenile mounds. She, in turn, declared war and produced sharp-edged Bauhaus sand models, all the while exclaiming, "Look how nice and neat, Marcus. And my hands are so clean from using my tools!"

What Ellen likes best about architecture, and has always liked best about architecture, is this: an arch, even one made without mortar (and thousands, millions were made without mortar) can be as thin as a sliver or as long as a train tunnel. No matter how hard you press on an arch, you cannot break it. It has an empty underside and still cannot be broken, regardless of the force. That an arch can be broken by the slightest push upwards or from the side concerns Ellen not at all. It is that needful marriage of stress and strength she loves. When she is aligning floor levels of pre-existing living rooms with proposed sun porches, when she is drawing plans for skylights and fireplaces, recessed bathtubs and glass-brick kitchens, she thinks of this arch. When she is designing the happiness of other people's lives, this ever-beleaguered, ever-more tenacious arch is what she likes best.

Ellen pounds the meat for veal marsala so hard that she is emitting short, yelling bursts as she makes impact with the cutting board. Leo calls in asking if she needs help. She does not and makes sure to continue quietly. It seems that the kitchen table is now giving off steam. Ellen's hair comes down in wet tendrils as she cooks.

Marcus eats only some ice cream to soothe his mouth. They eat again on the verandah, this time on the other side of the house, away from the ocean towards the sunset. The failing light and its colors replaced conversation adequately but now, with night fallen, with Marcus' slow, studied progress weakly licking the ice cream from his spoon, with little or no speaking, the silence seems amplified. They are outdoors and it is airless. Ellen's lungs are made of lead. When the phone rings, she feels she has broken the surface and starts to breathe again. She fairly flies into the kitchen to answer it.

"Hello?" she breathes heavily into the phone. She doesn't care who is on the other end.

"Hello, may I speak with Valerie please?" asks the voice.

"Valerie who?"

"Is this Valerie's house?"

"Let me check," says Ellen. "I'm just visiting. Hold on."

Ellen holds the phone for a while against her chest. She must calm down. Eventually she must let this woman on the other end off the phone, but she cannot slow her heart. She is sure the woman can hear it on the line.

"No, I'm sorry. No Valerie." She says with such hopelessness and apology that the other woman reassures her.

"That's okay," she says. "I'll check the number again."

"I am sorry."

"Who?" Leo asks when she returns.

"Wrong number." She scowls at him as if it were obvious.

"Do you know what I was thinking about this afternoon, El?" Leo begins. "Remember Asher Korner? The biologist? That summer he made up *'Menteur menteur, pantalons de feu'*? Remember how we laughed at that, we thought he was so clever? We said it all summer, *'Menteur, menteur, pantalons de feu.'* Remember?"

"No, not really." Ellen speaks through the fog of a coming headache. "Anyway, that means 'Liar, liar, pants *of* fire.' I hardly think we would have thought it was so clever. It's actually wrong. It should be something like *'pantalons brulants'* or something like that."

"I remember it," Marcus says. "Tom and I say it sometimes."

"Ah, Marcus has joined us for the evening, I see," she says, looking at him sideways. "How's the ice cream, Marcus?"

"Fine, Ellen. How's your drink?"

"Fine, thank you." Ellen eyes him skeptically. "You remember that? I haven't heard you say that since you came. I haven't heard you say much, actually." Ellen wets her mouth with her wine. Her tongue feels thick and gluey in her mouth. She is drinking too much this evening and does not care. She is feeling the hard-edged, funny nastiness brought on by drink that she used to at those dinners from the past. She is, truth be told, a little bit out for blood. The present company's will do, she has decided.

"I do remember it, I do say it sometimes. Not all the time, sometimes." He rises. "I'm going to bed. Thanks for the ice cream. Leo, I leave you to your wife." Marcus pushes his chair back and walks inside.

"I just think it's interesting when you choose to and choose not to chime in, that's all. That is all. That is all I am saying. Never too tired to disagree with Mom! Never too tired to make a fool of Ellen, huh?" Ellen yells at his retreating form, eager for a fight.

She is swinging wide now. She focuses on Leo across the table. She can see that he is looking at her uncomprehendingly. He does not know when this shift in her took place, at what point pleasantly buzzed at twilight turned into shrewishly soused for the evening.

"Fuck him if he can't take a joke," Ellen says and looks out into the night.

She dreams she buys a bottle of water in a shop. The water is so high-tone that it contains caviar. When she tips the bottle to her mouth, the fish eggs block up in her throat like small twigs in a sieve. Her thirst remains unquenched. She cannot find another shop to make a different purchase.

Ellen finally wakes and rises to get a drink. She feels like a salted plum—dessicated and crystalline. Her fingers will ping and snap off like stalagmites if she bangs them against the sink. She watches herself in the bathroom mirror. She thinks she can see her cells moistening and swelling as she drinks water. Her pores are wheezing and creaking at the effort of replenishment. They stop, gasp and wheeze again. She is a ship rolling and creaking on swells of water. She is watching her unmoving face all the while, fascinated at the labored sounds her body is making as it fills up, as the water races through her channels. Wheeze, rattle, gasp. This has never happened to her before. She must either have drunk more than she thought or her metabolism has changed radically with aging.

Things slowly focus and she sees her mouth is closed, her breathing even. She checks the taps for the sound. She lays her forehead uncomprehendingly on the porcelain edge of the sink.

"Not me," she thinks, "not the sink." She is sniffing around, eliminating possible sources of the noise. She fingers the folds of the shower curtain. She feels like a stroke victim, only getting it partially right, or one of the blind men with the elephant. The knowledge dawns on her before she is even fully awake. She has walked to Marcus' room before she even remembers she's at the beach house.

She turns on the light, touches her son, pulls her hand away, wakes Leo and tells him, "Marcus is on fire. Call Tom and tell him to call their doctor. We'll drive him to New York." She is weary and somewhat relieved. The way one greets rain after a day spoiled by an oppressive, threatening sky.

"Why don't we just take him to the hospital in Cambridge?" asks Leo.

"Because he doesn't live in Cambridge."

She has practiced these steps, this actuality, so often. All these actions feel apart from her and automatic. She is performing in a play she has rehearsed in her sleep for years. The anthropologist was wrong; there is a hypothetical case, although the scenario is reversed here: if a son is drowning and the mother and the lover are on shore, who will save him? And what if the sun is shining on the waves and the gulls have voices like razors and she can't see if it's even her son out there or what if she's already too damned tired and she knows he'll just end up back in the water anyway? They will drive him to New York.

It is 3 A.M. She has pulled on jeans and a sweater and is tending to Marcus. She sponges him down and looks at the naked body of her son—it is already vestigial. When her father was sick and dying, she bathed him, too. Seeing her old father's penis bobbing in the bathwater as she washed his back made her strangely nauseous in the base of her stomach. Looking at Marcus' penis, she feels nothing. It is a dewlap, a soft ear. When he first came out to her, Ellen had a dream of Marcus. His penis was huge and red as he held out a crooked bony finger to an unseen figure. She had woken shaken and sweaty and angry with her son. Leo stands outside in the hallway, naked as well but for socks, talking to Tom on the telephone. Her own clothes feel ludicrous to her.

"This is the time years ago when we'd all be skinny-dipping," she muses.

The night smells uncommonly good to Ellen as they drive along the Cape towards New York—like crackers. She only opens her window an inch at the top. If she opens it the whole way, she'll gorge herself on the night air and be sick. Marcus is wrapped in a blanket in the backseat. He had whispered once, "I'm sorry," as they locked up the house and Leo carried him out to the car, and then he dropped off.

When he was about eight or so, he broke his leg in a hockey game. Leo had gone down to the hospital to pick him up.

When they returned, Marcus was in Leo's arms as he was now, wrapped in Leo's overcoat. His face shone with pride. "I broke my leg!" he beamed at Ellen. She had felt embarrassed at the time, in the presence of Marcus' masculine pride. It felt oddly sexual and private to witness the pleasure her son was taking in his physical injury. She had the same feeling when, years later, she met Tom and Marcus for a drink in New York. When the pianist began to play "But Not For Me," Tom, who had been saying something to her, took Marcus' hand in his and placed both of them on his knee and continued speaking to Ellen. She did not want to be privy to this aspect of Marcus' life. She had been glad to get back to Boston after that. "I'm sorry," her grown-up son had said. "I'm sorry what?" she thinks. "Sorry's not good enough."

Leo puts in a cassette of the Weavers. Pete Seeger tells the audience at Carnegie Hall to harmonize, and they do—spontaneously, beautifully. Ellen sits in the dark listening to them sing "Good Night, Irene." She wonders if they all knew one another that night in 1955, if they were professionals sitting out there. Or was that one of those instances where life doesn't disappoint? Why not be a Communist, she thinks, if it means that kind of belonging? The road is bone white under the headlights.

"No one opposes Commissioner Moses. Even the fishes do as he wishes." Growing up in New York, Ellen recited this in primary school. She thought Commissioner Moses must be a very mean man, bullying everybody, even the fishes. Ellen had never liked the city, her whole life. It all seemed too crowded and squalid and she couldn't help feeling that Robert Moses had imposed his despotic will onto everything. Parks, beaches, roads. It all felt so much like what her own father did with his loud, autocratic hectoring. As a young child she had conflated the two of them; Moses was in the bible, her father was Jewish. "Don't tell your father," her Mother said about the most minor infractions of his will, usually involving something as inconsequential as a new pair of shoes, or the two of them having an ice cream at the Woolworth's counter before they returned home from shopping. The kind of man who yelled at fish; Swim faster! Swim slower! Go through the fake sunken castle!

New York doesn't thrill Ellen even now. Even though she successfully got out, she despises it and fights the panicked feeling that she will be detained whenever she has to visit. So much garbage everywhere. How does a sofa land up on the side of a highway with no buildings in sight? The traffic creeps, radios cut out in the tunnels, everything is covered in graffiti, people wear the paucity of quality in their lives like a badge of honor, laughing ruefully and contentedly when their subway tunnels fill with smoke. Ellen hates New York and New Yorkers. It is everything she was thrilled to leave behind when she left to go to college over forty years ago.

It is 7 A.M. when they reach the city. There is construction all the way down the West Side Highway. The Weavers sing for about the tenth time during their trip, "the Rock Island Line it is a mighty good road." Marcus is still asleep in the backseat.

"When the stores open in New York, we can buy some underwear and toothbrushes and stuff," Leo had said when they had just passed Boston.

"You can do what you like. I'm coming back to the Cape tonight."

People have been asking the same thing of Ellen for the past twenty or so years, ever since the culture got its paws into psychiatry: "Oh," they will say, "your husband's a psychiatrist? What must that be like? Does he analyze you just all the time?" or they ask "So, are you all crazy?" as if it were the funniest, most original joke that could be made. But the answer (the answer Ellen never gives; generally she will chuckle and say something like "Absolutely—as proverbial fruitcakes") is quite simple: "He wouldn't dare." Ellen knows that she has become, amazingly enough, not her mother, whom she defended and vowed she would never treat with anything but respect and compassion, but her own father. She bullies, she lectures, and she has kept her husband at bay almost since the day they met. She has come to think of her mother's passivity in exactly the opposite terms she used to. It sickens her. It makes her want to have lashed out more when she was alive. There are some days when Ellen would like nothing more than to have her mother back for even just an hour, but the fantasy always turns into Ellen dressing down her risen mother for some stupidity. By the time Marcus got sick, the lines had been drawn between

Ellen and Leo. Maybe once over the years, he had tried to get her to examine her own feelings about something, perhaps he had commented on her extreme efficiency in dealing with her father's estate after he died, she could not remember. She had levelled a gaze of such murderous censoring on him that he had retreated immediately. Leo's analyses of her and Marcus, whatever they may be, remain unverbalized.

"Yes, well then," Leo says in a tiny voice, "I think I will stay and you can go wherever." And then her husband begins to cry.

She does not even need to ask him to pull over, he is already swerving across two lanes. He stops the car and leans on the steering wheel and cries in earnest, the ribs in his back furling and unfurling under his dirty T-shirt.

Ellen almost puts a hand on him but stops herself at the last moment. She is overcome with the thought that this scenario ought to have the windshield wipers going as well, for maximum effect. She hoists her purse onto her shoulder and gets out of the car. Marcus has still not woken, lying across the backseat like a suit on a broken hanger.

Standing on the side of the road, Ellen thinks of her table display. Now nobody will get to see it. She hopes when she gets back it is blanketed with a carpet of flies. She hopes a family of mice are nestled into the hillocks and eating the soft rot of it.

In the distance, Ellen sees a cab. Leo's car still idles twenty feet behind her. The cab comes closer. A barreling yellow sun, its lights and grill smiling a greeting. Ellen raises her arm and opens her mouth to call and the air rushes in.

TRICKED

• ROBERT RODI •

In the movies, when an ominous, portentous moment occurs, you get ominous, portentous music to club you over the head with foreboding. When I met Elliot Shore, all I could hear was the pathetic tick of plastic champagne glasses and quadraphonic conversation about John-John Kennedy and the actress who played the mermaid. So where's Bernard Hermann when you need him?

I was riding a tsunami of self-esteem at the time, so maybe I wouldn't even have noticed an orchestral thrum of doom. I was at the Velma Stamen Gallery on Ohio Street, basking in the opening-night glow of my sixth one-man exhibition. And as if that weren't heady enough, I'd also just spent a ridiculously enjoyable half-hour expounding on the death of modernism to a Hippie Chick from Hell, a p.c. scribe sent by *ARTnews* to impale me on my own reactionary representationalism. I gave her plenty of ammo. What she didn't notice—and I did—was that her tape recorder was dead during my entire song and dance. Wish I could've been a fly on the wall when she got back to her desk and tried a playback.

But my anti-modernist spiel had attracted Elliot—a tall, lean, beautifully wiry youth with eyes that fizzed like Alka-Seltzer when he looked at me. And when I looked back, he blushed—blushed! like a schoolgirl, like a nun!—and turned away.

I sidled up to my rep (and best friend), Ottolina Probst, who was trying with much vigor and even more saliva to remove a chutney stain from her daishiki.

"Heads up," I muttered, nodding ever so slightly in Elliot's direction. "Babe alert."

Ottolina, who at fifty had discovered an unquenchable lust for teenage boys that she'd unfortunately suppressed during her own adolescence, flicked her head to attention as efficiently as any snapping turtle. "Oh," she muttered, disappointedly eying Elliot and returning to her stain. "Bit old, isn't he?"

"You're nuts! Can't be more than twenty-three."

"Like I said." She took a quick glance around her. "Lull in the festivities, Vance. Go on, have a go."

Now, I'm not a young thing myself—not anymore. At forty-seven, I have an insecure grip on my remaining hair—or, I should say, it has an insecure grip on me. My face is lined and weathered, the way I thought all painters' faces should look until mine actually got that way. And while I'm in good physical shape, my body is in daily battle with the great god Gravity, and defeat is both inevitable and imminent.

However, advanced age has brought with it a largish compensation: fame. I've been lionized by *Life*, analyzed by the *Atlantic*, and deified by "Donahue." I've painted presidents, pundits, pop stars, and princesses. To be sure, in the grand scheme of things my fame is still of the big-fish-small-pond variety, but the way Elliot was filching glances at me, I could tell he called that small pond home.

I ambled over to him, utterly confident within the armor of my celebrity. "Any questions, just ask," I remarked with debonair off-handedness, trying not to allow this youth's physical perfection to render me all gushy and *gamin*. "I'm the artist. Vance Zazlow."

"I know," he said, and it sounded as though he'd rehearsed it before a mirror for weeks. That single "I know" spoke volumes; it told me not only that he knew who I was, but that I fascinated and attracted him.

I decided to tease him by pretending obliviousness. "Well, of course," I said, shrugging. "My name and picture are by the door."

"I knew before that," he said, and he flicked his tongue across his lower lip. I thought I might faint. "I came here just for—just *hoping* to see you."

"How sweet," I said, meaning it, and I lifted my champagne glass to my lips. As I did so, I could see that it was empty, but by then it was too late. Brazening it out, I tilted my head and pretended to have a big old chug of the Widow Clicquot.

Elliot appeared not to have noticed my pantomime. He took one step closer and all of a sudden I could *smell* him—breathe in that dried-sweat-on-supple-skin musk of youth, that intoxicating scent of pheromones being pumped out as if by a Play-Doh factory going full tilt. I wondered what it would be like to grab and kiss him.

"I couldn't help overhearing your interview with that *ARTnews* reporter," he said. "I can't believe the courage it took for you to tell her all those things when you know how she's going to position them to her readers."

"Well," I said, reddening a little as I remembered her dormant tape-recorder, "less courage than you think."

"And you were so *right*!" he said, a little gasp in his voice. "It blows me away, how right you were! After all these decades of plumbing modernism to the very depths—all that stripping away of layer after layer of meaning just to see what's left—we've reached a dead end."

"Actually, 'impasse' is the word I used," I corrected him, smiling.

"Like, once we've said, 'Here it is, here is the "all" of painting, reduced to the irreducible,' what value is there in continuing to say that? Now that we know images are just colors and shapes, now that we know form is independent of content, isn't it time we started putting the layers *back*, one by one, to see what's there for us?"

"Past time," I corrected him again. "About fifteen years *past* time." A server came by with a fresh tray of champagne glasses. I grabbed two, and handed one to Elliot.

He took a swig and then rubbed his nose, as though the bubbles had tickled him. "Christ, it's so exciting just to be here *talking* to you like this."

From across the gallery, I could see Ottolina giving me the pinky-in-the-air wave that was our code for "Prospective Buyer." She was standing next to a woman in a rose Christian

Lacroix suit with an incredibly teary-eyed Shih Tzu in her arms. You could practically *see* the money falling out of her purse.

I scowled at Ottolina, in full view of the Prospective Buyer. The great thing about being a painter is that people *expect* you to be rude.

Then I turned to Elliot and said, "Well, enjoy the exhibit. And listen, if you'd like to stick around, we can continue our discussion afterwards."

"You mean it?" He swallowed a breath. "I'd like that, I'd like that a *lot*."

Now, here is where the oboes and the kettle drums should've come in at about forty gazillion decibels.

I scuffed my way over to Ottolina and played the tempestuous, difficult *artiste* for Mrs. Granger Sparks II for a half-hour or so, explaining—with Ottolina's deliberately less condescending annotation—that my championing of representational painting was a philosophical and historical choice. And that my series of notable men and women with their faces partially obscured by their hands was my way of commenting on the world's reluctance to see things my way. Which was of course a crock of shit, because the world was only too happy to see things my way. And Mrs. Granger Sparks II was no different. By the time she left, she'd commissioned her own portrait and her husband's as well, and was wondering out loud how she was going to manage to cover her face with her hands and still hold darling Koko.

That's when I noticed that Elliot was indeed still waiting. Windbreaker slung over his shoulder, champagne glass in hand, he was studying my portrait of the wife of the mayor of Boulder as though it held the key to the secrets of eternity.

Ottolina noticed him, too, and kept nodding towards him and opening her eyes wide, as if to say, Is what I think is happening, happening? And, giddy and giggly, I wiggled my eyebrows in reply. Because, fame notwithstanding, I'd never attracted anyone *quite* as young as Elliot; I'd fully expected the boy to come, flirt, and flee, the way boys his age usually do once they get an up-close look at the romantic hero of their dreams and realize he kind of resembles their dads. But I wasn't about to look a gift horse in the mouth, now, was I?

Now here, here is where a kind of synthesizer growl might've alerted me to what was coming if I weren't careful.

Elliot waited until the gallery closed, and then the two of us went out for coffee. But we couldn't find a café in the neighborhood, so we went to a dance bar instead and had margaritas and gyrated while Lisa Stansfield tried to wail like a singer of color, and then all of a sudden he was all over me—or maybe I was all over him—or maybe both. However it happened, I woke up the next morning, my head feeling like the Spin Cycle on a Westinghouse washer, and found his clothes scattered all over the bedroom.

I lurched out of bed like someone who'd been given a hotfoot, and, holding on to the wall for support, crept to the edge of the loft and looked down into the studio.

Something was wrong.

"Hey," I tried to shout. My voice was husky and dry. "*Hey.*"

Elliot appeared in plaid boxer shorts and nothing else, looking as brown and lean as a Jimmy Dean sausage. "Hi!" he chirped, waving with one hand. In the other, he held a lamp.

"Whad are you doon?" I mumbled, my head not yet clear.

"Just moving some furniture," he trilled. "I got up in the middle of the night to take a whiz, and I stubbed my toe on your bookshelf. And then I looked around and realized, the way you had things set up here was kind of like an obstacle course. So I decided to do you a favor." He swept his arm across the room to display his handiwork. The place now looked like a V.F.W. hall, everything pushed right up to the four walls. "You'll find you can move around a lot more easily now."

I felt a flash of irritation, then thought, Well, it's worth it to be able to look at him a little longer—and I can always move everything back when he leaves.

But he didn't leave. It was Friday morning, and I presumed he must have a job for which he'd have to depart, but he clung to me like a sheet of fabric softener to a sock. We ate breakfast side by side (which was difficult, as he'd shoved the kitchen table into a corner), then showered together (mmm), dressed together, and sat and read the paper with our arms around each other. It was a little weird, but in a way I was enjoying it.

Still, I eventually began to feel a yen for privacy. I had work to do, and I couldn't do it with Elliot's hands holding the brush alongside mine.

I turned to him, tousled his hair, and said, "Listen, I've got to go out now. But this has been great. It really has. It's meant a lot to me." I gave him a peck on the lips.

"It doesn't have to end," he said, eyes as wet as a fawn's. "I don't have any plans."

I grinned sadly. "Alas, I do."

"What?" he asked, and his tone was a hair too proprietary for my taste. This is where a jagged violin riff would've ripped into the soundtrack.

"Well, errands to run," I said. "Supplies, food. That kind of thing."

"I'll come with you." His big, blue eyes bore into mine like a tractor beam from the U.S.S. Enterprise.

What could I say? I shrugged and muttered, "Well, great. Okay."

He put on my denim jacket.

"Oh, hey, that's mine," I said. I pointed to his windbreaker, which was lying atop the Lifecycle that sat beneath the far south window. "Remember?"

"Oh—I just wanted to wear something of yours," he said, straightening out the shoulders. "It's okay, isn't it?"

"Well—yes, but then you'll have to come b— See, I wasn't intending that—" I took a deep breath. "Sure, I guess. I mean. Hell."

As we descended in the elevator, he hugged my arm and said, "We have to get some whole milk. I can't drink that skimmed stuff you've got."

"So don't," I said cheerily. "Listen to you! Sound like you're moving in or something." I laughed, to convey the ridiculousness of the idea.

He laughed, too, but didn't respond; he just kept smiling.

"I mean, hey," I said, desperately trying to elicit some clue to his state of mind, "it was *only* one night."

"So far," he growled, and he bit my shoulder.

I felt trapped. Cornered. Hamstrung. How had this happened? Why did I feel so out-of-control? I made a mental note never to have casual sex again.

A moment later something hit me. What if he'd swiped my keys? I felt my pockets. Empty!

Then I remembered. I'd left them in the denim jacket. Had he known that?

The elevator was now just two floors above the lobby.

I panicked. I said, "Come here, you," and gave him a hug, and as I was hugging him I deftly removed my keychain from the jacket pocket.

Feeling a small measure of relief, I allowed him to hold my hand as we strode out of the elevator and into a bright, crisp summer cityscape.

Once we were outside, however, I tried to be more circumspect. I mean, I believe that publicly displaying affection is as constitutionally protected a behavior for gay men as it is for straights. But the fact is, there are people who disagree. Violently. And for that reason, holding hands with another man is a political act, and like every political act, it has potential repercussions. And if I was going to risk life and limb by committing a political act on the mean streets of Chicago, I was sure as hell going to make certain it was with someone I *wanted* to hold hands with. Which, at this point, wasn't Elliot. But damn if I could wrench myself free from his triathlete's grip.

Fortunately, we inspired only a few catcalls as we walked; even so, by the time we reached Kady Art Supplies, I was not only eager, but anxious, to have my private sphere restored to me. As we walked down the store's aisles, me carrying one of its red plastic shopping baskets, I had to resort to saying, "Elliot, do you mind? I need both hands for this."

"Huh? Oh, sure." He released me, but put his hand on my back and rubbed me as we walked.

Feeling frightened now, I tried to steer him into conversation, hoping that he might thus reveal himself to be basically normal—just a little high-strung and overly affectionate, like a lovably annoying Labrador. I said, "You know, Elliot, I don't know a thing about you. Where you live, what you do—your whole story." As I was talking, I climbed a ladder to reach a bin of brushes. Elliot's hand stayed in place as I climbed, so that it slid down my back and ended up resting on my tush. Startled, I abandoned the brushes and hurried back down.

"There's nothing to tell," he said when I was again at eye-level. "My life began last night."

I laughed nervously. "No. Come on."

"I'm not a liar," he said, a bit prickly. "I mean what I say."

I was now so rattled that I couldn't stand his touch a moment longer. I handed him the basket and said, "Could you hold this, please?"

"Anything, for you." As soon as he had it, he started sorting through the tubes of paint. "These for me?"

"What?" I asked, stopped in my tracks, astonished. "They're for *me*."

"I know that, silly. I mean, are these for your *portrait* of me? Because—I don't know." He fingered the tubes dubiously. "I don't really see my coloring reflected here. My hair, especially. More of an amber, I think. But maybe you're better at mixing than—oh, God. Of course you are. You're a genius. Forget I said anything."

"You want me to *paint* you?"

"I want you to do *everything* to me." He licked his lower lip again, but the erotic sizzle was gone. Now, he just looked like a hungry, man-eating panther.

I shook my head in disbelief. "Elliot, do you have any idea how much I charge for a commission?"

"I'm sure we can take it out in trade," he purred, and he grabbed my crotch with a leer.

My heart was pounding faster than the rhythm track of any Paul Jabara tune ever recorded. This. Boy. Was. Trouble.

I cleared my throat and said, "Uh, Elliot, do me a favor and get started ringing those up, will you? I just need to grab something in back."

And then—

—I hate to say this—

—I ditched him.

I darted into the rear storeroom, scooted past some fairly surprised clerks, and exited through the back door to the alley behind the shop. Then I ran all the way home, panted and wheezed on my way up in the elevator, and locked myself in my apartment.

I saw his windbreaker. I checked it for a wallet, for keys, for anything he might have to return for.

Nothing.

Fine, then. He could just have the denim jacket in trade.

I threw myself onto the couch and stretched a pillow across my face.

No more casual sex, *ever*.

Eleven minutes later, the telephone started ringing.

I threw off the pillow and stared at it, as though it were Pandora's Box, and if I dared to lift the receiver—

Before I could think of disconnecting the answering machine, it kicked in. "This is 555-4122," my voice droned. "Leave a message after the tone." *Beep.*

A strangulated pause. "Vance? It's Elliot."

My heart jumped into my mouth, and I had to gulp to get it down again.

"Um—I don't know what to think. You disappeared from the store, and—was it something I said? I hope it wasn't something I said. Listen. If it was something I said—uh—" What was that? What was that? Was that a sob? Could that have been a sob? "I can't believe this. If I really did fall in love with one of the most titanic geniuses in the world, only to lose him not a day later—I—I couldn't face it. I don't know what I'd do. To myself. To both of us. I just don't."

I clutched my collar and felt my hair stand on end. This is, I think, where a shrill flourish of harpsichord would've been suitably threatening, but by now I was beyond the help of any soundtrack, theoretical or otherwise.

"I copied your number off your desk phone at home," Elliot continued. "While you were asleep. Hope you don't mind."

I wondered how long it would take to have it changed.

"I bought your supplies for you," he said. "I'm kind of not employed at the moment, so it's pretty much wiped me out. I at least need to know how to get these to you. And, you know, get paid back. Not that that's imp— Well, it *is* important, but in comparison to— I mean, nothing compares to—" Another long pause. "Um—guess I'll head over to your place. Maybe I'll run into you on the way. Uh—bye."

I leapt to my feet and started running around the studio. "Oh, shit!" I hissed, in a blind panic. "He's coming! He's coming!" I ended up tripping over the goddamned coffee table he'd moved, and the floor knocked some sense back into me.

By which time the phone was ringing anew. I let the answering machine take the call, and listened from my place on the floor. "It's me again," said a much-relieved Elliot. "I just figured out what happened. You got a sudden inspiration for a painting, right? And this creative fever just overcame you. And you just *had* to get back to your studio immediately. So you left, and I was so busy with the clerk at the cash register that I didn't even see you go." He sighed. "I know artists are like that. You don't owe me an apology, baby. I don't want you to think you owe me anything. Ever. I want to devote my life to serving *you*, and being your muse. So from now on, don't worry about me, about leaving me behind or anything. I'm sorry if my first call made you feel guilty, or mad, or whatever. Because—I mean, hell, I know where you live, I know where you're exhibiting, I even know where you shop for supplies. I can always find you. Don't worry. I'm here for *you*. Not the other way around." Then, with a little more iron in his voice, "I still can't figure out why you're not *answering*, though. But never mind, I'll be there soon enough."

The moment he hung up, I grabbed the receiver and called Ottolina. "I have to come and stay with you for a couple of days," I burbled hysterically.

"What? Out of the question. I have Frankie here this weekend."

"The Boy Scout? This is more important, Ottolina."

"He's a Scout *Leader*, thank you very much. And nothing's more important."

"Oh, no? Sit down." And I collapsed on the couch and spilled the whole sordid story, beginning with our departure from the gallery (had it only been the night before?) right through the phone calls of only minutes earlier.

When I'd finished, she sighed deeply. "So your little trick turned out to be a starfucker. Big deal. Happens to everyone at least once. Just send him packing."

"You aren't listening! He refuses to hear anything but what he wants to hear! And he's out there now, *stalking* me." I curled into the fetal position.

"Well, there are laws against that. Sic the police on him."

"I thought of that. I'm pretty sure you have to be stalked for a couple days, at least, before they'll do anything. I mean, they're not going to arrest this kid because he's been bothering me since breakfast."

"So, wait a few days, *then* sic the police on him."

"I can't *do* that—I can't live like this for that long, my phone ringing, someone out on the streets watching for me. It's too creepy."

"Well, maybe he'll get tired and eventually give it up."

I considered that. "I don't think so. He says he loves me. And I think in some loony way, he really *does.*"

She sighed, then said, "All right, listen, you're plainly too dis— Just a minute. What, Frankie? It's on the second shelf. The *second* shelf. I can see it from *here*, for God's sake. Count Chocula—plain as day." Then she returned her attention to me. "Listen, you're plainly too distraught to think clearly. Come on over for lunch and we'll work something out."

"You're a doll. I love you."

"Well, you're a pig and I hate you. So I guess we're even."

It was more than an hour to even the most liberal approximation of lunchtime, but I couldn't just sit here, waiting for Elliot to come haunting my doorway. I made up my mind to get out of there at once, and just wander the city till it was time to see Ottolina. I washed my face, donned my leather jacket, and slipped down the back stairs. Since I live on the tenth floor, the exertion pretty much winded me. No way could I go back *up* that route.

Once I'd emerged from the laundry room at the side of the building, I started making tracks in the direction of Ottolina's Lincoln Park digs. But something stopped me. I had to know just how serious this was.

I backtracked till I was just around the corner from the front of the building.

Then, slowly, I stuck out my head and looked.

And there he was. Elliot. Not ten yards away, buzzing, buzzing on the bell, a bag of Kady art supplies under his arm.

Then, as if he'd received a psychic signal, he turned and looked my way.

I yanked back my head and ran like a goddamned bat out of goddamned hell.

When I reached Ottolina's neighborhood, I began to feel safe, so I slowed down and began strolling, taking in the shops and restaurants. It was the middle of a workday, and the streets were filled with the aged and the infirm, making incremental progress on their daily errands, trying to get as much done as possible before the power-suited young descended on the area and filled it once again with hurry, hurry, hurry. In such surroundings, I could almost make myself believe that I was taking Elliot much too seriously; maybe Ottolina was right, and he *would* tire of the chase and move on in a day or two. But then I turned a corner and found myself confronted with someone who on first glance seemed to be Elliot, and the way my throat and stomach and testicles constricted with fear told me that this cut a little deeper; instinctively, I knew the boy couldn't simply be dismissed. And I found myself running again.

I arrived at Ottolina's terraced Shangri-La looking sweaty and pale and fearful, but her doorman admitted me all the same. I thanked him profusely and stumbled over to the elevator.

Ottolina, her head swaddled in a turban and wearing a T-shirt that said NUMBER ONE BITCH, welcomed me into her chintz-gone-mad apartment with a shake of her head and a perfunctory hug. I could hear the television blaring in the background. "Now, come along and let's talk while Frankie's busy with 'The Monkees,' " she said. She led me into her kitchenette, where she'd set a place for two. She pulled a particularly mutilated leg of lamb from the refrigerator.

"Leftovers?" I said, aghast, trying to be funny.

"I'd appreciate your help getting rid of it," she said, setting it on the counter. "Frankie only likes hamburger. Now, let's get right to it. I think I have a solution to your little problem."

"It doesn't involve having him hit, does it? I couldn't have him hit."

"No, it involves you acting like a *mensch*, for God's sake. Listen, this is a boy we're talking about. He's, what, twenty, twenty-three? Over-the-hill by my standards, true, but we're not talking about me. Anyway, you're this big, glamorous, internationally acclaimed painter. *You're* supposed to be the one who sets the pace here." She took a salad bowl from a cabinet.

"He won't let me!"

"Your fault, dear." She yanked a head of lettuce from the refrigerator and started shredding it into the bowl. "But never mind, it's too late now to try to assume any kind of authority. You've already given him the upper hand. So you're going to have to use more devious means."

"Like what?"

"Well," she said, rinsing her hands under the faucet, "you could make yourself unattractive to him."

"I—could—what do you mean?"

"You know what I mean. Put your goddamn vanity aside for a moment. This boy, he has an image of you as an exciting, so-phisticated figure. All you have to do is show him you're really dull and petty and crude, and that's it, the illusion disappears and so does he." She started hacking off bits of meat and toss-ing them into the salad bowl.

I felt shamed. Such a solution never would have occurred to me. As much as I wanted to be rid of Elliot, my pride wouldn't have allowed me to consider making him not *want* me. "You're a genius," I said, cozying up to her and giving her a kiss.

She giggled and pushed me away, then continued cutting the lamb. "Have you had a meal with him yet?"

I thought for a moment. "No; we only drank together last night." I shrugged. "There was breakfast this morning, but that was just a bagel and cream cheese."

"Then here's what you do," she said, pouring a bottled Par-mesan dressing over the salad and carrying it to the table. "Take him to dinner tonight. Be a complete slob—no manners what-soever. Make it embarrassing for him to be seen with you."

We sat, and I tucked in a napkin. "Wonderful!" I enthused. "I wish for your sake there was a Nobel Prize for diabolicality."

"I wish for your sake there was such a *word* as 'diabolicality.' " She spread her napkin over her lap. "Now shut up and eat. And no practicing the slob routine till you're out of here."

I returned home with some trepidation, but, miraculously, Elliot wasn't waiting in front of the building. There were, how-ever, nineteen messages on my answering machine. I only had the nerve to listen to the first four, which got progressively more hysterical and more possessive (the fourth saying that he hoped I didn't "wind up sorry" for how I was treating him) be-fore calling the number he repeated like a mantra after each.

He answered on the first ring. "Hello!" he barked.

"Aha! Now I have your phone number," I said, trying to be

breezy and teasing. "I'm getting to know more about you all the time."

He let a quivering sigh escape him. "That's not what this was all about, was it? It wasn't just some weird strategy of getting my phone number? I mean, I'd have given it to you."

"Well, I don't know about that; you're pretty reluctant to give me *any* information about you. But, no, as it happens, I went missing for precisely the reason you mentioned."

"But—I've been calling for *hours*. You never answered. I even rang your doorbell!"

"I never let anything interrupt me when I'm working. Sorry, you're just going to have to get used to that. No one ever said dating an artist was easy."

A pause. "I guess."

"Don't be upset. Listen, I'll make it up to you over dinner tonight."

"You mean it?"

"I mean it. Meet me at Angelina's at eight."

"Oh, God. I'll be there. I swear."

"Good. I'm counting on it."

He looked radiant when I met him there; almost enough to make me reconsider what I was about to do. But I had to ignore his aquiline nose and ring-coiled hair and the glinty stubble on his cleft chin, the front tooth that crossed attractively over its mate, and the soft cottons and wools that enveloped the wiry, fighter's body I'd felt hard and hot beneath my hands just the night before. No, no—I had to be strong.

I began with the bread the waiter had laid out for us. I slathered a piece with olive paste and shoved it whole into my mouth. "So," I said, my words barely distinguishable through the mass of doughy pulp, "you gonna tell me 'bout your life, or do I hafta have your phone number traced an' start following *you*?" Olive paste dribbed down my chin and settled into a fold in my crotch.

He stared at me in disbelief. "There's not much to tell," he said, quietly, searching my eyes for some way to make sense of my behavior. "I'd much rather just sit and listen to *you* talk."

I gulped down the barely chewed glob of bread. "About what?" I asked, snapping up my fork and using it to pick my teeth. A woman two tables away tsked at me.

Elliot was trying not to be put out. "Um—about art, and life, and philosophy, and the future," he said, folding his arms over the table and smiling dreamily.

"*That* crap," I said, shaking my head. I leaned forward. "Can I let you in on a little secret? I don't know *shit* about any of that."

He looked stricken. "But—but I *heard* you—that woman from *ARTnews*—"

I waved in dismissal. "Oh, *that*. Ottolina, my rep, wrote all that for me. Made me memorize it, so I could spew it out at the drop of a hat. Figured it'd impress prospective clients. Thing is, we artists, all of us, we're fucking primitives." To accentuate this point, I blew my nose into my napkin. "The ideas just come *through* us, and we put them down. It's up to other people to figure out what's in there. All that philosophy stuff. For the birds, you know what I mean?" I waved a new piece of bread at him; olive paste leapt into his waterglass. "Know what *I* like? Just hanging out and watching 'The Monkees.' " I made a mental note to thank Frankie for the inspiration.

The waiter interrupted us, and asked if we'd like to order drinks. I loudly asked for the cheapest white Zinfandel they had, then sent him away.

For a time, Elliot sat with a dubious grin on his face while I expounded on which of the Monkees I thought the most beddable. From there I went on to the Beatles, the Beach Boys, and the Dave Clark Five, and had just started to expound on Paul Revere and the Raiders ("Mark Lindsay's ponytail was to *die* for") when our appetizer came: a nice, light Insalata Caprese. We split it. I finished my share in just under seventeen seconds, leaving my shirtfront spattered with olive oil. Then I belched as loudly as I could—which, to my glee, was considerably loudly. Several other diners half-turned their heads.

By the time we'd finished our entrees, I'd managed to hold forth on the joys of newspaper crossword puzzles for almost an hour, and had strands of linguine in my shoes. Elliot was graciously trying to maintain the polite fiction that I had not in fact coughed a steamed tomato across the table and onto his sleeve. I, however, was becoming too much a mess even for myself. I excused myself, and Elliot seemed only too grateful to see me go.

I spent nearly ten minutes in the men's room, trying to get the worst of the carbonara stains out of my seersucker trousers, and hoping against hope that Elliot would use the time to figure out that he could now up and ditch *me*. But when I returned to the table, he was still sitting there, patiently, adoringly.

"You were gone a long time," he noted as I resumed my seat.

I met his eyes warmly and said, "I was picking my nose and it started to bleed."

On the way home, I ran out of absurd topics of conversation, and was trying to make my final few comments on Jacqueline Onassis's hairstyles last the rest of our walk, when Elliot stopped short and started weeping.

I turned back to him (passing through the trail of garlic I'd left hanging in the air) and put my hand on his shoulder. "What's wrong?" I asked with concealed ecstasy. Clearly, I'd made the boy miserable.

But when he managed to pull an answer from among his wracking sobs, it was, "I'm not worthy of you! I didn't realize till tonight. You're so wonderfully unpretentious—so—so *bohemian*!" He let loose a feathery gasp, then fell onto my chest and hugged me. "You've *got* to give me a chance—a chance to let go of all my pompous ideas and just *live*. Like you do!" And then he continued bawling.

Utterly defeated, what could I do but agree?

Back at home, in bed, I decided to give it one final shot. "I don't recall what happened last night, when I was drunk," I whispered to him as he lay next to me, electric with expectation, "but the thing is, sexually, I'm a little—well—unconventional."

His eyes blazed with excitement. "I don't care," he said. "I'm yours. Whip me. Beat me."

"It's not like that," I said, hoping my nose wouldn't grow *too* much for the whopper I was about to tell. "Thing is, I like it quiet."

A moment's pause. *"Quiet?"*

"Yes. You know. No noise. And in complete and total darkness."

"In—the dark." He shifted under the sheets.

"Yeah. No stimulus other than touch. Not sight, not sound,

nothing." I shivered. "Ooh! Turns me on just thinking about it."

He turned away from me and shook his head, as if expressing disbelief to some invisible onlooker. Then he turned back, and, his voice drenched with misgiving, said, "I suppose we can give it a try."

As soon as he doused the light, we began fumbling around like two virgins in the back of a minivan. Neither of us dared to do more than breathe heavily. He kept aiming his mouth at me, but I was deliberately jerking my head around so he ended up biting my pillow, or licking the basebaord. After ten minutes or so of this, both Elliot and I were still as flaccid as water balloons.

I rolled over and gasped, "It's just no good."

"What?" he panted. "Baby, I *know* I can get used to this. Just let's keep trying for a little long—"

"It's not you, it's me." I pointed to the window, which was allowing a dribble of moonlight into the room. "It's just too fucking *bright* in here!"

There was a long spell of silence. At any moment, I expected Elliot to get up, grab his clothes, and bolt, having had quite enough of his piggish, priggish portraitist.

But instead, he laughed. "This is *ridiculous*," he said. Then, before I could object, he straddled me like a cat and clambered up my body. He pressed his knees into my armpits, then raised himself up till his suddenly engorged penis was suspended over me like the sword of Damocles.

Then he angled himself an inch or so to the left, and all at once moonlight was spilling over his erection like milk.

"Oh, damn it," I moaned, stirred by the sheer poetry of the sight. "God damn it to *hell*."

And after that—well. A *lot* of noise.

Two days later I stumbled into Ottolina's office.

She rose to her feet and helped me into a chair. "You look like *hell*," she said, putting her hand on my forehead.

"He's a vampire," I gasped.

"Who?"

"Who else? Elliot. He's an incubus."

She crouched next to me, all her jewelry jangling at once. "Stop it. Talk sense."

"My grandmother from Croatia used to tell me about his kind. They come from nowhere—from the land of the dead. Just like Elliot. Did I tell you I had his number traced? A phone booth. He waited that whole day for me to call him back at a *phone booth*."

She turned her head and barked a command to her assistant. "Kelly, green tea. Strong. With honey and lemon. Two cups."

"These vampires, you know what they do? They pick one person, and they attach themselves to you, and they suck you dry." I displayed my pale, disheveled person to her. "Case in point."

"You're exceptionally melodramatic today, Vance." She checked my pulse. "You eaten anything lately?"

"Granny Zoia always said that back in her village, the old folks would warn the young people not to dress too fancy or make too big a deal of themselves, because that would attract a vampire, and then they'd be doomed. And look at me—big, famous painter. Face all over the media. Of *course* he'd come for me."

She grabbed my cheeks. "Stop this now or I'll take a cattle prod to you."

"Don't mention cattle prods to Elliot! He'll want to use them during sex."

She got to her feet. "I take it you haven't gotten rid of him."

"How? Granny Zoia used to say try a crucifix, but I haven't got one. Do you?"

"For God's sake, Vance! Besides, Elliot's Jewish. Would a crucifix even work?"

"I suppose not. Nothing will. That's why I have to let him move in."

"*What?* Are you *crazy*?"

"Or maybe he's moved in already. I don't even know if he *has* any stuff of his own. Vampires usually don't."

"If you say 'vampire' one more time, I'm going to drive my cellular phone through your heart." She returned to her chair.

"I can't help it. He's got me. Resistance is futile."

She put her hands flat on her desk and leaned forward. "I just want you to know, you're reinforcing every stereotype straight America has of weak-willed gay men in thrall to easy sex."

"You mean my parents were right?" I clasped my hand over my forehead. "That, *too*? Oh, God—save me, Ottolina!"

"How the hell am I supposed to do that?"

"I don't know! Give me something else to try. Something new. I'm *desperate*. And I'm tired of dribbling food on my best shirts."

"*I'll* give you something to try." She stood bolt upright. "Get out, go home, throw that cheap little trick out, and start painting again."

I looked at my fingernails, and mumbled, "I *have* been painting."

"What? Him?"

"How'd you guess?"

She snorted in disdain. "I repeat: Get out, go home, and throw him out. Or you and I are through."

"Oh, don't say that!"

"And stop sniveling. Now, move!"

"I haven't had my tea yet."

"*Move!*"

But of course, I didn't do as she said. I didn't throw him out. I couldn't. He wouldn't go. He wouldn't hear me. In a fit of anger, I tried to push him out the door, but he pretended to interpret that as a new way of initiating rough sex. Which is what it turned out to be. My jaw still doesn't close right.

He kept saying that he existed only to serve me, so I told him he'd have to remain silent while I tried to paint. But it was the loudest silence I've ever heard. He'd walk around in his boxer shorts making not even a rustle, not even a murmur. Like he was floating a few inches above ground. It'd be so eerie that I'd have to look. And there he'd be, half-naked, browned and ready to serve. And that led to you-know-what.

Once I asked him to put some clothes on. He came up to the easel so that his fur-frosted navel was exactly two inches from my nose, and said, "Okay. If you want. Just say the word." And that led to you-know-what, too.

By the end of our second week together, I'd given up all hope. And I'd given up painting. Except for my portrait of Elliot—Elliot with his hands before his face, all right, but extended outward, as if he were blowing a kiss. A poison kiss. Like a breeze from Chernobyl.

The day I finished it, I rolled it up and gave it to him. "For you," I said, knowing he'd just take it anyway.

He held it to his breast. "This means more than I can put into words," he said, and there were actually tears in his eyes.

Two nights later, we went to the opening of a retrospective exhibit of works by one of my old mentors, Karl Shrenck, who was just back from a triumphant tour of six European capitals, including Prague, from whence his ancestors hailed. Word had it he'd even had a commission from Vaclav Havel. He'd returned the world's darling, and a heartthrob, too; he was a strapping sixty-eight, his head a shock of snow-white hair, his biceps like softballs. When I greeted him at the gallery, he laughed and said, "By God, you look older than I do!"

"Where's the champagne?" I asked in my now habitual whine. He pointed me in the right direction.

Elliot returned from checking our jackets. "So that's Karl Shrenck," he said, and when I turned to tell him, Yes, that's Karl Shrenck, I could see that his eyes were whirling like Tibetan prayer wheels.

I heard Ottolina's laugh, which was unmistakable—like a parrot crossed with a machine-gun—so I sought her out. We chatted briefly—not about Elliot; she refused to as much as utter his name—before I noticed that one of her lengthy brass earrings had gotten caught on a thread of her collar. I ushered her into the corridor and helped her fix it.

When we reentered, I saw that Elliot was standing very close to Karl. And that Karl had drawn up to his full height, and was holding forth on something or other—surrealism as a genre instead of a school, deconsructionism as a decadent movement, or one of his other pet topics.

Something bloomed inside my breast; at first I thought it might be heartburn (which wouldn't have surprised me, given the excess of grain mustard on the London Broil sandwiches), till I noticed that my hands were ruddy and red again. I went to the men's room and checked my face. The wanness had gone; I looked forceful and hearty, like I was wearing stage makeup.

I returned and continued watching Elliot and Karl, who

stood at the center of the gallery like twin suns around which a host of planets swirled. When Karl was momentarily drawn away, I went and tugged on Elliot's sleeve and said, "Can I have the ticket for my jacket?"

He looked at me as though I were only half there. "What? Oh, sure."

He reached into his pocket and pulled out two tickets—the one for my leather jacket, and the one for the denim jacket he'd all but appropriated from me. He handed over both.

"Thanks," I said, smiling.

"No problem," he replied, and he turned to await Karl's return.

I was on my way to the coat check when a busboy walked by carrying more champagne. Deciding to have a glass for the road, I deftly lifted one from his tray and started to sip it. Slowly.

After all, there was no hurry.

And as I sipped, I wished Karl oboes, and kettle drums, and shrill flourishes of harpsichord.

"SUMMERTIME, AND THE LIVING IS EASY . . ."

• REGINALD SHEPHERD •

I am sitting in the library of Marshall's parents' house reading a book about beauty: another sentimental education. The book isn't mine, but I want it. The house is huge, three floors of rooms tastefully decorated with ormolu clocks and reclining bronze figurines on mantels: things I will never own. I envy Marshall the rows of pristine hardcovers lined up shelf over shelf, dust covers unmarred by the indignities of hasty packing in stolen milk crates, the two circular staircases made of banded Siena marble, one with Venetian cut-glass chandelier, the guest bedrooms and small rooms in the back that were once servants' quarters (now they hire people with my skin to do things and leave). I envy him the luxury of hating it. None of it is mine, not even Marshall.

Marshall is my best friend. We had a brief affair, before we became friends. Marshall would say we slept together, once, twice (we've put all "that stuff" behind us, he says), but I say it's all in how you look at things. Marshall says I am out of touch with reality, but I am the one who grew up in a housing project and he is the one who grew up here; we have different notions of what constitutes reality. He doesn't like me to talk about things like that, his money, for example, but as far as I'm concerned that is as good a reason as any. Our relationship relies upon a certain degree of mutual annoyance. I am annoyed that Marshall is rich and white and beautiful, and he is annoyed that

I constantly remind him of it. He'd like to enjoy his abundance of blessings without feeling it is anything out of the ordinary. He wants to feel normal. I, on the other hand, want him to feel guilty.

The book doesn't say much about any of this, though it does talk about longing. The author finds beauty in strange places: Czechoslovakia and northern Minnesota. The book is about the beauty disease. What the book doesn't say is that beauty costs money.

I am lying in my room, one of the guest bedrooms, listening to the Smiths. It's ninety-five out and muggy, and I want to go swimming, but it's thundering and a deceptively blue plastic tarpaulin covers the pool. So it won't attract lightning, Marshall says. Marshall's parents are vacationing on some Caribbean island (one of the Grenadines, I think, or Guadeloupe) and I have yet to see anyone but a gardener (his skin like mine, like that of the smiling people left behind on that vacation paradise when the tourists have gone home for the season), but this house is full of invisible presences stripping and making beds, stocking the pantries with heat-and-serve meals, and rolling protective tarpaulins over the pool. Marshall is asleep; he finds thunderstorms relaxing. Yet another way in which we're not alike.

Marshall's family has two dogs, some mix of terrier and golden retriever. The family rescued them from the pound as puppies; this house takes in all kinds of waifs.

The dogs are Marshall's excuse for being here; he will take care of them, avoiding an expensive and probably incompetent kennel. Marshall's family have known people whose dogs died in kennels; Bob Barker's cat received a permanent bald spot while in the care of Pets of the Stars. I, on the other hand, have no excuse. Or, Marshall is my excuse. Though the incidence of first-born sons dying while their parents are on vacation is doubtless lower than that for dogs.

I understand that golden retrievers are among the stupidest of dogs. Marshall told me that as well; he finds it funny. He loves his mutts.

Marshall calls them mutts.

The dogs are afraid of thunder. They are probably afraid of lightning. One of them noses his way into my room, where I am lying on the floor trying to make the most of the air conditioner's artificial breeze, and I take great satisfaction in kicking the door closed. I can hear the dog paw at the door, then stop. It has probably climbed into the bathtub, but the airconditioning filters out the scratch of nails on porcelain. It rained last night also, and the dog was cowering in the tub after midnight when I went to pee. I yelled at it until it left; I never touch these dogs.

Marshall was far away, dreaming of dusty softball games in spring, or damp soccer matches in fall. I will never do those things.

Life is an affair of places, isn't it? I love it here. There is the pool and there are the books and there are the kinds of food the titled rich are served in Proust, whom I refuse to read. For dessert there is invariably ice cream: kumquat currant, persimmon lime, macadamia poppyseed yam. Marshall is a connoisseur of ice cream, an emperor. There is the central air-conditioning and the home entertainment center that takes up half a wall. There is the VCR and the videotape library (that is what they call it) of all the classic films I have ever promised myself to see, the ones that play Tuesday matinees at revival houses in Somerville. And there is the illusion that I have Marshall to myself.

We go for walks and for drives in the country, to the beach, to town with its three-block-long main street and to the mall ten miles from town, where I wonder whether I am imagining the strange looks we get together (can they be wondering if we are lovers, or adopted brothers?), the lingering glances when I enter a store alone. When I meet their eyes the proprietors always smile and look away. At home Marshall and I play chess and Parcheesi and backgammon and Chinese checkers, and Marshall always wins; he is the one who grew up with hundreds of well-scrubbed friends with whom to play those games. I had black and white TV. I endure the humiliations of losing stoically, since it is I who like to sit for hours watching his face scrunched in concentration. But I always win at Scrabble, and in general I am much the better cheater. We argue about the economy and whether socialism in one country could work, we watch music videos with the sound off while I massage his shoulders, sore from a morning's game of racquetball. We play old Smiths albums as the soundtrack to *Imitation of Life*. The remake featuring Lana Turner and a white actress as the tragic mulatto Troy Donahue beats up when he discovers the girl he's been dating is a nigger's daughter. To be honest, I prefer to hear the dialogue.

I am bored all the time, and luxuriate in my boredom. It's not often I have the opportunity to lie by a pool for weeks at a time and ponder the utter pointlessness of life. It's quite pleasant to know that when I wake up near noon (I prefer to read at night) and can't think of a reason to get out of bed, I don't have to. My melancholy is as cool as the fresh orange juice I drink quarts of each day, as warm as the azure skin of the pool when I break the surface tension with my toe, just playing, really, not quite ready to commit myself to the colder water waiting beneath that glittering canopy. I can take all day to decide. I can postpone decision until the end of the summer, when my life will begin again.

Marshall is full of plans to improve himself. He is not wondering how he will make September's rent on a stifling apartment with a window opening onto a brick wall. Come fall he won't have to ask himself each morning how to ignore the pimply-faced kids with greasy blond hair and Metallica T-shirts who shout epithets from the playground across the street whenever I come home or leave. It really doesn't matter what they call out, "Hey Mike! Hey Michael Jackson!" or "Get the Vaseline out of your ass yet?" whether they make fun of my skin or my clothes or the way I walk: it's one of the only neighborhoods I can afford. Those kids are too old to be hanging around in playgrounds.

Marshall will not be looking for another job staring at a computer screen for eight hours a day plus an hour's unpaid lunch, because it pays better than retail and sometimes includes partial health insurance. He is always proposing rounds of tennis, squash matches; maybe we can go riding. I tell him I don't feel like it. I don't know how to do those things, I don't want to learn how to do those things, I would prefer not to. I'd rather lie here beside the pool and think about my problems, knowing that for the immediate future I need do nothing about them.

One afternoon Marshall goes on one of his outings without telling me. He knows I hate to be disturbed when I am reading, or sleeping, or masturbating. "Where did you go?" I ask accusingly when he returns, well after dinnertime. "Why didn't you ask me if I wanted to go with you?"

I ask myself, "If Marshall didn't love me, why would he invite me here?" and respond, "If he loved me, he would sleep with me." Marshall always says, "Of course I love you; you're my best friend." We're not speaking the same language at all.

I put on "Parade" by White and Torch, another British duo, moody like all the music I love, and close my eyes, listening. I keep the blinds drawn tight. Wearing nothing but one of Marshall's old Madras shirts, too big for me, I like to pretend I am reclining on a divan in the atrium of a stone house in Marrakech, protected from the desert sun by a maze of fine latticework shutters, lazy dust motes floating on the few stray threads of light that infiltrate the cool enclosure, the silence perturbed only by the singer's thin, almost broken voice, a barely discernible English accent filtered through an adolescence in a provincial Northern town spent listening to American soul music. A boy I like to think is gay (all pretty English pop singers are, you know), whose records no one in America buys but me, singing of love abandoned, false love once imagined to be true. *Looking through your eyes, you won't even notice me.*

When Marshall knocks on the door I don't answer. I don't carry a torch for anyone.

I condescend to Marshall only to keep him in his place. If he were not so wealthy, so handsome, if only he were not so white, I could afford to be kinder. But he is, so it must be understood that I am the more intelligent.

In deference to my host, my obscure object of desire, my muse and nightmare Marshall, shall I describe him, imagine him as if he led some life beyond my desire-filled resentment, my resentful desire? Marshall lifting a tennis racket to test the heft of it before his serve, Marshall tilting a glass of milk to barely parted lips while an unruly curl pokes from beneath the plastic snaps of a backwards blue corduroy baseball cap, or biting into a half-peeled pomegranate, licking the tart juice and a pulp-cased seed from his lower lip with his tongue. Marshall browsing the ethnic snacks section of the local grocer with his Brooks Brothers chinos and untucked pink buttondown Oxford, or checking his "goddamn cheap Rolex" with a scratch on the face. Marshall shaking the sweat from his hair after he has come back from running, his grey tank top clinging to the skin that sheathes his sternum and covered with a fine sheen of dust.

By the standards of one who has been the same height since the seventh grade, Marshall is quite tall. He has a slim muscular build, a swimmer's body they call it (in high school he was captain of the team), and a great devotion to keeping fit. Marshall has always been what our college catalogue called a scholar-athlete. He has a thin line of fine hair between his pectorals, and large pink nipples that stand out from his chest. Very sensitive nipples, I recall. He has black curly hair and green eyes and his ears are small and almost translucent. The left side of his mouth doesn't quite match the right, and his face looks a little lopsided when he smiles. I like to see him smile; it makes me hate him less. His teeth are perfectly even, and obscenely white.

I'm sorry I ever started this.

Most of my love goes to the pool, which has been for the past week unwrapped, unrolled, uncovered, revealed in all its hyaline glory. This is an affection Marshall and I share. He does laps; I float.

There is, apparently, someone who cleans the pool. I have never seen him. Marshall is driving through the country and I am lying by the pool reading Jean Rhys. It's comforting to read about the sufferings of the first Mrs. Rochester on an island where people whispered that she must be part-black, an island like the one on which Marshall's parents are summering a thousand miles away, with ivory beaches I can see myself lying on if I close my eyes. Jean Rhys smashed up her life and I have no life to smash up, but we both have our islands and that is what matters. Through the speakers I have carried onto the back patio Dionne Warwick insists I make it easy on myself and I am taking her advice.

After all, in a week Kyle will be here.

I'm under no illusions. Kyle's presence will bring discomfort and anxiety. Like everything, I suppose. To Marshall, of course, it will bring someone to sleep with every night.

Kyle and I do not like one another. Kyle dislikes me because I am snide to him and often rude. I dislike Kyle because he is Marshall's lover.

Ever since I have known him, and before, since our freshman year, when he was just a Homeric myth I watched play volleyball on the Green out the windows of the dining common, Marshall has had a succession of boyfriends named Travis or Justin or Shane; I'm sure there must have been a Lance, but I can't recall him just now. With each succeeding one I have simultaneously asked myself, "How could Marshall go out with someone as stupid as Trent?" and "Why couldn't Hugh be interested in *me*?" Few of Marshall's boys (that's what we called them, I and my small band of bookish young men who never got laid, who never thought of sleeping with each other) had IQs larger than their waist sizes, but they all knew how to carry themselves. Marshall was always valiant in praise of their hidden virtues, though as far as anyone could see (and anyone could, even I), their virtues were only too apparent. But then, I can vouch for intellect's lack of allure. One of Marshall's boys was named Cameron; he rowed crew. "Call me Cam," he always said; I never did.

Each had his own distinctive charm. None of the relationships worked out, not for long, but all of those boys did. Trent played rugby, Shane was a wrestler. (Discretion, when required, has always been one of Marshall's virtues. I leave that sort of thing to him.) Late at night in my dorm room, Marshall would ask me what he should do about Skip or Ashley, while I played Echo and the Bunnymen and diffidently rested a damp open palm on his knee while gazing empathetically into his eyes. Our relationship was not off to an entirely healthy start, but I always gave excellent advice.

Marshall slept late after our talks, and I got up to work the breakfast shift at the snack bar. Cameron always ordered four eggs, and extra butter on his toast.

Kyle is the worst of a bad lot. He and Marshall have been dating for a year.

I'm Marshall's best friend. I'm allowed to say such things. He laughs good-naturedly and agrees.

When Kyle is gone, I will still have Marshall. I don't know if that comforts me.

Kyle has just returned from a month in Europe, a birthday present from his grandmother. At dinner he tells me about his trip; he's trying to open up to me. He wants me to be on his side. He was mugged in Amsterdam, Nice was filthy and noisy, and the water in Marseilles made him sick. I hate people who complain about their trips to Europe. What Kyle doesn't understand is that there is only room for one on my side.

I am floating in the pool listening to Marshall and Kyle argue. It's their main activity when together: that, and having sex. I suspect it's only the fighting that maintains the attraction; the fights make them feel different from one another. Every bout of raised voices and mutual recriminations is followed by a lengthy silence; I keep the air conditioner turned up.

As far as I can tell, they argue about nothing, who's been unfaithful to whom in whose absence, even if only in his unspoken desires the other can read like a Dr. Seuss primer. Did Kyle sleep with Jonathan in Zurich? Was Marshall in Disneyland with Evan on Kyle's birthday? (I tell Kyle he's being silly, why would Marshall do that? I show him the 101 Dalmatians souvenir figurine Marshall gave me, but can't remember when.) Marshall always turns to me for counsel, as he has for years. I eagerly prize out every detail; it makes them seem more real, the two of them. Marshall tells me, "We have our best sex after we've fought. Sometimes we won't speak for almost a week, but still have incredible sex two or three times a day. You don't think that's too weird, do you?" I try to explain to him that healthy relationships are based on more than just sex.

Marshall tells me Kyle is jealous of us. "Sometimes I think he doesn't really understand what friendship is." I tell him he's being hard on Kyle; Kyle can't help being who he is.

I try to imagine them in bed, the ways their bodies fit together: what Marshall's body does to Kyle's, what Kyle's does to Marshall's. At times, I confess, I've listened at the door of Marshall's bedroom, desperate at least to hear. At times I'm sure Marshall must know. At times I think he likes it.

I can imagine the bodies, but never the people. When the shouting stops I decide to swim some laps. I have never swum a lap in my life, but there's a first time for everything.

Downstairs, they are quarrelling again, but I never see either of them anymore. When I'm not in the pool I'm in the library, and when I'm not in the library I am sleeping. Thunder doesn't comfort me, but the calm steady hum of the air conditioner does. I turn it up high, then bury myself in blankets, sinking into a white linen pillow of sleep to a soundtrack of white noise. I read profiles of the hot young writers and actors in the Hip Issue of *Interview* and tributes to Marilyn Monroe and Dr. King in *Life*. I keep myself an informed voter with *Time* and *Newsweek*, and then my fingers slacken and my head lolls back. When I wake up the magazines have slipped between the bed and the wall, or dropped behind the headboard. I don't look for them. There is no shortage of magazines.

This afternoon I am reading, out of sequence because that leaves more room for me, a series of letters I found just after graduation in the room next door to mine. A tall blond boy who people whispered was Edie Sedgwick's cousin, and half-insane, lived there; he should have graduated, too, but he went to Italy instead. Each letter is a tortured demand for love from someone who had spent the year travelling over Europe, and when she returned had given them all back, because she'd decided she was a lesbian. I imagine myself that girl, probably foreign, perhaps even Italian (he'd gone there in search of her ghost), sitting by the cliffs on Corfu or at a sidewalk café in Budapest with a sad smile because all the quotes from Baudelaire in the world could not make me love this man again, could not make me love any man. That boy spent the last month of school throwing knives at the wall we shared, but the letters were beautifully written.

Marshall comes to see me, sitting on the edge of the bed as if I were a sick relative he is obligated to visit once a day. Affecting not to notice the stale smell of semen hanging in the room, he says he worries he's neglecting me. He knows I'll always be here when he knocks. He can indulge me when I sulk.

Sometimes we laugh and he hugs me; sometimes we hold hands. It makes Marshall uncomfortable to know that underneath the covers I am naked.

It seems that Marshall and Kyle are not speaking again. I pretend to be busy packing my clothes and my records and my favorite books from the downstairs library, tokens of this summer of playing house, consolations for my imminent return to life. I can keep myself occupied with this for years. Every night for the past week, Marshall has come to my room to tell me the latest twists of their arguments, to ask me what he should do. Every night I tell him I don't know, I've never had a relationship like theirs, and every night after he leaves I dream of his large pink nipples. Once I dreamt I was kneeling in front of him and he detached his penis and handed it to me, walking away. It was made of wood and very hard and I held it in my hand for a long time before I woke up.

I ask Marshall why he and Kyle can't at least be civil. I tell him it's not fair that the two of them should ruin the last days of the only real vacation I have ever had. I know they're not sleeping together and I'm glad.

All my things are finally packed and I am rewarding myself with a final afternoon in the pool; as I have for almost three months, I am wearing one of Marshall's bathing suits. Kyle is leaving for California this afternoon; he and Marshall have agreed to patch things up before his flight. I allow myself to be carried by the pool's vague eddies; I'm memorizing every movement of the warm, clear water.

I can hear them yelling and then doors slam. A cab honks and before long takes off; Kyle is gone. Marshall is standing on the patio, shading his eyes against the glare. I wave slowly and he waves back. Like in a movie, there is no sound. I don't move. I have to go back in the morning and look for a job, but now I smile and close my eyes, floating on nothing at all, and wish again this place were mine. I feel happier than in months.

TOILET TRAINING
(THE ABC'S)

• D. LEE WILLIAMS •

A couple of days into summer, it rained. Me and Nikki were still in Eugene, by the Rose Garden Park, and a ways into the night—by ten, ten-thirty or so, maybe—it'd stopped, and looked like it was going to stay clear for a while. We ditched our spot under the Washington-Jefferson Bridge, headed up the riverbank, past the bum camps, into the Rose Garden, and to the bathrooms right by the bikepath.

The mud squished loud and Nikki almost slipped but we made it through the grass, shortcutting to the bathroom lights. We toured around the johns—me, mostly ahead—Nikki keeping back but keeping eyes open. I did a quick check on the boys' side, and all the stalls were empty, pretty much as we figured, as early as it was, but two of the middle stalls had empty Coors cans, and the last stall had a few stubbed out butts and a lot of new smoke.

I came out of the johns and Nikki was drinking at the water fountain right in front. I looked long around—down the bikepath, to the fuck-trees off to the side, way over to the lights by the school district building, back to the park, to the bushes and dark on the other side, by the park's parking lot, then up the bikepath, and the bushes and trees next to where we came from. I didn't see anybody. Nikki looked up, wiped her mouth, and said, "Let's bench-it," which meant we'd grab a bench in the dark part on the other side, sit and scope and wait because she hadn't seen anybody either. My stomach bitched loud—I grabbed a drink of water—and we squished over to a bench pretty far out of the parking lot light, parked it, Nikki pulling my arm around her.

She pulled out a hunk of Snickers bar from her back pocket, broke it in two and I took the hunk with the most nuts, too big, broke it apart some more, gave her back some, but she said, "Take it." We munched and my stomach still bitched so Nikki bitched back at it, told it to shut up, thumped it, then—spotting something—got off my arm and stomach and said, "There he is," pointed to a kid coming up the bikepath, going into the boys' side john—a kid we'd seen, four or five nights ago, cruising a couple nights in a row.

"Maybe a cop," Nikki said.

"Too young," I said. And, "He's a kid. He's just like us."

"Maybe," she said. And then, "Check him out?" so I got up—but the kid'd come out—was already off and out of sight, cruising the outskirts. I turned around, popped buttons, peed in some roses by the bench. Nikki said, "Prob'ly a cop."

"He's way young," I said.

"A dope cop," she said. "He's scoping for deals," and then, "or maybe he's a dealer."

"He's just like us," I said, shaking my dick. There were other voices—two older guys—coming past the fuck-trees up the bikeway, and when they got to the bathrooms, they stopped talking and looked around, stood and waited till one of them—smoking—took a last couple of drags, stubbed out his cigarette—then they went in.

I was already buttoning up, set to jam when Nikki said, "Shit!" and I turned around, saw the other kid cruising up fast out of nowhere and already into the boys' side. "He's takin' 'em," Nikki said.

"I fuckin' told you," I said.

"Fucker can't do both," she said.

"I'm going," I said, got out of the bushes, started up to the johns. I heard her say, "Watch out," real low, looked back, saw her climb up, park it on the back of the bench, start spitting down into the seat cracks.

I squished around and up to the john lights. When I got to the open john doors, I looked back again—seeing if I could see Nikki—and couldn't—she was hidden in all the dark. Car lights came up, in the parking lot behind her, and a couple of cars came through, but nobody stopped, came in.

There was a splashy clank, clank—from the johns—and when I stepped in I saw the Coors empties rolling around and out from under a stall—the back, back stall—and then another one, fairly full, rolled after it, nailed the empties, spilled Coors, and made a quick puddle that spread big and squished loud when I moved up to the last stall.

There were shoes under the last stall—drowning in beer, but not moving—and when I looked around the stall wall the two guys standing (one holding a Coors, drinking) and the kid that beat me there (holding one dick, sucking the other)—didn't move, didn't look back or around. The guy with the beer drank, kind of looked back, handing the can to the other guy, who didn't turn around at all, didn't drink, just put the beer on the kid's head, and with his other hand, pulled the other guy's dick out of the kid's mouth, put in his. The other guy wanted more, put his dick back in too, and the kid couldn't really handle, take, suck both, slipped off the pot, to his knees—squishing around in the beer puddle till he got so he could take them both. My foot pinched a can—a cracky, small crunch from me peeking around, checking out how the kid was doing it, how it was done—but nobody turned, looked up, so I scooted back, stepped back over the rolling empties, and out of the john.

There was smoke outside, right in my face—a guy by the water fountain blew out a big wad of it, then soaked his butt in the water, looking at me the whole time—but I squished around the cloud and him, new lights from the parking lot coming up, and two cars coming in slow, over by the school district building, and a couple more dinky lights coming down the bikepath. When I got to our bench in the bushes, I checked back—and with all the other lights coming in—the bathroom lights didn't seem that bright anymore.

Nikki asked what's going on, and I didn't say anything, so she hit my arm, said, "So what the fuck's goin' on?" and I didn't look at her, just kept eyes on the bathroom, just said, "He's no cop."

Kid was in for a while—ten minutes probably—and then the two johns came out, but not the kid. The two guys split a beer, wandered behind the bathrooms, off down the bikepath, drank, walked, chucked the empty, and the kid still hung inside.

New guys—maybe four, five, half a dozen—wandered, roamed in the john-light, but nobody went in, nobody wanted to pay. One—the one who'd blown smoke at my face—came back, smoked by the fountain again, was there for a while—like he was willing to pay, had cash—drowned and flicked his butt, then went in.

"Jam," Nikki said—and I was already up the path—at the johns even before his smoke cloud'd blown away. Smoker-guy hadn't made it back to the stalls yet—he was up front, pissing or playing with himself at the first wall-pisser—didn't look up, was into whatever he was doing, so I got to move on him first, and I went right beside him, stuck my head into the sink, turned the spout on, got a long drink.

He had his face kind of turned, and his hands were really going on downstairs, belt buckle jingling. I stopped my drink, tried to check him out, but he kept most of his head down. I grabbed a paper towel from the other wall, started drying, warming the hands, spying the kid's shoes still sticking out, still in beer, empties around them, no pants around his ankles, so there was no way he was for real dumping, really using the pot—knew he was waiting, still working it—so I moved in, up behind wall-pisser guy, was just about to say, "Man, need a hand with that?"—some line, then the rates, how much a hand or whatever'd be—and then his face came around and up from his dick—smiling pretty big—and nothing—just shit—came out of my mouth—"Oh man!"—stutter shit—"Oh, shit, man—no way, no day"—and I jammed.

Nikki wasn't back at the bench, was wandering around the roses, behind the bushes, looking over to the parking lot light, checking for any new cars and cops. She said, "Shit, that was fast."

"I didn't do him."

"Fuck!" She turned, spit quick in the roses.

I said, "It's Asshole. The Asshole."

"Oh, *fuck*. Sonafafuck," and she came over, back into my dark spot, started to say—"The dick that—" but I cut her close, said, "Yeah—right before the rain."

"What'd he do? Did he fuckin' try anything? What'd he try?" She was pulling at my arm, looking around me, up to the johns, then jumped on the bench to look around, see more. "He's still there, right?" she said. "Asshole's still in there?"

I said yeah—said they both were.

"Cool," she said. "Way fuckin' cool."

"Why cool?" I said.

She hopped down, told me to just watch the bathrooms—johns were coming up from somewhere, squishing around in the raingrass, and a couple more were floating close to the fountain, but nobody was going in. And Nikki—up behind me—said, " 'Cause that sonafafuck that tore your shit's probably stiffin' that new kid right now is why." Her arms—fairly to really warm—came around my middle, and she talked up, low into my ear, "Dissin' the competition is why," she said, pulled her arms down low to my butt, and scooted me, started me moving, started us walking up the john path, said, "C'mon—let's get closer."

We went around, came up on the grass behind the johns, squishing over to and parking it on a picnic table off to the side, in enough bathroom-light to see, but still mostly invisible. We listened close—Nikki said she heard the *Uh-humm*'s and *Oh yeah-yeah*'s of a deal being cut or going on already. One of the two guys that'd been floating around floated over to our table, sat on the other side, said, "Summer at last, maybe, humm?" and "Looks like the rain's gone at least," then asked for a light but we just heard him, didn't look at him, saw the other floater slip into the johns and come out way fast, head low, looking around, and Nikki giggled, said, "Oh yeah—it's goin' on in there," and I just watched.

Less than a second after her last giggle, we heard "You *fuck*! You old fuck!"—and the Asshole was out—jangling his belt buckle and pants together, and walking fast—an old man's running—out of the john-light, off into the rest of the dark park. The kid came out—a couple seconds after him—yelling more *You old fuck!*'s, and the floater at our table got up, took off, squishing fast away.

Nikki was cracking up and I kind of laughed—mostly just watching the kid. He spit a lot—shirting his mouth dry—then spit some more, then stomped over to the water fountain, got drink after drink—not swallowing—turning—spitting mouthful after mouthful. His last spit came close to us.

"Somethin' fuckin' funny?" he said. "You fuckin' think I'm funny?" and he started coming over, another john—coming up behind him on the bikepath—turned around, walked away. "You think that old fuck's funny?"

I shut up, Nikki giggled some more—one more time big.

He squished up closer to Nikki. "Hey babe," he said, "aren't you in the wrong fuckin' park?"

I scooted up closer, right next to Nikki, said, "She's with me." And then, "Zat alright?"

"You think I'm funny, too?" he said, getting into my space. "You dicks know that old fuck, maybe?"

"He's a sonafafuck," Nikki said.

The kid took a couple steps back—"You know him? You know that dickwad?"—looked at me—"He do you or somethin'? He fuck you over? Hey—you get fucked over, too?"

I looked over to Nikki—her face getting spotlighted by a string of car lights coming through—then looked back at the kid, said, "Yeah, I know." I said, "Fucker'd give you twenty-five for fuckin' you—big fifty if you let him . . . took his load. . . ." Kid didn't move. Stayed, no squishing. "So then he gets you flat up," I said, "pants down—and he's got this . . . gotta monster fuckin' dick, right?—and he's goin' at it, and does it—blows it all in—and everything—then he jams. Just fuckin' takes off. No cash—total nothing. Right? Pretty much?"

He backed up more, wasn't looking at me or Nik, was looking off and squishing around, backing off. "Just head," he said, wiping his shoes in the grass. "It was head for a ten spot, and twenty for takin' it."

I looked at Nikki.

"Head's all?" she said—another car light catching her—only this time, the light stayed and she stared at it. "Cop," she said, and we looked over, saw the cop car stopped and searchlighting the park.

Me and Nikki jumped off the table—"C'mon"—the kid said—"Fuckin' follow me"—he said—"My place"—and we followed him, squished around the johns, down the bikeway, then off the path and down a bank, to a clearspot in the river bushes—the big light coming around, flashing everything above ground again. "This'll be cool for a couple seconds," he said, moving around, clearing some of his shit—shirts, a black jacket, tapes, a Raider's cap, couple *Penthouses*, Walkman, Pop Tart box—and crouching back against the big weeds. Other voices came down the river and I looked through the weeds, saw bums crawled up from their bum camps, peeking over the bank for cops.

"Lazyass motherfuckers," the kid said. "These cops don't even get out of their fuckin' cars," he said. "Usually."

Nikki said, "Usually," then, "So—what's your name?"

He said Branch, and Nikki asked what the fuck kind of name was Branch.

"Californian," said Branch.

The bums were laughing and I looked past Nikki, watched them through the weed slits crawling back into their space. The searchlight'd stopped and there was only some glare left from the closed mall across the river. Branch got up and whizzed into the weeds. I snagged a *Penthouse* and Nikki inched up the bank to peek over the bikepath.

"I think he's still there," she said, and sure enough the big light came around again. Nikki slid down, and Branch finished, crouched back with us. I squinted at the mag—used the big light when it came around—making out a few lines of a JO letter—hard-up guy puts peanut butter on his dick, gets dog to lick it till he comes—and Branch asked who we were, where the fuck we were headed.

"Dave and Nikki," said Nikki, checking out his tapes, and "We don't know where—do we, Dave?" and I said, "Anywhere but here," squinting at the pics now, checking out big center-beaver.

"I'm going more north," he said. "Portland. I know people in Portland."

I looked up to Nikki, already staring at me. I dropped the mag.

"What?" Branch said. "You guys thinkin' 'bout Portland?"

Nikki picked up his Raider's cap, said, "Thinking about it."

"You know that's *real*," Branch said—looking at the hat—"That ain't no fake. I'm from there. That ain't no fake."

Nikki put the cap on. The big light'd quit. She climbed back up, looked around, said the cop car'd left, said it was totally dark, and had to be eleven-thirty, and Branch said, "Why eleven-thirty?" and Nikki said, " 'Cause the john lights go out at eleven-thirty." Then said, "Shit. I don't fuckin' believe it, no way," and then, "Get up, get up here," and me and Branch crawled up, looked over the cement to the bathrooms.

There was nobody around—scattered and scared off by the cop car—nobody except for one guy, right by the water fountain, smoking in whatever was left of park-light.

"He's back," said Branch.

"No shit," I said.

"Sonafafuck," Nikki said.

Branch slid down and so did I. Branch said, "That's him, yeah that's him—the fuckin' balls. *Man*, what fucking balls."

I roughed around for rocks, found a couple, then three fairly flat ones, stood up and whizzed one out through the river weeds, hearing it *plop-plop-plop* straight out, then I skipped another one up river, waking the bums, a couple or more of them grumbling *fuck*'s.

"We gotta fuck him over," Branch said. "Take him out of this scene. You wanna fuck this guy over?"

"Roll him?" Nikki asked, still up the bank, looking out.

"No—rip him," Branch said. "Just a mind fuck."

"That'd be hard," I said. "I mean—he knows us all," and Nikki, looking down, right at me and Branch, said quick—"Asshole doesn't know *me*"—and Branch reached up, flicked Nikki—right on the Raider's brim—said fast—"Choice fuckin' hat, huhn?" and I skipped my last rock.

Me and Branch sat low on a bench behind a tree by the bikepath, facing the Willamette. Nikki stood behind us—on the path.

"He's still there, right?" Branch said.

"Uh-humm," she said.

I peeked around—watched her stuff a few loose pieces of hair back into the hat. Branch slugged me. *"Don't fucking stare,"* he said. "Don't let that dickwad see us." We were fairly close to the johns—and even though the john lights were out, a few path lights up the way still glowed. I turned back, stared at the river again, the closed mall lights, heard Nikki rustling the hat some more, screwing with and zipping up Branch's black jacket.

"Okay," she said, "check me out, I'm ready."

We peeked around. I stared.

"Whoa," Branch said.

"You look like. . . . You're maybe my little brother," I said.

"You got a brother?" Branch said.

"No," I said.

"How's my hair?" Nikki asked.

"In-fucking-visible," Branch said.

She said " 'Kay—cool," kissed me fast, started to the johns.

"Keep your head low," I said low, and Branch said to her, "Scratch your dick."

We waited quite a while—watching the water—before looking back again. Big-dick-john was leaning against the water fountain, just lighting up again, lots of smoke around the johns and Nikki was cruising him pretty good, head low, hands in her pockets.

"Walks like she got a dick," Branch said, and, "Knows how to work it."

"Been watchin' me," I said, and monsterdick was cruising Nikki right back, eyeing the Raider's hat, Nikki's almost boy-butt.

She walked slow, started into the men's side, then stopped, leaned up against the wall by the open door, kept her head real low. John stood up real straight, smoking and watching her.

"He's totally buyin' it," Branch said.

Nikki coughed—good, hard, from the balls—itched her crotch, and then went in.

John reached around, squeezed the water on, doused his cigarette, flicked it, and followed Nikki's boy-butt inside.

"Sold," Branch said.

"Let's get closer," I said.

We squished straight across the grass, sat up on the picnic table me and Nikki'd been on. Branch said he couldn't see good enough—I said me neither—so we jumped off, pulled the table around, till we were just about facing the doorway to the men's side. Car lights came up, I jumped, looked around—a new john was coming out of the roses. He came up, cruised around us, checked us out, started for the johns.

"Occupotto, man," Branch said—nice and low—and I said "Big-time occupotto," and the guy wandered back around and off. I scanned the rest of the park, cars came through the lot, but nobody else was coming in.

Branch said—"Listen"—and I looked back—"He's cuttin' the deal. He's goin' for head again"—and I could hear Nikki saying all the right *Uh-humm*'s and *Right*'s real deep, waging the deal perfect. I slid off, walked closer to the doorway, Branch behind me, and we both looked slow around the corner.

Carlight made us shadows for a second—on the far wall in the john—our heads spotlighted under a big black patch of graffiti, but Nikki and john—down in the last stall—must not've seen anything, weren't talking at all. We heard an empty rolling, and a *clink*—belt buckle coming undone, then a *clank*—belt buckle going down on concrete, then his *Good-good-yeah-good*'s with Nikki's low and deep *Uh-humm*'s, and we moved in closer, inching from stall to stall—then into the next-to-last stall—right up against them.

I looked around, Branch looking around me—just at a growly *Hmmm* from him, while Nikki was doing him—the Asshole's monsterdick jamming into the dark under her hat—and his hand, going over her head—stroked and pulled—till it finally flicked the hat off, and her hair came down everywhere—all over him—and she giggled, laughing on his dick, and john's fingers froze in her hair, and "A fish—a goddamn girl!" came out, bouncing loud all over the stalls, and monsterdick died into nothing—right there—soft and gone, and Branch was laughing now, slapping me over, clanking me down into the empties and onto john's pants and shoes and belt buckle, and the guy yelled another round of *Goddamn*'s—pissed that I was on top of the clothes he was trying to pull up. He kicked empties around, kicked me off, pushed Nikki, grabbed up his clink-clanky clothes and *Godamn*'d out—Branch pulled me up, Nikki pushed behind me—and we took off after him, outside, but just to the edge of the grass, stopping and watching him squish off—going for the kind-of-lit bikepath, then turning, changing his mind, jamming over to the bright parking lot—and out of the park.

Nikki ran back in—came right back out with the hat—held it tight, stood flat against the wall and said—"Next."

We scrounged around the water fountain for a while, checking the ground for good, smokeable stubs. Branch said he'd been jonesing for one all night. Lights came up, cars rolled in and out of the parking lot, one—coming in by the school district building—parked, and the driver-guy got out, started in.

Branch said, "This is stupid here, a total waste of time."

Nikki said, "Got one," stood up, held up a big stubby.

I watched the guy head into the park through the roses.

"Nobody's got any money here," Branch said. "Nobody fucking pays."

"It's a small fuckin' town is why," Nikki said. "Branch—you got a light?" and Branch said, "You guys should hitch with me. Portland's bigger—way bigger. Straights, breeders, Beamerfags—everything," and Nikki said, "Maybe. That's maybe where we're headed," then—"Davy, what d'you think?" and I stopped staring at the bushes, got a quick drink from the fountain. I looked at Nikki and wiped my mouth. I said, "Yeah, cool, the big city."

"Sure?" Nikki said, and I said "Yeah," again, said, "We're not makin' shit here," and Nikki said to Branch again—"You got a light or what?"

"Somewhere," Branch said, and they turned to go back to Branch's camp—Branch saying, "I got places," and "I know people," Nikki asking about the park scene up there—me staying back—still by the johns, hanging at the fountain, watching the new lights coming up, watching the new john cruise closer.

"What're you doin'?" Nikki said loud, turned around.

I put my hand on my stomach—it'd just gone off—and rubbed up and down. "I gotta dump," I said, and started into the john, and Branch said a loud "Lookout for assholes," took them both back over the bank.

I kicked out one last empty left on the floor in the last stall, popped buttons, pulled my pants down, sat down on the cold pot. A car light came up and a shadow came in. I held in my load. The guy came down, around the stalls, stood in front of me, crunching his crotch.

"How much for this thing?" he said.

"Nothin'," I said. "Free."

He unbuckled and unzipped. I tightened my butt to the pot.

He poked around in the dark in front of my face, poking my eye, hitting my nose, then touching dick to lips. I opened my mouth and let go. Everything blew out—*plop-plop-plop*—smell coming up everywhere.

"Christ!" he said, "You pig—you fucking pig!" and he pulled out, zipped up, jangled out—rolling, kicking, crunching the empties. Carlight came in—right after him—and I caught something on the wall—graffiti on the wall where the guy'd been standing—"Smile if your shit stinks."

I grabbed some paper. Giggled, wiped and flushed.

ABOUT THE AUTHORS

Paul Bonin-Rodriguez is a performer and writer living in San Antonio. The story included in *Men on Men 5* is part of a performance piece, *Talk of the Town*, which with *The Bible Belt and Other Accessories*, he has been touring across America. He is at work writing *The I Love Lunacy Show: Love in the Time of College*, the third part of a projected novel. The winner of a fellowship from the National Fund for Lesbian and Gay Artists, Bonin-Rodriguez teaches at Palo Alto College and is a member of Jump-Start Performance Company.

Liam Brosnahan is the son of a bricklayer and an ex-nun. He is the author of *The Outrageous Limerick Book* and *Rhymes Without Reason*, a book for children. His work has appeared in *Christopher Street* and *McCall's*. He lives in New York where he is often spotted peering across the Atlantic Ocean toward his own private Ireland.

Peter Cashorali lives in Los Angeles with his lover, Caesar Bonilla. They celebrated their twenty-second anniversary last Halloween. His interests are domestic life and the other world. His story "The Ride Home" appeared in *Men on Men 3*.

Clifford Chase is the author of *The Hurry-Up Song*, from which "Leaving the Beach" is excerpted. His work has appeared in *A Member of the Family* and such journals as *The Yale Review*,

Threepenny Review, and *Boulevard*. Born in Stamford, Connecticut, he now lives in Brooklyn, where he's finishing a novel.

Justin Chin is a writer-performer. He is the author of *And Judas Boogied Until His Slippers Wept, Go, or The Approximately Infinite Universe of Mrs. Robert Lomax*, and *M. Cockroach*.

Jameson Currier is the author of *Dancing on the Moon: Short Stories about AIDS*. His writing on AIDS has appeared in *The Philadelphia Inquirer Magazine*, *Art & Understanding*, and *Christopher Street*, among many other journals. He has also written the documentary film *Living Proof: HIV and the Pursuit of Happiness*, based on the Carolyn Jones photography project.

Joshua David is a writer living in New York City.

Wesley Gibson was born in Mobile, Alabama, and now lives in Richmond, Virginia. A graduate of Virginia Commonwealth University and Brown University, he has been a fellow at Yaddo, VCA, and the Cummington Community. He is the author of the novel *Shelter*.

Gary Glickman is the author of the novel *Years from Now*, several short stories, a comic opera, *Orlando or Love of a Leg*, and a musical setting of *Twelfth Night*. He is working on a screenplay of his novel *Sylvia Threefoot*. He lives in New York City with James Still.

Raphael Kadushin is an editor at the University of Wisconsin Press. His work has appeared in such magazines as *Christopher Street*, *Bon Appétit*, *Lambda Book Report*, *Our World*, and *Isthmus*. He is currently working on a novel featuring the characters in "Boys on Fire."

Brian Kirkpatrick recently moved to the Netherlands. "Hot Chocolate Drips" is his first published story.

Adam Klein is a graduate of the University of Iowa's Writers' Workshop and is a poet, essayist, and fiction writer. He works for the State of California placing ex-offenders in jobs. He lives in San Francisco.

Michael Lowenthal was born in Washington, D.C., and now lives in New Hampshire. A former editor at the University Press of New England, he was the first openly gay valedictorian of Dartmouth College. His work has appeared in *Flesh and the Word 2* and *Sister and Brother: Lesbians and Gay Men Together.*

Jaime Manrique is a Colombian-born writer. His novel *Latin Moon in Manhattan* was a Lambda Book Award finalist. He is at work on a novel, *Twilight at the Equator*, a biography of Federico García Lorca, and a book of poems, *The Nat King Cole Years*. He is associate professor of writing in the MFA program of Goddard College.

Richard McCann was raised in Silver Spring, Maryland, and was educated at Virginia Commonwealth University, Hollins College, and the University of Iowa, where he received his Ph.D. in American Studies. He now codirects the M.F.A. program in creative writing at the American University in Washington, D.C. His fiction and poetry have appeared in *The Atlantic, Esquire, American Short Fiction*, and *Ploughshares*, as well as in many anthologies. He is the author of *Dream of the Traveler*, a book of poetry, and a forthcoming novel to be published by Pantheon, from which "Some Threads Through the Medina" in this volume and "My Mother's Clothes: The School of Beauty and Shame" in *Men on Men 2* are derived.

John L. Myers was born and raised in North Carolina, where he was graduated from the University of North Carolina at Chapel Hill. He now lives in Washington, D.C. "All Who Are Out Are In Free" is an excerpt from his novel *Run Mourner, Run*. He is the author of *Holy Family*, a mystery.

David Rakoff was born and raised in Canada. He attended Columbia University, where he studied Japanese. In Tokyo, he worked as a translator for an art publisher. Now an editor for HarperCollins, he works on a novel, performs his own theater pieces, directs other people's plays, and draws comic strips.

Robert Rodi is the author of *Fag Hag*, *Closet Case*, and *What They Did to Princess Paragon*, and is working on a fourth novel, *Drag Queen*. He lives in Chicago with his lover and partner, Jeffrey Smith, and their dog, Nelson.

Reginald Shepherd was born and raised in New York City and is a graduate of Bennington College, Brown University, and the University of Iowa's Writers' Workshop. His collection of poems *Some Are Drowning* won a 1993 Associated Writing Programs' Award and will soon be published. Recipient of a 1993 "Discovery"/*The Nation* Award, his poems have appeared in *The Antioch Review*, *The Kenyon Review*, *The Nation*, *The Paris Review*, and *Poetry*. His essay "On Not Being White" appeared in *In the Life*.

D. Lee Williams was born in Portland, Oregon, and has lived in Eugene, Oregon, all his life. After he is graduated from the University of Oregon, he plans to enter the M.F.A. program at the University of Washington.

David Bergman, editor, is the author of *Gaiety Transfigured: Gay Self-Representation in American Literature* and *Cracking the Code*, which won the George Elliston Poetry Prize. He is the editor of many volumes, including John Ashbery's *Reported Sightings: Art Chronicles 1957–87*, Edmund White's *The Burning Library*, and *The Violet Quill Reader*. He lives in Baltimore.

PLUME (0452)

GREAT SHORT FICTION

☐ **MEN ON MEN:** *Best New Gay Fiction* **edited and with an introduction by George Stambolian.** "Some of the best gay fiction, past, present and future . . . It's a treat to have it conveniently collected. And it's a treat to read. Hopefully the word will now spread about the riches of gay writing."— Martin Bauml Duberman　　　　　　　　　　　　(258820—$12.00)

☐ **MEN ON MEN 2:** *Best New Gay Fiction* **edited and with an introduction by George Stambolian.** "This collection includes some of the hotest (in other words, coolest) stories I've read anywhere. *Men On Men 2* is a rich late-eighties mix of love and death."—Brad Gooch, author of *Scary Kisses*.
(264022—$12.00)

☐ **MEN ON MEN 3:** *Best New Gay Fiction* **edited and with an introduction by George Stambolian.** This diverse, collection continues to explore the universal themes of fiction—love, family, and conflict—from the perspectives of such leading authors as Paul Monette, Philip Gambone, Robert Haule, Christopher Bram, and sixteen others.　　(265142—$11.00)

☐ **MEN ON MEN 4: Edited by George Stambolian.** As in past volumes, a powerful volume of literature that puts gay fiction on the cutting edge of contemporary art, allowing us to experience some of the most dazzling, revelatory, and provocative prose in print today.　　(268567—$12.00)

Prices slightly higher in Canada.

Buy them at your local bookstore or use this convenient coupon for ordering.

PENGUIN USA
P.O. Box 999, Dept. #17109
Bergenfield, New Jersey 07621

Please send me the books I have checked above.
I am enclosing $_____ (please add $2.00 to cover postage and handling).
Send check or money order (no cash or C.O.D.'s) or charge by Mastercard or VISA (with a $15.00 minimum). Prices and numbers are subject to change without notice.

Card # _____ Exp. Date _____
Signature _____
Name _____
Address _____
City _____ State _____ Zip Code _____

For faster service when ordering by credit card call **1-800-253-6476**

Allow a minimum of 4-6 weeks for delivery. This offer is subject to change without notice